OF SILVER AND SHADOW

D1057496

OF SILVER AND SHADOW

JENNIFER GRUENKE

flux ®

Mendota Heights, Minnesota

Of Silver and Shadow © 2021 by Jennifer Gruenke. All rights reserved. No part of this book may be used or reproduced in any manner whatsoever, including internet usage, without written permission from Flux, except in the case of brief quotations embodied in critical articles and reviews.

First Edition
First Printing, 2021

Book design by Jake Nordby
Cover design by Jake Nordby
Cover images by Marina Sun/Shutterstock, CoffeeTime/Shutterstock

Flux, an imprint of North Star Editions, Inc.

This is a work of fiction. Names, characters, places, and incidents are either the product of the author's imagination or are used fictitiously, and any resemblance to actual persons living or dead, business establishments, events, or locales is entirely coincidental. Cover models used for illustrative purposes only and may not endorse or represent the book's subject.

Library of Congress Cataloging-in-Publication Data
Names: Gruenke, Jennifer, 1992- author.
Title: Of silver and shadow / Jennifer Gruenke.
Description: First edition. | Mendota Heights, Minnesota: Flux, 2021. | Audience: Grades 10-12. | Summary: "Ren Kolins, a magic wielder in hiding, strikes a deal with a broody rebel plotting to overthrow the tyrant king"— Provided by publisher.
Identifiers: LCCN 2019054449 (print) | LCCN 2019054450 (ebook) | ISBN 9781635830545 (paperback) | ISBN 9781635830552 (ebook)
Subjects: CYAC: Magic—Fiction. | Revolutions—Fiction. | Fantasy.
Classification: LCC PZ7.1.G7957 Of 2021 (print) | LCC PZ7.1.G7957 (ebook) | DDC [Fic]—dc23
LC record available at https://lccn.loc.gov/2019054449
LC ebook record available at https://lccn.loc.gov/2019054450

Flux
North Star Editions, Inc.
2297 Waters Drive
Mendota Heights, MN 55120
www.fluxnow.com

Printed in Canada

To my parents, for all you've done.

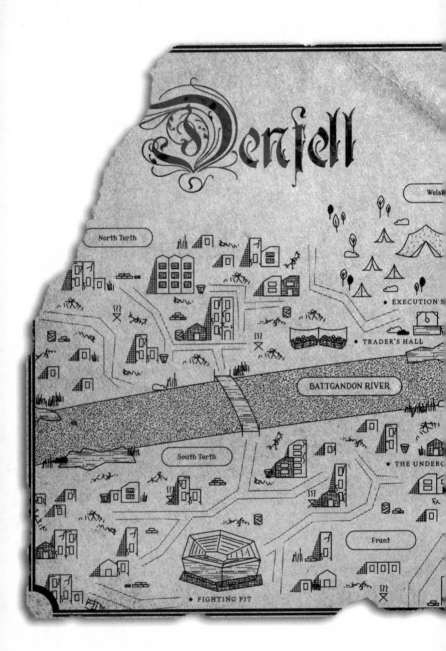

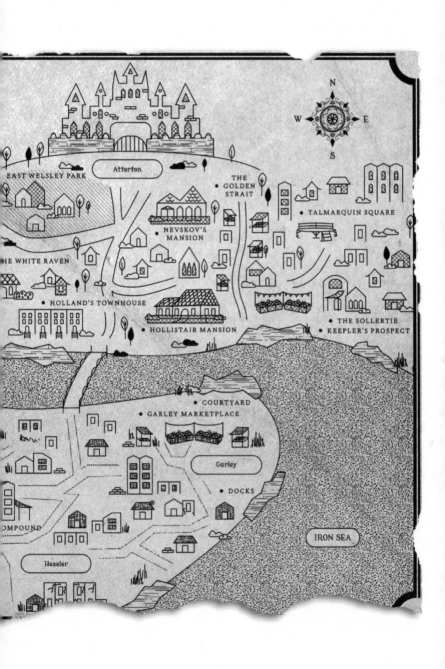

PART ONE

CHAPTER
ONE

The player slapped his cards against the table, leaned back in his chair, and grinned.

"Impressive hand," Ren said. She would know. She'd crafted it. "But better luck next time."

She fanned out her winning cards, and the man's smile waned, his arrogance falling away like an unclasped cloak slipping from his shoulders. The other two players whistled low. They had long ago folded, but not before parting with a dozen gold coins and a handful of silver. It was enough money to keep Ren comfortable for a week.

Standing from her seat in the crowded tavern, she swept her winnings into a pouch and shrugged on her black coat. She tipped her head at the table. "Gentlemen."

The losing player jumped to his feet, his hand latching on to her arm. "How about another round?"

When Ren looked pointedly at his grip, he released her but offered no apology. Entitled and cocky, with a taste for gambling and more than enough money to support the unfortunate habit, he possessed all the qualities Ren looked for in an opponent. But she had grown rather tired of him. He'd spent the game complimenting her *pretty poker face*, while his eyes not so discreetly darted to her low neckline every other second. He was so relentless she had started to wonder if it was possible to be killed by aggressive flirtation.

"Tempting," she said. "But I have places to be and your money to spend."

"Come on. I can't go home with empty pockets."

Ren was already walking away. "Looks like you'll need to ask for an advance on your allowance."

Chilly winter air greeted her outside the tavern doors. Slipping on thick leather gloves, Ren set out into the dark streets of Denfell. As she made her way through the city, she fingered the coins in her pocket. The man really hadn't thought she would win. They never did. Not when she'd played her first game at twelve, her black hair ratty and matted, limbs scarcely larger than the cards in her hand. Definitely not now. She was six years older, her long hair shined like fresh ink, and she'd packed on a fair amount of lean muscle, but now she wasn't a threat because she had the breasts to fill out a corset.

It didn't matter if people underestimated her or not. She would win either way.

Ren had a matter to attend to, and afterward she was heading to a fighting pit just across the river, but she didn't have anywhere to be for another hour. The tavern she'd chosen tonight wasn't far from the Golden Strait, a long stretch of road where the city's wealthiest shopped and dined. It emptied after dusk, and though guards made their rounds, if Ren timed it right, she could avoid them entirely. If she timed it wrong—well, she knew how to deal with it.

When Ren arrived at the Golden Strait, she was relieved to find the guards were nowhere to be seen. It wasn't that she was opposed to taking care of their presence; it was just a massive pain in the ass. Once, she might have objected on moral grounds, but that was a long time ago.

Ren pulled out a watch, clocked the time, and estimated she had at least seven minutes. She'd need no more than five.

Sweeping down the cobbled stretch of road, she blended into the shadows beneath doorways and overhangs. She slipped past windows of expensive fabrics, passing by jewels glittering in the moonlight, and stopped in front of a shop boasting clothes of some of the finest make in Denfell. There were dresses she would never have a place to wear and painful-looking velvet shoes. If she'd been feeling self-indulgent, she might have considered trying them on, but tonight her attention slid past the glamour to the far-right side of the display and the burgundy coat she'd been eyeing for two weeks.

Tossing a glance around the deserted street, Ren stepped up to the barred door and the heavy padlock. She turned up a palm, and a wispy ball of silver light formed in her hand. It grew dense, the faint silver becoming something more solid, and shot into the keyhole. With a flexing of her fingers, Ren worked the inside of the lock, prodding until it popped open. She unchained the bars and pulled them outward, then directed her silver to the door, guiding it under the crack, into the shop, and up to the lock on the other side. One twist of the wrist, and the shop was hers.

She stepped inside, her silver vanishing like smoke on the breeze as she removed her old, ratty jacket. The coat caught her shirt, dragging the collar sideways, and Ren quickly tugged her sleeve back up to cover the uneven skin marring the top of her right shoulder. Then she pulled the new jacket from the display, the silk lining shining like water and just as smooth to the touch. As she'd suspected, the coat was a nearly perfect fit, save for the sleeves, which were slightly too short, but it was nothing gloves couldn't fix. The front ended just below the slight curve of her chest and the long coattails, which fell to her heels, highlighted her tall frame nicely. In conjunction with the leather corset she'd paid a fortune to commission (a bodice that failed to cinch in her waist but fared quite nicely when it came to storing small daggers), Ren had to admit she looked good.

Before departing, she checked for a coin box or purse, but the merchant wasn't stupid enough to leave their money overnight, so she settled for pocketing the jewelry, which she'd hawk at the Underground later. She took one last moment to drape her old coat on the display where the red one had been, then slipped out of the shop, her silver locking the door once more. The bars and padlock went back in place, and Ren continued down the street. She caught the faint click of heeled boots, the swish of winter cloaks, and she ducked around a corner just as the guards appeared, gone a moment before they knew she was there.

Ren crossed a stone bridge over the Battgandon River,

a wide body of water that ran through the center of Denfell like a spine. It separated the generally pleasant northern half of the city from the rougher southern side, but some places, like the Terth slum in the west, were shitholes through and through, regardless of direction.

Ren had just stepped off the bridge when she sensed she was being observed. Without slowing, she glanced back and spotted a tall man on the opposite side of the river. He was mostly obscured by the night shadows and doing a spectacular job of acting casual, but Ren had lived on the streets long enough to know when she was being followed.

She ducked between two buildings and picked up her pace, but before she'd reached a fork at the end of the alley, she heard the pound of footfalls behind her. Cursing under her breath, Ren took a right and broke into a sprint, her long coattails rippling behind her like red streamers.

The streets of Denfell had been her home for nine years. She knew the straight lines, wide roads, and bright paint of the wealthy districts just as well as the dull colors and crooked alleys of the slums, and she never lost her way as she ran in what she hoped was a disorienting pattern. She darted over bridges spanning the Battgandon and slipped into gaps between buildings, their candy-colored hues bright enough to put sweetshops to shame. Finally, she found the passage she'd been searching for. It was only a couple feet wide and next to invisible in the darkness to anyone who didn't know to look for it, but she slipped in easily. She backed into the shadows and held her breath. Five seconds passed, then ten. It was another thirty before she loosed a breath and still thirty more before she moved. Ren slid between the walls and popped out onto a narrow pathway running beside the river, illuminated by a few scattered streetlamps.

"You're quite the card player," said a voice.

Ren whirled, simultaneously withdrawing a dagger from a hidden slit in her corset. She came face-to-face with not a man, but a boy, who she doubted was any older than her. He really didn't look like much of a threat. In daylight, he was probably downright pleasant, with darker skin, round eyes, and thick black hair, but strangers chasing her around the city were bad news, no matter how attractive.

"Why are you following me?" Ren asked, backing away with her knife held aloft.

"I'm sorry if I scared you."

"I don't scare easy." Her fingers twitched at her side. "Why are you following me?"

"I just want to talk."

"Go to a confessional."

Ren flung her dagger. It plunged into the boy's shoulder, and he staggered sideways, biting back a shout of pain. Pulling out a second blade, she stalked forward, but before she could make certain he wouldn't be following her anymore, something smashed into the back of her head. She dropped to the ground, and darkness took her.

CHAPTER
TWO

The first thing Ren was aware of was a fierce pounding in her skull. It was bad enough that she felt as if someone had taken a hammer to her head, which perhaps wasn't far from the truth. Next, she registered the rope and the fact that her hands were tied behind a chair.

Ren resisted a groan as she lifted her head and blinked her surroundings into clarity. She was sitting in the middle of an abandoned building, some kind of warehouse by the look of it, with boards nailed haphazardly over broken windows, bits of debris and rotted wood scattered across the stone floor. High above, the rafters were barren, and swaths of moonlight filtered in through weatherworn holes in the ceiling. It was as silent as a boneyard, and when Ren strained her ears, she heard nothing from the streets outside. Though the place was deserted, the air was neither stale nor dusty. It carried a telltale tang of salt, which meant they must be near the Battgandon River, but as to where exactly they'd taken her, she couldn't say.

The pouch of gold in Ren's coat pocket pressed against her side, and she breathed a shallow sigh of relief. At least she hadn't been robbed. She wasn't dead yet, but she definitely would be in a day's time if she lost that money. And while the daggers were gone from the slits in the front of her corset, her captor had missed the ones in the back, as well as the knife she kept hidden in her boot. Hands tied to the back of the chair, Ren curled her fingers and sent a thread of silver slithering into the knot at her wrists, hoping the moon would hide the glow.

By a set of metal doors across the room, two tall figures were murmuring, their heads bent together. Ren stared for several seconds before one noticed. He broke off, jerking his chin in her direction, and when the other turned, she was unsurprised to find the boy who had been chasing her. He'd removed his coat, and a good portion of his white shirt was wet with blood. As he approached, his left arm was stiff at his side. Good. If she was royally screwed, at least she was inflicting some pain on her way down.

The boy stopped ten feet in front of her chair, a chunk of black hair falling over his forehead. His soft eyes were a strange contrast to the shadows and the shuttered building. He looked like he should have been at a tavern with friends, not tying girls up in empty warehouses. "I'm sorry about this," he said.

"What do you want?" Ren asked.

"Like I said, I just want to talk."

"Do you tie up everyone you want to talk to?"

"Only the people who stab me."

Ren cocked a brow as if to say, *Do you expect an apology?*

His mouth quirked. "Don't worry. My brother patched me up."

Ren eyed the man leaning against the door. His hair was tied back in a knot, and a black overcoat fell to his knees. With a shadow of neatly trimmed facial hair, he was clearly the older brother, but the two did look a lot alike. Same sharp jaw, same towering build, same hair color. He met her stare with an unreadable expression.

"I guess you have my undivided attention," Ren said to the younger one. "So talk."

He watched her for a moment, as if considering, and in the quiet, Ren half expected to hear a bat stretching its wings in the rafters. "What do you know about the Silver Purge?"

Ren stiffened. She knew all about the slaughter of every magic wielder in the kingdom of Erdis. The story might have been erased from the history books, but it was as well-known as any folk tale. A century ago, King Tallis Lyandor, a wielder himself, had been so terrified of losing power that he'd outlawed the use of magic by anyone but the royal family. He'd sent his armies across Erdis, burning villages of wielders, hanging magical families, beheading anyone caught fleeing. The Silver Purge was the reason the only magic left in the kingdom belonged to the crown, why the only silver wielders in the past one hundred years had been Lyandors.

"I know enough," she said. She didn't like where this was going, and she definitely didn't like the way the boy hadn't stopped staring at her as if she were a map he wanted to memorize.

He let a few endless seconds pass. "We know you're a wielder, Ren. We've been looking for you for a while."

Shit.

Ren's heart skipped one beat and then another. How? How could they possibly know the secret she'd spent her life protecting, the one that could get her killed—that almost *had* gotten her killed nine years ago? She forced herself to focus on the silver still working its way through her bindings. Without being able to see them, she was having one hell of a time getting the ropes undone.

She had to get out of here. Now.

"How long have you been looking for me?" she asked.

"A few months. Everyone thought you were dead, but then my father heard rumors about a girl with a burn mark across her shoulder. You fit the description; you're the right age. He thought it was worth checking out."

"Your father?"

"He was a friend of your parents before . . . when they used to live here." A pause. "You changed your name."

"You would, too, if the king wanted you dead. How did you find me?"

"People talk," the boy answered. "Especially about girls who like to frequent the fighting pits."

"Are you going to turn me over to the king?"

"No."

"Then what do you *want*?"

His gaze was steady. "We want you to help us overthrow the throne."

She could have laughed. She would have if she hadn't

been chased, knocked out, and dragged around the city by two strange men. "You want me to join the rebellion? You can't be serious."

The man by the door finally spoke, the deep rumble of his voice carrying across the empty room. "Why would this be a joke?"

"Because I'm not a patriot? Because I don't give a shit about this country?"

He pushed off the wall, and where his younger brother moved casually, this man was all tension and purpose. His booted steps echoed in the hollow space of the warehouse. "Do you know why a rebellion has never succeeded?" he asked.

"Poor organizational skills?"

He gave her a stony look. "The king has the entire country convinced he's all-powerful. He's feared as if he were a god. Not to mention that one King's Child is more effective than twenty commoners with pitchforks. They make certain rebellions fail before they begin."

Ren knew of the King's Children and was smart enough to stay away. They were the king's personal warriors, lost and stolen kids raised by swordpoint in the castle armory. By sixteen, they could hit any target from impossible distances and kill a man in no less than a hundred different ways. They were brutal, deadly, and loyal to no one but the crown.

"The people have lost hope," the older brother said. "They've been beaten down too many times to stand back up. And without the people on our side, it'll be impossible to take the throne. *You* can give them cause to keep trying."

"You clearly don't know me very well," Ren muttered. She had been accused of a lot of things, but inspiring confidence was not one of them.

"If the king is to be believed, nothing is as powerful as the crown," he said, scowling hard. "You can prove otherwise. Ren, you are the only thing in all of Erdis that King Mattheus Lyandor is afraid of."

"Plus, we could use skills like yours, silver and otherwise," the younger brother added. "My brother will never admit it, but you're a talented thief and a good fighter. That could come in handy."

"This is insane. *You* are insane. Both of you. I'm one person. I can't bring a country to its knees."

"The king thinks you can," the younger one pointed out. "Look at history. The Silver Purge happened because the Lyandors were threatened by other wielders. They were worried their rule might be challenged. One hundred years later, and magic is still illegal because it poses too great a danger to the crown."

Ren was shaking her head, so the older brother pushed harder. "Did you know magic disappeared from your family centuries ago? It's what saved your bloodline from destruction in the Silver Purge."

Of course Ren knew. Silver was passed down by blood and blood alone, and it would have been impossible for her to wield magic without an ancestor who had. It was a long-dead grandmother who'd been a wielder, but her children had been born without any silver, and their children after them. By the time the Silver Purge took place, everyone had forgotten her family had once possessed the magic that King Tallis was eradicating. Ren had learned this from her parents when she was just a girl—before the fire, before she'd gotten them killed.

She glared up at him. "Don't talk about my family."

He took two steps forward, moving away from his brother's side and closer to Ren. His entire body was tensed. "I've never heard of magic returning generations later, but yours came back to you. It's a miracle, a gift from the gods. And what have you done with it? You've become a thief. You cheat, you steal, you lie. You've done nothing but spit in the faces of the gods."

"Darek," his brother warned.

"And the worst part is, you don't care." His voice was gruff and full of heat. Ren could tell he'd been wanting to say this since the beginning of the conversation, but he'd been holding himself back. "While people starve and suffer and die at the hands of a tyrant, you gallivant around Denfell, taking everything that doesn't belong to you and nothing you deserve." She opened her mouth to fight back, but he didn't seem inclined to let her. "You could be anything, do anything, but you only care about yourself."

"Stop," his brother said, grabbing his arm to wheel him away.

Ren finally managed to free her hands. The pressure eased, the ropes dropped to the floor, and she shoved to her feet. "The gods can go to the ninth hell. The king sent men to burn my home because of my *gift*. My parents died in that fire. I was nine when I started living on the streets. *Nine.*" Ren spat the number out like it was poison. "You have no idea what I've been through, so don't insult me by speaking of starvation and suffering like you understand it. I've done what I needed to survive, and I won't apologize for it. Not to you and not to your gods."

He ripped out of his brother's grasp and descended on her so quickly she nearly fell back into the chair. "They're your gods, too."

Although she was tall, he was even taller, his build towering over her, but Ren held her ground, her hands practically vibrating with energy. He better thank his gods that her silver wouldn't act without her say-so, because if it could, it would be wrapped around his neck right about now. When she spoke, her voice was low and simmering with rage. "Get out of my face."

They stood there, Ren's green eyes refusing to shift from his brown ones, while long seconds ticked by.

He made a noise of disgust. "You're right. You're not fit to inspire the people. You're a coward with a few tricks up her sleeve. Erdis deserves better."

Pivoting away, he stalked toward the exit. His palms hit the doors, and he pushed them open, allowing in pale streaks of yellow lamplight from the street outside. But he paused in the doorway, a gruff curse spilling from his mouth. He turned back and shoved his arms over his chest, glowering at Ren as the doors fell shut behind him. The clang reverberated around the room, barreled into shadowed corners, and ricocheted off rafters.

Silence crept in, tense and unsettled, and Ren glared back. She didn't have many weak spots, but the man—Darek—he'd found a good number of them, whether he'd meant to or not. His words stung in all the wrong places, places that were best avoided and ignored. Maybe if she was lucky, he'd get hit by a carriage on his way home.

"Ren?" said the younger brother.

"Why are you still here?" she asked, flexing her fingers.

"Because I have no sense of self-preservation, apparently."

She tore her eyes from the older brother. The younger one's face showed the hint of a placating smile. She didn't return it.

"I'm sorry about my brother. He's very"—his eyes flickered toward the door—"passionate."

"He's an ass." Ren shot the man a pointed look. It was too dark to tell for certain, but it looked like his jaw may have been ticking.

"Yes, he's that, too. I'm Markus."

"Charmed," Ren said flatly.

"Look, I know you don't trust us, and I understand. I do. But will you listen to what I have to say? I promise Darek and I prepared different monologues." Ren nearly smiled at that, and he took it as permission to continue. "The Lyandors have always been your typical tyrants. They keep the poor too hungry, tired, and sick to rise up. They ply the rich with gold, and they kill their critics before they ever become a problem. But political tensions are at a high. We've heard the rulers of Jareen, Eslind, and Orian are demanding King Mattheus sign a treaty. It sounds like they're trying to strong-arm him into agreeing to keep his armies out of their countries. The king is none too pleased. No one can predict how he's going to react. It could spell disaster for Erdis. We need you, Ren. You can help us prevent a war."

Politics and war and disaster—such weighty words. But they held no meaning for Ren. What did she care if the kingdom went to war? Erdis had never been kind to her. She didn't owe it any favors.

"And if I refuse?" she asked. "Will you turn me over to the king then?"

"Of course not. My brother may love to huff and puff, but he'd carve out his own eyes with a spoon before handing a wielder over to the king."

Darek let out a grunt that could have been called a laugh if it weren't so devoid of humor.

Ren lobbed another glare in his direction. "Thank you for that lovely image," she muttered, looking back to Markus. "It's a suicide mission."

"It's not."

"It is." She smoothed down the front of her new coat and went about inspecting it. If they had so much as torn the fabric, she'd bring the wrath of all nine hells down on them. "You're more than welcome to get yourself killed, be my guest, but leave me out of it."

"Will you just think about it?"

"I don't have to. I'm not interested in your revolution."

"You'd really turn your back on this kingdom?"

Ren narrowed her eyes. So much for different monologues. "Here's one thing to know about me: my morals died with my family."

She fished out her watch and flipped it open. It looked like she still had enough time to tend to her errand and make it to the pit, as long as they hadn't taken her too far from the Golden Strait. Hells, she was feeling a little reckless tonight, so she might just head west and check out a fighting pit there instead. She'd never been to the pit in the Terth, where matches concluded in either death or mercy. Winning fighters received more gold than anywhere else in the city, but it wasn't usually worth the gamble, seeing as most people who frequented the place were not inclined to mercy.

"Well, Markus, it's been a pleasure. I hope I never have the misfortune of meeting you or your brother again."

She was halfway to the warehouse doors, and Darek wasn't moving, standing there with his arms crossed, looking like a guard at the gate to one of the hells. Fine by Ren. She had no qualms about going through him rather than around. But Markus's voice called her up short. "Two hundred and fifty thousand gold pieces."

She halted, her stare locked on Darek's. His face was stone-hard. "What?" she asked.

"Two hundred and fifty thousand gold pieces," Markus repeated. "That's how much we'll give you if you help."

Gods, that was a lot of gold. Even her more daring

bouts of thievery couldn't bring in that much. The greedy part of her wanted it, but her rational side warned her to heed caution. She turned her back on his brother. "Dead women can't spend money."

"Five hundred thousand," Markus offered.

Ren sucked in a breath. *Heavens above and hells below.* She'd never have to play another card game again. With that kind of money, she could pay off her debt, buy a house for every orphan she knew, and have enough left to move to the countryside and raise a herd of show horses. Not that she was particularly interested in that scenario, but it was always nice to have options.

"Seven hundred," Ren countered.

There was shifting behind her, a boot stepping forward. "Markus—"

"Darek, just please shut up," Markus told his brother. To Ren, he said, "Five hundred and fifty."

Ren chewed on her lip. If this worked, if they managed to overthrow the king and by some miracle she made it out alive, she would be a very rich woman indeed. It was so much gold Ren couldn't begin to fathom what she'd do with it all. She had always wanted to travel.

"Six, and you give me half now."

"Six-fifty, and you get it all when this is done."

She sucked on her teeth a moment, Darek's presence like a hot iron at her back. She could feel his gaze, disapproval rolling off him in simmering waves. She blew out a breath. "When I check your bank account, will I find it full of gold or cobwebs?"

"You can check our bank account?"

Ren raised a brow. "I'm about one of a thousand people in this city who can get a look at your account."

His face drew into a startled expression, as if he'd never considered the possibility that his money wasn't safe. "Our account is plenty full."

Ren nodded. "I'll still be checking, of course."

"Of course."

She looked him up and down, from his expensive boots to the face that seemed too young to be part of a revolution. Ren knew she wasn't much older, but the streets followed their own laws of time. Eighteen years old, and she felt as if she'd reached middle age.

"You better hope I survive this, because if I don't get my money, I'm haunting your ass until the day you die." She tossed a glance over her shoulder. "Yours, too."

Darek's expression didn't crack; his stance didn't shift.

"And if the king kills us all?" Markus asked.

"If you think I'm annoying now, wait until you're stuck with me in the afterlife."

He laughed. "You drive a hard bargain, Ren Kolins." He stuck out his palm. "Six hundred and fifty thousand gold pieces, it is."

"If we survive," Ren felt compelled to point out. She gripped his hand and shook. The warehouse doors creaked open and clanged shut a moment later, signaling Darek's departure.

"We will," Markus promised.

CHAPTER
THREE

The rebel sympathizer was a sniveling mess. Every one of his nails was missing from his left hand, and after she'd removed them, Adley had moved on to breaking his fingers. She'd snapped his thumb and now gripped his index finger. She jerked it back. His scream split the air. If anyone on the night-covered street heard, no one dared investigate, not with the leather-uniformed King's Child stationed outside the broken front door.

"What do you know of the rebellion?" Adley asked, calm, level, bored. She spoke in the voice she'd spent eleven years perfecting, the voice of a King's Child, the crown's most lethal and devoted weapon.

"N-n-nothing," the man whimpered. It was the same word he'd said over and over since she'd kicked in his door and beaten him until he could hardly see. Then she'd dragged him from the dimly lit hallway into a cramped kitchen with scuffed floorboards and sagging cabinets. While she strapped both his wrists to the arms of his own chair, Lesa stirred the embers of a dying fire. Now flames licked the edges of the hearth, providing enough light to see, and the smell of charred wood filled the small room.

Dancing shadows distorted each of their faces. It seemed appropriate, somehow, that none of them looked quite human.

Adley trailed a hand over the sympathizer's mangled fingers, across his heaving chest, and down to the knuckles she hadn't touched. His sobbing spilled into hysterics as she taunted, a predator playing with her food.

"Please," he whispered.

"You can make it stop," Lesa said. She leaned against the doorframe and used a dagger to clean her nails. Even without the lion stitched on her top, she would have been recognizable as a King's Child. It was in the way she held her shoulders, the scars along her muscled arms, a look in her dark eye that flashed like a warning. "All you have to do is tell us about the rebels."

"I don't know anything, I swear."

"You don't expect us to believe that," Lesa said. Her face was blank and cold, a mirror of Adley's own. But while Adley wore her unflinching cruelty like a mask, she saw no flicker of emotion from Lesa, no indication that what they were doing might have been difficult to stomach. "You're a known rebel sympathizer."

"I'm not," the man said. His swollen blue eyes looked into Adley's—pleading, begging. Everything she'd done to him, every broken bone and agonizing moment, was staring back at her. Judging her.

"I think I'm rather tired of snapping your fingers," Adley said. She stood, reaching back to pull an arrow from her quiver. She stroked the head as if petting a house cat, then leveled it over the man's thumb. He jerked his arm, but the rope held firm. "Don't make me maim your other hand, too."

A sob wracked his body, and he rasped out, "I don't—I don't know a-a-anything."

She shoved her arrow into his thumb, all the way through, and pinned it to the chair beneath. A scream ripped from his throat. Tears, saliva, and mucus leaked down his busted face, and Adley's mask threatened to slip. No matter how many times she did this, the crying was always the worst. It slipped through the smallest of cracks and scratched at the person she was beneath the leather uniform and the calloused hands and the cruelty.

She freed another arrow from her quiver and tapped the sharp tip with her forefinger. "Tell me what you know about the rebellion."

"I don't know anything!" the man shrieked. His chin fell to his chest, and the sobbing started again.

"We'll make you a deal," Lesa said, tossing her dagger into the air and catching it by the hilt. Her pale-blonde hair, chopped without fuss at her shoulders, swayed with the movement. "Tell us everything you know, and we'll kill you now."

Adley hid a jolt of surprise. They had their commands. Once the sympathizer talked, they were to throw him into a prison cell. He wasn't slated for execution for another week. Adley didn't know if Lesa had made the offer out of clemency or because she found special joy in defying orders.

The man made no indication he'd heard her, so Adley stuck her arrow beneath his chin and forced his head up. "What do you say?" It would be a mercy killing. He had to know that. His eyes caught hers, and beneath the swelling and blood, she saw hesitation. The fire danced at his back. "Yes?"

"There's a tavern," he gasped. "In the Atterton District. Rebels meet there."

The Atterton District? That was the wealthiest neighborhood in Denfell, and its residents carried quite a bit of favor with the king. Most rebels they'd caught before had been operating out of dilapidated poorhouses and abandoned buildings in the Terth. The destitute had most reason to be dissatisfied with the king, but they had no resources. The wealthy, on the other hand . . . If they led an uprising, it could change the game completely.

"What tavern?" Adley asked.

"I don't know the name," the man croaked, and his chin began to quiver again.

"That's inconvenient," she said, running her arrow over the back of his hand in thoughtless patterns. The man shook from the tips of his scuffed boots to the top of his dry hair. She just had to finish this. Get him to talk, and it would be over. For both of them. "What about rebels? Do you have any names?"

"N-n-no," the man stammered.

Adley paused her aimless doodling. She applied pressure until the arrow broke his skin. Blood dribbled out, trickling down his hand and onto the wooden floor.

"I swear I told you everything I know! I've never met a rebel! I don't know anything!"

"Pity," said Lesa. She flung her dagger. The blade whipped across the room and drove into the man's foot. It pierced straight through leather, flesh, and bone, and embedded in the floorboards. He screamed again—and kept screaming. How he mustered the energy for it, Adley didn't know. He was going to blow out his vocal chords soon.

Wiping flecks of blood from her hands, Adley fought a wave of nausea, knowing all too well the kind of agony they were putting him through. In their training, the King's Children had practiced torture techniques on one another, since firsthand experience was supposed to be the best way to understand what would break a person the quickest without killing them. When her turn had come around, Adley had passed out in less than five minutes. Armed with her arrows, as always, she had been sure to return the favor as soon as she'd been released from the infirmary.

"You done with him?" Lesa asked.

Adley glanced at the wreck of a man tied down behind her. He hung his head against his chest and cried, spittle dripping onto his lap. "I'm finished."

Lesa turned on him with a saccharine smile, but Adley grabbed her by the arm. "Wait," she whispered. "We said we'd kill him if he told us what he knew."

"So?"

"So he told us what he knew."

Lesa held her gaze, and for a moment, it was just the

two of them. Eyes flickering down to Lesa's lips, Adley wished that were true. Wished they were anywhere else but here. Wished they were any*one* else.

"He's a traitor to the crown," Lesa said at last. "Our promises mean nothing to men like him."

Adley didn't really have an argument for that, so she released Lesa's arm. Lesa withdrew a blade more wicked than her smile and sauntered up to the man's chair, shadows skittering over the walls. "You and I are going to have such fun."

The screaming didn't stop until he lost consciousness.

CHAPTER
FOUR

Darek was as irritated as ever when he arrived at the White Raven. He nodded to the guard sitting on a stool outside the tavern, the man's figure like a shadow against the white brick facade, and tugged open one of the wooden doors. Candlelight and fragmented conversation spilled into the pristine empty street. The Atterton District, the wealthy neighborhood where Darek and his family lived, was always barren after the sun went down. That was when the respectable residents turned Denfell over to the gangs and pit lords, the thieves and con artists. At night, the city belonged to people like Ren.

Darek felt a bit bad about knocking the girl unconscious. He hadn't been planning to, but she'd flung a dagger at his brother, and she'd clearly had every intention of finishing what she'd started. He should have taken the knife as a sign. Or possibly some kind of omen.

He wasn't sure why he'd expected their first meeting to go better. He and Markus had spent the last couple weeks tailing Ren, tracking her as she slipped cards up her sleeves and broke into a dozen different shops. He'd watched from a shadowed alley as she dropped a sapphire necklace into one pocket and a ruby-studded ring into another, and didn't hesitate once. But Darek had thought maybe when they spoke she would show a hint of compassion, an indication that she cared about more than stolen jewels and card games—something resembling decency. Anything. He'd hoped she'd surprise him.

She hadn't.

The only language she seemed to speak was one of greed and gold. Of all possible people, the gods had given this girl magic. Darek couldn't believe Ren was supposed to be their salvation. Maybe she was right. Maybe her silver wasn't a gift, and it was all just a coincidence.

He snapped the door shut a little harder than he meant to and shot a glare heavensward. Or maybe the gods had a terrible sense of humor. He was probably being punished for something.

Inside the White Raven, a fireplace provided respite from the promise of snowfall, three crystal chandeliers illuminating the spotless walls and framed paintings. The oak floor was polished, the scent of something savory floated from the kitchen, and the piano in the corner was actually in tune. All said, it was a tavern fit for the Atterton District. No one bothered the patrons of the White Raven. Every one of them was a rebel and a traitor to the throne, but the King's Children didn't look twice at the quiet building with the white rosebushes out front.

Darek had learned that money was good for quite a lot, disguising rebellions included.

He sometimes felt guilty about the fortune to his name,

money he hadn't lifted a finger for. His mother had been from Ticharra, the perpetually warm country that bordered Erdis in the south, where her family owned desert land rich with a volatile sand-like substance called *fragor*. His father was just as well-off. Possessing an exceptionally keen eye for business, his investments were wide-reaching and varied. There were tea shops and tanneries, imported jewels from Sirica, fabrics from Orian. He'd even managed to snag the queen's interest. She'd been working with him since before Darek was born.

At least his family was doing something useful with their money. That helped to assuage the guilt he felt when he traveled south, when the disparity of wealth became tangible, when he could breathe in poverty like a lungful of smoke.

Darek peeled off his gloves and shoved them into a coat pocket, making for the bar. Only about a dozen people were gathered at tables scattered around the room, their chatter no louder than water running through a brook. Darek didn't stop to talk, but he did offer the occasional nod in greeting.

Although the rebels who visited the White Raven rotated each night, Darek was familiar with every face. He had to be. One slipup, and a plan decades in the making would fail. Darek wasn't about to let that happen.

Before he reached the counter, he was waylaid by his father. Laurin Hollistair was as tall and broad as his sons, with the same sharp nose and jaw, but that's where the resemblance ended. He was fair-skinned and light-eyed, his straight brown hair streaked with gray. He wore it styled back from a face that had become lined by both laughter and grief over the years.

"How did it go?" he asked.

Darek looked over his father's shoulder and caught the barmaiden's eye, holding up one finger. With a smile, the young woman produced a clean glass and began to fill it with ale. He turned his attention back to his father. "She stabbed Markus."

His father gave a short, surprised laugh, and Darek gaped at him. "Did you just *laugh*?"

"She sounds just like her mother. Kara Avevian was the most spirited person I've ever met. A lot of fun at parties. She never stabbed me, but I think there were times when she wanted to."

Spirited was one word for Ren, but not one Darek would have chosen. "Father. Your son was stabbed. With a knife," he added, in case the point needed to be driven home a little more.

"Well, since you're here, it must not be too critical."

Darek glowered at him, and his father chuckled again.

"Always so serious. You take after your mother like that."

As usual, Darek's heart panged at the mention of his mother. The twinge had become less painful over time, but he doubted it would ever disappear entirely. When she had died in a raid on a rebel safe house in the Terth, he'd been there. *Take care of your brother*, she'd said, shoving his gangly thirteen-year-old body into a crawl space. *And don't let this revolution fail. However long it takes, see that it's done.*

I promise, he'd said. She shut him into the wall, and the next time he saw her, she was lying faceup in a pool of her own blood.

"Believe me," Darek said now, "once you meet Ren, you'll understand."

"Actually, that's why I'm here. I might not get to meet the girl for a while. One of my deals in Sirica was meant to close this week, but with this whole treaty business, Sirican merchants are wary of making new deals with Erdis. I need to go smooth this over."

Darek ran a hand across his neck. It was poor timing. Their revolution was coming closer and closer to a head. Darek could feel it like the final days of fall when the air turned crisp, a warning that winter was on its way. And now that Ren had agreed to work with them, it wouldn't be long before they could make their move for the throne. He wanted his father here when that happened, but the truth was, he didn't need him. For a while now, Darek had been acting as the rebellion's unofficial leader, a title that had originally belonged to his mother, then passed to his father after her death. But in recent years, his father had turned to funding their efforts behind the scenes. Laurin was tired after so many years of fighting, but Darek was just getting started.

"Weren't you supposed to be going to Lan Covve tomorrow?" Darek asked.

Lan Covve was a country town a day's ride from

Denfell, where the queen of Erdis had an estate. For months, his father had been planning a meeting to discuss the business ventures the two of them were wrapped up in. Queen Ellisa wasn't a politically minded woman, only making public appearances at high-profile events like the upcoming Royal Carnival, nor was she all that compassionate. Darek's father had come to know her well over the years, and he'd learned she left the ruling to the king, not concerning herself with the bloodshed staining their name so long as she had money to keep her comfortable and a closet full of dresses.

"Yes," his father said. "And you know we can't cancel. So I'll need you to go in my place. I've already told Jaston to draft up papers for you."

He nodded. "Of course."

His father was silent for a moment, and then he set a hand on Darek's shoulder, giving a small squeeze. "I'm proud of you. No matter what happens. You know that, right?"

Emotion surged in Darek's chest. Placing a hand over his father's, he squeezed back. He missed his mother every day, but in the wake of her death and in the midst of his own grief, Laurin had more than stepped up to the task of raising his sons. Darek would never stop being grateful. Sometimes, an extra prayer of thanks to the goddess of the family didn't feel like enough.

"I know," he said. "What time do you leave tomorrow?"

"My ship departs at dawn."

"Markus and I will see you off."

His father laughed again. "Best of luck getting your brother out of bed."

"We'll see you off," Darek insisted. He'd drag Markus from his sheets and carry him to the docks if he had to.

With a fond smile, his father clapped him on the shoulder one last time before turning to depart the tavern.

When Darek finally arrived at the bar, the drink the barmaiden had poured for him was waiting. "Any news from the castle?" he asked, sweeping it up.

"Not as far as I've heard," she replied, pushing a piece of copper-colored hair out of her face with the back of her hand. "The Orian emissary is still at court. King Mattheus hasn't signed the treaty, and it doesn't look like he plans to."

Darek rubbed his jaw, his stubble rough against his palm. "I was afraid of that."

The rebellion didn't have any of their own people inside the castle, but everyone knew someone who was willing to spill details here and there. It seemed the king had finally overstepped his bounds. Ever since the Silver Purge, Erdis's borders had been closed to immigration under the pretense of protection; the crown claimed they were preventing the spread of a disease that had decimated the silver wielders a century ago. No one, not even the schoolchildren who read about the plague in history books, believed it, and still the crown continued their poorly disguised attempt to keep magic out of the country.

Other kingdoms were paying the consequences. When civil war broke out in Ticharra and King Mattheus refused to accept the neighboring country's refugees, it drove hundreds of thousands of people across the Iron Sea to Orian and Jareen. It wasn't long before illness swept through Orian, which was overcrowded and ill-equipped to handle its sudden growth in population. King Mattheus reacted by sending an army under the guise of providing humanitarian relief to the fever-ravaged country. Then he sent a second army to Jareen, claiming he wanted to ensure disease didn't also spread into their lands. Darek didn't know why anyone was surprised that he'd abandoned the humanitarian shroud and was now attempting to use his armies to gain a political foothold in both Orian and Jareen.

Word was Orian's king had had enough. With an army half the size of Erdis's and no feasible way to take a stand on his own, he'd proposed an alliance to Jareen and Eslind, the latter of which bordered both countries on the east and was most likely to fall victim to King Mattheus next. Together, the three kingdoms had prepared a treaty and were threatening to bring war to Erdis if the king didn't agree to their terms and withdraw his armies from their lands.

"What does this mean for us?" the barmaiden asked, filling another glass.

"It means we're running out of time."

She sighed and set a second mug in front of him. "For Riko," she explained, nodding across the room. "He and Jaston are over there."

Darek raised a brow. "How many drinks has he had?"

"Three," she said immediately.

"Liar."

She bit her bottom lip to hide a smile and ran a rag over the spotless counter. Shaking his head, Darek picked up the second mug of ale—Riko would no doubt talk the barmaiden into putting it on Darek's tab at the end of the night—and headed for a low table on the other side of the tavern.

Jaston was leaning back in his seat, arms crossed over his thin torso and sandy hair brushed away from his forehead. He was eyeing Riko, who gesticulated wildly, his black brows and dark eyes as expressive as the rest of him. When Riko noticed Darek approaching, he dropped his arms. Both he and Jaston straightened in their seats.

Darek deposited the glass mugs on the table and shrugged off his overcoat. He yanked a chair back and sat, popping open the buttons on his vest and shoving his sleeves up to the elbow. He grabbed his ale, leaning back to take a drink.

"Well?" Riko prompted. "Is she everything you dreamed she would be?"

At the mention of Ren, Darek's scowl returned. He swallowed. "She's worse."

Riko chuckled. "That good, huh?"

"Are you sure we need her?" Jaston asked.

"Unfortunately," Darek said, training his dark stare on his drink. He had a second gulp.

"I was thinking," Jaston said, "about shadows. And how many generations in her family went without magic before she was born. Do you wonder if Ren—?"

Darek waved a dismissive hand. "Doesn't seem likely. Whose would she even be?"

Jaston frowned, while Riko asked, "What does her silver look like up close?"

"It's silver. What do you think it looks like?"

Riko pushed aside an empty mug and grabbed his new one. "Someone's in a mood."

"Isn't he always?" Jaston observed.

Darek took a second to glower at them both, then asked Jaston, "Did you get the hycanthian flowers?"

Jaston pulled out a small jar filled with dried-and-crushed petals that strongly resembled pale-blue tea leaves. "Those cost a fortune," he said, setting the glass container on the table. "Real pain in the ass to track down, too. The princes better drink them; otherwise, I wasted months of my life."

Darek inspected the contents of the jar, then he stowed it in the pocket of his trousers. "My father needs me to go to Lan Covve tomorrow. I should only be gone three days."

"Send my regards to Her Majesty, the Queen," Riko said.

"Be careful, Darek," Jaston added. "I'll have the papers for you in the morning."

Jaston possessed a real talent for forging documents, a useful skill they hadn't had at their disposal until he joined the rebellion four years ago. He'd proven himself invaluable, and Darek had no doubt that the fake papers would stand up to the scrutiny of the Queen's Guard.

"Appreciate it. Once I get back, I'm taking Ren to the

Underground. You both should be there. Start spreading some of the rumors we've been talking about."

Riko lifted two fingers to his temple and saluted. "You got it, boss."

"And please keep an eye on Markus while I'm gone. Make sure he doesn't do anything stupid."

"Of course we'll watch out for him," Jaston said. "You know that half the people in this tavern would die for that boy."

Riko's attention drifted to the door. "Speak of a devil."

Darek's seventeen-year-old brother had just stepped in out of the cold. As the tavern doors drifted shut, his gaze roamed the room until it landed on Darek, and it suddenly hit him that Markus was no longer a little kid. Darek was five years older, but pretty soon he wouldn't look it. At least his jaw was perpetually stubbled. If his little brother stopped shaving, that was when Darek would have to put his foot down.

Sometimes, he resented himself for letting Markus take part in this revolution, when death was such a likely outcome. But Markus was their mother's son. Rebellion swam in his blood, and if Darek had forbidden it, Markus would have become involved in a more dangerous way. And Darek couldn't break his promise to their mother. He couldn't lose his brother. He would rather lose his soul.

Markus meandered their way, smiling and offering better greetings than Darek's half-hearted nods. He grimaced when a woman wrapped him in a hug, and gestured to his shoulder. Waving away her apologies, he disengaged himself from a budding conversation and continued through the room. He arrived at the back table and took a seat, his hands immediately picking up a drumbeat on the buffed wood. The tap of his fingers and the low cadence of background conversation were the only sounds between the four of them.

"So?" Jaston finally prompted. "How much gold did it take to get her to agree?"

Markus's hands went still. His eyes flicked to Darek, and a beat passed before he answered. "Six hundred and fifty thousand."

Riko gave a loud, surprised laugh. "The girl knows how to make a deal, doesn't she?"

Darek took a long swig of ale. Ren was going to be trouble—that much was clear. He only hoped she wasn't going to be more trouble than she was worth.

CHAPTER
FIVE

Ren stood in the middle of a large foyer, a dull ache at the back of her head from whatever had knocked her out an hour earlier, and regarded her surroundings: deep-purple-and-black wallpaper with a curling design, silver candelabras mounted at eye level, a table resting in the middle of the room bearing a vase of white calla lilies. To the left, a spiral staircase led to the second floor. Though every candle was lit, the place was still dim. It was always dim in Izram Nevskov's home, be it the middle of the day or the dead of night. Ren suspected the lack of light was an intentional aesthetic choice.

She had first set foot in the gang leader's house three years ago. It hadn't changed at all, down to the flowers on the foyer table—even their color was the same.

A hand came down on Ren's shoulder. She grabbed four large fingers, jerking them back to just shy of the breaking point. The owner of the hand gave a pained hiss. Ren was calm as she met the man's reproachful eyes and debated whether snapping his wrist would be worth the fuss he'd make.

She was in a bad enough mood to do it. Up until an

hour ago, she'd thought Freya, her one and only friend, was the sole person in all of Erdis who knew about her silver. When she pictured someone else finding out, she imagined the king taking off her head. Maybe some good, old-fashioned torture beforehand. She never considered that she might be dragged into an idiotic revolution by a couple rebels. She wished she could kill both brothers, shove a knife into their necks and be done with it. Corpses couldn't talk.

Another thing corpses couldn't do: go off on diatribes against her. She wouldn't easily forget the things Darek had spewed in that warehouse. She pictured his stormy expression as he told her, *You're a coward with a few tricks up her sleeve.* He could go to the hells and take his high horse with him. Ren would point the way down.

But if she killed Darek or his brother, she didn't think she would be getting her money.

Her grip tightened. The man cursed at her.

"Ren, darling, what have I told you about maiming my investments?" came a deep, smooth voice.

In an expensive velvet vest with a silver chain snaking across one side, Izram Nevskov stepped into the foyer. Slim and tall, he was in his forties but looked ten years younger. His thick head of hair was as black as Ren's, his eyes a clear blue, and there was hardly a wrinkle on his pale skin. He had strangely perfect features, save for his nose, which was bent in the middle like it had been badly broken and never healed properly. But this detail only made him more attractive. Without it, he might have resembled a porcelain doll come to life. He gave Ren a look somehow both warm and cold, and if she hadn't detested him with every breath in her body, she would have asked how he managed it.

Investments. That's what Nevskov's men were to him. Not gang members or thugs or murderers. She shot this one a look edged with ice and released his hand.

He took two quick steps back. "Bitch," he muttered, rubbing his wrist.

Her answering smile was tight-lipped and immensely sarcastic.

"Now, now, Fetz," Nevskov chided. "That's no way to speak to a lady."

The gang leader lifted a finger and beckoned Ren forward, then turned and glided down a hall branching off from the foyer. Ren followed him to his office. Like the rest of the mansion, the room was larger than it needed to be, sparsely decorated, and shadowed, despite the burning candles on the wall. Outside the windows, the sky was a deep, unending black.

Nevskov settled into a leather chair behind his black oak desk. He waved to a smaller, matching seat across from him and said, "Please, sit."

Ren pulled out a pouch weighted down with gold and tossed it onto the desk, the coins inside jangling. "This isn't a social call."

"Indulge me." He picked up the small bag.

Because no one really had a choice when it came to Nevskov, Ren lowered herself into the chair. The leather was butter-soft and easy to sink into, but she remained perched on the edge like a bird prepared to launch into flight.

Once upon a time, Ren had known one of Nevskov's *investments*. She was nine when she met Aidann. He was also living on the streets after a fallout with his family, and he had a habit of taking lost children under his wing. But he fought in the pits for Nevskov, and he belonged to the gang. When he borrowed more money than he won and subsequently fell behind on payments, five of Nevskov's men beat him to death. Ren was fifteen.

For six years, Aidann had been the only semblance of family she had left, and then he'd gone and gotten himself killed.

After that, Nevskov planned to take what Aidann owned from his family. He would have been devastated. So Ren told the gang leader to transfer Aidann's debt to her name. She didn't know why she'd cared. Most days, she was convinced she'd made a huge mistake.

Gold clinked as Nevskov dumped out the contents of Ren's pouch. He began to count. "Still visiting the fighting pits?" he inquired.

"You know I am," Ren said. Every few days, it was a different fight, a new opponent to beat, more money to win. She could have said she didn't enjoy the pits, that the sounds of crunching bone and split flesh were as unappealing as groaning metal, that she fought because she had to, because she owed a gang leader a huge sum of gold and she had no choice.

But that was a lie if she'd ever heard one.

Ren fought not just because she needed the money. She fought because she liked it.

Nevskov slid a coin across his desk. "If you ever change your mind about fighting for me, my offer still stands."

"I'm not interested. I—"

"You fight for yourself, I know," he finished. "But you and I are both aware that your debt isn't going away any-time soon. Fight for me, and you'll find I can be a generous man."

Ren was silent. She wanted to tell Nevskov that the day she fought for him would be the day he shit gold, but she held her tongue. He'd always been lenient with Ren's caustic comments, but she wasn't about to push her luck, not when it came to one of the deadliest men in Denfell.

"What's your secret?" he asked. "I know you have one."

Ren went still. She sucked in a silent breath. Two more coins scraped across Nevskov's desk.

For as long as she could remember, Ren had been guarding her silver as closely as a bank vault. But she'd learned it was a volatile magic, always clamoring for atten-tion, and if she went too long without using it, the silver would find a way out on its own. So she'd made herself a contradiction of recklessness and caution. When she wanted extra money (or a gorgeous red coat), she used magic to steal it, as long as the street was abandoned, the eyes trained elsewhere, the doors closed. It wasn't just the king she was worried about. Silver was powerful enough to murder a crowd of people and level cities. If her magic became public knowledge, Nevskov and every crime lord like him would try to take Ren for their own.

"What secret?" she asked.

"How you win so many fights," Nevskov said.

Ren started breathing again. A bit of the tension melted off her shoulders.

"A pretty little thing like you—you must have something up your sleeve."

She watched his fingers slide gold over dark wood. Growing up on meals of stale bread had left Ren thin, and she had long ago learned that she wasn't strong enough to win fights with brawn, so she'd developed a few strategies for the pits. She tired out her opponents, she bluffed and manipulated her way to victory, she used their strengths against them. Simply, Ren won fights the same way she won card games: because no one expected her to.

"Aidann was a good teacher," she said, an irritated note to her voice.

Nevskov's mouth ticked down. "He died three years ago, Ren." His baritone was as smooth as ever, but he'd stopped counting her money. "When are you going to get over it? He was foolhardy and irresponsible. He brought it on himself."

Ren couldn't help it—she snapped a little. "So you're the only one allowed to maim your *investments*, then?"

"Aidann was a poor decision. A good businessman cuts his losses while he's ahead. That boy was dead weight."

Dead being the operative word.

Ren jerked her chin at the gold scattered across his desk. "Are you almost finished?"

Nevskov counted the remaining coins and returned them all to the pouch. He plopped it down in the middle of the desk, then leaned back in his chair, folding his hands over his stomach. "I must admit, I had hoped you would have paid back more by now."

Ren stiffened. "I've never been late on a payment. Every month, I give you everything you ask for."

"I won't deny you've been consistent," Nevskov conceded. "That's more than Aidann could have said. But it has been quite some time now." He paused, and the air in his study thickened. Ren swore she heard his pocket watch ticking. "Have you heard? Our king has been given a treaty to sign. But Mattheus Lyandor is a temperamental man. Very stubborn. I suspect things are about to get a lot less pleasant around here. I can only be patient with you for so long."

Was everyone in this city obsessed with that damn treaty? It was tainting her night like a rancid smell. The rebels wanted her magic; Nevskov wanted her gold. Next thing she knew, the king was going to walk through the door and force her to fight in his army. For someone who didn't follow or care about political affairs, she was certainly becoming wrapped up in them.

"Get me my money, Ren," the gang leader said, his voice like poisoned wine.

"I'm working on it," she grit out. She just had to overthrow a king first. After she got her gold, Nevskov would have his damn money, and she would never have to see his crooked nose or the inside of his mansion again.

"That's good to hear. I would hate for something bad to happen to you." Nevskov leaned forward and picked up the pouch, his clear eyes unwavering.

CHAPTER
SIX

Adley and Lesa stared down at the slack body of the rebel sympathizer. Beneath a bloodied-and-torn tunic, his maimed chest rose and fell in a shallow rhythm. He sagged sideways, his raw and swollen wrists straining at his ropes. If he hadn't been tied down, he would have fallen out of his chair long ago.

Adley handed Lesa the cloth she'd used to clean the blood from her hands. Lesa wiped her dagger clean and shoved it into a sheath strapped to her thigh.

"I should get back to the castle," Adley said. "Take him to the prison?"

A crease formed between Lesa's brows, her eyes dark. She reached for a piece of hair that had fallen free from Adley's loose braid, and when Adley didn't immediately pull away, Lesa tucked the brown strand behind her ear. "You shouldn't return alone," she said, letting her hand linger on Adley's neck.

Now Adley did step back, putting a few feet between them. She dropped her gaze and tugged a pair of gloves from her jacket pocket, slipping them over calloused fingers stained with red. She spent far too much time and energy fighting this dangerous thing growing between the two of them. Lesa knew as well as Adley why it had to be this way. They were King's Children; they were forbidden to love. If they fell in love—with each other or anyone else—the crime would be punished by death. Their feelings were embers and needed to be stomped out, not stoked into an uncontrollable fire.

"You deal with him," Adley said, nodding at the man. "The interrogation ran late. King Mattheus is going to be impatient for our report."

"But—"

"Just take him to the prison, Lesa. I'll meet with the king."

Adley turned away and swept through the door, acknowledging the King's Child waiting outside with a tilt of her chin. The winter air felt colder than it had an hour ago, and she quickly did up her double-breasted trench coat, cinching the belt around her waist. She swung up onto her waiting horse, gathered the reins, and nudged him into a canter. Horseshoes clicked against cobblestones as Adley guided the animal along the Battgandon. The river cut through every major neighborhood in Denfell and flowed out to the Iron Sea, a gray body of water hugging the southeastern corner of the city.

As she wove through the streets, Adley had only moonlight and a salty breeze to keep her company. Night was a dangerous creature in Denfell, and most citizens who lived to the north of the Battgandon spent the hours after the sun went down locked in their homes. The few who had braved the darkness and impending cold front ducked their heads when Adley rode by, headed for the castle on the hill. The looming structure overlooked Denfell, its turrets clawing at the sky like sharpened fingernails, and no matter where in the city she went, its presence followed her like a shadow.

By the time she pulled to a stop at the castle stables and dismounted from her horse, the clock was chiming fifteen minutes before the hour. She handed her reins to a younger King's Child lingering in the training yard with an order to take care of the animal and headed into the castle at a brisk pace. As she made her way to the council chamber, her thick boots echoed through stone hallways that were as tall as they were long, torches and tapestries lining the dizzying maze of corners, turns, and stairwells. The castle was so large that it took her ten minutes to arrive at the chamber. A couple guards in maroon-and-gold uniforms pulled the doors wide, but Adley only got one step farther before her feet faltered.

Two men and a woman stood in the middle of the room, ragged and dirty clothes hanging off their bony shoulders. They faced the king, the crown prince, and a dozen advisors seated at a large lacquered table. Bronze chandeliers dangled from the vaulted ceiling, lit sconces flickered along the walls, and a fire roared in a giant hearth at the king's back, bathing the room in shades of yellow and gold. It was much too warm for the scene unfolding in front of them.

"Your Majesty, I beg of you," the woman was saying.

"People in the Terth District are dying. We don't need much. Food. Blankets. Anything."

In a gold crown encrusted with rubies the color of fresh blood, King Mattheus Lyandor watched the woman from his carved seat at the head of the table, the chair's twisting prongs framing his dark-brown hair like stag horns. His hands were clasped in his lap, and a gold ring in the shape of a lion's head—the symbol of the Lyandor family—sat on his forefinger. It was the same lion all the king's men wore, the same image Adley had sewn on the chest of her uniform.

The guards moved past Adley to close the chamber doors. She stepped fully inside and took up a place at the edge of the room.

The youngest of the two men stepped forward. "Please, King Mattheus. Send gold to the slums. You have more than enough to spare."

The older man pulled him back, maneuvering him behind his body. "Apologies, Your Majesty. My son means no disrespect. We come to you with admiration. We ask only for your goodwill. Your people are suffering."

The king stared at the starving family and said nothing for a very long time. The council chamber was so quiet Adley thought she might have heard the woman swallow.

Eventually, the king said, "I confess myself confused."

"Your . . . Your Majesty?" the father stuttered.

"I am confused because you referred to the scum living in the slums as *my people*. I assure you: they are no such thing." He cocked his head, as if contemplating an interesting painting. "They are miscreants, thieves, and criminals. Half of them are addicted to drugs and liquor, and the other half are selling the poison. I won't waste money on anyone who refuses to follow my laws. If your district is dying, you have only yourselves to blame. You'll find no sympathy here."

Adley shifted her weight. Her eyes wanted to stare at her boots, but she made herself watch.

The crown prince, seated at the king's right, leaned forward. "Father, if I may?" His voice was smooth, pleasant even, though he was anything but. Heath Lyandor donned pretense like clothing, his kindness and charm falling away as easily as removing a hat at the end of the day. He had sentenced as many people to death as his father, and he was only twenty-two.

"You may not," the king snapped, never turning his head toward his son.

A look of contempt passed over Heath's face, a muscle twitching in his jaw. Half a moment later, the emotion was gone, erased so completely it might not have been there at all.

"I'm afraid you've wasted not only your time, but mine," the king told the family.

"My sincerest apologies," the woman said, wrapping one hand around her son's arm and latching the other on to her husband's shirt. When she started to pull them away, four guards stepped into their path.

"I won't tolerate insolence," said King Mattheus. He extended his hands as if in supplication. Silver appeared in his palms, swirling and shimmering as the mass of magic grew larger, while the guards pushed the family to their knees. The king paused, and the entire room went still. Even the fire dancing in the sconces seemed to freeze.

He curled his fingers in, and his silver crept forward as slowly as morning fog rolling into Denfell. The magic approached the struggling family, and with a slow rotation of his wrists, the king forced silver down his subjects' throats. The guards released them, stepping back while they choked, hands clawing at their necks. King Mattheus might have been smiling as he extended his fingers and the family dropped to the ground. They writhed, eyes and noses glowing, heads thrown back and silver spilling out of wide mouths as they tried to scream, but couldn't.

No one spoke. The only sound in the whole room was the sound of three people having their insides ripped apart. They coughed up blood. It trickled from their noses and ears, fell from their eyes like tears. Adley couldn't take it anymore. She'd seen enough pain for one day. Tomorrow, she would wake up, and she would put on her leathers and be the soldier she was trained to be, and she'd do it again and again and again until she finally made it out of this place—if she ever made it out of this place—but for tonight she just wanted a breath of relief. So she gave in and looked down. And as she waited for it to end, she swore their dying sounds would haunt her dreams that night.

Only once the choking had stopped did Adley lift her chin again. The family lay supine on the floor, faces covered in blood and wet pools of crimson around their heads.

Guards grabbed their arms and began to drag them away, streaks of scarlet painting the pale stones like a twisted work of art.

Their dirty shoes weren't out of sight before the king called Adley's last name: "Farre." The chamber door fell shut, and he turned his blue eyes on her.

Adley pushed the dead family out of her mind. Silently, she stepped forward and bowed her head.

"Where is Lesa Ghan?" he asked.

"Dropping the rebel sympathizer at the prison," Adley said.

The king assessed her, his council watching in silence. Most of the men wore placid expressions, as unflinching in the face of violence as their ruler, but there were a few council members who did look pale, like weary, seasick sailors wishing for land. "I take it the interrogation didn't go well?"

"We learned of a tavern in the Atterton District where rebels have been meeting, but the sympathizer had no name for the alleged tavern, nor did he have names of any rebels."

King Mattheus rested his hands on the arms of his chair and seemed to ponder her words. "My best interrogators have been searching for rebels for weeks, and yet you've gleaned nothing useful. How very disappointing." He assessed her like a butcher who couldn't decide what to do with a piece of raw meat. "I'm feeling generous today, so I'm going to let you off on a warning. You would be wise to remember my clemency and do better next time."

Adley forced all expression from her face and said, "We'll go back out. We'll find them, Your Majesty."

"Yes, I suspect you will." He drummed his fingers, his large iron ring glinting. "I've decided it's time for a little extra motivation." He looked to a guard. "Gather the King's Children in the training yard."

The king stood, the rest of the table following suit. As he swept across the room, he flicked a hand upward and sent a stream of silver shooting forward. The magic banged the doors open, and he strode from the chamber, Adley and his council flanking him in a flurry of booted steps.

Ten minutes later, and they were in the training grounds. Dozens of torches ringed the edge of the large square yard, and on the walkway high above, more fire flickered at the edges of the stone parapet. A group of King's Children dressed in leather stood at attention, feet planted wide in the dirt. Their faces were shadowed, their silhouettes feathered orange. The king had recently sent one hundred warriors down the eastern coast to Anteran, a major port city that would undoubtedly fall under siege in the event of war. Roughly two hundred King's Children remained, just over half their total number. Lesa was standing at the front of the pack, surrounded by muscled men and women, only a few among them approaching fifty years in age. Adley took a place beside her and waited for King Mattheus to speak.

"I find myself in need of a new Fang," the king said, his red cloak rustling in a weak breeze. "Someone who will act as my right hand to enforce my rule swiftly and without mercy. Who better for the job than one of you?"

Adley pulled her spine straighter, as did half the King's Children in the yard. The king had been without a Fang for over six months, and they'd all been wondering when he was going to replace the woman who had previously held the position. By the time she had completed her required twelve years of service as King's Fang, she had as much blood on her hands as the king himself, but she also got to walk away from the castle with enough gold to keep her comfortable for the rest of her life.

No one really talked about what happened when a King's Child lost their finesse with a weapon and their body began to fail, but everyone knew. The king worked his Children until they outlived their usefulness, and when their aim was no longer true and their sword shook in their hands, he sent them to an early grave. He kept a few favorites around to train the younger ones or sit on his war council, but he never let any of them go. It was a special kind of cruelty, to dispose of them when they no longer suited his needs. Setting them free would have cost nothing, but if there was anything the king was not, it was merciful. Becoming Fang was the only chance any of the King's Children had at escaping the castle. Adley held her breath. She'd been waiting her entire life for this opportunity.

"As you know, you will be second in power only to myself, and you will be paid handsomely for the position," the king continued. "Bring me the leader of Denfell's newest rebel group—alive—and you will be made my Fang."

King Mattheus let his words hang in the air. No one shifted a finger as his eyes swept over the assembled warriors, the men and women who had grown up with a knife in one hand and a bow in the other. For as long as there had been Lyandors on the Erdis throne, there had been King's Children. Some were picked up off the street, others were taken from orphanages, and many were outright stolen from their families if they showed promise. But few kids survived the first weeks of brutal tests and daily beatings. Fewer still made the cut.

"You're dismissed," said the king.

Amid the shuffling boots and flapping leather coats, King Mattheus's voice called Adley up short. "Farre."

Adley stopped and turned back to the king of Erdis. She waited before him with a straight spine and her hands clasped behind her back, face entirely devoid of expression.

"My son has disappeared from the castle. Again."

Adley's eyes flicked to the crown prince at his left. Tall and lean with blond hair, elegant features, and a smattering of freckles over his tanned nose, Heath was the opposite of his younger brother in every way but appearance. The crown prince cared about politics and the affairs of the kingdom. His presence at court was not discussed in whispered giggles, nor did he have a reputation for drink and scandalous women. Heath was wholly prepared to inherit the Erdis throne, but he was as ruthless as his father. The only thing toward which the younger prince seemed to exhibit cruelty was Denfell's liquor supply.

"His guards are utterly incompetent, so you are to find him," King Mattheus continued. "It shouldn't be difficult. The nearest brothel isn't far. Return him to his chambers and see to it he stays there this time."

A shallow wave of disappointment washed over Adley. There were a hundred ways she could spend her time and plenty of tasks far more suited to her skills, such as unearthing that tavern that the sympathizer had mentioned. But instead, she was being dispatched to track down a prince with an attitude problem.

She schooled her features and dipped her chin.

"That will be all." The king turned his back on her and retreated from the dark yard, his son and council members trailing behind.

Adley walked over to Lesa's side. Both of their uniforms were covered in streaks of dried blood, the red visible even in the night shadows. Adley fingered the front of her coat. "I should change before I leave."

They stepped into the torchlit glow of the castle, and as they moved in silence down the long corridors, Lesa kept her lips pressed together, her fingers brushing over the hilt of the knife at her thigh. Half a minute after they had left the ground floor behind, she burst, apparently unable to hold her tongue any longer. "Unbelievable!"

Adley threw a glance behind them. "Be careful."

"You're routinely shoved aside and underestimated. Doesn't it bother you?"

"I'm a King's Child," Adley said in a low voice. "Nothing bothers me."

Lesa stopped. She grabbed Adley's elbow. "You're getting that position. I'll kill every Child who stands in your way if I have to. You deserve to be Fang more than anyone."

Adley stared into Lesa's eyes, aching to reach for her. It was a dangerous urge she spent far too much time fighting. And she was a good fighter, but when Lesa looked at her the way she was now, she found herself not wanting to fight at all. Lesa was all she had in this godsforsaken world. She could be cruel. She was unflinching and violent at times. But if she needed to be those things to make it from one day to the next, then Adley couldn't fault her for it. Lesa may not have been good, but she was good to Adley, the only good thing she might ever have.

"Thank you," Adley whispered.

Lesa swallowed, and for a second, Adley feared she was going to lean in and kiss her, but then Lesa tore her gaze away and took off down the hall. "The king doesn't seem to care that it's been four years since anyone outshot you on the archery range. You could kill a blasted dragon, and he might shake your hand for it."

"Dragons don't exist," Adley pointed out, following after her.

"The closest you'll get to admiration from him is if his son decides you're worth bedding."

Adley's heart gave a painful wrench. Lesa rarely spoke of her nights with the crown prince, but Adley had heard enough. She'd seen the bruises. "Lesa . . ."

"Don't," she said, continuing up a flight of stairs and entering the corridor that housed their rooms. Dozens of wooden doors lined the walls, and though a few torches were set up, they were rarely lit, the hall brightened instead by moonlight floating in through a lone window. But the corridor wasn't empty. Ethen Delano, one of the favored King's Children, was leaning against the stone wall, examining his sword. The edge was sharp, the metal glinting in the faint light.

He took a moment to run a finger over the blade, then he lifted his chin. A piece of dark-blond hair brushed his brow. Adley supposed some people might consider him attractive—the gods knew he thought himself the best-looking man in Denfell—but those people didn't know Ethen. She did. She'd grown up with him, fought by his side, fallen victim to his sadism in the training yard, and she'd seen that his insides were as vile as the rats crawling through the sewers in the Terth. He'd never have to worry about the type of death sentence that hovered in the shadows of every moment Lesa and Adley spent together; she doubted Ethen knew how to love anyone.

He slid his blade back into its sheath and crossed his arms over his broad chest. "Adley. Lesa."

"What do you want, Ethen?" Lesa snapped. Her hand dropped to her thigh, hovering by the blade strapped there.

"Nothing much. Just came to talk." He looked at Adley. "I know you want to be Fang."

"So what if I do?" Adley asked.

Ethen smiled, but there was malice hidden behind

the soft lines of his lips. It was as if he were incapable of displaying kindness, like his face wasn't made for it. "It'll never happen."

Lesa took a half-step forward, placing herself between Ethen and Adley. Her fingers went from brushing her knife to curling around it. "Is that a threat?"

He gave an amused chuckle. "Down, girl. I'm not threatening anyone. Only telling Adley what she already knows." Dropping his arms, he straightened off the wall and casually strolled forward. "Being able to shoot an arrow doesn't make you fit to be Fang. So why don't you leave the rebels to the grown-ups and go babysit the prince?"

He stepped around Adley, his large body closer to her than was necessary, as if he'd come to make a threat after all. Then his boots were thudding down the stairs and out of earshot. Ethen was conceited and awful, and the fact that he was skilled enough to present a challenge in the training yard had always been a little infuriating, but Adley wasn't easily intimidated. Ethen could lurk in the corridors all he liked, but that wouldn't stop her from searching for the rebels.

"Gods, I hate him," Lesa said, glaring at the stairwell he'd disappeared into. She turned away and headed for Adley's door, her pale hair swishing as Adley trailed her down the hall. When Lesa stopped to look over her shoulder, she was smiling playfully, a hand wrapped around the door handle.

"I need to go find the prince," Adley pointed out.

"The prince can wait," Lesa said. She pushed in Adley's

door, grabbed her hand, and tugged her into a small room mostly devoid of personality. The bedsheets were wheat brown and made of rough cotton, standard issue to every King's Child. No art adorned the walls, and Adley had never acquired any trinkets to display. The only things that hinted at the room's occupant were the books. They were stacked haphazardly in corners and atop every available surface. Her wooden chair was yet another storage space. Adley never sat in it.

The door snapped shut, and Lesa pressed her against the wood. "Lesa," she breathed. The name sounded so different on her lips than it had only a few minutes before. It was a plea and desire and hesitation all at once.

"Shh." Lesa pushed the coat away from Adley's shoulders, and she shrugged it all the way off. The soiled leather dropped to the floor, leaving her in nothing but a tight leather shirt with a tie running up the front, a lion head stitched over the left breast.

"We shouldn't," Adley breathed.

Lesa leaned down to place a kiss on her collarbone. "I know."

"It's dangerous."

Lesa moved to her neck. "I know."

"The king would have us killed if he found out."

"I know."

Their mouths met, the world coming undone bit by bit. Lesa nipped at Adley's bottom lip, and if she hadn't been so firmly pressed into the door, she would have dropped to the ground then and there. Lesa tugged Adley's shirt off her shoulder, kissed the golden-brown skin.

"Someone could walk in," Adley gasped, barely managing to get the words out.

"Adley?" Lesa mumbled against her shoulder.

"What?"

"Shut up."

Lesa trailed her lips and fingers across Adley, knowing too well all the things that made her tick and sigh and shudder. Breath hitching and heart hammering in her chest, Adley leaned her head against the door. Lesa moved down the front of her body. She kissed Adley's neck, her collarbone, her chest, fingers gently tugged her braid loose.

Oh, to hells with the king.

Adley pushed Lesa toward the bed. They tumbled down onto the mattress, but when Lesa landed on her back, her wince and curse jolted them to a stop. "Bleeding hells," Lesa said, pulling a book from beneath her. "It's like you've never heard of a shelf."

Adley was also lying atop a few books. She rolled aside, tugging tomes free of the bedclothes. Once she'd stacked them in a small pile, she leaned over the edge of her bed and dropped them on the scuffed floor. Although she was aware she had what some might consider an unreasonable number of books, she couldn't seem to help herself. She'd always liked stories, even as a little girl running through the hilly roads of Sirica, but then she'd been brought here, and books became more than just stories. They were a reminder that the whole world wasn't a bleak tapestry of violence, and while she might never see anything beautiful again, at least she could read about kinder things. It was easier to breathe between the pages of a book. They helped her forget about the blood under her fingernails.

"The shelves they give us are tiny," Adley complained. "They hardly fit anything."

"Maybe you don't need so many books."

Adley gaped at her, and Lesa laughed, the sound like a warm breeze in a meadow. Adley wanted to bask in it all day. "Look at you," Lesa said. "You'd think I just told you to give up chocolate."

"I'd rather give up chocolate than my books."

"Are you feeling all right?" Lesa lifted a palm to Adley's forehead, brow wrinkling in mock concern. "You're completely delirious."

Adley tugged her hand away from her face, but instead of letting go, she laced their fingers together and placed her lips to the back of Lesa's hand.

With the book still laying in her lap, Lesa flipped through the pages. "What's this one about?"

Adley smiled, studying the way their fingers linked together. She loved that Lesa always wanted to hear her ramble on about books. She was reading a new one every few days, so the gods knew she never ran out of fodder, but Lesa listened. She always listened. Maybe she secretly liked the escape, too. "So this young girl finds a crow egg . . ."

As she regaled Lesa with the story, Lesa pulled her close and went quiet. She was silent for so long that Adley was surprised when she spoke; she thought maybe Lesa had fallen asleep. "Adley?"

"Yes?"

"I want to tell you something."

Adley went rigid. She didn't turn her head to look at Lesa, but she didn't need to. She knew her lines like a painting she'd studied for years: the slope of her small nose and the exact shape of her lips. Her angular eyes were the night sky, a brown so dark they looked black, with a perpetually troublesome starlike twinkle. As well as she knew Lesa's soft curves and hard muscles, Adley knew where she was headed right now. Where they'd both been headed for months, if she was being honest with herself.

"Please don't," Adley said. "Don't say it."

"Why?"

Adley sat up and set the book aside. "You know why."

Things between them had come on slowly. They'd both been brought to the castle after the king's men had raided a slaver's ship and found them stuffed belowdecks. That was eleven years ago now, when Adley was seven and Lesa was eight. The two of them had bonded through nothing more than proximity and a shared fear of whether they'd make it through the next day alive.

They were so different. Lesa was hard, and Adley was soft. Lesa didn't care enough, and Adley cared too much. And maybe if they had met in any other circumstances, they never would have wound up wrapped around one another. But somewhere along the way, things had slid into place. When the first kiss had happened a year ago, it had almost felt inevitable. So Adley had set rules to protect them both. They could kiss, and they could spend nights together. They could laugh and whisper and share bedsheets. They could bare their skin, but they could never bare their souls. Because those three words, spoken aloud, they would mean the swing of an executioner's ax.

Lesa was silent for a while. "You're right," she said. "I'm being careless. Forget I brought it up."

Adley nodded. She retrieved a clean coat from a hook on the wall and tugged it on, freeing her waving hair from the collar. She didn't want to leave. She wanted to be here, with Lesa, always with Lesa. She wanted to lie in her arms in a safe place that didn't exist.

But wanting was a dangerous game, so Adley shoved down her desire and left the room. She walked calmly out of the castle and into the night.

CHAPTER
SEVEN

The pit lord waited for two men to drag the bloody, half-dead fighter from the ring, then he swept across the red-stained sand, his cloak billowing behind him like a trailing shadow. "Next fighters!" he called. "A reminder of the rules." He held up a finger. "No outside interference." A second finger went up. "No weapons." He lifted a third finger. "Fights end in death or mercy."

The moment he finished speaking, a muscular woman hauled herself over the pit's short wooden railing and landed with a heavy thump in the sand. Shale, one of the pit's strongest female fighters. She didn't lose often, and she showed mercy even less. The dirty crowd was already buzzing like the flies they were, placing bets even though Shale didn't yet have an opponent. They'd be screaming for blood soon, blood they would no doubt receive.

Beneath the black mask covering most of his face, the pit lord's annoyance was plain. He was dreadfully bored of Shale and her antics. He might as well hand over her winnings now.

"Let go—"

His eyes shot to two girls arguing at the edge of the pit.

Or, rather, a girl with deep-brown Jareen skin and curly hair was pleading with a tall, thin girl removing a slew of knives from her clothing. She shrugged off her coat, which was the same dark color of red as the blood beneath his boots, shoved everything into the smaller girl's arms, and turned to face the pit.

Surprise jolted the pit lord. She was young—probably younger than him—and cleaner than most people in this place. At first he wondered what she was doing anywhere near the Terth, a neighborhood that made every other slum in Denfell look pleasant, but then he peered closer and noticed the hardness beneath her surface, the strength in her stance, the grim determination about her. She held her chin as if bearing the weight of a crown.

She took a moment to tie back her long hair. Though fires burned along the cracked stone walls and in creaking iron fixtures up above, the lighting in the pit was dim at best, so it was impossible to say whether her mussed strands were black or just a dark shade of brown. After that was done, she braced her hands on the railing and hauled herself up to swing a lithe leg over the divide. The crowd fell silent as she lowered herself into the pit.

Was that a *leather corset*? Now that was something the pit lord hadn't seen before, and he'd seen quite a lot. She would probably look even better out of it, but he'd never get the chance to see for himself if Shale killed her.

His pit wasn't like others in Denfell. Neither needing nor caring about money, he gave his investors and winning fighters a larger cut than any other pit lord, and in doing so he attracted the city's finest scum. While he accepted the reality of the pits, he wasn't interested in leading a lamb to slaughter.

The pit lord grabbed the girl by the arm and hauled her away from Shale, who was practically salivating at the sight of her. "Did you not hear what I said about a fight to the death?" he hissed in her ear.

She gave him a rather impressive glare. "Tell me, are you fond of your hand?"

Feisty, too. Good. She'd need it.

The pit lord looked her over. Her arms were thin, and her waist was too small. Up close, he could tell her eyes were a rich shade of green, made brighter by heavy black cosmetics, her skin alabaster pale. *If she's so set on killing herself*, he thought, *who am I to stop her?* He dropped his grip and stepped aside. The girl shoved past him, knocking into his shoulder as she went.

The pit lord crunched across the sand and jumped out of the ring. He took his place at the front of the shifting crowd, sinking back into a thick aroma of sweat, blood, and dirt. He turned to face the fighters and paused for the length of a breath.

"Fight."

The word rang out like a hammer striking an anvil.

Shale snapped to action, rushing her opponent head-first. The girl twirled aside and bounced out of reach before circling back around. But she wasn't watching the other fighter. Her eyes were trained over Shale's shoulder on the girl she'd been arguing with. The gesture wouldn't have been noticeable to anyone paying less attention than the pit lord—he barely caught it, as it was—but she dipped her chin in the smallest nod.

When Shale came for her a second time, she barely moved. Shale rammed her into the wooden railing and cut a fist to her side. The girl twisted, avoiding a liver shot, and the blow connected with the rail. At his back, the crowd leered and lunged.

The pit lord slid his gaze to the Jareen girl, who paid little attention to the fight. Instead, she was placing bets with the men around her. She went from one to the next with her small shoulders back, easily holding her own among a group of ruthless men who thrived on the smell of carrion.

In the ring, the girl was stumbling around like a drunkard as Shale attacked again and again. To pretty much everyone else in the room, she was losing spectacularly. Maybe if he weren't so damn interested in her and her leather corset, the pit lord wouldn't have picked up on it, either, but as he studied her and the way she avoided the worst of Shale's damage, he had his suspicions.

Shale's feet were more sluggish than usual as she followed her zagging opponent around the pit, and when she went in for another attack, the girl hooked a leg around Shale's ankles and yanked. The instant Shale went down, the girl was on top of her. She drew her arm back and jabbed like a crossbow firing, straight and quick. Blood sputtered from Shale's nose. The crowd screamed and surged forward, feet pounding against the uneven ground, people leaning over to bang fists on the inside of the railing.

Shale bellowed and rocked up, throwing the girl over and slamming her into the sand. The girl's head smacked the ground, and Shale punched her in the cheek. Her head snapped to the side. Shale delivered another hit, then another. The blows continued to fall, and the girl twisted uselessly, her teeth gritting. Blood poured from a gash at her brow, coating half her face and wetting her dark hair. The pit lord couldn't hear a thing over all the screaming.

His chest deflated. Things were just getting interesting. What a pity.

He was steeling himself to declare Shale the winner when the girl, impossibly, found an opening. As Shale drew back to deliver another blow, the girl bent her knees and hooked her ankles around Shale's calves, locking the other fighter's legs beneath hers. She bucked her hips, twisted sideways, and threw Shale onto her back. Straddling Shale's chest, the girl jammed a thumb into her eye and buried it knuckle-deep. A scream ripped from Shale's throat, blood spurting from her eye socket as the girl twisted her finger. Shale clawed at her arm, but the girl grabbed on to her wrist with her free hand and jerked. The bone broke. Shale let out another scream.

Face covered in blood, one hand stuck in Shale's skull and the other gripping her broken wrist, the girl seemed so far past mercy that the pit lord wondered if the gods could have sent an avenging spirit down to punish Shale for her crimes. Fire blazed in her eyes, and her cheekbones were sharper than combat daggers.

And then she pulled away. The girl wrenched her hand free of Shale's eye and pushed herself to her feet. Shale put her unbroken hand to her bloody face, rolled to her side, and curled into a ball. The girl stared down at her with a sneer of contempt and not a sign of remorse, blood dripping from her thumb. There was a tear in the seam at her right shoulder, where a nasty swirling of scar tissue peeked through. The crowd was deathly silent and just as still.

When she finally lifted her chin at the pit lord, it took him a few moments to find his voice. "Victor," he declared.

The girl directed one last glare at Shale, the likes of which would have put the god of wrath to shame, and trudged over to the pit lord, her gold-buckled boots dragging a little through the sand. Her hair was wild, half of it torn free from the braid and clinging to the blood on her face. The pit lord marveled at her. She should have been on the ground by now. She should have been dead. But her gaze was strong, steady, defiant even.

Forget the corset. He'd never seen anything like her.

She paused in front of him, holding out a hand. The pit lord removed five gold coins from his pocket. "Who are you?" he asked, his stare tracking over her sticky face. Blood was still dripping from the wound on her forehead.

"It's not important." While she did an impressive job of hiding it from her expression, the girl's voice was laced with pain.

"It is to me." When she said nothing, he pressed the

coins into her palm. "Stay away for a while. Shale doesn't take well to losing."

On the other side of the pit, a section of the crowd began to rumble. The pit lord whipped his head toward the raised voices. With clenched fists and flexed arms, a group of men encircled the winning fighter's friend, a man wearing a nasty grimace looking two seconds from skinning her alive. He withdrew a knife, latched on to her arm, and yanked her into his chest. She lurched sideways with a cry, but went abruptly quiet when he put a serrated blade to her neck. The tall girl whirled, green eyes flashing, but the pit lord was already vaulting over the railing and sprinting across the sand. By the time he reached the other side, his sword was drawn. He leveled its point on the man's neck.

"Drop it," the pit lord said.

The man's eyes went wide, but he didn't move. A thin trickle of blood slid down the girl's throat and disappeared beneath a large black collar. Her cheeks were wet with tears, her hands trembling.

The pit lord increased pressure on his blade. "Don't make me say it again."

The man swallowed visibly. He lowered the knife but kept his hold on the girl's arm, his knuckles white. He was probably bruising her. "You got any idea how much this bitch won?"

"I don't think I care. Hand over her winnings, or I'll carve their weight from your flesh."

As quickly as he had snatched her up, the man shoved

the girl away. The pit lord's face was masked, but he made sure to meet every eye in the little mob. "That goes for all of you."

No one dared grumble their complaints as they shoved coins into the girl's hand. The pit lord tried not to gape as she collected more money than most people usually made in five fights. Whoever these girls were, they would be eating well tonight.

After she'd pocketed the money, the pit lord offered her a hand. She hesitantly took it, allowing him to help her over the railing. He didn't sheathe his sword until she was standing in the pit, the bottom of her purple skirts brushing the sand. Her old black coat was at least three sizes too big, and she was still holding on to her friend's red jacket and knives. She looked delicate and lost, like a flower dropped in the weeds. The pit lord couldn't believe she'd come here on purpose.

The girl may have been free from the crowd, but the winning fighter wasn't satisfied. She snatched a dagger from her friend, barreled forward in a storm of furious energy, and latched on to the tunic of the man still holding his knife. She yanked, slamming his stomach into the rail. The man started to shout, but his mouth snapped shut when she put a blade to the skin beneath his eye.

"Touch her again," the girl hissed, "and you'll be praying to gods you didn't know existed."

Her friend rushed forward to grab at her shoulder. "Stop. Ren, *stop*. It's not worth it."

The man whimpered like a dog under her stare. The

pit lord had seen his share of threats and withering gazes, but there was something dark inside this girl, something forcefully muzzled and barely controlled. He hoped to be far away if it ever got out.

A full minute had to pass before the girl—Ren—released the man. When she turned her back on him, it was as though the entire pit let out a collective breath. The man gave a relieved sort of chuckle, but he really should have waited until she was out of earshot.

If she had moved any faster, she would have been a blur. She turned, whirling like a demon escaped from the hells, and slammed her dagger into his cheek. The man gave a garbled yell and fell back into a crowd not considerate enough to keep him on his feet. Knife buried hilt-deep, blood gushing something fierce, he tumbled to the grime-slick floor.

"Next time, it's going in your neck," she warned.

The other girl said nothing, only placed a gentle hand on her friend's arm and guided her from the silently gaping crowd. The pit lord watched them disappear through a group of onlookers who moved aside to create a path. He glanced down at the man moaning on the ground, clutching his bleeding cheek and the dagger stuck there.

Well, shit.

He'd never seen this *Ren* before, but he sure as hells was going to find a way to see her again.

A couple hours later in a much more pleasant-smelling room, the pit lord stared at Holland as she slipped a pink silk robe over her porcelain shoulders. Snaking an arm around her waist, he tugged her back onto the rumpled duvet, but she didn't giggle or even smile as he nuzzled his face into her neck. She only pushed him away and sat up again. He fell face-first into the ivory covers.

"Out," she said.

He groaned and rolled over onto the pillows, staring up at a canopy the color of dusty roses. "You should know that I'm beginning to feel used." He moved to rest his chin against her shoulder. The scent of flowers and sugared icing lingered on her skin. "Tell me about your family. Did you have a dog when you were a child? I've always wanted a dog."

He really didn't care, just as Holland didn't want to know the trivial details of his life. Neither of them had much interest in talking at all. He was only trying to prolong the inevitable, and she knew it, too.

Holland shrugged him off and tied her bright-red hair into a knot on top of her head. "Go home. You can't avoid your life forever."

She stood up and glided barefoot across the large bedroom. The walls and fireplace were white, the lamps and chandelier were gold, and everything else was a different shade of pink. Holland disappeared into the bathing room. The door slammed shut.

Heaving a sigh, the pit lord pushed himself up and shrugged into his clothes. He slipped his mask from a vanity table crowded with twinkling jewels and perfume bottles. His fingers ran over the silk. "Holland?"

"Why haven't you left yet?" she shouted through the closed door.

He chuckled. She was impossible. It was what he liked about her. "Do you know a pit fighter by the name of Ren? Tall, dark hair, some kind of scar across her right shoulder?"

The door popped open. Holland crossed her arms, the action pushing together her full chest, and leaned a shoulder against the frame. Her robe was short, barely covering her round thighs, and if he didn't know better, he'd think she was trying to get him into bed again. "What makes you think I know anything about pit fighters?" she asked.

"You know everything that goes on in this city."

As the daughter of Denfell's most popular baker, Holland had met damn near everyone. She'd crossed the bridges and streets a thousand times over to make deliveries, and with a keen set of ears and a penchant for gossip, she traded in secrets as much as she traded in bread. If something was happening in Denfell, odds were the baker's daughter was aware of it.

She examined her nails. "I don't make a habit of visiting the fighting pits, but if I did, I'd tell you the girl you're referring to is an orphan. She helps run a boardinghouse of sorts in Hessler."

Now *that* was interesting. He could maybe buy her small friend as a street rat, but with the way Ren carried herself, not to mention her expensive coat, leather corset, and shining hair, the last thing she looked like was a starved child eking out a pathetic existence. But if someone was going to be in charge of a group of orphaned kids, he supposed it would be her. She had shoved a knife into a man's head as if sticking a chicken for that night's dinner.

"Any gang affiliations?" he asked.

"She owes Izram Nevskov a ton of money, but as far as I've heard, she's paying off the debt and she's doing it without pulling any jobs for his gang," Holland said. "What do you want with her?"

The pit lord shrugged. "She won a fight against Shale tonight."

"That brute of a woman?"

"Shoved a thumb into her eye. Probably blinded her."

Holland arched her brows as if reluctantly impressed, but said nothing. Still propped up against the white door-frame, she moved to cleaning the nails on her other hand.

"Do you know where I can find her?"

She remained silent, and the pit lord eyed her curiously as he retrieved his cloak from the floor, the wooden boards shining in the chandelier's warm light.

"You should stay away from her," she blurted.

"Why?"

Holland went quiet again. She bit her lip and stared at her nails.

"What do you know?" he pressed.

"Nothing."

"Holland . . ."

"I don't know anything," she insisted. "I just heard

she's bad news, that's all. She's not the kind of person you want to be associated with."

He shook out his cloak and flung it over his shoulders. "Is someone jealous?"

"Hardly."

He did up the silver buckles at his neck, then strolled across the bedroom to plant a kiss on Holland's cheek. He was quick enough that she didn't have the chance to bat him away.

"Get out of here, you great sap," she said, hiding a smile.

The pit lord made his way to her bedroom door, boots tapping softly. "I'll see you tomorrow night."

"So presumptuous. Maybe I'm tired of you."

"And maybe the king taught his horses to fly," was his farewell.

The moment he stepped out of the warmth of Holland's opulent townhouse, the cold pummeled into him, a sure sign the first snow would be arriving soon and with it, the Royal Carnival. That was a week he wasn't looking forward to, what with all the pomp and circumstance he'd be forced to endure. Maybe he could find an excuse to travel abroad. His father was always complaining that he never made himself useful. A diplomatic trip might do them all some good, and there was a courtier in Brede he wouldn't mind seeing again.

He tugged on his gloves and stepped out onto the wide, cobbled street, his mind churning. A salty breeze flicked his hair over his forehead. Glowing lamps dotted the dark road.

"It's about time." The voice sent him whipping around, his hand shooting to his sword. "I thought you were never going to come out."

It took his eyes a few seconds to adjust, but then the pit lord recognized the warm Sirican features of the girl leaning against Holland's front gate. A bow and quiver of arrows were slung across her back. He dropped his hand. "Adley."

She had one leather-clad leg kicked up on the gate, and her arms were crossed loosely over her stomach. She dipped her head, but didn't take her eyes off him. "Prince Kellen."

CHAPTER
EIGHT

"**Y**ou'll be lucky if this doesn't scar," Freya said, digging a needle into Ren's forehead.

"Yeah, wouldn't want to get one of those," Ren said dryly. She leaned back in her chair with her eyes closed and tried not to flinch while the needle wove through her skin.

"Your ribs aren't broken, but they're close," Freya went on. "What were you thinking, Ren?"

"I don't want to talk about it."

Bracelets jingled close to Ren's ear, and amber incense prickled her nose. There was a soft tug on her forehead as Freya knotted off the thread, then she applied some truly remarkable salve over the stitches, and the smarting wound went numb. Ren had no idea what was in the stuff, but it saved her from a face of nasty scarring, so she made sure to steal multiple containers every time she hit the local infirmaries.

Ren heard Freya drop into a seat, and she peeled open the eye that wasn't swollen shut. Curly haired and small, Freya sat on Ren's sagging red couch with her arms shoved over her chest and her mouth pressed into a thin line. The frill of her flowing top hung off dark-brown shoulders, exposing collarbones that seemed to jut out more severely than usual, like they, too, were upset with Ren.

"What's the deal?" Ren asked. "I won, didn't I?"

"Only barely. We don't go to that pit for a reason. She could have killed you. She would have, if she'd had the chance."

"I knew I could win."

"No, you didn't! You were upset, so you did something stupid and self-destructive. Well, did it work? Do you feel better?"

"I doubt you'll be so mad when you're spending all my money," Ren snapped. Freya's face crumpled like used parchment, and Ren sighed, closing her eye again and trying not to breathe too deeply. She hurt down to the ninth hell and back. "I'm sorry. I didn't mean that."

"What is going on with you?"

Ren didn't want to get into the way Darek had reached inside her and pulled at all the wrong threads. She didn't want to admit that it had stung. She hated him. For bringing her into a budding revolution, for putting so much weight on her shoulders, for voicing every ugly thought she'd ever had about herself.

Ignoring the pain in her side, Ren stood and grabbed a glass off the scarred table. Freya didn't protest when she poured herself a drink, even though the liquor was supposed to be for cleaning wounds. She swallowed it in one gulp. The burning in her throat didn't help much.

Ren stared around the small, crowded room. The mismatched curtains were faded shades of gray and black, and a giant fraying rug covered the dull floorboards. Random trinkets she'd nicked and taken a liking to dotted the shelves, scattered among the handful of books she'd read over the years and particularly enjoyed. A painting of a rose garden rested above the wooden fireplace; Ren had stolen that from an art gallery. She was supposed to sell it, but when she'd brought it back, she hadn't been able to tear her eyes from the sprays of reds and pinks, the dots of white and the pale-green leaves, so she'd kept it.

"I've joined a group of rebels," Ren said.

A beat of silence. "What?"

It all came rushing out. Ren told Freya about Markus and Darek, how they wanted her to inspire the people to rise up and overthrow the king. How, in exchange, she'd be six hundred fifty thousand gold pieces richer. But she kept what Darek had said to herself: how he'd called her a coward, said Erdis deserved better than someone like her. She knew Freya would disagree, but assurances and soft smiles were kindnesses Ren didn't deserve. She was terrible and rusted. She was the kind of thing that gave you an infection if you were unlucky enough to scratch yourself on its edges. If Freya's faith in her weren't so misguided, it would have broken what was left of Ren's heart.

"I'm asking to get my head chopped off," she finished. "They're insane to think this will work."

"I don't know . . ." Freya said. "I think I agree with them. People still tell stories about magic, you know. If you show them that the Lyandors aren't the only wielders still here—that *you're* still here—you could very well start a revolution."

"Of course you would say that," Ren muttered, dropping into a chair that had lost most of its stuffing. Freya was more idealistic than a kid who'd grown up in the slums had any right to be. She'd always been that way, since the moment they'd met in an alley nine years ago. Hours earlier, Ren had awoken to flames eating her home, blown out a window with her silver, and run. She was terrified and alone, and she'd liked Freya immediately—but that was mostly because she'd given Ren a tonic to ward off infection in the burn on her shoulder.

"What did you want me to say?" Freya asked.

"Maybe that I've lost my mind. I was hoping you would talk me out of it."

From her seat on the couch, Freya watched Ren closely. "The king destroys everything he touches," she said. "You're probably the only person in this kingdom with the power to stop him. You can't do nothing."

"I've been doing nothing for nine years, and it's never bothered you before."

"You couldn't do it on your own, and I knew that, but now you have a real chance to change Erdis for the better. You have to take it."

Damn Freya and her ethics. If they weren't friends, Ren thought she might hate the girl.

"Just to be clear, I'm doing this for the money," Ren said. "I don't care one way or another who sits on the throne. A godsdamned winter sprite could rule this kingdom, and it wouldn't make a difference to me, as long as I got my gold."

"Glad you cleared that up. Imagine if someone thought you'd gone and grown a conscience."

"The horror," she said dryly.

A knock came at her door, followed by the hesitant voice of a young girl. "Ren?"

"Go away!" Ren barked.

Freya shot her a stern look as she got to her feet, walking across the sitting room to pull open the creaking wooden door. Ren didn't listen to the conversation that followed.

Several dozen orphans lived in the building dubbed the Compound. Three stories tall, the place sat in the heart of Hessler, a poor district that was one step up from the slums and one step down from pretty much everywhere else. A kitchen, living room, a couple bathrooms, and ten small rooms made up the first two floors, while the third was comprised of two suites. One belonged to Freya, and Ren rented out the other. The Compound was about as nice as anything else in Hessler, but the drafts were mostly boarded up, the windows and doors locked, and it even had running water.

Owning an orphanage had been Aidann's dream, not Freya's and certainly not Ren's, but when he'd died, Freya had made it her mission to open one. It took a year of saving and all the money Freya had to her name to afford the place, and when she ran into some trouble securing the building from the bank, Ren had lent a hand by bribing the right people into overlooking Freya's age. Two years later, and the place was managing to pay for itself. Freya hadn't wanted to charge the kids a boarding fee, but Ren convinced her they would all starve if she didn't. The Compound officially belonged to Freya, but every so often—usually in the winter when the rooms were full and the kitchen was sparse and things seemed to fall apart quicker than Freya could fix them—Ren succumbed to a rare shred of decency and gave Freya the funds she needed to keep the doors open. And then after she did it, she wondered if she was ever going to settle her debt with Nevskov.

When Freya returned, Ren said, "I need you to do something for me."

"Aren't you interested in what she wanted?"

"Not particularly."

Freya gave her a familiar look of exasperation. "I need to lower my expectations when it comes to you."

"I've been telling you that for years."

After a quick roll of her eyes, Freya asked, "So what is it you need?"

"Get me information on Darek and Markus. Make sure they're legitimate. I know they live in the Atterton District." She recited an address in Denfell's wealthiest neighborhood. It had been about the only thing Markus had given her before they'd parted, along with the command that she come by in a week. "And check their bank account."

If the brothers crossed her, everything Ren had on

them would be fed to one of Nevskov's men. She may have avoided joining up with his thugs, but she had her contacts. Any one of them would do. While Ren had committed to working with Darek and Markus, she didn't trust anyone but Freya on principle.

"Of course," Freya said. "You know I would have done it even if you hadn't asked."

"I know."

Where Ren's specialties revolved around manipulating card games and throwing punches, Freya's way of making money was a little more subdued but no less dishonest: she peddled out fake fortunes for Denfell's gullible citizens. Using powers of conjecture, her connections, and a gift for acting, she gave readings that were both unnervingly accurate and convincing. Ren had no doubt she could keep up with fortune-tellers from Glynn, who claimed to be the real thing. Freya had always been skilled at digging up information. It was a damn handy talent.

Arms crowded with tinkling bracelets, Freya gathered the bloody rags and supplies piled on Ren's sitting room table. As she tidied, she shifted her long curls so they fell over one shoulder to expose the injured side of her neck. The slice wasn't deep, but it looked inflamed.

"How's your neck?" Ren asked.

"Okay," Freya said, hauling everything to the set of countertops and shelving that barely passed as a kitchen. The fine mesh of her purple skirts swished, bits of gold-and-silver string sewn into the top layer glittering as she walked.

Not for the first time, Ren was impressed with Freya's commitment to her act. No matter the season, she dressed in the flowing layers and shoulder-baring tops the mystics favored. Jewelry, both crystals and metal, crowded her fingers, arms, and neck. She made her own faint music whenever she moved.

"You didn't need to hurt him like that," Freya added.

"Yes, I did."

Ren would be damned if anyone believed she was all bark and no bite. Freya nodded like she understood.

"I'm going to bed," Ren announced. It was an effort to get up from the chair. She couldn't remember the last time she'd fared so badly in a fight. She always tried to pick matches she would win, not because she particularly cared about her health or because she was averse to taking a beating. It wasn't even pride. It was the money. She needed a victory. So if she was being honest with herself—which she avoided, as a general rule—she'd concede that Freya was right and that she had let her emotions get the better of her. Ren believed there was a line between recklessness and straight-up stupidity, and she stayed on the right side of it, straddled it on occasion, but she didn't cross over. Most of the time.

Ren slowly made her way to her bedroom and eased the door shut. A mattress piled with dark blankets took up most of the floor, and moonlight drifted in through the window. The vanilla-and-cedarwood smell was stronger here than the rest of the suite, a perfume Ren had stumbled upon in a shop on the Golden Strait. It had been two years, and the shopkeepers still couldn't seem to figure out how bottles kept going missing.

Her ribs screamed as she pulled her clothes off and dropped them to the floor. A mirror was propped up in the corner of the room, and when she caught sight of her reflection, she sucked in a breath. A cloud of bruises covered the left side of her torso, blossoming over her ribs and extending down to her hip. In a strange way, she appreciated them. For once, the scar across her shoulder wasn't the ugliest thing on her body.

But the bruises would fade soon enough, sooner than they would if she were anyone else, if she didn't have silver taking up residence in her bones. But thanks to the magic, Ren healed twice as fast as was normal. She didn't know how it worked—virtually all books on wielding had been banned, then destroyed in the Purge—but she imagined silver rushing through her veins, frantically pulling her body back together.

Her silver was not a gift from the gods, but it had its uses.

Ren slipped on a large shirt and collapsed onto the bed. She grabbed an armful of blankets and rolled, tugging them over her bare legs, hoping tonight she would be spared from dreams of the crown prince. For years now, she'd been dreaming about Heath Lyandor. It had been happening since her parents had died and possibly before—she couldn't remember for certain—a blond boy only a little older than herself appearing in her head at night. She hadn't realized who he was, not at first. She must have been twelve when she spotted him touring the Naval Fleet at the docks. That was when she realized the kid in her dreams wasn't a figment of her imagination, but a Lyandor, the prince of a throne seeped in blood and the spawn of the man who'd sent soldiers to burn her home. He never approached her in the dreams, never spoke to her or looked at her. It was as if she were receiving glimpses of his life, usually not very pleasant ones, at that. Heath was not a kind prince. The dreams were like some kind of sick, cosmic joke, but she couldn't get them to stop. Ren didn't know what that said about her. Maybe she was torturing herself, or maybe it was a sign she needed to let go of the past. She only knew that she hated being forced to watch him over and over again, as if his family killing hers hadn't been cruelty enough.

As she drifted off to sleep, she heard cabinets creaking and the sink filling with water—Freya cleaning up in the kitchen.

CHAPTER
NINE

While most people were uncomfortable around the King's Children, nothing bothered Kellen much, deadly archers included. He was at ease beside Adley as they walked back to the castle. They weren't what anyone would call friends, but he had known her since she'd arrived at the castle over a decade ago, when he was only eight years old. He'd heard her full name was Adalena, but she never seemed to go by anything but Adley.

"My father is wasting your talents," Kellen said, his breath puffing in the winter air. His ears were numb with cold, and his gloved hands were buried deep in his coat pockets as they trekked up a path of stone steps set into the grassy hill. He'd sent a ball of silver bobbing ahead, the swirling magic lighting a path in the night.

Adley wasn't making a sound beside him, as if she'd been crafted by shadow. Her steps didn't crunch like his, her breath didn't hitch, her trench coat didn't even rustle. The wind was louder. The people said what they would about the king and his Children, but there was no denying that their training was effective.

"You can hit a moving target from six hundred feet away."

"Nine hundred," she muttered.

"Further illustrating my point."

"You know, I wouldn't have to waste my time running around Denfell if you'd stay in the castle."

"The castle is boring." And depressing. The place made Kellen want to drink, maybe lend some truth to the rumors people were constantly spouting about him. Despite all the talk, he wasn't actually a lush, but if he had to spend more time there than was absolutely necessary, he'd be at risk of turning into one.

"Come now. There must be a few courtiers you haven't bedded yet."

"Don't talk to me about the courtiers. They're more boring than the castle."

Adley huffed, but by the way her lips gave a slight twitch, Kellen had a hunch she agreed with him. As she should. The courtiers were terrible.

"Besides," he added, raising his brows, "the most interesting women at court are sleeping with each other."

Adley's foot missed a step, and she froze. Kellen stopped to give her a sideways look. The warmth had drained from her face so completely you'd think the executioner had put his ax to her neck. He frowned. "Relax. I don't give a shit who you spend your nights with."

"How did you know?" she asked so softly he almost didn't hear.

"I saw the two of you once." Kellen had assumed

whatever was going on between Adley and Lesa was only lust, but was it possible there was something more between them? If there was . . . Gods, he hoped his brother never found out. "It was only a jest, Adley. Forget I said anything."

Kellen continued up the hill toward the castle, where walls and turrets loomed against a black sky dotted with stars. He didn't say, *Your secret is safe with me,* though it was.

While he would never describe Adley as animated under the best of circumstances, she was markedly subdued when she caught up with him, watching her feet and kicking rocks with the toes of her laced boots. Moonlight shimmered in her waving hair. "Where do you go when you sneak out?" she asked. "When you're not with Holland."

"Opium dens. They have the loveliest décor. Excellent carpets. I'm thinking of purchasing a few for the castle."

"Funny."

"Oh no." Kellen was grave. "Interior decorating is serious business."

"In that case, you really should reconsider getting together with the courtiers. I suspect you'd have much to talk about."

Kellen beamed at her. "A marvelous idea."

As they took the stairs in silence, Kellen watched Adley out of the corner of his eye. She really was pretty, with her smooth brown skin and soft eyes. She was half a foot shorter than him, all lean muscles and wide shoulders, and though she was as talented at killing as the rest of the King's Children, there was something different about her. It was like she'd managed to hold on to a shred of warmth despite her training, which was intended to render her as cold as the mountains of Glynn. She hid her heart well, but Kellen suspected it was still there. He wasn't so sure about the other Children.

"How do you slip out of the castle?" Adley asked.

Kellen wasn't about to tell her that at the age of thirteen, he'd cleared the rubble from a collapsed tunnel and created an escape route. For the first twelve years of his life, he'd been a reasonably happy child, ignored by his father but doted on by his mother. She left the ruling to the king and advised Kellen to do the same, dressing him in expensive clothes and showing him off at social parties disguised as charity events. His life was surrounded by nice things, pretty things, kind things. And then when he'd gotten too tall to be considered an adorable accessory, his mother had cast him aside in favor of a dog that shed an ungodly amount and barked far too much. It didn't take long for the castle walls to become suffocating. Kellen had needed out. To this day, he was the only one who knew about the tunnel, and since the king would lock him in his rooms if he learned his son was running a fighting pit in the slums, Kellen wanted to keep it that way.

"And here I thought the King's Children were supposed to know everything," he said. "Honestly, I haven't the faintest idea why anyone is scared of you."

Though he hadn't meant it as a challenge, Adley was in motion in half a second. She whipped her bow out and unsheathed an arrow in one moment, pulling the string taut and letting loose in the next. The arrow flew into a tree some few hundred feet away. It was dark, with only the light of the moon and a little ball of silver to see by, and she hadn't paused to aim, but a bird dropped to the ground nonetheless, skewered on the wood. No more than a breath had passed.

Kellen stared at the dead bird while the trees rustled in the wind. "No one likes a show-off, Adley."

At the top of the hill, the castle guards bowed low to Kellen and pushed in the wide front gates. His magic faded to nothing as they made their way through the torch-lit inner courtyard, passing by a preposterously large fountain with two roaring lions perched on top. As Adley and Kellen approached the castle's grand entryway, the doors groaned open, spilling light over the steps.

They stepped out of the crisp air and into the glow of the castle, and Kellen felt the change immediately, even if Adley didn't. There were dozens of walls between him and his father, and yet his presence was everywhere, as if the king's disapproval had seeped into the walls. Kellen was already less content than he'd been down in the city, so far away from his life as a prince. It was a life he couldn't seem to fit into, one he wished he could leave behind. But a crown wasn't as easy to shrug off as a pair of worn shoes.

Once the castle doors thudded shut, Kellen said to Adley, "Well, this has been grand. Let's do it again sometime." He turned away—and was jerked back by the collar.

"Not so fast," Adley said.

Kellen rotated on the spot, brows rising. Never in his life had he been yanked back like a dog forced to heel. He really didn't mind it. He should spend time with Adley more often.

"I'm to take you to your chambers and keep you there."

"If you wanted to see my bedroom," Kellen purred, "all you had to do was ask."

"Don't be disgusting." Adley shoved him down the arching hallway.

As they wound their way to his chambers, Kellen kept up a constant stream of complaints. The castle was too cold, the food was inedible, there was a frightful draft in his rooms, the artwork was ghastly and he had a headache just looking at it. In admirable fashion, Adley ignored him, except for a roll of her eyes now and then.

He was in the middle of a rant about the state of the garden roses when a murmur of voices drifted from a cracked door. He recognized the deceptively smooth tones of his brother and came to a stop.

"What—" Adley started.

"Shh." He slunk down the hall and peered into the room.

". . . completely unacceptable," Heath was saying to an Orian emissary. The man had arrived at court a week ago, carrying a treaty put together by Orian, Eslind, and Jareen that demanded the king of Erdis keep his armies out of their countries. Kellen was surprised it had taken this long. Since he was a child, the king had been keeping a close eye on the rest of the world, waiting for disaster to strike and then springing to action, sending his men across borders carrying humanitarian excuses, when providing aid was the last thing on his mind. He had yet to sign the treaty, and he probably never would. He'd see it as a show of weakness, bowing to the whims of foreign rulers.

The emissary's mouth was a hard line, and his shoulders were tense beneath a dark cloak. Heath was equally stiff in his black-and-gold jacket with buttons done up to the chin. His blond hair—hair Kellen hated, only because it was so like his own—was ruffled, as if he'd been running his hands through it again and again.

Oh, his big brother was very, very stressed. Interesting.

"Prince Kellen," Adley whispered. "What are you doing?"

He pulled back and pressed himself to the wall outside the doorway, putting a finger to his lips. This was no ordinary meeting, and Kellen wanted to know the details.

Adley blew out a shallow breath. She bit her lip, glancing down the empty hall. After a beat, she leaned against the wall beside him.

"These are not unacceptable terms, Your Highness," the emissary said. "On the contrary, I'd say they're very reasonable."

"*Reasonable*?" Heath repeated. "Your king is threatening to wage war."

"I've given you an alternative, but you don't seem interested in the desert."

"No. Not yet. I'm considering my options."

Kellen wrinkled his brow. The only desert that came to mind was the Desert of Lost Souls, but that land had been forsaken by both the gods and the devils. It drove men to lunacy, turned them to monsters. Every terrible creature in every storybook had come from the vast stretch of dead land at the southern end of Erdis. Sometimes, men made it out alive, only to butcher entire towns days later. Traders from Ticharra, the southern kingdom across the desert, spent a month traveling around the sands, rather than risk a week's journey through. It was madness to even think about stepping foot in it.

There was a pause, then the emissary said, "War will come, whether you like it or not. If not from outside your borders, then from within. We hear you have something of a rebellion on your hands."

"That's none of your concern," Heath snapped.

"Maybe not. It certainly doesn't change the fact that Orian, Eslind, and Jareen *will* attack if you don't accept our terms. It's time your father chooses a side."

Heath's voice was venomous as he said, "Let me make this perfectly clear: There is the wrong side, and there is my side."

"You mean your father's side?" the emissary corrected.

"No, emissary," Heath said slowly and clearly, "I do mean *my* side."

"You Lyandors," the man scoffed, hardly ruffled. "You think your silver entitles you to an unchecked rule. Think again, Your Highness."

"You're walking a thin line." If possible, Heath's voice was colder than before. In all his life, Kellen had never seen his brother grow heated. Heath was always something darker and calmer. He was calculated and controlled, his anger like frozen iron.

But the emissary either didn't notice or didn't care. "Orian remembers how your family cemented their claim on the Erdis throne," he said, and Kellen wasn't sure if he should be worried for the man or impressed by his composure. "Don't make the mistake of thinking anyone has forgotten the Silver Purge. Magic would be thriving if it weren't for King Tallis."

The Silver Purge. Now *that* was one of Kellen's least favorite topics, lower on the list than the state of the castle sewers, but not by much. He'd learned at a young age that his great-grandfather was the one who'd ordered the genocide of the other silver wielders. No one believed the crap his family peddled about disease and plague. The outlaw of silver, the strict immigration laws—everyone knew that the only thing the king was trying to prevent was the spread of magic. Uprisings sprouted here and there, people with idyllic dreams of a better tomorrow taking a stand in the face of tyranny, but they'd always been dealt with by the King's Children before they could make much of a fuss.

Before the Purge, Erdis was an epicenter of magic, drawing wielders from all over the world to make their home within the kingdom. Infirmaries were run by wielders, who used their silver to help heal patients more quickly than tonics and tinctures. Some particularly creative wielders turned their magic into art, and Kellen had heard that street performances were such a common occurrence that Denfell's roads shone all night long. Magic had facilitated some of the city's most impressive pieces of architecture, supporting builders as they took structures to impossible heights, like the Royal Theatre, a glass-domed building that sat in the middle of the city and sparkled like a diamond when the sun was high in the sky. The castle itself had been built by wielders, with spires so tall they pierced the clouds.

It was estimated that at the height of silver, seventy percent of all wielders lived in Erdis. And maybe that was their mistake. When so many people were gathered in one place, they became much easier to exterminate.

"If you're attempting to threaten my family, you're doing a piss poor job of it," Heath told the emissary.

"It's not a threat, only a fact."

A silence filled the room, so terse it seemed to flow out into the hallway. Kellen glanced at Adley. She was staring at the cracked door, but it was impossible to tell what she was thinking.

"Sign the treaty," the emissary said to Heath. "My king is losing his patience."

The door jerked open, and the emissary appeared, his silky black hair tied in a bun at the base of his neck. He pulled up short at the sight of Kellen. "Little Lyandor," he said. He'd been calling Kellen that since he arrived, even if Kellen was nineteen, just three years younger than Heath. The emissary glanced back at the room. Heath had taken up a place in the doorway and was watching the Orian man with narrowed eyes. The man looked back to Kellen. "Do your kingdom a favor and convince your father to agree to the terms of our treaty."

Kellen raised his brows. He didn't know if there was a single person in Erdis less equipped to convince his father of anything. The last time King Mattheus had listened to something he had to say, Kellen must have been ten years old and deciding on a moniker for his new horse. Even then, when Kellen had chosen the name Hermies, his father had been less than impressed. *That's a ridiculous name for a horse*, he'd said and swept out of the stables.

"Sure," Kellen told the emissary.

The Orian man appeared annoyed with the short response, but before he could add more, Heath said, "I think it's time you got back to your chambers, emissary."

The emissary shot Heath a final look, then he gave a curt bow and took off down the low-lit hall. He turned a corner, the quick tap of his footsteps fading into the depths of the castle.

"So, Kell, what do you think?" Heath asked. "Should Father sign the treaty?

"Well . . ." Kellen trailed off. If he were king, he would have signed, but he wasn't king. He never would be. Heath had been preparing for that role his whole life, and he was far more suited to it. Kings were ruthless. They had hearts of ice and wills of unyielding steel. Their job wasn't to be kind; their job was to rule. His family hadn't kept their hold on the throne for centuries through benevolence. His father hadn't become the most powerful leader in the world by showing mercy. As far as Kellen was concerned, Heath was welcome to the Erdis throne. Wearing his father's ruby-studded crown was about as appealing as cleaning out the stables.

His brother was watching him, still waiting for a response.

"No?" Kellen said, though it sounded more like a question than an actual reply.

Heath's laugh was short and not all that kind. "It's a good thing you're not king. Otherwise, we'd all be doomed." Heath stepped fully into the hall, closing the chamber door behind him. "Go to bed, Kell."

After his brother had walked away, it was silent for a long time. Kellen pushed a hand through his hair. This was exactly why he ran off to the city every night. The Terth was dark and violent, and it smelled a little rank, but whenever he stayed in the castle, he always found a way to fall short. He'd said a grand total of three words, and he'd still managed to mess them up.

"We should get you back to your chambers," Adley said. She didn't sound all that concerned, but maybe talk of battles to come was casual dinner conversation for one of the King's Children.

On the way to his rooms, they passed through a long hall lined with paintings. Each gilded frame depicted a battle gone by, a fight won or lost, the glory of war. Every color, from blood red to death black, was vivid, as though the paint was still drying. The hallway seemed to go on forever, as if there were no beginning or end to the fighting, as if it was simply part of life, as inevitable as the sun rising in the morning.

"Do you think we're really headed for war?" Kellen asked Adley.

She didn't say anything, and that was all the answer he needed.

CHAPTER
TEN

"**O**f course they have a view of the river," Ren grumbled to herself, glaring around the clean, sparse streets of the Atterton District. Across the cobbled road, the Battgandon River lapped quietly in a cold breeze.

She turned her eyes on the Hollistair mansion. The thing was absurdly huge, as was the iron gate enclosing the front yard. Against the house's sapphire-blue paint, gold trim glinted in the late morning sun like a coin and windows caught the light bouncing off the river, the whole place glittering as brightly as a chest full of treasure.

And the stink of salty fish was barely present here. It seemed unfair that the residents of the Atterton District should have both piles of money and fresh air. Yet another reason to hate Darek Hollistair and his brother. As if roping her into a rebellion weren't enough.

A couple out for a morning stroll slowed as they passed by. The woman's nose wrinkled while she took in Ren's appearance, from knee-high boots to eyes lined with black. The man lingered on the cropped front of her burgundy coat and the leather corset beneath. His gaze slid up to her face, and he gave a start when he found her staring back.

"What?" she snapped.

The couple quickly looked away, picking up their pace. They hurried off, heels and boots tapping against the paved walkway. Ren watched them go, then pushed open the gate, her side aching slightly from the movement. Though the bruises coloring her ribs had healed to pale shades of yellow and green and Freya had removed the stitches from the gash on her forehead, she still had a couple more days before all traces of last week's fight in South Terth were gone. She was just glad the swelling around her eye had mostly subsided, even if the delicate skin was still reddened and it hurt a little to apply her cosmetics. That didn't stop her from doing it, though, much to Freya's chagrin.

The gate swung in, creaking on its hinges, and she traipsed down a walkway lined with bare trees and bushes that probably flowered like mad when the weather turned warmer in the spring. As the gate drifted shut behind her, she treaded up the porch steps and reached forward to knock, but paused at the sound of a carriage coming to a stop on the street. Horse hooves clomped and went silent.

She turned. The door of a simple carriage popped open, and Darek ducked out, a thick traveling cloak around his shoulders. Brown boots hit the pavement, and he straightened up, throwing a satchel over his back. He was so tall that he didn't even have to stretch to hand his fare to the driver.

Ren narrowed her eyes. Like his house, he was so much *larger* than was necessary.

Darek started forward, but faltered when he caught

sight of Ren waiting. At his back, the driver flicked his reins and the carriage pulled away, rattling wheels and clicking horseshoes filling an otherwise silent street. Once they were gone, it was just Ren, Darek, and the river.

Adjusting his satchel on his shoulder, Darek swung in his front gate. "You're here," he said.

"Surprised?" Ren moved to the side, making room for him on the porch.

He dug around in his coat, pulled out a key, and slipped it into the lock on the front door. "A little," he admitted, shouldering the door in. He crossed the threshold, then held it open for her. His gaze lingered on her damaged eye, but if he was curious about what had happened, he didn't ask. She gave him an annoyed look as she stepped through.

The door swung shut, and Ren took in the mansion. The foyer was open and airy, an unlit chandelier dangling from the high ceiling. Gold railings wrapped around the upper floors, a massive white staircase was straight ahead, and gold leaf painted dozens of doors. Sunlight shone through tall windows, falling across the marble floor and plush area rugs. The house was warm enough that more than one fireplace must have been lit, and Ren popped open the buttons on her coat. She tugged it off and held it out to Darek. He took it without comment, adding it to a rack by the front door where he'd hung his cloak. The stubble along his hard jaw was more unkempt than it had been the night she met him, and his hair, which was tied back in a knot, seemed messier, too.

"Where were you?" she asked.

"Lan Covve."

Ren raised her brows. Many of Denfell's wealthy residents owned second homes in the small country town. They often visited for "a brief respite from city life." Ren didn't know what that was supposed to mean, considering most people who could afford property in Lan Covve were as rich as Darek.

"Why?" she asked. "Needed a break from your life of hardship? Is it just positively exhausting to spend all day letting servants feed you grapes and fan you with palm leaves?"

A few moments passed, during which Darek stared at Ren with the same indecipherable look he'd worn a week ago, before he'd tried to bite her head off. He sighed, popping open the buttons on his vest as he stepped around her. "Come on," he said. "I'll make tea."

"Boiling your own water?" she asked, following him across the foyer. "How *common* of you, Darek."

At the back of the house, he pushed through a swinging door, and she trailed him into a room lined with white countertops and rows of glass cabinets crowded with dishes. A fire flickered in a hearth, and the scent of warm spices lingered in the air. It was immaculate, everything clean and in its proper place, apart from a worn leather sketchbook sitting on top of a table in the middle of the room. Ren wondered who the artist of the family was. Darek certainly seemed moody enough for it.

While he filled a kettle with water from the sink, Ren

said, "I'm impressed you found the kitchen. Next thing I know, you're going to tell me that you can cook."

He grabbed a towel and hung the kettle over the fire, then turned back to her. His expression was flat. His jaw pulsed once. "Are you about finished?"

Ren would never be finished. She could keep at it forever, so long as it annoyed him. "For now." She ambled around the room, running her fingers over the spotless surfaces. Pausing at a glass bowl piled with vibrant winter fruits, she selected a persimmon and leaned back against the counter. She tossed it in the air and caught it, watching Darek watch her. A small part of her—a very, very small part—liked the look of him, his height and his eyes and his sharp jaw. Probably the same part that insisted she only kiss men who weren't any good for her, but were good enough for a night. "So why were you in Lan Covve?"

He tossed the towel on the counter. "I was visiting the queen."

Ren had been about to throw the fruit again, but paused. "*Really?*"

He came to her side, opening a cupboard above both their heads to grab two teacups and a metal canister. Silently, he unscrewed the container and shoveled a concoction of autumn-hued tea leaves into the cups. Their scent left a trail of nutmeg and clove.

"Why?" Ren pressed.

Darek returned the tea to its place on the shelf. His jaw was clenched tight.

"Fine," she said, raising the persimmon to her lips.

"Don't tell me." She bit into the fruit's soft flesh, and sweet juice flooded her tongue.

Darek's brows furrowed, pulling his face into a scowl. While she chewed, he assessed her for what felt like the tenth time in the last five minutes. She didn't miss the way his eyes flickered down to her corset and stayed there a beat too long, like maybe he liked the look of her, too. Averting his stare, he reached for a jar of sugar and pulled it across the counter. "I wish I didn't have to trust you," he said.

"You don't," she replied, inspecting the fruit. "You only have to pay me." She took another bite.

"When you say things like that, it makes me trust you even less."

"Why? Greed is about the only thing you can count on around here."

His face was as stony as ever, but since he didn't come up with a response, Ren assumed she'd won whatever game they were playing. Leaving his side, she leaned her hips against the table in the middle of the room and kicked one ankle over the other. "So are you going to tell me why I'm here, or are we just going to stare at each other all day?"

He mirrored her, falling back on the counter and shoving his arms over his chest. They faced one another, neither of them speaking until eventually he said, "I wanted to talk about your silver."

Ren couldn't stop her heart from kicking up its pace, but she forced her shoulders to relax. "Fine, but before we do, I want to know how you found me."

He blew out a breath through his nose, as if annoyed

by the detour. "It was because of that big fight you won a few months ago. There was a ton of money riding on it, and your victory was enough of an upset for word to trickle back to us: the eighteen-year-old girl who came out of nowhere to win."

Ren remembered that fight. The pot was huge—and her opponent, just as large. It was a bitch to get him down and even more difficult to keep him there, and she'd broken a finger in the process, but the pain had been worth the heavy pouch of gold. She'd had money that month to make her payment to Nevskov and also repair some drafty spots in the Compound before winter hit. "It still doesn't explain how you figured out I had silver. I don't use it at the pits."

"It was just a hunch from a friend who tracked you down. She told us you might be worth our while, so my brother and I started following you. That was when we saw it."

Well, that was unsettling. Ren had thought she'd been careful with her magic, but apparently she hadn't been careful enough. She hesitated to call herself lucky, seeing as she'd been drawn into a revolution that may very well get her killed, but there were worse people who could have caught her.

"So how does the magic work?" Darek prompted.

She pressed the persimmon to her mouth for a few moments, and then lowered it from her lips. "I'm not entirely sure," she admitted. "It's not like there's been anyone around to teach me. My parents tried to help when I was younger, but I learned to wield myself."

Although Ren's parents had loved her fiercely, they were clueless when it came to her magic. Neither of them had expected it when their five-year-old's hands had started glowing at the dinner table. Her mother had run a business of some sort—Ren was never entirely sure of the details—and her father had been a professor at Denfell's university. Nothing had prepared them for Ren. They did their best, tracking down what little information they could on silver, helping her to control the magic, shielding her from the king. But then their house went up in flames, and everything they'd done was a waste because they were in the ground and Ren's magic had put them there.

"You really taught yourself?" Darek asked with a tilt of his head. "How?"

Ren shrugged. "It wasn't that hard. Silver is a part of me. I was born with it. I guess I just think about it like any other part of my body. I tell it what I want it to do, and it does it. It's mostly about concentration and moving your hands the right way. Practice helps."

She didn't confess that when she was ten years old, she'd been overeager and a bit too enthusiastic with her hand gestures and had accidentally blasted apart a brick wall, nearly taking a building down with it. That was when she began to understand just how dangerous silver could be. A couple of experienced wielders could get together and destroy armies if they really wanted to. Ren, she favored the more subtle aspects of the magic. It made a damn good lockpick. Slipping coins from pockets was as easy as twitching a finger.

"But it won't do anything by itself," she added. "And if you can't use your hands, you're screwed."

He nodded. "What can you do with it?"

Ren could do quite a lot with her silver. She could twist it into any shape she liked. She could reach cups on high shelves and tear apart men from the inside out. "What do you want me to do with it?" she inquired.

Over the fire, steam was shooting out of the kettle. Darek picked up the towel again and went to remove it from the flames. "For the next few weeks, we want you to make a series of public appearances with your silver. We'll start tomorrow—"

Ren set the half-eaten fruit on the counter and headed for the door. "No. Absolutely not. You can keep your money."

If the king found out she hadn't died like she was supposed to, gold wouldn't mean a thing. She could hardly spend it from the grave. She'd find another way to pay off her debt to Nevskov. If she had to, she'd take him up on his offer to fight for him. It was moronic, and she'd probably never escape his crooked nose or dimly lit house, but at least she'd be alive.

"No, Ren, wait—" There was the sound of the kettle hitting the floor, followed by, "Ow. Shit." Booted steps rushed across the room, then Darek grabbed on to her arm. "Stop."

She yanked free of his hold, whirling back around. "I won't be your damn martyr."

He stepped away, palms raised as if in surrender. "No one is asking you to be."

"If King Mattheus finds out I'm alive, he'll finish what he started nine years ago. He'll kill me."

There wasn't much the people of Erdis agreed on, but everyone knew how the Lyandors felt about magic: it belonged to them, and them alone. They'd claimed it a hundred years ago, and they weren't letting it go anytime soon. In one of her recent nightmares about the crown prince, he'd been torturing someone, drowning them slowly. Letting them catch their breath for only a moment before shoving them under again. Over and over and over, she'd had to stand there and watch. She suspected her own fate wouldn't look too different. As long as Ren had silver, there was a price on her head.

"He won't find out, not until we're ready," Darek said. "We told you we wanted you to inspire the people. What did you think that meant?"

"I certainly didn't think it meant extended magic displays around the city. Word will get back to the king."

"It won't—"

"The only reason I'm still alive is because I haven't been acting like a circus performer. I won't start now."

She made to leave again, and Darek gripped her elbow. "Please, Ren. We have a plan. Just listen."

She jerked her arm out of his hold. "No." She swept to the kitchen door, smacking it with her palms and pushing through. As the door swung behind her, Darek grumbled something unintelligible but undoubtedly rude.

Ren was halfway down the hall when he came rushing after her. He jumped in front of her, blocking the path to the foyer. "You are the most unreasonable person I've ever had the displeasure of meeting."

Ren glared up at him. Why in the name of every god were his eyes such a warm shade of brown? It was infuriating. "Yes, well, you're no charmer." She rammed into his side, shoving him out of her way.

He let out a curse under his breath. "I'll give you another fifty thousand gold pieces."

She stopped in her tracks. They were both quiet for a while, then Ren groaned. "You have too much godsdamn money," she said, turning back.

Darek's towering form took up a good deal of the hallway, and his stare was so hard that Ren wouldn't have been surprised if he was attempting to set her on fire through sheer force of will. "Well?" he demanded.

Ren crossed her arms and considered him. The afternoon sun shone through a window at the end of the hall, creating a halo of light around his messy hair and broad shoulders. "You've been with the rebellion for how long now? Years?" His only response was frowning deeper, so Ren took it as confirmation. "Yet you need *my* help badly enough that you're willing to part with a small fortune. Is that right?"

"Do you have a point?"

"Have you considered that maybe you're not cut out to be a rebel? Perhaps you should pick up a hobby. Like pottery. Or knitting."

"Is seven hundred thousand enough for you?" he bit out.

She inspected her nails and said, "Tell me your plan first, and I'll consider it."

"We'll start at the Underground," Darek told her, his words gruff and short. "Nothing that happens there gets back to the castle, and don't argue, because you know it's true."

Ren gave him a dirty look. He was right, of course. The Underground was an illegal marketplace deep in the Terth, and events in or near the slums never reached the castle's ears. Quite frankly, the southwestern portion of Denfell ruled itself. King Mattheus didn't seem to care about the poverty in his city. He didn't send guards to patrol the graying and jagged streets, buildings fell into disrepair, crime ran rampant. Ren was fairly sure he was waiting for the poor to die off, since it was easier to oppress them until they faded away than give them resources. In any case, they seemed to have given up on asking for help. They were all too busy trying not to starve.

"We want to start a trickle of rumors, and the people who visit the Underground have their own network of communication," Darek added. "They have a way of passing along information without it getting back to the castle."

"I'm aware," Ren said.

His lips pulled down, like he didn't care for the reminder of who she was and where she came from. "Your identity will remain a secret until we can make our move for the throne. The people will learn about you slowly.

They won't even know you're a girl, not at first. All we need is to set off the rumor that there's another silver wielder living in Denfell."

Ren wasn't happy to admit it, but it wasn't a bad plan. Announcing her presence with all the grace of a fragor explosion would certainly make a statement, but statements didn't overthrow kings.

"So do you agree or not?" Darek asked after she'd been quiet for a long time.

"Fine." By the front door, she took her jacket from the coatrack and pulled it over long, billowing sleeves. "I'll meet you at the Underground at ten tomorrow morning, unless you do us both a favor and throw yourself into the river before then."

She left the Hollistair mansion, making her way down the steps and through the front gate. As she walked away, she shot one look back at the blue paint. *Honestly*, she thought, *who needs a home that large?*

CHAPTER
ELEVEN

A fire roared across from Adley as she pored over a map of Denfell, her loose braid swinging at her shoulder. A few days ago, the map had been littered with pins, marking every tavern in the Atterton District that could possibly be serving as a meeting ground for the rebellion. One by one, Adley had gone through and removed the pins as she crossed establishments off the list. Now, she pulled the pins out of two more taverns and set them aside. Her eyes caught on her hand as she braced it atop the table, the nails crusted with dried blood.

Adley curled her fingers in and straightened up, rolling out her shoulders and popping her neck. She was no stranger to the castle's interrogation cells, but since the announcement of the King's Fang competition, she'd found herself down there more than ever. With the help of Lesa and a few other Children who had no interest in becoming Fang, she'd brought in anyone who might have a connection to the rebels, no matter how nebulous. The dead ends and mistakes were the worst. Those nights, Adley would lie in bed and feel guilt swimming in her stomach for torturing an innocent person who had as much to do with the rebellion as Prince Kellen. But then she'd catch a break: She'd find someone who did know something, and she'd get one step closer to the rebels. One step closer to King's Fang and eventual freedom.

She often thought about what she'd do if she ever got to leave the castle, leave and never look back. There wasn't a confessional large enough to contain her sins, but she knew she would have to atone for the things she'd done. A lot of people probably didn't think Adley deserved forgiveness, but she had to believe that wasn't true. There were nine heavens and nine hells, each mirroring one another, and though Adley didn't know where she'd belong when all was said and done, she hoped the gods would understand that her actions had been for her survival. She might have lost a little bit of her humanity along the way, but she would get it back. Somehow.

The tea she'd prepared for herself had long gone cold, but she grabbed the cup and swallowed it down anyway, grimacing at the bitter taste. Her eyes scanned the map again, studying the remaining pins: Foxglove Tavern, Full Moon Howl, The White Raven, Retribution, The Willow Room.

She was so close. Which one was it?

Lesa had suggested they perform some raids—go in with swords drawn and cut down a few people until they found the right place—but Adley didn't want to scare the rebels off. If King's Children started raiding taverns in the Atterton District, it wouldn't go amiss. The rebellion would move base, and Adley's one lead would be gone. No, she had to play this close to the chest. She couldn't let the rebels know she was on their trail until it was too late.

"Well, what do we have here?" came a deep, conceited-sounding voice from the open doorway.

Turning to face Ethen Delano, Adley dropped her hand to the knife at her waist, wishing for a sheath of arrows on her back instead. She never walked around the castle completely defenseless—none of the King's Children did—but after she'd finished up in the dungeons, Adley had discarded most of her weapons, thinking she wouldn't have a need for them anymore tonight. Clearly, she'd been wrong.

"Ethen," she said.

He ambled into the room, eyeing the map sprawled across the wooden table.

Adley shifted her body in front of it. "Can I help you with something?"

Ethen's stare slid over to her own, and something dangerous sparked in his eyes. "I thought I told you to leave the rebellion alone."

"Scared I might find the rebels before you?"

His laugh was soft and slightly sinister. "That's cute."

Adley came very close to pulling her dagger from her hip and slamming it into his thigh, but as tempting as it was, getting into a knife fight with Ethen in the middle of the night was not in her best interest. "Go away, Ethen. I'm busy."

"I can see that." As if out for a casual stroll by the river, he moved toward her, coming closer, too close. She took a few steps back, but Ethen only followed until her back was pressed against the wall and his massive frame was dwarfing hers. "Make no mistake. I will be King's Fang."

"Have you found the rebels, then?" she asked, keeping her voice steady and her chin high. Try as he might, Ethen couldn't intimidate her. She wouldn't let him. "Do you even know where to look?"

There was that laugh again. He touched the end of her braid, his calloused fingers playing with her hair. "Oh, Adalena. There's so much you don't know."

Before she could ask what in all nine hells he was talking about, a blade whizzed past his head and slammed into the wall above Adley. A breath hissed through his teeth, and he put a hand to his ear. When it came back, his fingers were wet with blood. His eyes flashed, his whole body jerking toward the door and away from Adley. Around his back, Adley saw Lesa leaning an unbothered shoulder against the doorframe, her long coat slung over one shoulder and bright-blonde hair swaying.

"What the *hells*, Lesa?" Ethen cursed.

"What?" she asked innocently. "It slipped."

"You are psychotic," he seethed. His muscles were tensed, the veins in his neck standing at attention.

"You're one to talk," Lesa replied.

Blood was beginning to slide down his tanned neck and into his leather top. With something close to a snarl, he turned back to Adley, a look on his face that reminded her of a predator who enjoyed toying with its food. "I was done here anyway," he said. "Stay out of my way, Adley."

Ethen rotated, striding past Lesa and into the depths of the quiet castle.

As Lesa made her way across the room, Adley yanked the dagger out of the wall and held it out hilt-first. Lesa accepted it, sliding the blade back into place on her thigh. "Did he hurt you?" she asked, her dark eyes tracking Adley's face, her arms, and her body.

Adley shook her head. "I can handle him."

Lesa nodded, dropping her coat on the chair where Adley had thrown hers. They matched in their uniforms, with their black pants and sleeveless laced shirts, the golden lion stitched on the chest shining in the firelight. "Ethen talks a big game, but Tarrus told me he hasn't made any strides in his search for the rebels. We're pretty far ahead of him."

"We need to keep it that way," Adley said, stepping over to the map and eyeing it again, the few remaining pins calling to her like targets in the training yard. She knew staring at them wasn't going to help her find the rebels any more than staring at the sea helped to catch a fish, but that didn't stop her from doing it.

"When was the last time you ate?" Lesa asked as Adley ran a tired hand over her face.

"This afternoon? This morning? I'm not sure."

Fingers brushed over Adley's lower back as Lesa came to her side, and though the room was warm from the fire, a shiver broke out across her exposed arms. Lesa's hand whispered over Adley's, drawing her around. They were about the same height, making it easy for their gazes to meet. Lesa's eyes softened, something they only ever did around Adley. "You need to rest," Lesa said.

Fondness tugged at Adley's heart. Her life had gone so horribly wrong, but with Lesa, one thing had gone right. Maybe it was luck or a small mercy from the gods that she'd found someone who cared about her in a place where it shouldn't have been possible. Adley had never really had a home. Whoever her parents were, they were gone before she could remember, having died or abandoned her, she didn't know which. She'd been left alone on the hilly streets of Sirica, white stucco houses against a backdrop of azure water. When she'd been tossed onto a slavers' ship and later taken by the king's men, she feared she would never find a safe place to rest. But then Lesa had come along, and though Adley still didn't know what home felt like, she imagined she might have found it in Lesa's arms.

"Will you come with me?" Adley asked. "In twelve years, after I'm done being Fang, will you leave the castle with me? We could go anywhere."

Lesa's eyes flickered between Adley's. "You know the king would never let me."

"It's twelve years, Lesa. A lot could change." Adley would figure something out. She had to. Though she desperately wanted to escape the king, could she really go without Lesa?

But Lesa only bit the inside of her lip, and Adley worried that maybe she didn't want to leave. Lesa didn't like the king, but she'd always had a sense of loyalty to him, even if it was somewhat tenuous and she pushed the boundaries of obedience as far as she could. Adley couldn't quite understand it, even after Lesa had explained that she felt he'd rescued her from a life of the gods knew what; they never had learned where the slavers were taking them. But the king had given them food and clothing, beds to sleep in, and shelter from the cold. They had received a basic education and the finest weapons. It was more than many people ever had.

Adley disagreed. Most days, being a King's Child felt like another form of slavery.

Staring at Lesa now, she remembered the look on her face when they'd tortured the sympathizer—not a flinch or a stutter the entire time. Adley had never been able to go there, to discard the mask entirely and embrace the cruelty. But each of them became who they needed to be in order to wear their uniforms every day and not be crushed by the weight of them. Adley had chosen to bury her heart. Lesa had discarded hers entirely. And maybe that should have bothered Adley. Maybe in another life it would have. But in this life, Lesa was the best thing Adley had. She was all Adley had.

"Where would you want to go?" Lesa suddenly asked.

"Sirica," Adley said.

Lesa raised her brows in question, her fingers slipping between Adley's where they rested on the table.

"I don't have fond memories of my childhood there, but it's a beautiful country. Did you know that at night, the sea glows?"

"It glows?"

"Because of all the sunstones. The waves are constantly moving them around, and when it gets dark, the sea lights up." Sunstones were a pebble found only in the waters of Sirica, named after the way they emitted a faint golden light when jostled, and though they were no more magical than fireflies, they were appallingly expensive. But if you could afford it, they were nice to have on hand in case you found yourself in a bind and needed light. Adley smiled to herself. She didn't want to live forever with tainted images of the country. She wanted to go back, fix things, pick up the broken threads of her life and mend them. "I'd like to see it again. Make some new, better memories." She glanced up at Lesa. "With you."

Tilting her head, Lesa lifted her lips into a soft, innocent smile she only showed Adley. It wasn't the smile of a King's Child, but the smile of a girl Adley knew was buried beneath her leather uniform and sharpened knives. It was a girl Lesa could be if given the chance.

"That sounds nice," Lesa said.

Hope surged in Adley's chest. Twelve years was a long time to wait, but it wasn't forever. It wasn't never. And then the things they felt would no longer be dangerous, and they wouldn't have to hide. They could stick their toes in the sand and love one another the way they were supposed to. "Yeah?"

Lesa wrapped a hand around the back of Adley's neck and brought their lips together. The kiss was tender and longing, tinged with dreams for the future. Adley could almost smell Sirica's warm breeze, almost taste the fruit picked fresh from the trees.

Lesa pulled away and ran her thumb over Adley's bottom lip. "Let's find those rebels."

CHAPTER
TWELVE

U p on the third floor of his house, through wide windows and thick ivory curtains, Darek had a view of Atterton's many hues. Buildings were painted bright and scrubbed clean, trees and streetlights lined the cobbled streets, and the river shined in the sun. From here, it was easy to forget that not all of Denfell shimmered, and easier still to forget that the slums were a contained disease. King Mattheus plied the residents of Darek's neighborhood with enough gold to *make* them forget, gold that should have been going south to the people who needed it. Darek could only imagine what Ren had been thinking when she'd come by the day before. But she should know his family wasn't so easily bought.

Darek pulled a heavy black cloak from his armoire. "I'm meeting Ren at the Underground in a couple hours," he said, fastening the gold buckles at his neck. "I have to run an errand first."

"I'll be there," his little brother replied, not looking up from his work. A thick brocade robe knotted at his waist and his hair in disarray from sleep, Markus was seated at Darek's desk, drawing in one of his many sketchbooks.

They were scattered all over the house, turning up in random places like gifts brought by a winter sprite during the night. Just yesterday, Darek had pulled a sketchbook from beneath a cushion in the library couch.

"You have charcoal on your face," Darek told him on his way out of the room. He paused to ruffle his brother's hair.

Markus grunted and jerked his head away.

"Be careful at the Underground. I'll be too busy with Ren to watch your back."

"I will," Markus said, sitting back to study his half-finished sketch of the animals at Kanning Heart Stables, where their family boarded their horses.

"I'll meet you back here later."

Darek padded down the staircase, his hand gliding along the metal bannister. Morning light flooded the front porch, along with the bite of a winter breeze. Pulling the front of his cloak tighter, he set out for Keepler's Prospect, a courtyard in front of the city's largest art museum, the Sollertie.

As Darek left the quiet of his neighborhood, Denfell came awake. One clopping horse became three and then five and then too many to count. Voices drifted by, both friendly morning greetings and irritable snaps from people who would much rather be asleep. Beneath rolling gray clouds, fishermen in thick scarves were guiding boats down the river. Merchants and tradesmen waited in line at tea stands before heading to shops, marketplaces, and Traders' Hall.

When he got to the Golden Strait and its glittering storefronts, the smell of sweet rolls wafted through the air, strong enough to overpower the ever-present tang of salt that clung to the city. Across the road was Denfell's most popular bakery, Noble Finch. Darek caught a flash of blazing red hair behind the glass door, and a second later, Holland stepped out of her mother's shop, crimson curls spilling over her shoulders and a set of white boxes tucked beneath her arm. With her free hand, she pulled her fur collar high around her neck. When she lifted her chin, she noticed Darek watching. He offered her a nod before continuing on his way.

The Golden Strait was only a few blocks behind him when he came upon a horde of people gathered at the river's edge. A dozen men and women in black leather were standing atop a bridge halfway down the road, their backs to him as they stared over the other side. The crowd was as silent as a church in prayer, and hot, acidic dread pooled in Darek's stomach.

When he was close enough to see what was going on, he stopped cold. Five people were hanging from the bridge by their wrists. The men were shirtless, the women stripped down to their underthings, their feet bare. Water dripped from their hair and drenched clothing, shivers wracking their bodies. Two King's Children forced one last man onto the railing. In only a pair of rough-spun trousers, he crawled up and stood there, shaking in the frigid air, hands bound in front of him. A gust of wind ruffled his hair. No one on the street moved.

The King's Children pushed him over.

The splash cut the silence like a clashing symbol as the man plummeted into the Battgandon River, disappearing beneath the blue-gray surface. The water churned, bubbling and rippling.

"What happened?" Darek whispered to a woman beside him.

"Heard they were spreading illegal propaganda," she explained, staring out at the river. Everyone knew that in Denfell, *spreading illegal propaganda* meant one thing: speaking out against the king. "Poor bastards."

Up on the bridge, the King's Children yanked the rope taut and began to tow the man up. Clenched fists emerged, then tied wrists and forearms. His head broke the surface, and he sputtered, gasping for air as the Children pulled him out of the water. Once his feet were clear by a yard, they secured the rope to the railing, then all twelve Children turned and left. They never spoke a word.

The men and women dangled from the bridge, chins to their chests. They didn't struggle, their bodies drifting back and forth like creaking doors in a shifting house. A mumbled prayer snaked through the gathered crowd. Silently, Darek added one of his own.

Though he'd never witnessed the practice up close like this, he knew the gist of it. This particular execution was unique to Denfell in winter. Overnight, the water would freeze on their skin, and what remained of their clothing would turn to sheets of ice. Their noses and fingers and toes would shift to blue and black. By morning, they would all be dead—and still hanging from the bridge by their wrists. It would be weeks before they were cut down.

Darek swallowed. He ducked his head and pushed his way through the onlookers. He didn't glance back.

He arrived at Keepler's Prospect just as a faraway clock tower was striking the hour. The courtyard was circular, as white as fresh snow, and made entirely of marble. The semicircles of towering columns, the scattered statues, the steps leading up to the museum—all were entirely colorless. It was empty and oddly silent. Darek shivered, trying to push the scene at the river from his mind.

The woman he was meeting, a young dancer with the Royal Ballet, appeared from behind a statue across the courtyard. When he saw her, Darek slipped between two columns and into a walkway, the woman stepping in moments later. They met each other halfway. A white wall carved with images of the gods loomed at their left, shadow and sunlight streaking the marble.

People in Denfell worshipped the gods in a hundred different ways. Some attended church each morning during an hour many considered holy, though Darek had never understood why he should pray during one time of day over another. Private confessionals were popular but not required, a safe place where people could speak to the goddess of forgiveness. And then there were some people, like Ren, who either didn't believe in the gods or didn't care about them. Darek was not like Ren. But he also wasn't one to worship in designated spaces. He knew the gods would hear him, no matter where he was.

He produced a pouch of gold, but the dancer waved him off, pulling folded parchment from the back of her skirts. She shoved the papers at his chest. "I told you: I don't want your money. Take them and go."

"Everyone wants something," Darek said. He smoothed open the choreography for the Crown's Demonstration, an event that marked the official end to the weeklong celebration known as the Royal Carnival. During the demonstration, the king and his sons displayed their silver for the entire city to see. It was a painfully obvious attempt at intimidation, and damn Darek if it didn't seem to work.

"I want the same as you," she said quietly. "I want the Lyandors off the Erdis throne."

When Darek looked up, her eyes were downcast. "But why? If anyone finds out you gave me these, you'll be punished. You won't dance again."

The dancer wrapped her slight arms around herself and didn't respond.

Darek went back to the choreography, mind already turning to the ways in which he could use it to his advantage. They were so close. Now that Ren had joined them, their plan was weeks away from unfolding. He had very little time to get the pieces into place. They couldn't afford mistakes.

"I love dancing," the woman said suddenly. "So do a lot of men. For an extra fee, they can see us offstage, too. But it's never just dancing they want." She paused, staring out at the white courtyard. She didn't look sad, only resigned.

"Prince Heath comes by sometimes. He never has to pay, of course. The king knows. He doesn't stop it."

"I'm sorry," Darek said. He meant it with everything he had, but the words felt as weightless as cotton on his tongue.

"We all have our reasons," she said and left him with only the statues for company.

CHAPTER
THIRTEEN

O h, how Ren despised the cesspool that was the Underground. Black mold covered the crumbling tunnel walls, it was damp and smelled like piss, and she suspected at least half the men and women creeping in the shadows were carrying infectious diseases.

While she waited for Darek to show up, Ren decided to pay a visit to one of the weapons dealers; she needed to replace the knives she'd lost the night the Hollistair brothers had knocked her unconscious. "Morning, Jac!" she called into the depths of a spectacularly cluttered stall. It looked like it had been on the brink of collapse dozens of times and patched up with whatever was nearby: a broken chunk of wood, one huge iron spike, a slab of bent metal.

"Gods almighty, girl, you go fishin' with your knives or summat?" the weapons dealer grumbled, hobbling out of the shadows to greet her. Jac wasn't all that old, but he was missing an eye, a leg, and most of his teeth, all of which he claimed to have lost in a gang fight. The only thing he had a full set of was arms.

"Don't be absurd," Ren said. "I get the handsome boys to catch the fish for me."

Jac scrutinized her with his one eye, then hawked spittle on the ground. "What'll it be this time?"

"Five of those fixed-blade combat daggers you know I love and four boot daggers." Ren had a feeling she was going to start losing her knives quicker than she could buy them, so it was best to stock up. "Oh, and a couple neck daggers."

Jac gave a disgruntled huff as he went about rounding up her weapons. Metal clanked and clattered inside his stall. "What's a pretty girl like you need with so many knives?"

"Haven't you heard? A lady never reveals her secrets."

He grunted in response.

The low cadence of voices filled the Underground, as soft and dangerous as a sinister wind. An incessant dripping came from somewhere unknown. The stench of rot floated by, and Ren wrinkled her nose, glancing over her shoulder to spot the culprit. When her back was turned, someone approached and stopped at her side, a too-tall someone she was not very pleased to see. Ren rotated slowly.

Darek wore a black cloak similar to the one he'd had on yesterday, but while that had been a rougher material made for horseback and traveling, today's was fine and thick, with a set of gold buckles at the neck and chest. A gray fur lining peeked out from the edges. His hair was the messiest Ren had seen it, as if he'd knotted it back while running down the stairs and hadn't glanced in a mirror since. She was mildly annoyed by how well it suited him.

"I've been looking for you for ten minutes," he said, scowling.

"You found me. Congratulations."

Jac reappeared from his stall. He rolled his one eye over Darek before setting it on Ren and listing her price. She shook her head. "Why are you always charging me an eye and a leg?"

"Hardy-har," Jac said, adjusting himself on his remaining foot and holding out a palm. "And the sayin' is 'an arm and a leg.'"

Giving her best smile, Ren handed over her coins in exchange for the blades. "A pleasure as always, Jac."

"Yeah, yeah." As if swatting at fleas, he waved a lazy hand and returned to the darkness of his rickety stall, muttering all the while.

After she'd slipped her new knives into the various pockets and hidden slots in her clothing, she turned to Darek. His eyes snapped up from her corset, as if he'd been caught looking somewhere he shouldn't, and his expression darkened. He frowned so much Ren was beginning to suspect it may be permanent.

"Are you done shopping, or do you have some stolen jewels to buy first?" he asked.

"Why? Need more diamonds to bathe in?"

Darek's mouth didn't even twitch. He produced an extra cloak and something that looked like a cloth mask, and pushed them at her. "Put these on."

They stepped out of sight, disappearing into a smaller tunnel that branched off the Underground's main stretch.

The cloak swallowed Ren like a shadow in the middle of the night, hiding her form well. She tied the mask over the top half of her face and pulled the hood forward. Darek raised his hood, as well, and they returned to the dingy light of the larger tunnel.

Side by side, they made their way through the dank marketplace. It was crowded with makeshift stalls and carts looking one moment from buckling under the weight of their wares. This far beneath the streets, the whole place was as dark as a dungeon. Torches and lamps were burning so low that it was impossible to properly make out anyone's face.

Ren dodged a heavily scarred man who had been getting too close for comfort, then flung her sharpest glare at Darek. He should have had the decency to be a little less attractive. The fact that he looked the way he did, all sharp edges and hard angles, offset by round eyes and fuller lips, was entirely unfair. It made her body curious about his, even though her head had no interest in him or his self-righteous attitude. "There are about a hundred places in this city we could have gone." She wrinkled her nose at a man who leaned out of a stall to sell her what looked like a dead spider on a chain. "If you were going to subject me to your company, the least you could have done was picked somewhere cleaner."

"You're not exactly a joy to be around, either," Darek said.

"At least I managed to brush my hair this morning."

A hulking bald man pushed a cart toward them, the

wheels rattling to high hells on the crater-ridden floor. Darek and Ren each stepped to one side, and the man passed between them. His malice-drenched stare slid to Ren, but when he found a cloak and not a girl, his eyes drifted forward.

As his cart clattered away, Ren and Darek came together again and continued on. "I don't know why you hate this place," Darek commented. "With your manners, you should fit right in."

"Manners are nothing more than a polite form of dishonesty."

"Since when do you care about honesty?"

Ren leaped over a puddle of what she chose to believe was dirty water. "Are you always so blunt?"

"Are you always so petulant?" he returned.

"Only when the mood strikes."

Darek waved off an old woman who was wandering toward them from a stall lined with unlabeled bottles of what were probably a hundred different types of poison. For a brief moment, Ren wondered which would be best suited to murder. She supposed it would depend on whether the poisoner wanted to make it look like an accident, and then there was the type of accident to consider. Allergic reaction? Heart attack? Seizure? The options were endless.

When they came to the mouth of a tunnel, Darek slid past Ren and stepped into the dark. "I'll be back here," he said in a low whisper. "I don't care what you do with your silver as long as you put on a good show, but keep your hood up and mask on. Don't let anyone see your face."

"I'm a thief, Darek, not an idiot."

He ignored the comment. "When you've got enough attention, create a distraction, and we'll slip out this way." He gestured down the pitch-black tunnel to some exit Ren couldn't see, and then retreated into a darkness so dense he may as well have vanished entirely.

Turning her back on the tunnel, Ren faced the Underground. She lifted her hands, black leather covering her long, thin palms and fingers. She stared around at all the patrons and shopping carts. This was it. This was the moment she lost her mind.

With her pulse racing in her ears and heart thudding like a bass drum, she took in one deep breath. *Seven hundred thousand gold coins*, she thought. The number would become her mantra if it had to.

She called her silver. It swirled in her palms like thunderclouds rolling in from the sea, shifting and twisting and beginning to take shape. It morphed into the form of a small deer, only half a foot high. With a curl of her fingers, Ren sent the animal bouncing into the crowd and straight into a man's line of vision. He gave a start. His eyes followed the deer as it trotted back and settled in her hand once again.

Ren prodded her silver, and the deer transformed into a tree. It grew upward, branches stretching toward the crumbling ceiling. By now, she had succeeded in catching a decent amount of attention, and a small crowd amassed in front of her. As silver leaves rained down, the branches growing bare as if preparing to receive a heavy winter snow, Ren caught fragments of conversation.

"Who is it?"

"One of the princes, you think?"

"What in the 'ells would a bleedin' prince be doin' 'ere?"

"Must be a trick."

Ren's heart began to settle. Tension leaked out of her shoulders. She really did enjoy proving people wrong.

The crowd had tripled in size, and it only continued to grow as the branches of the tree fused together, the silver stretching and morphing into a new shape. Ren lengthened the distance between her hands, calling more silver to create the scene. The whispers escalated, and now people were shouting to their companions, the stallkeepers, and complete strangers to come watch.

By the time she'd finished building her castle, there were enough people assembled that she could no longer see the stalls of the marketplace behind them. She sent the silver structure drifting forward, pulling it to a stop between her and the crowd. Her magic hovered in midair, an unmistakable rendering of the stone monstrosity up on the hill. Her audience watched in a mix of wonderment and confusion.

Ren steeled herself with thoughts of her parents. They'd lived a fairly quiet life in a nice part of the city to the north of the river, two people who'd been sentenced to death for nothing more than the misfortune of having her as a child. In one night, two-thirds of the Avevian household was gone. Their home had been modest in size and the color of dandelions, with blooming flower boxes below the windows. Ren had little reason to visit her former home, but she avoided it nonetheless. She didn't want to see what had become of that yellow house, what the king had done to her childhood.

With resentment simmering in her gut, Ren lit the castle on fire.

It went up in a blaze of silver, and she swallowed back a sudden burst of nerves. She reminded herself that she was wearing a hood and a mask. She was unrecognizable.

Seven hundred thousand gold coins.

As flames consumed the scene, the crowd dropped into silence. It was as tense as the moment before the royal executioner swung his ax. Although patrons of the Underground were far from model citizens and many surely shared in Ren's fantasy, they were also fond of their heads. No one spoke out against the king and lived.

Seconds ticked by while fire ate at the castle. A voice came from the crowd, awed, wondering, a tremor of fear. "Who are you?"

That was her cue.

Still thinking of the fire and her scars and every dream she'd had of the crown prince since that gods-awful night, she twisted her hands and urged the burning castle to collapse in on itself. Energy built inside her as she raised her arms, lifting the ball of silver higher, and shoved it forward. The crowd ducked. Her silver sailed over their heads and smashed into a stall, which she had expected to contain something like cow tongues or illegal exotic plants. But then the stall went up in a burst of flames and a boom that shook rocks free from the wall.

Ren cursed. She hadn't intended to cause quite so much damage. The last thing she needed was Darek accusing her of melodrama. But what was done was done, and before the remnants of the stall had finished raining down, Ren was running. The crowd, shouting for water and blankets to douse the flames, was too distracted to follow.

Darek fell into a jog beside her, a wisp of silver lighting their path. "I told you to create a distraction," he said, "not destroy the Underground."

"Next time, be more specific!"

They didn't have to run far before Darek came to a stop at a heavy iron door. He slipped a key into the lock and yanked it open. Ren rushed through, with Darek quick on her heels. Once he'd locked the door behind them and shoved the key away, they took off down the new tunnel.

Ren pulled the mask off her face but kept the cloak on for warmth—it felt even colder down here than it did on the streets. She couldn't begin to guess where they were. While she was plenty familiar with the layout aboveground, this part of Denfell was entirely foreign. "Are you sure you know where you're going?" she asked.

"Yes."

They twisted their way through the tunnels, Ren's silver lighting up crumbling walls so riddled with holes it was a surprise they hadn't collapsed. A layer of moisture gleamed on the stone like sweat, though water hadn't run through the Terth in years, and the air was heavy, as if unaccustomed to visitors.

"How do I know you're not about to feed me to a vengeful spirit?" Ren asked. She herself was tempted to hand Darek off to the first ghost they saw, just to be rid of his brooding.

"Something tells me if anyone is a match for a vengeful spirit, it's you," he said.

"Why, thank you."

"Wasn't a compliment."

The tunnels that connected to the Underground had been abandoned for so long no one seemed sure of their original purpose. Some said smugglers used them to bring illegal goods into the city, others claimed they were to get slaves out, and still more insisted they had been torture chambers. Most believed they were haunted. Only the brave, the stupid, and the desperate visited the Underground.

But the only ghost Ren believed in was her past. She didn't like the illegal marketplace because it was, quite simply, disgusting.

Silence settled between Darek and Ren. Broken bits of rock crunched beneath their feet, the sound echoing through curving walls that twisted around one another like a bed of snakes.

"You don't seem impressed by my silver," Ren commented. She still felt strange speaking it aloud to someone who wasn't Freya. *My silver.* She'd been hiding for so long.

"Should I be?"

"I am the first common wielder in a century. Some people would call that impressive." In the dark, Ren had barely enough light to see as Darek gave a shrug, his face impassive. "Come on," she pushed, though she had no idea why she cared. "Did you see what I did back there?"

"Tricks don't impress me, Ren."

She hated to admit it, but she sort of wanted to know what did impress him. "*Tricks*? I'm not a dog."

"No," he agreed. "Dogs are better behaved."

Ren tensed. Somehow, Darek always seemed to know how to get under her skin. Even if he wasn't saying it, the accusations he'd spewed the night they met clung to every one of his stony looks. She could hear him again now, calling her a coward, claiming Erdis deserved better than someone like her. Maybe he was right, and Ren hated him for it.

He hadn't taken another step when her silver lashed out. It twined around his ankles, and he careened forward, barely getting his hands in front of him before his head smacked into the wall. He went still, his back rigid and his breathing hitched, palms braced against the dirty stone.

It was a few seconds before he turned to face her. "Did you just trip me?"

Ren twirled her silver and watched it dance. "I daresay I did."

From the corner of her eye, she assessed him for signs of anger, the flared nostrils or the ticking jaw, and performed a mental check of every knife she was carrying. Four in the corset, one in each boot, another in her right pocket—and that wasn't even counting the ones she'd just bought. It was an automatic train of thought, but it wasn't necessary. Darek knew what she was. This wasn't like the streets, where too many watching eyes and blabbing mouths meant she couldn't use silver to defend herself. If he attacked, she could crush his windpipe with a flick of the wrist.

But Darek only stared at her. "I suppose I deserved it," was all he said, and he set off down the tunnel once more.

With silver swirling in her palms like mist caught in a wind, Ren watched him walk away and wondered, *That's it?* She should have been relieved, but some twisted part of her couldn't help wishing there had been more. Freya liked to complain that Ren was always looking for a fight. Freya wasn't wrong.

She ran to catch up. "How did you become a rebel?"

"It's none of your business."

Ren's laugh was humorless. "I beg to differ."

"Maybe I don't want to talk about it."

"You know everything about me," Ren protested. Of course it wasn't true, but that was hardly the point. "It's only fair."

"Has anyone ever told you life isn't fair?"

"I think I remember that one. My parents may have mentioned it sometime before their home burst into flames."

Something flashed across his face, a brief show of emotion, though she couldn't have said what it was.

"Ren."

"Darek."

She glared at him long enough that he heaved a reluctant sigh. "An Erdis free of the Lyandor rule was my mother's dream. I'm just trying to finish what she started."

He didn't rush to fill in the details, their echoing footsteps suddenly loud in the empty tunnel. Ren called up more silver, and the angles of his face came into full view. He stared straight ahead, the line of his mouth hard. She had already known Darek's mother was dead, but what she didn't know was how. Whatever had occurred, it was wrapped too tightly for Freya and her many sources to dig up.

Dead mothers were something Ren was plenty familiar with. Fathers, too. Nine years, and the pain of missing them still hadn't gone away. When she was young, Ren's father had always told her that she was so very much like her mother. *Spirited* was the word he used when he was in a good mood, and *a pain in my ass* when he thought Ren wasn't listening. But she'd taken after her father in coloring, with her black hair and pale skin, except for the eyes; she had her mother to thank for their bright-green hue. She wondered if, when Darek looked into a mirror, he also saw his mother. It was strange to think that the two of them might have something in common.

"What happened to her?" Ren asked.

Darek's jaw ticked. Without warning, he took a corner, forcing Ren to stumble back so she could follow. She watched his broad shoulders as he stalked through the dark tunnel, the way his arms swung at his sides. He could have been entirely unbothered, but Ren knew a front when she saw one.

"Darek?"

He turned on her abruptly, and she took a few steps back. Sometimes, she was very, very thankful for her height. His frame would swallow her whole if she were any shorter.

"Listen," he said gruffly. "I don't want your sympathy, and I want your friendship even less."

Ren shoved her glowing palms into his chest and pushed him back with the aid of her silver. Once there were a few feet between them, she forced herself to drop her hands. It was taking every ounce of will she possessed to keep herself from lashing out again. She knew if she did, she might actually hurt him. Had he been someone else, she wouldn't have cared, but if Darek wound up dead before they overthrew the king, she'd have to find another way of getting seven hundred thousand gold coins.

She thickened her silver, turning it brighter. It bounced off the wet-and-broken walls and cut across Darek's face, casting his eyes and the hollows of his cheeks in darkness like some distorted shadow puppet. He squinted into the light.

"What did I ever do to you?" Ren demanded. She was none too fond of him, but at least she had a reason. She didn't take kindly to strangers who knocked her out, tied her to a chair, and flung insults at her as if she were target practice. He, on the other hand, seemed to hate Ren on principle.

"Me?" he asked. "This isn't about me."

"Then what—"

"Gods, Ren. You really don't get it." He lifted his hands like he wanted to shake her, but settled on rubbing one over his jaw. "You walked away. You could have done something about this festering rash of a kingdom, and you turned your back on everyone in it."

Ren heard it again, the word that trailed her everywhere like a flea-infested mongrel in search of food: *selfish*. She didn't want to have this fight again. She didn't need to defend herself to a man who had grown up in the wealthiest neighborhood in the city while she had fought for scraps on the other side of the river.

"Tell me," he went on. "If it weren't for the money, would you be doing this at all?"

"I'm sorry, when have I ever given you the impression that I care about your cause?"

If winter hadn't already arrived, his stare could have ushered it in. "You're pathetic. My mother—" He broke off.

"Your mother what?" Ren snapped back. "Were you going to say she would be ashamed to have you for a son? Can't even plot a rebellion without paying off someone to do all the work for you. Imagine her disappointment if she could see you now."

A calm look overtook Darek's face, his eyes piercing her like an arrow finding its mark. "My mother died fighting for this cause. She died doing what you wouldn't. But you don't care, do you? Not when there are coats to steal and cards to cheat at. What's the life of one woman?"

Ren's silver died in her hands, the dark flowing in to

take its place. Dozens of feet beneath the ground where sunlight never reached, the tunnels were an endless, unwavering black. The silence was so heavy it was palpable, suffocating. A phantom pain flashed through her shoulder.

Her mother. Her father. The fire.

It was only seconds before she spoke, but it felt like much longer. "What was her name?" she asked.

"What?"

"What was your mother's name?"

Ren waited while Darek shifted his weight. When he answered, his voice was softer. "Alyah."

"I'll add her to the list." She brushed past him, calling up only enough silver to see a few feet in front of her, half expecting to run into the bones of some lost and forgotten soul.

"The list of what?"

"Deaths that are my fault," she said. Tears didn't sting her eyes. Ren had shut down that particular impulse a long time ago.

It took Darek so long to come after her that she began to think he intended to let her find her own way out of the tunnels. But in the end, he did follow, only staying close enough for Ren to just make out the crunch and scrape of his boots on the rocky ground, so that she would know he was there. She kept her back to him, all the while wondering how badly he wanted to shove a knife into it.

CHAPTER
FOURTEEN

The fighters were beating the ever-loving shit out of each other, the crowd's rumble nearing a deafening pitch. With his arms crossed and chin tilted back, Kellen watched from the other side of the short wall that served as a barrier between the grainy sand of the pit and the rough stone flooring of the rest of the room. Fires burned high in their iron sconces.

His pit would make a killing tonight. Of course, this had never been about the money, but something a little less tangible. He had been sixteen when he'd first stumbled on the fighting pits, seventeen when he'd turned a shuttered building into a ring, and eighteen when his pit had transitioned from a humble bit of sand to what it was today. For the better part of a year now, Kellen had been operating the most ruthless and profitable fighting pit in Denfell. The entire endeavor was vile and a little depressing, but he didn't let it bother him. The alternatives—holing up in the castle or drowning in alcohol—were worse. And it had all started because he had a point to prove.

Although he'd heard of pit fighting, it was never something he'd endeavored to witness. It was boredom, plus a few glasses of cheap liquor, that had driven him to that first fight three years ago. But then the match had started, and Kellen saw the way the pit lord smiled down on his fighters, the blood in the sand, the sweat and screaming and sheer brutality of it all. He couldn't think of anything less soft. And so he decided, without giving it much consideration at all, that he'd reside over his own fighting pit. At his pit, he could don a mask and become someone else, someone harder and more ruthless, someone his father wanted him to be, even if it was only for a few hours when the stars came out.

In the sand now, one man's fist connected with another man's nose. Flesh split, bone crunched, blood dyed skin red. The larger of the two fighters hit his opponent a second time and a third. The smaller man was doubled over, his feet canting like a ship in rough water. He dropped on the next punch. The audience screamed so loud Kellen suspected he'd hear ringing for the rest of the night. The larger fighter studied the other man, decided he wasn't getting back up, and threw his fists in the air. Roars pummeled against the cracked walls.

Kellen jumped over the railing and came down with a crunch in the sand. He assessed the winner. "Victor!"

The man sauntered over like he was the richest bastard in Denfell, his lips lifted in a nasty smile to reveal half a mouthful of rotting teeth. Kellen avoided actually touching the man by dropping the gold into his waiting palm. He didn't like to worry himself with where the money would be going. Bars, brothels, or a drug-induced haze, it made no difference to him. But he did sort of hope the man would overindulge and choke to death on his own tongue.

Kellen headed for the loser drifting in and out of consciousness on the sand and nudged him with a boot. The man gave a feeble groan. "Someone get this pathetic excuse for a fighter out of my pit." Bored arrogance seeped through his voice. The persona he'd crafted for South Terth Pit Lord wasn't so different from that of Entitled Prince, except where the prince was flippant, the pit lord was menacing. It was easy enough to switch from one to the other.

Two men entered the pit and began to half drag, half carry the beaten opponent away, but they stopped when the metal doors groaned open. Everyone went quiet as a dozen burly men entered the room. Arms shoved over wide chests and hands balled into fists, they stood like statues in the doorway, rendering the exit impassable. One last man with a bent nose and black hair stepped inside. The gang leader known as Izram Nevskov glided between his thugs and took up a place at the front of his pack.

Unease prickled over Kellen's back. Tension sat in the room like still water.

Kellen walked across the sandy pit and vaulted over the railing on the other side. The crowd parted, creating an aisle for him. "Gentlemen," he greeted, adopting a tone like they were old friends. "What can I do you for?"

Nevskov shed his coat, tossing it to one of his men. "Good evening, lord," he said, unbuttoning his dark sleeves and rolling them up. He pulled out a pair of black gloves. "I have some business to settle with a few of your patrons.

It'll only take a moment." He slid the gloves over long, pale fingers and nodded at an impressively muscled man to his right who Kellen knew went by the name Fetz. The gang member trudged forward, and the audience surged away as one, a few people rushing the doors. Nevskov's men threw them back as Fetz plunged into the crowd, hooked on to a bulky fighter who frequented Kellen's pit, and yanked him out by the neck.

"Please—please don't," the man begged. "I'm sorry. I'll return it. I just need a few days—a day. One day!"

Fetz threw him onto the stone at Nevskov's feet.

"Don't—please—" the man said, crouched on his hands and knees. "Please, sir, I will—I'll get your watch back. I'll return it."

The gang leader stared down his jagged nose. "It's too late for that, I'm afraid." He reached into his dark velvet vest and pulled out a bottle of what looked like black syrup.

"No!" the man screamed. He fell back on his elbows and began to crawl away. The rest of the pit watched the scene from the edges of the room. No one moved.

Nevskov took one step forward, then two, and Fetz grabbed on to the man's head, forcing him to the ground. As Nevskov pulled the stopper out of the bottle, Fetz wrenched the man's jaw open. He writhed, legs kicking.

"I don't appreciate men who steal from me," Nevskov said.

The scent of sugared blackberries wafted from the bottle, mixing with the pit's usual tang of sweat and grime, except it was too sweet, sickly and unnatural. Kellen breathed through his mouth.

Nevskov crouched down at the man's side. In gloved hands, he swirled the black contents of the bottle and said, "I take no joy in this, but you've left me no choice."

He poured the poison into the man's mouth. The man jerked, his limbs spasming. He tried to scream, but only managed a gargled, choking noise. Once the bottle was empty, both Nevskov and his thug stepped back, watching the man contort, his back arching up and slamming down against the stone floor. He thrashed like he was possessed, the veins in his neck bulging.

Then, as suddenly as it had all started, he went limp.

He lay faceup on the ground, eyes wide and shot with black. The dark syrup bubbled in his mouth, the poison popping and churning as it overflowed and dripped down over his jaw and neck. Kellen thought he might vomit, but he also couldn't seem to look away. He'd seen a lot of violence in his pit and desensitized himself to most of it, but he hadn't seen a poison quite like this. It reminded him of something his father would have used.

He didn't snap out of his trance until two more of Nevskov's thugs started forward, making to pull more people from the crowd. Kellen slipped into his pleasant, unbothered tone and held his palms up to the gang. "Take it outside, gentlemen. You're bringing down the mood."

"I have no fight with you, lord," Nevskov said, stepping over the body of the dead man on the ground. He glanced around the pit. "In fact, I'm rather impressed by what you've done with the place. I'd love to chat about a business arrangement sometime, but for now, I suggest you leave."

While Nevskov handed the empty bottle to one of his men, Kellen glanced around the room, the sconces and iron light fixtures giving off a hazy glow. Dozens of men and women in ragged clothes stared back at him. The air was heavy with unease, and Kellen was very conscious of how outnumbered he was, even with his guards hovering at the doors. Maybe Nevskov was doing them all a favor. Most people who visited this pit were about as close to model citizens as the man's thugs.

Turning to the gang leader, Kellen surrendered with nothing more than a nod, and as he did it, he became acutely aware that just because he ran a fighting pit and called himself a lord, that didn't mean he was one. He knew an actual pit lord wouldn't have given up their domain so easily. But Kellen wasn't interested in a fight or risking his life over a bit of sand and a fake title. The realization hit him hard—he was only a prince playing at a pit lord, and apparently he wasn't very good at either role. He just couldn't seem to find his place anywhere. Nothing he tried on was the right size.

The gang let Kellen pass. Once he was outside, the doors were pulled shut, and the clang of metal on metal rang through the barren alley walls. It wasn't long before another round of pleading started up. Making a note never to enter into any kind of agreement with the gang leader, Kellen ducked his head and took off, more than ready for a distraction.

When he arrived at Holland's townhouse, he didn't knock. He never did. At her own suggestion, he walked in like he lived there. She could usually be found warming herself by the sitting room fire or lounging in her bed upstairs, but tonight she wasn't alone. Voices were coming from the kitchen door, which stood open in the middle of a hall papered in pink. As Kellen approached, the sweet smell of cake grew stronger. The scent was such a fixture at Holland's house that Kellen could no longer separate girl from dessert. Whenever she wore her floral perfumes, all he could think of was a rose-flavored cake rising in the oven.

He paused outside the kitchen door and listened.

"You don't know a thing about this girl," Holland was saying.

"We know enough," a male voice replied.

"Is that so? I've heard what they say about her, and most of it isn't favorable. She's a liar and a thief. Last week, she stole a coat worth five hundred gold pieces. I don't even own a jacket that expensive."

"Are you jealous of her clothes?"

"Very funny," she said dryly. "My point is, she could have taken anything, and she chose the most expensive coat in the city. She's unnecessarily self-indulgent, and I don't like what that says about her."

Kellen couldn't begin to guess who they were talking about, but if Holland had something against self-indulgent people, it was a wonder why she had any interest in him.

"You sound like my brother," the man said.

"Don't compare me to your brother. Darek has a stick up his ass." There was a tense silence, then Holland snapped, "I'm just telling you the truth. Putting all your hopes in this girl is unbelievably stupid, even for you."

"Even for me?"

"You're too optimistic for your own good."

"I have faith in people."

"You're an idiot."

Kellen smirked. He'd go to his grave loving her blunt temper.

"You were the one who found her," said the man. "Why did you tell us about her if you didn't want us to go looking for her?"

"Trust me, I've been asking myself the same question."

A beat passed, and the man asked, "Does this mean you don't want to help anymore?"

When Holland didn't answer right away, Kellen debated announcing himself. She would skin him and feed his carcass to a pack of rabid wolves if she knew he was listening in, but she was the one who'd left her door unlocked. It was her own fault.

"We're already making progress," the deep voice pushed. "This could actually work, Holland. People are talking about her. Rumors are spreading."

A sigh, then Holland said, "I've heard."

Talking about who? Heard what? Nothing out of the ordinary had reached Kellen's ears, and not for the first time he wondered just how Holland knew the things she did. Who were her contacts in the city? And who exactly was she, for that matter, other than a baker's daughter? He never had gotten a straight answer, not on the night they had met at a castle ball and not in the six months since.

"Oh, for the love of the gods," Holland finally muttered. "Of course I still want to help. I'll always want to help. You know that. Always."

There was a raw, honest edge to her voice, and Kellen leaned forward. The hilt of his sword smacked against the doorframe. The kitchen went still.

Cringing at the inelegant way he'd announced his presence, Kellen stepped into a brightly lit room bursting with pastel colors. Glass containers full of sweets dotted countertops and shelves, and sure enough, a cake with yellow frosting sat in the middle of an island table, a slice missing. Holland's eyes narrowed into an expression that told him she was hoping for his immediate and painful demise.

Her mystery guest wasn't a man, but a boy of no more than seventeen. He was tall, taller than Kellen by a few inches, with golden Ticharran skin and thick hair brushing his ears. By the look of his black coat, with its long tails and shining silver buttons, he was as wealthy as Holland. He seemed pleasant enough, but he didn't rush to introduce himself.

Thankful he hadn't removed his mask, Kellen didn't make the first move, either. His eyes flicked to Holland. "Who's your friend?"

"No one," she said quickly. "He's no one, and neither are you." She turned to the boy. "Tell your brother I want to meet her."

"Thanks, Holland," he said, leaning in to peck her cheek. He gave Kellen a brief nod and slipped out of the colorful kitchen.

Kellen waited for the front door to open and shut before he spoke again. "Really, who was that?"

"How much did you hear?"

"Not much. Who was he?"

Holland pinched the bridge of her nose like he was working her last nerve. "That's none of your business."

"Who's Darek?" he tried, pulling off his mask and slipping it into his pocket.

"That's also none of your business."

"What about the girl?"

"If you're going to pester me all night, you can just leave."

Holland brushed past him, aiming for the kitchen door. But before she could get there, Kellen flicked out a hand and sent a burst of silver for the open exit, successfully using his magic to push the door closed. He quickly stepped forward and snaked his arms around her soft waist, pulling her into his chest. The breath caught in her throat. He swept her hair off her neck and put his lips to her delicate skin.

"What qualifies as pestering?" he murmured. He kissed her neck. "Does this?" He moved to her shoulder and pulled the frail material of her dress aside, nipping the exposed flesh. He smiled as her breathing hitched. "What about this?" He trailed his lips back up her throat and stopped at her ear to whisper, "How much do I bother you, Holland?"

"I hate you," she said, flipping around in his arms. Her bright eyes flicked to his lips. One look, and Kellen knew there was no chance they were making it to the bedroom.

He backed her into the kitchen wall, pressing his body against hers. "What do you think, Holland?" he said, his breath heavy. "Still want me to leave?"

"Oh, be quiet." She hooked a hand on the back of his neck to pull his lips down to hers, sucking the breath right out of his lungs. His body hardened against her, and she sighed, slipping her hands beneath his tunic at the same time his own roaming fingers found their way under her beaded ivory skirts.

Kellen forgot all about his fighting pit. He forgot about the castle, the disappointment and disapproval waiting for him inside it. Whenever he was with Holland, he forgot about everything plaguing his mind, his shortcomings and failures. With her, he didn't have to try to be someone he wasn't, to be something more than simply himself. He wasn't a prince or a pit lord. He was just Kellen, whoever that was. She didn't ask anything more of him than that.

He slipped a hand into her red curls and tilted her head farther back, deepening the kiss. As she sighed against his mouth, the only thing on his mind was her and her beautiful rose-painted lips.

CHAPTER
FIFTEEN

B ow and arrow in hand, leather archery gloves wrapped around her forearms and fingers, Adley stood with her boots planted wide in the dirt of the castle's training grounds. Winter air prickled her cheeks as she lifted the weapon and pulled the string taut, taking aim. Scraps of fabric tied to poles across the yard flapped in a gust of wind. Dusk had long since fallen, and the white cotton was barely perceptible in the night shadows, but barely perceptible was perceptible enough.

Adley released her first arrow, then reached back for a second. She fired a third, a fourth, and finally a fifth. She lowered the bow to her side, and the poles stood empty. Beyond them, each of her arrows pinned a piece of cloth to a span of wooden fencing on the opposite side of the yard. They formed a perfect line.

Adley turned to the three kids staring at her with a mixture of awe and terror, not an uncommon expression for the youngest of the King's Children. They had their own bows in hand, a bucket of old arrows sat between them, and a burning torch provided a bit of light. The kids—two girls and one boy—couldn't have been more than eight.

Their weapons were too large for them, and their leather uniforms, which had been crafted for a muscular build like Adley's, gaped at their chests. They were as obviously out of place as a young girl playing dress up in her mother's jewels and silk shoes.

"Your turn," she said. None of them moved, and Adley tried not to laugh at their wide-eyed expressions. She shuffled them into position in front of targets fifty feet away, not five hundred like the ones she'd shot at. And even then, she could have hit those with her eyes closed. Adley's record was nearly thirteen hundred feet, and she was itching to break it.

She stood between the two girls. "Like this," she said, lifting her bow and nocking an arrow a second time. It was a fluid motion, thoughtless after all these years. The weapon was like an extension of herself. There were times when she didn't know where she ended and the bow began.

The young King's Children slowly did the same, and Adley moved among them, adjusting their stances and grips. "Good," she said. "Now shoot."

They did. And they missed.

The Children dropped their eyes, their shoulders curving in, and one of the girls cringed like she expected Adley to strike her. It twisted Adley's heart a little. These kids were new to the castle, which meant they'd recently been put through every hell and had been lucky enough to come out alive. They'd been brought in a month ago, taken from some village the King's Children had raided on their way down the coast to Anteran. The king was demanding more and more Children every day, yet another sign that war was on the way. He clearly had no plans to sign any treaty.

Adley dropped into a crouch before the kids. One of the girls had a long gash on her cheek that looked about a week old, the edges clean, as if sliced by a knife. In the light from the torch, the deep cut was black. "You want to know a secret?" Adley asked. The boy lifted his chin enough to meet her eyes. She smiled softly. "When I was your age, I missed, too."

Now both girls looked up. The one who had flinched said, "I thought you never missed. That's what everyone always says."

"I don't. Not anymore. But I used to. All the time. And you want to know another secret?" All three kids nodded. "Any archer worth a damn has missed a thousand shots." The boy drew his brows together, and she added, "You have to miss a lot if you want to be any good, kid."

"So if we miss a thousand shots, we'll be as good as you?" he asked.

Adley stood. She raised her bow and withdrew an arrow as black as ink. She winked at the little girl with the cut on her face. "No one is as good as me," she said and loosed her arrow.

The hour was nearly up, and not one of the kids had made a single shot when Lesa barreled into the yard. Her trench coat flapped furiously around her legs, and her hair had mostly fallen out of its short braid, pale strands sticking to her face. She was breathing hard.

Adley stepped away from the young Children. "What is it?" she asked.

Lesa smiled wickedly. "We've found that tavern the rebels have been meeting at," she said. "It's the White Raven."

CHAPTER
SIXTEEN

With her booted feet kicked up on the table and her chair tilted back on two legs, Ren shuffled a deck of cards. She slipped them up her billowing sleeves and worked them back in effortlessly. The aces and the clubs, the diamonds and the hearts, they were nothing but a blur in her quick fingers. Now that she'd healed from her fight in South Terth, she'd been able to get back in the sand, and her knuckles stung, freshly bruised and split from a pit fight the night before. But the pain was as familiar as the bite of salt in Denfell's breeze, and Ren tuned it out.

While she loaded the deck, Ren watched the cards, Markus watched Ren, and Freya watched them both with an amused expression on her face. They were seated at a table in the corner of Markus and Darek's personal library, an enormous room lined with white bookcases nestled flush against the walls and a ceiling painted with gold leaf. Settees and chairs upholstered in ivory were scattered about the room, and a mahogany ladder leaned against one of the shelves. A large bay window overlooking the garden showed a thick mass of gray sky quickly darkening to black. Just last night, the clouds had delivered the first snowfall of the season, and Denfell was powdered white.

Ren slipped the last card into the deck. She swung her legs to the floor and brought her chair forward with a thump. She made to deal, but Markus stopped her before she could. "Wait!" he exclaimed.

She stilled and raised one brow.

"Let me see up your sleeves first," he demanded, and so she showed him the inside of one shirtsleeve, then the other. Placated, he motioned for her to continue. As she distributed the cards, his gaze never wavered from her long fingers, not even when she placed the deck in the middle of the table, right beside the silver coins they'd all set down for the blind, and swept up her own hand. Freya picked up her cards, too, but Markus only stared at his small pile like he thought they might be hungering for his fingers.

"Go on," Freya urged.

Frown lines etched on his brown skin, Markus looked to Ren again. "You're not going to cheat?"

Oh, dear, sweet Markus, she thought. "I promised, didn't I?"

He slipped his cards off the table, organizing them into a messy fan, and they began to play. New cards were drawn, and old ones tossed down onto the buffed table. The pile of coins grew. When it was too dark to see by the light of the fireplace alone, Markus lit the lamps, drawing the pale curtains closed. A soft glow swept over the library.

As they continued their game, Markus's decent hand became a good one, and he threw in more and more money, a grin inching onto his lips. Just when his luck was about to turn, Ren dropped her arm beneath the table and tapped Freya on the wrist. Her friend folded. Markus was next. He pulled a card from the pile, and his smile vanished.

Gods, he was bad at this.

"A bit of friendly advice?" Ren said. "Don't go gambling. You'd put your family in the poorhouse." She glanced around the ornately decorated room and slipped one card up her sleeve. Then she discarded two and drew another from the pile in the middle of the table. "Which would be quite the accomplishment, really."

"Ha ha," Markus said. As he was reaching for the deck, the library doors glided open. His hand froze in midair, eyes darting across the large room.

Heavy footfalls stopped short. "What in all nine hells are you doing?" Darek's deep, annoyed voice demanded.

Ren studied her cards. "Gambling. Care to join?"

He came up to the table, saw how much money his little brother was about to lose, and turned his scowl on Ren. "I didn't ask you to meet me here so you could play a game of cards."

"Well, you were late."

"So you decided taking more money from my family was the best way to pass the time?"

Ren sighed and placed her hand facedown on the table. She tilted her head back to look at Darek. His hair was tied in a messy knot, his black coat unbuttoned and hanging open over a navy vest with gold buttons, as if he'd only just stepped in out of the cold. "Why do you insist on spoiling my fun?" she wondered out loud.

"It concerns me that robbing my brother blind is your idea of fun."

"Is there anything about me that doesn't concern you?"

Markus rose from his chair and stepped over to Darek. Ren glanced between the brothers: one rugged, and the other softer. Good gods, they looked even taller standing side by side. How was that possible?

"It's okay, Darek," Markus said. "The game was my idea. And I think I was winning."

"About that . . ." Ren said, tugging a couple cards from her sleeves. She placed them on the table and slid them toward him.

Markus gaped. "You promised you wouldn't cheat!"

Now Darek's glower was on his brother. "And you believed her?"

Markus looked at Freya. "And you! You were in on it!"

Freya's smile was a little guilty. But only a little. "Sorry."

With an indignant huff, Markus turned and stalked out of the library, muttering something that sounded like, "Girls."

Once his brother's footsteps had faded into the depths of their mansion, Darek turned his attention on Freya. Now that Ren considered it, she did look a bit out of place, her layers of jewelry and the worn fabric of her flowing skirts at odds with the wealth of the library. Darek frowned. "I don't think we've been introduced."

She stood, but it really didn't make much difference,

since the top of her head still only came to Darek's chest. "Freya Akaychi," she replied.

He stared down at her with a hard expression that Ren was coming to know so well and said nothing.

"This is the part where you give her your name," Ren told him, still seated at the table, where cards and silver coins lay abandoned. "Or are we waiting on a butler to announce it for you?"

His dark stare cut to her. Brown eyes glided over her long frame, from her mussed black hair down to the golden buckles on her boots. As usual, she couldn't guess at what was beneath his stony surface, and some treacherous part of her wondered if he ever thought about what it would feel like to dig his hands into her hair. She had. She hated him, his superiority and pointed barbs, and she didn't know why the image pervaded her thoughts late at night when she was lying in her bed. She'd also suspected Darek was good with his hands, probably better than half the men she'd been with before, none of whom had meant anything to her. And then she would groan and shove a pillow over her head because she must have been losing her damn mind.

But she didn't expect him to abruptly say, "Grab your coats."

"Why?"

"I asked you to come over, remember? There are some people I want you to meet."

Ren was curious enough that she didn't argue. She and Freya shrugged on their jackets while Darek slipped a vial of sunstones into his pocket. Of course he owned sunstones. Ren wasn't even surprised. He certainly had enough money to get his hands on them. He left the room before Ren and Freya had finished doing up their buttons. Freya freed her mass of curling hair from her collar and leaned in to Ren. "You said Darek was insufferable, but you failed to mention how attractive he is," she whispered.

"Please," Ren scoffed, tugging the cropped front of her coat straight. She agreed, but she wasn't going to tell Freya that.

Freya tugged on a pair of thick wool gloves. "You don't think so?"

Ren drifted toward the library shelves, where hundreds of spines faced out. She pulled down one that had caught her eye and thumbed through the pages. "He hates me, and he doesn't hide it, so you'll understand if I'm not swooning over someone who has made a hobby of reciting my many failures."

"I see your point." Freya glanced at the library doors he'd disappeared through. "I amend my previous statement. He's rude, and he's hideous."

Ren snapped the book shut and raised two fingers to her temple in a salute. "Thank you for your solidarity."

Darek reappeared in the doorway. "Are you two about ready?"

Ren and Freya exchanged a glance before following Darek outside. Undisturbed snow covered his yard, dusting the bushes along the front walk and glittering on bare branches. Ren's breath puffed in the air, cold seeping through her sleeves. She fished out her black gloves at the same moment that Darek flipped up his collar. Fresh snow crunched beneath their boots as they made their way down the walk.

"It's a good story," Darek said to Ren.

"Excuse me?" she asked.

"The book you stole," he explained, pulling open his iron gate.

Ren silently cursed herself. She hadn't thought he'd noticed her slipping it into her coat.

"I think you'll enjoy the story," he added, holding the gate wide.

Ren stepped through, searching for a reply. She settled on "I didn't steal it."

Darek raised his brows.

"I was going to return it when I was done. Thus, it's borrowed, not stolen."

He latched the gate, and they started down the street, lamplight bouncing off the white road, and the river shining an inky grayish-black. He sounded like he might have been amused when he asked, "You're really arguing semantics?"

"Thievery is all about perspective, Darek."

"Whatever you say, Kolins." He went quiet. A street or two away, horse hooves clacked, and carriage wheels rattled.

Ren rolled her eyes to herself and tugged the book from the inside of her coat. If she was going to have to spend the evening with Darek, she didn't want him scowling at her the entire time because she'd stolen from him. "Here," she said, holding it out.

He eyed the book for a moment. "Keep it."

Ren blinked. "What?"

"You can keep it until you're done with it."

She shot him a wary look. "I can?"

Darek shrugged. His eyes met hers for a beat before he shifted his gaze forward. "It's just sitting in the library, collecting dust anyway." He cleared his throat and took a couple long strides, leaving her side.

Freya linked her arm in Ren's and smiled knowingly.

As they followed him through the wide streets of the Atterton District, Ren tried not to watch him, but every once in a while, her gaze flitted to his tall frame. His black coat flapped at his legs, and his shoulders were hunched up near his ears. Like many men and some women in Denfell, he wore a sword at his hip.

She wasn't quite sure what had just happened. Maybe it had something to do with the last time they'd really talked to each other, in the shadowed tunnels beneath the city, when she'd made some cruel comments and he'd returned them in kind. She'd seen him twice since then, first in an alley in the Terth, her silver lighting up the dirty walls with an image of a burning lion. Next, they'd met in the doorway of an abandoned building, a large audience gathering as she shattered crowns and thrones into silver pieces. But they hadn't much spoken again until now. He had a real talent for getting under her skin, and as they'd made their way through those damp tunnels, she'd revealed more than she would have liked, a sliver of vulnerability she preferred to hide. But Darek had managed to dig it up. Had he been surprised by what he'd found? Was that why he'd let her keep the book, as some kind of peace offering?

Whatever the reason, it didn't change the fact that he was judgmental and serious, and he really was far too tall. She'd get a crick in her neck just trying to kiss him. But that was if she wanted to kiss him. Which she didn't.

Feeling the press of the book against her side, Ren reminded herself that she couldn't stand the man.

CHAPTER
SEVENTEEN

"**W**hat in the hells, Darek?!" Ren shouted. She couldn't *believe* him. She wanted to call up some silver and wrap it around his neck, which she could have done without anyone at the table blinking an eye, seeing as the bastard had gone and told his friends about her.

Every patron in the expensive tavern Darek had brought her to was staring at them. Only a couple dozen people were gathered inside the White Raven, and there was no din of noise, no scraping chairs or raised voices to hide her outburst. People shifted in their seats, trading glances, and the barmaiden, a young girl with shining copper hair and a smile kind enough to get her killed in the Terth, concentrated on cleaning an already spotless glass.

Darek tried to maneuver Ren back into her chair, which she'd nearly kicked over when she'd shot out of it. "Sit down, Ren," he hissed, a hand on her upper arm. "You're making a scene."

"Shove off." She jerked her shoulder free and turned to the two men across the table. The shorter one with warm-brown skin and heavy features—Darek had introduced him as Riko—watched her with amusement. A skinny, pale man named Jaston was far less cordial, staring at her like he'd just been served his least favorite meal. Had Freya been there, she would have countered Ren's tension with a kind smile and a soft comment, and this whole thing would probably have gone down more smoothly, but Freya had been hired to give readings at a party tonight, and she'd parted with Darek and Ren outside the tavern doors.

Darek had some nerve. It was bad enough he and his brother knew about her silver. Riko and Jaston were an unnecessary risk. If she didn't need seven hundred thousand gold pieces so badly, she would have been tempted to kill them just to be on the safe side.

"If either of you tells anyone about me, I swear to every god in the heavens there will be no safe place for you in this city," Ren threatened.

Darek grabbed her arm again and finally managed to pull her into the chair. He sat down beside her. "You're being dramatic."

"You're being an ass."

"Riko and I won't say anything," the man called Jaston said. "We need you. We're not looking to get you killed any more than Darek is."

"You can trust them," Darek added.

"I don't even trust you," she said, glaring at him.

He reached inside his vest and produced a few pieces of folded parchment, then pushed the half-empty mugs of amber ale aside, creating an empty space in the middle of the table. "I assure you, the feeling is mutual," he said, unfolding the papers. He smoothed the creases against the wood, his eyes scanning lines of black ink. "This is the choreography for the Crown's Demonstration. Look over the cues for the silver, and tell us if anything seems out of place."

"Ever heard of the word *please*?" Ren asked, picking them up.

"I have, but I didn't think you had."

Riko snorted into the mug of ale he'd lifted to his lips, and Ren shot them both sharp looks before turning her eyes to the choreography. The Royal Carnival was starting up in just a few days, with the Crown's Demonstration concluding the week of music, dancing, and performance. During the demonstration, King Mattheus, Crown Prince Heath, and Prince Kellen put on a show for the city, twisting their silver in front of a massive crowd. Or so Ren had heard. She'd never actually attended the demonstration. Watching that circus act was about as enticing as visiting the sewers.

She scanned the last sheet of parchment, her frown deepening.

"What's wrong," Darek asked.

"Nothing's *wrong*," Ren said. "It's just strange. This looks more like a step-by-step guide to silver wielding than choreography. It's unnecessarily specific."

"What do you mean?" asked Jaston. He'd pushed his mostly full mug aside and was leaning across the table to see the papers in Ren's hand.

She set them down and pointed at a set of directions.

"No wielder needs to know how far to twist their wrist or which fingers to flick."

"No?" Riko asked.

She shook her head. "You can definitely screw up, but as long as you use it regularly, silver isn't *that* hard to control. It's natural. At least, for me it is."

"Maybe Prince Kellen is particularly stupid," Jaston mused.

"I don't doubt it," Riko agreed. "He probably only learned how to read the street signs so he could find taverns and brothels."

Darek took the choreography from her hands and went about inspecting it. Jaw as hard as ever, he was immediately engrossed. Ren would have asked him how he'd gotten his hands on the papers, but she doubted he'd tell her.

Her eyes roamed the tavern. She'd walked by the White Raven's colorless facade a few times and attempted to get in on one occasion, but the bouncer had refused to let her through. She'd tried to bribe him, thinking she could make up the loss inside, but he hadn't even glanced at the money. His stony expression would have done Darek proud. Gilded-framed paintings decorated the walls, and the glasses winked in the light from a set of crystal chandeliers. Every so often, a whiff of sweet cinnamon and browned butter drifted by, like something was baking in the kitchen. Opulent and expensive, it was the kind of place you'd expect to find kids with too much time and money on their hands, not a group of revolutionaries.

Once he was done scrutinizing the papers, Darek

shoved them away. Ren studied his vest, gold buttons laying flat over his torso. She definitely did not think about popping open those buttons . . . or the bare skin underneath. "You going to tell me what that was all about?" she asked, nodding to his vest pocket where the choreography had disappeared.

"Do you care?"

Ren picked up her ale and took a drink. She shrugged. "As long as I'm still getting my money, I guess I don't care if you plan to fashion a headpiece out of starfish and crown yourself a merman king."

Riko chuckled. "Now there's an image."

Darek leveled one of his scowls on her, but Ren was so used to it by now that Jaston's dark look caught her attention instead. She met his gaze. "Can I help you?"

"You really don't give a shit about this revolution, do you?"

"I really, truly don't."

Jaston's shoulders were stiff while he assessed Ren, his stare disapproving. Riko cleared his throat, and the whole table glanced at him. He held up a deck of cards. "How about a game? It could help"—he split the deck in half—"cut the tension."

Darek groaned at the joke. "Riko, that was terrible."

He grinned, but his attempt at levity didn't seem to have an effect on Jaston. "I am not playing her," he said.

"I can't say I blame you," Ren commented, leaning back in her seat. "I wouldn't want to play me, either. I rarely lose."

"That's because you're a cheat," he said.

"I'd say I'm a woman who is very good at what she does," Ren countered.

Riko's laugh was deep and rumbling. "Oh, I think I like you." He downed the remainder of his ale and took a full glass that had been sitting neglected on the table. "I don't trust you, but I like you."

"Most people neither trust nor like me, so I suspect we're well on our way to becoming dear friends."

"Gods, I hope not," Darek said and drank from his own mug.

Jaston's eyes were on the burgundy jacket slung over the back of Ren's chair, the line of his mouth taut. It was like he expected it to stand up and start waltzing around the room. "Want to try it on?" Ren asked. "Though I have to say, I don't think red is your color."

His gaze turned to her. "I don't know why you need so much of Darek's money. You seem to be doing rather well on your own."

The last of Ren's humor faded. She narrowed her eyes, her stare sharpening like one of the daggers tucked into her corset. He was right. He didn't know why she needed the money. He didn't know that when she was fifteen she'd taken on as much debt as Darek's father made in a year. He didn't know that if she failed to pay it off soon, the city's deadliest gang would come to collect, and if they couldn't get gold, they'd take their payment another way. He didn't know a damn thing.

"Okay, what is your deal?" Ren demanded. "Are you and Darek part of the I Hate Ren Kolins Club or something?"

"I am not part of that club, just for the record," Riko piped in.

Jaston gave his friend an irritated glance. "As much as we need you, I'm wary of petty criminals."

"Am I not sophisticated enough for you?"

"It's not about that."

"Then what is it about, exactly?" When he hesitated, she said, "Out with it. Don't get shy now."

"Jaston," Darek said, a low warning in his voice. "Don't—"

"Fine," Jaston spoke over him. "Thieves like you are self-serving opportunists. Frankly, Ren, I don't trust your judgment, and I don't trust you."

Ren clenched her jaw and released. Then she asked as evenly as she could manage, "Is that so?"

Darek cast his eyes upward like he was calling on the good will of the gods. "Heavens help us."

"Look, I'm sor—" Jaston began.

"No," Ren stopped him. "You're going to listen to me now. While your governess was busy wiping your ass, I was on the streets. I was in the fighting pits." Ren was a lamp turned up too high, glass heated to a breaking point. "Tell me, Jaston, have you ever gone to bed uncertain if you'll wake up in the morning? No? I have. More times than I can count." She leaned forward, and Jaston paled, his smattering of freckles stark across his nose. "Do not make the mistake of believing you know a godsdamn thing about me."

She was sick of this, sick of people looking at her like she was dirt they'd tracked into the house, sick of the accusations and assumptions. She'd done the best she could with what she had, and she'd challenge anyone to do better. It was true she was a thief, a cheat, and a liar, but she wasn't ashamed of it. Why should she be? If life was what you made of it, Ren thought she'd done a spectacular job, given the circumstances.

Jaston looked like he might not have been breathing, but Ren wasn't finished. "You call me a petty criminal, but rest assured, there is nothing petty about me. I could keep up with every gang in this city if I desired. My talents could ruin you." Ren pushed herself up from the table and tugged her coat off the back of her chair. "I think I'm done here."

She slung the heavy red fabric over an arm and headed for the tavern doors. The handful of patrons gathered at the shinning tables were quiet as they watched her go, and just before she was out of earshot, she heard Riko say, "Hot damn. Where do you think that girl came from?"

Outside the White Raven, Ren shrugged into her coat and went to work on the buttons, covering the corset none of the men had commented on, even if she'd caught all three noticing it. The cold night air snapped at her nose and cheeks, but Ren loved Denfell in the winter, if only because the snow toned down the ever-present tang of salt and fish. In the summer, the smell was so bad it was as though the warm weather brought along the stench for company.

Ren freed her hair from her collar and pulled her gloves out of a pocket. She was about to take off when she caught sight of a girl leaning against the facade of the White Raven. Her generous hourglass figure was clad in tailor-made pink silk and layers of delicate lace, vibrant red hair cascading in perfect waves over a huge fur shawl.

The girl glanced past Ren to speak to the guard. "Give us a minute, Rutger?"

The guard inclined his head. He opened the door, and a burst of laughter spilled out, a square of candlelight falling over the cobbled stones. Once he'd stepped into the warmth of the White Raven, the door snapped shut, and Ren was alone with the girl.

She was in no mood for whatever this was. She tugged on her gloves, turning away.

"Ren Kolins."

Ren wasn't even surprised. First Darek, then his friends, now this girl. She only wondered who else in this godsforsaken city was aware of her existence, because right now the number was dangerously high. "You have me mistaken for someone else," she said over her shoulder.

"I don't think so. Unless there are two silver wielders living in this city, but I find that unlikely."

A breath died in Ren's throat.

Not again.

She rotated slowly, slipping a hand beneath her coat to grip one of the blades stashed in her corset. The air shifted. It felt charged in the way it was before a storm rolled in, and every hair stood at attention on the back of Ren's neck. "What do you want?"

"I'm Holland," the girl offered. "I'm a friend of Darek's."

"That's nice. What do you want?"

"I—"

The doorway of the White Raven exploded. A flash of red curls was the last thing Ren saw before raining debris smashed into her skull.

CHAPTER
EIGHTEEN

Since Ren had left, Jaston had been staring grimly at the White Raven doors, silent as the soft clatter of the tavern went on around them. He tore his eyes away and turned to Darek. "Are you sure about her?" he asked.

Darek grabbed his mug, the neglected ale inside slowly going flat. He rolled it between his hands just to give himself something to do. It was a loaded question if he'd ever heard one. "I haven't been sure about Ren since the moment I met her."

"Maybe we can find a way to do this without her."

Staring at the gently sloshing liquid, Darek shook his head. "You know we can't. We need her. There's no one else."

The pieces of this plan had been falling into place since before Darek could remember, and he wasn't about to let Ren and her attitude ruin it. Everything hinged on the appearances she'd been making with her silver, appearances more and more people were talking about every day. It wouldn't be long now before they could make their move for the throne.

"That was actually something I wanted to talk to you

both about. The Terth won't shut up about Ren, but no one to the north has caught wind of her, and we can't overthrow the king with only part of the city, especially the part he doesn't care about. We need to think about setting her up somewhere new. Not here in Atterton—it's too soon for that—but nearby."

"Don't change the subject, Darek," Jaston said. "I know we need Ren, but I really hate that she's a criminal."

Darek sighed. "And you're a student, and Riko's a drunk. Your point?"

"I'm not a drunk!" Riko protested too loudly. He lowered his voice and repeated, "I'm not a drunk."

"You certainly do your best imitation of one," Darek said.

Riko lifted his mug to his lips and muttered something crude.

"Darek," Jaston said, "I don't mean to question your leadership skills here—"

"Then don't."

"But have you thought this through?"

"You were aware she was like this," Darek pointed out. "I told you everything I knew about her."

"Hearing it and seeing it are two different things."

"Jas, please," Darek said wearily. "Just stop."

Darek thought he'd had Ren figured out, but he was starting to realize she was not as unshakeable as she pretended to be. He didn't know if the fire had done it, or if the streets were to blame, or if she was tearing herself apart because she thought she deserved the pain, but there was something a little bit broken inside of her.

Jaston was studying Darek with far too much attention. "Are you sleeping with her?"

"What? *No.*"

Riko lowered his mug, a smile turning up his mouth. "This conversation is finally getting interesting."

"No, it's not," Darek said, "because I'm not sleeping with her."

Fine, so maybe he'd thought about it once or twice—and who could really blame him when Ren wore her anger so well, her heated green eyes and her pursed lips—but, *gods*, that was never actually going to happen. Ren was as inflammatory as her magic, and Darek liked relationships. He couldn't see her in one of those, especially not with him.

His past was an easy one to map out: three women he'd seen the possibility of a future with, three women he'd been intimate with, three relationships that hadn't worked out for one reason for another. He didn't see Ren becoming number four. They hated each other, and even if their bodies might have fit together, they would never work in all the other ways that mattered.

Darek enjoyed the physical, but he needed more than a night. Not the promise of forever, but not temporary, either. He didn't go to bed with anyone unless he knew there would be a tomorrow and many days after. That wasn't Ren. He suspected she didn't even know how to be vulnerable without lashing out.

"She's the girl from the wrong side of the city," Jaston

continued. "I get it. She's dangerous. For the gods' sakes, she was wearing a *leather corset.*" He emphasized the last two words like Darek had failed to notice the bodice that would drive plenty of people a little mad. But of course he had noticed. He noticed so much that sometimes he worried she'd catch him staring.

"Books are written about romances such as these," Riko added a bit wistfully.

"But our lives are dangerous enough as it is," Jaston finished.

"Are you really trying to give me a lecture?"

"You obviously need one. Do us all a favor and get your kicks somewhere else."

"I'm not sleeping with Ren," Darek repeated. "I don't even like her. She's barely tolerable on her best days."

So what if he'd let her keep his book? That didn't mean anything. He was just doing something nice for her. She clearly needed it. He'd realized that down in the tunnels, when he'd thrown his mother's death in her face, and her tough exterior had given way to something more delicate. It had been a mistake. Although Ren had many faults, there were a lot of people he blamed for his mother's death, and she wasn't one of them. Darek could take whatever caustic comments she lobbed his way, but maybe she couldn't take all of his. He didn't want to be responsible for pushing her over the edge she was so clearly teetering on.

Riko leaned back in his seat, lacing his fingers behind his head. "Well, if you're not bedding her, mind if I do?" Darek glowered at him, and Riko burst into laughter. "For someone who says he doesn't like the girl, you're awfully touchy when it comes to her."

Darek didn't get to defend himself, because that was when the barmaiden screamed. With a head-rattling boom, the doors crumbled in a cloud of splintered wood and flying stone. Debris knocked the guard who had recently stepped inside to the ground, and Darek lost sight of him as the tavern descended into madness. Some people rushed to the pile of rubble that had once been the doors, while others sheltered beneath tables. Another explosion went off. The chandeliers rattled, and every table shook like the floor was opening up a passageway to the hells. From the sound of it, the back door had been blown out.

Darek, Jaston, and Riko surged from their seats. "Come on!" Darek yelled over the cacophony, already aiming for a back exit.

Jaston went opposite, toward the rocks that used to be the front of the tavern. "I'll help! You go!" he shouted, and before Darek could protest, he darted away.

Darek and Riko turned and dashed across the room, dodging bodies running this way and that, no one seeming to agree on where they should go. There were two more exits, but only the one in the kitchen was well-known. The door to the wine cellar was barely a door at all and easy enough to miss from the street. Odds were the kitchen would be the next to go, so Darek headed for the stairs. He caught arms as he went, pulled bodies off the floor, pushed and prodded and sent people toward the cellar, but the tavern was pure chaos, and he couldn't corral the whole room. When he tried to shout, his voice was lost.

Riko grabbed his arm and started tugging him away. "We have to go!"

Darek hesitated for only a moment. These people were rebels. They knew the risks. He couldn't protect them all.

He tore his eyes from the ruined wall and ran for the cellar, where he took the stairs two at a time, Riko on his heels. Crates of wine and liquor, barrels of ale, and spare glasses were packed into every corner of the room. They hurtled over stray bottles and empty containers on their way to the cellar ladder, its metal doors already open to the night sky and a pair of feet disappearing onto the street above. Darek reached it first. He scaled the rungs quickly and pulled himself onto the cold cobblestones. He was turning back to help Riko through when he noticed the pile of fragor outside the cellar doors and the flames eating up oil-drenched ropes.

"Get down!" Darek yelled into the cellar. He flung himself around a corner, hit the street, and threw his arms around his head. The fragor ignited. The blast assaulted his ears, the ground beneath his cheek rumbling as stray chunks of stone rained down, nicking his bare hands and forearms. It felt like minutes until the world stilled.

With the ground tilting beneath him and his ears ringing, Darek pushed himself to his feet. He stumbled back toward the cellar doors, now nothing but a pile of crumbled stone, a mixture of what had once been the cobbled street and the white brick wall of the tavern. The metal doors stuck out at odd angles, the entrance entirely obstructed by debris.

He braced a hand against the wall to steady himself, his breath steaming in the air. Riko had been right behind him, and others were still fleeing to the cellar. His first thought was to dig, to shift away the rubble until he could get back inside, but that would take hours of time he didn't have. He needed to leave. He shouldn't even be standing here contemplating this. He should have already been running. But he couldn't find it in himself to leave his friends behind.

Darek hadn't heard a fourth explosion, so he headed for the kitchen doors. At the corner of the building, he paused to glance down the alley, and dread knotted like string in his stomach. Two King's Children were standing guard outside the kitchen doors, unmistakable in their black leather uniforms and the loaded weapons belts at their hips. Darek ducked back into the side street.

Shit. Shit, shit, shit.

He took a deep breath through his nose. He'd spent the last fifteen years training with a master swordsman, so he knew how to handle a weapon, but he wasn't foolish enough to think he could take on two King's Children. If he tried, he'd only get himself captured or killed.

He didn't have a choice. He had to leave. Without Riko and Jaston.

Darek took off down the street, sending a prayer to the god of protection as he passed the collapsed cellar, and made for an alley up ahead. Down it was a door that led into the underground tunnel system. From there, he could get anywhere in the city, navigating by the map in his head.

He ducked into the space between buildings, but he didn't make it ten feet before a man appeared from a gap in front of him. "Halt!" he shouted, drawing a sword.

Darek skidded to a stop. The man was dressed in a fitted maroon jacket, a lion stitched on the cloth at his chest. Darek's hand went to the hilt of his sword, and the blade slid free with a whine. Setting his shoulders, he bore down on the royal guard.

"In the name of King Mattheus, I command you to halt!"

Darek could've laughed. He'd throw himself into the Battgandon and let the river rats feast on his flesh before he did anything in the name of a Lyandor. He swung. Their swords clashed, metal screeched against metal. Darek attacked again and again, pushing the guard deeper into the alley. But the man parried with a finesse to match Darek's own, and when he feinted right, Darek fell for it. The mistake cost him a slice to the thigh.

Leg growing wet and warm with blood, Darek was careless the next time he lunged forward. The guard swiveled out of the way, and as Darek's sword shot past him, the man hooked on to his arm. He pulled Darek into his body and smashed an elbow in his nose. Pain flooded Darek's face, his sight going hazy. The guard pushed him away, and Darek careened into the wall with a grunt, blood dripping over his mouth and falling like splattered ink onto his shirt.

"By order of King Mattheus, you are under arrest for conspiracy to commit treason," the guard said.

Darek spit red on the ground. "You can take your king's order," he said thickly, "and shove it up your ass."

He launched himself at the guard, got in one decent swing, then his feet were knocked from beneath him. He dropped to his knees with a thud that sent pain shooting through his legs, the cut on his thigh screaming. The guard pressed his sword into Darek's neck. There was the sting of a blade and the warmth of blood sliding down his throat.

"You are under arrest," the guard repeated, shoving Darek's face into the ground. His nose was hot with agony as the man pressed a boot into the space between his shoulder blades and wrenched his arms back. Metal clamped around his wrists. Darek jerked his shoulders. This couldn't be it. They were *so close* to being rid of the Lyandors for good, to winning this whole damn thing. His mother's revolution wasn't supposed to end with handcuffs in a dark alleyway.

He thrashed on the cobblestones, his skin burning as his wrists strained against the cuffs. The guard gripped on to Darek's hair, yanked his head back, and slammed his face into the ground. Black exploded across his vision, blood flooding his mouth. He groaned.

"You're making this harder than it needs to be," the guard said, yanking Darek up, first to his knees, then onto unsteady feet. The dark walls swayed, and Darek came dangerously close to tipping sideways, but he managed to keep his legs beneath him. He blinked the haze of pain from the forefront of his mind, forced himself to focus, to think. He could still get out of this, he just had to find his opportunity.

Holding on to the handcuffs, the guard forced him forward. "Walk."

Darek shuffled ahead, head hanging and shoulders slumped, as though his last ounce of resistance had been spent. The guard didn't know that Darek was an unending well of revolt. Rebellion existed in him like a second pulse. He very well may have entered this world with fists swinging.

When he felt the guard relax, Darek snapped his head back. Drawing on every bit of strength he had left, he connected violently with the guard's skull. The man cried out, releasing Darek's hands and tripping away. Darek's own head was throbbing, but he pushed his legs into motion and hurtled down the alley, away from the castle guard. His hands were still bound behind his back, but he would take care of that later.

The guard rammed into him. They went down with all the force of a thunderstorm. Darek slammed into the ground at a bad angle, and blinding heat shot through him as his shoulder was knocked free of its socket. The world went dark, and then the guard was shoving Darek over and pinning him down with his knees. He pulled a dagger from his belt.

"Don't you give up?" the guard asked.

Darek swallowed down a wave of nausea and gasped, "Not as long as King Mattheus sits on the throne."

The guard held his knife above Darek's eye, his face filled with contempt. "The king ordered all rebels brought back alive, but he said nothing about what state you had to be in."

If he'd had any energy left, Darek would have spit in the man's face. When the guard lifted his knife, he bit down and told himself he wouldn't scream, even though he knew he would.

A blade pushed through the guard's neck, and the man's eyes went wide. Blood poured from his mouth, thick as paint. He swayed for a beat, toppled over, and thudded against the ground beside Darek, a sword stuck in his throat. The guard's breathing came ragged and gurgling for one, two, three seconds, then ceased.

Darek didn't know what he was more shocked by: the dead royal guard lying beside him, or his little brother, staring at the man he'd just stabbed with a look of horror on his face.

"I killed him," Markus said. He sounded dazed and far away.

With his hands cuffed behind his back and one dislocated shoulder, Darek awkwardly got to his feet. "Markus."

His brother looked at him, eyes as lost as his voice. "He's dead."

Darek's heart threatened to cave in, but he refused to let it. "Listen to me: it was him or me. You had no choice."

Markus glanced back at the dead man. He swallowed. Nodded.

"Good. We need to go."

A grimace flashed over Markus's face as he stooped down to pull a set of keys off the guard. He turned his back on the dead man and unshackled Darek's wrists. The cuffs dropped to the ground with a clank, and Darek limped as quickly as he could to the door down the alley. He procured a skeleton key that unlocked most everything in the system of tunnels snaking beneath the city streets and slipped it into the rusted lock. Ignoring protestations from his injured arm, he hauled the heavy door open, followed Markus through, and yanked it shut behind them both.

The darkness was sudden and absolute. From a pocket, Darek withdrew the sunstones he'd grabbed earlier, which were already emitting a faint yellow sheen. He shook the vial until it was a soft golden color. Sunstones didn't compare to a torch or lantern, but he could make out both his brother and a set of stone stairs disappearing down into shadow.

"I need you to put my shoulder back in," Darek said. "Think you can manage that?"

Markus looked faintly ill, but he pulled his spine straight and lifted his chin. "Come here."

Darek positioned himself in front of his brother, and Markus gripped his elbow in one hand and his forearm in another. Darek grimaced but made no noise as Markus slowly manipulated his shoulder. In one practiced move, he popped it back into place. Another surge of pain, then the softer flow of relief. Darek cradled his arm into his body, knowing he'd be as sore as a devil soon enough, and he'd need to make a sling when he could.

"Thanks. Let's go."

The stairs led down into three inches of standing water, the result of a minor leak from the river. Wrapped in a faint bubble of light, they splashed through the tunnel, brackish water lapping at curved stone walls, an odor of mildew clinging to the air. When they came to a branch, Darek chose the tunnel leading south, away from the Atterton District.

"Where are we going?" Markus asked.

"We can't go home right now. Atterton is going to be crawling with guards and King's Children for days. I don't want to risk being questioned."

"King's Children?" Markus repeated, startled.

"Someone told them about the White Raven. They were behind the attack. They knew rebels would be there." Darek glanced at his brother. Markus's mouth was set, his eyes downcast. "Did you hear the explosion?"

"Yes. I didn't even know you were there. I just wanted to see what was going on, and when I showed up, you were fighting with the guard, and I—I just . . ." He stopped in his tracks, water rippling out from his boots. "Ren. Was she with you?"

Until now, Darek hadn't a spare moment to think about Ren. He didn't know where she was, if she'd taken off immediately or lingered outside the tavern doors long enough to be blasted away with them. He couldn't worry about that right now. If he did, he'd lose his hold on the little bit of calm he had left.

"She left before the attack," Darek said.

"Is she okay? Where did she go."

"I don't know."

"You don't know? Darek, we need to find her. If she's hurt—if she's dead—we—"

"One thing at a time. As Ren likes to remind us, she knows how to handle herself. Right now, we need to get somewhere safe."

"I don't think there's a safe place left in this city," Markus muttered, mostly to himself.

As their splashing echoed against the damp walls, Darek said nothing, even if he couldn't help but agree.

PART TWO

CHAPTER
NINETEEN

The castle's interrogation cells sat deep beneath the ground, below the general cells and the solitary wing, and closer to the hells than anywhere else in the castle. The walls weren't made of bars, but slabs of iron two feet thick. A blazing torch barely kept the dark at bay, and blood stained the rough stone floor. Sometimes, when she was down here, Adley swore she could feel fire burning her feet.

She dumped the rebel she'd pulled from the basement of the White Raven into a large wooden chair mounted in the middle of the cell. She didn't pause to chain his hands or feet. To keep him in his seat, she pulled an arrow from her quiver and brought it down on his right hand, shoving through flesh and delicate bone and driving deep into the chair's arm.

The rebel screamed.

He was Sirican, like her, with golden-brown skin and waves of dark hair. He'd been disoriented when she and Lesa had cleared away the rubble from the cellar doors they'd blown out. Half of his face was slick with blood from a deep slit across his forehead and brow, and his left eye was swollen shut.

"Who's leading the rebellion?" Adley asked, easily slipping into the stoic voice of a King's Child, as if it were no effort at all. "I want a name."

"Piss off," the man gasped.

Adley grabbed the arrow sticking out of his hand and gripped his chin. Forcing his gaze to hers, she began to twist. He gritted his teeth. Adley could tell he was trying to keep from screaming, but she twisted as slowly as a second hand ticking around a clock, and a pained grunt escaped his throat.

"Want to try again?" she asked.

The man spit blood in her face.

Adley didn't wipe it away. She just pulled out a second arrow and shoved it into his other hand. The rebel threw his head back, the cords in his neck straining, and screamed. The sound rippled through the air and struck her ears like an out-of-tune instrument.

"The name of your leader," Adley said when he'd quieted and all that came out of him were wet gasps. Tears leaked from his eyes, running tracks in the blood covering his face.

"All right." His voice cracked. "All right."

Adley waited while he took in a shaky breath.

"Bobo Balkinson," the rebel said.

She gave him a look that had made bigger men piss themselves. Bobo Balkinson was an exceptionally dumb character in *The Knave's Heart*, a play put on every year during the Royal Carnival. "Funny," she replied. She slid yet another arrow from the quiver on her back and twirled it between her fingers. Arrows didn't always have to puncture. They could be as detailed as blades, as long as you knew how to use them. And Adley . . . she'd known how to use her arrows since she was seven years old.

She set to work.

The man's screams were an orchestral score from the ninth hell. It seemed like they would never end. Adley was flaying the skin on his foot when he finally passed out. With a small feeling of relief that it was over for now, she let the arrow tumble from her wet fingers to the bloody stones and stood up. Turning her back on him, she crossed the cell to heave the door open. "The old candle factory on Hiatt Street. Go," she commanded, stepping out into the hall. Two members of the Royal Guard turned and hurried up the rough stone stairs, their heeled boots clicking.

She went to run a hand over her braid, then stopped when she remembered her fingers were wet with the rebel's blood. She pulled a cloth from her pocket and wiped her hands and face, but she couldn't get it all; red was stuck along the edges of her short nails.

"An old candle factory?" Lesa asked. She was sitting on the ground, one arm propped up on a bent knee, a dagger in her hand. She flung it at the wall with a jerk of her wrist. The blade sunk into a chunk of wood, just a hairsbreadth from two daggers already embedded there. She picked up another knife from the pile laying on the ground beside her and took aim again, almost carelessly, her throwing arm still resting on her knee.

"It's probably a fake," Adley acknowledged. "But I'm checking up on everything."

Lesa flicked her wrist. The knife drove home. "Think you've gotten anything useful out of him?"

Adley fell back against the dungeon wall. "Doubtful. He keeps insisting the rebellion's leader is called Bobo Balkinson."

"Maybe you're not giving him enough incentive," Lesa said, twirling a blade in her hand.

"If I gave him anymore incentive, he'd be dead."

"I fail to see the problem," Lesa commented.

Information was Adley's route to becoming King's Fang. Once she got a name, she could bring in the rebel leader and claim her position as the king's right hand. In twelve years, she'd walk away from the castle and never look back, Lesa hopefully by her side. This was the only shot at freedom they'd ever have, so she needed to break the man, not put his body in the ground. A corpse was useless.

"It's not as if I can torture his ghost into giving up their leader."

In the hours since their raid on the Atterton tavern, both Adley and Lesa had interrogated several rebels who were proving more difficult to break than a distrustful wild horse. Like the man she'd been maiming for the past half hour, all they seemed to give up were false leads and fake names. Adley suspected their confessions were scattered with truth, but like too many colors mixed together, everything was so muddled she had a difficult time discerning what was false and what wasn't. It was a technique she herself had been taught.

No one had held up so strongly under interrogation by a King's Child. These rebels were of a newer, more dangerous breed. They were the type of animal that wouldn't stand for muzzles and clipped claws, a thing that bit when a hand refused to feed it, and the king should be very, very worried.

Lesa picked up her last three blades. She threw them at the wall in quick succession, and each found the same mark. "These people are annoyingly loyal."

"Do you think we're ever going to find their leader?"

Lesa pushed herself up from the floor and strode over to the wall she'd been using as target practice. She yanked her knives free. "Yes," she said, handing Adley the weapons. The dungeons were too busy for them to touch, too many guards and King's Children rushing in and out in the wake of the raid, but Lesa's black eyes said everything their hands couldn't. Their look was fierce and tender and unwavering all at once. "You'll be made King's Fang. I'm sure of it. Use these."

Adley accepted the blades and turned back to the interrogation cell. She removed her jacket and dropped it to the ground, then pulled a chair from the corner of the windowless room and set it in front of the rebel. She seated herself backward, straddling the chair with leather-clad legs, and waited.

When he came to, her bare arms were resting on the top of the chair, muscles obvious even when relaxed. In her hands were Lesa's knives, each as wicked as the next, their sharpened edges razor thin. They were the best knives in the castle. Lesa had made sure of it, and she took stone to them every night, as if she were part of a particularly violent religion and sharpening the blades was a prayer.

The rebel groaned, a pained, almost inhuman sound, no longer at the mercy of unconsciousness. The coppery smell of his blood bit at Adley's nose. His good eye fluttered open.

"Who is leading the rebellion?" she asked again.

His mouth was a line, and he lifted his chin in silent defiance. Standing, Adley moved to look down at the rebel. Still pinned to the chair by his hands, blood had dripped onto the floor and formed two small pools at his feet, which were bare and soaked crimson, the skin flayed.

She held up the knives, examining them in the torchlight. "Which one do you think?" she asked and glanced down at the man. "What? No more funny comments?" She selected the second knife and stowed the other four in her weapons belt, then lowered the blade to his forearm. She paused just before piercing the skin. "I'm tired of repeating myself. Give me a name, and we can both get some rest."

He refused to speak. Adley began to cut.

She blocked out his screams and forced herself to imagine his arm as nothing more than dead pigskin, because if she let herself see a man and not an obstacle standing in her way, she might give in to the small voice begging her to stop. So Adley carved away at his forearm and pretended. Pretended just like she had every day since those slavers had taken her from the sun-drenched shores of Sirica. Pretended for her own sanity. For her survival. People did terrible things to stay alive, but they could be forgiven. Dirty hands could be washed clean. Adley told herself that every time the water in the sink ran red with blood that wasn't her own.

When a good inch of his arm was only blood and raw muscle, Adley paused. "A name."

"You'll never find her," he mumbled, the words low with pain. "You know how many pits there are—" He cut himself off, and the look of horror that crossed his face was short-lived, but Adley caught it.

Using the tip of her blade, she forced his chin up. "Your leader is a woman?"

Aside from his ragged breathing, the rebel was quiet. "She's not our leader. She's no one," he croaked out.

She smiled, and it was a sickly sweet thing. "Oh, I doubt that." She lowered her knife to his arm again. "A name." When an answer didn't come, she continued where she'd left off. She kept at it until he lost consciousness a second time.

He never did give her a name, but Adley didn't mind, because now she knew she was on the hunt for a woman. Even if the woman really wasn't in charge of the rebellion, Adley was certain she could lead her to whoever was.

And all she had to do was comb the fighting pits to find her.

CHAPTER
TWENTY

The castle was on high alert tonight. When Kellen returned from his fighting pit, he'd had no idea what to make of all the guards roaming the halls, the whispering staff and skittish courtiers. Everyone was tense. At first, he thought something had happened to his father, but then the news reached him: King's Children had gone looking for rebels, and they'd found some.

The rebels, with their half-cooked plans and their meager resources and their hope. Kellen didn't have anything against them, really. He didn't much care for his father, either, so he could hardly fault the rebellion. He simply thought they were idiots, fools wasting their energy on a fight they would never win. They rode horses made of faith, and nothing tired so quickly. No, they weren't just idiots. They were worse. They were suicidal idiots.

Kellen did kind of admire their persistence, though.

On his way to his chambers, Kellen recalled his brief, strange visit with Holland. He'd shown up at her home to find the front door locked, and when he'd knocked, she took so long to respond he thought she might be out.

"You need to leave," Holland had said the second she

opened the door. She was covered in a fine layer of dust, her usually styled hair a disaster of curls. A bead of blood seeped from a nick above her right eyebrow.

"What—"

A rustle came from inside the house, and Holland glanced over her shoulder. "Don't!" she'd exclaimed, shutting the door in Kellen's face without another word.

What had Holland gotten herself wrapped up in? First, there had been that meeting with the boy in her kitchen, a meeting Kellen was obviously not supposed to have overheard, and now this. The dusty clothes and the cut brow and another mystery visitor she didn't want him to know about.

He mulled it over while he wound his way through the castle's pale halls and drifted up the wide stairwells. The corridor he shared with his brother was quiet, fires burning low in their sconces along the wall and arched windows displaying the city down below, where thousands of windows glowed yellow. Heath's door was closed. Kellen pivoted toward his own chambers, which stood at the opposite end of the hall, and picked up his pace without entirely meaning to.

He hadn't taken more than a few steps when the door behind him squeaked open. "Kellen!" Heath called. "Come in here for a moment, will you?"

Kellen glanced down the staircase, but found nothing coming to rescue him from being alone with his brother. Usually, he avoided most everyone in the castle, grateful for late nights and quiet halls. It was easier that way, when all his presence seemed to illicit was irritation. He'd stopped trying to be a better prince years ago, since his attempts were only rewarded with snide comments and cool looks, but right now he wished for a council member to round the corner and ask to pick his brain about the treaty. Even if that was about as likely to happen as a successful rebellion.

He pushed a hand through his hair, turning back around, and walked into Heath's chambers.

"Close the door," Heath said. His hands were braced on the edge of his writing desk as he studied a large piece of parchment sprawled out before him. A fire crackled in its hearth, orange-and-yellow light flashing across diamond-patterned windows set into one wall. Kellen slowly shut the door.

"Will you take a look at this?" Heath asked. "It's the choreography for this year's demonstration at the Royal Carnival."

Kellen's shoulders relaxed half an inch. "Sure."

Heath moved aside, making room for Kellen so he could look over the layout of the stage that was currently being erected in Talmarquin Square. He studied the directions marked on the overlarge sheet of parchment, then turned to the written details of the Crown's Demonstration. Someone from the Royal Theatre had laid out the choreography in painstaking detail, each step written in language so clear and repetitious that Kellen thought his father should maybe be offended. The whole demonstration, during which Kellen, Heath, and the king would swirl their silver and generally intimidate the shit out of the city, was planned down to the minute. It was slated to last nearly twice as long as last year. Kellen frowned.

"What do you think?" Heath asked.

He flipped the paper over, where the choreography continued down the back. "This is a lot more complicated than demonstrations we've put on in the past."

"I know. It's father. He insisted. I think he's trying to scare the rebels into giving up."

"That's stupid. The rebels already know we have silver. They're not going to call it quits just because we're waving our arms more vigorously."

Heath gave a cold, mirthless laugh. "On that, we are agreed."

Kellen glanced up. "I don't think you've ever agreed with me on anything."

Heath's eyes flitted to Kellen and back to the stage layout. "You're not around enough for me to find anything to agree with."

"Father doesn't want me here," Kellen said. *You don't want me here. Mother doesn't pay enough attention to know if I'm here or not.*

"Can you blame him?"

Well, that stung.

"Is he intimidated by my good looks?" Kellen mused.

"Oddly enough, I don't think your cheekbones are the problem." Heath faced Kellen and crossed his arms over his chest. In the dim light of the hearth, his hair was a dark gold, his eyes shadowed. "You're smart, Kell, but you don't think with your head. You think with your heart. And hearts are dreadfully weak things."

Yet without them, we'd all be dead, Kellen thought.

"Stop being so soft. Your opinions will count for more."

When Kellen wore the mask of pit lord, he usually succeeded for a few hours in convincing himself he was someone he wasn't, someone cold and malicious. But then he'd take the mask off. He'd come back to the castle and find he was still the same kid his mother had raised and tossed aside when he no longer suited her tastes. Kellen wished Heath would tell him how he was supposed to stop being soft, how he was supposed to tear his beating heart from his body and discard it like a broken toy. How he was supposed to stop being *him.*

"I'll try," was all he said.

"Or better yet, find someone to marry. You'll be more useful if you form an alliance. A strong one. The gods know we need it. The treaty was bad enough, but the rebels are coming out of Atterton now. I never thought I would miss the days when they were just street scum from the slums."

That caught Kellen's attention. "What?"

"The King's Children raided the White Raven tonight. Apparently, it's a meeting place for rebels."

Kellen went still. "Is that the tavern on Hershing? White brick with a bunch of rose bushes out front?"

"That's the one. Its patrons have more wealth than they know what to do with, and unfortunately, funding the rebellion seems to be their chosen course of action."

Kellen looked down at the parchment. He swallowed,

fighting the urge to sprint from the room. "So this chore-ography is pretty involved, but if we practice a few times, we should manage just fine."

Heath took the papers and frowned, a worry line above his nose. "Are you certain?"

"It'll be fine, Heath. It always is."

With that, Kellen turned to leave his brother's chambers.

"I have these dreams sometimes." Heath's voice came quietly, and when Kellen looked back, he found his brother staring at the choreography, a faraway expression on his face, as if he were speaking to no one but himself and maybe the gods. "About a dark-haired girl. It's that silver wielder, the one father killed. She just . . . she won't go away." He glanced up at Kellen, firelight in his golden hair. His voice turned bitter. "I feel like she's haunting me."

Kellen remembered that night, when his father had sent men down into the city with orders to set fire to the girl's house. He was only ten at the time, but he remem-bered the story. The little girl had been caught doing magic in her own home, glimpsed through a window that should have been curtained. She was ratted out by an untrust-worthy neighbor who'd seen the display from afar. The man had received a nice sum of gold from the king as a reward.

Kellen wasn't surprised Heath was dreaming about the girl. He was more surprised she didn't visit them all every night. If anyone deserved to be haunted by a spirit, it was his family.

"No one is haunting you," Kellen told his brother. "It's just a dream."

Heath was quiet for a while, his cold eyes going back to the papers. "You're probably right."

Kellen hesitated in the doorway, torn between asking Heath if he was all right and getting out of there as fast as his feet would carry him. He knew he should ask—it was the brotherly thing to do—but there were more pressing matters to attend to, and Heath probably didn't want his concern anyway. So in the end, he left without another word. When he was out of earshot, he pushed his legs faster and bolted down to his tunnel, pulling out his mask as he went.

CHAPTER
TWENTY-ONE

Ren awoke in a room she didn't recognize, disoriented, with something covering half her face. She bolted to her feet, clawing at whatever was wrapped around her head. A wave of nausea hit. She swallowed it back and yanked off a thick bandage coated with blood.

"Don't!" yelled a girl's voice.

Ren's eyes shot to a set of open doors across the room and a lamplit foyer beyond. A red-haired girl shoved the front door shut and rushed toward Ren in a flurry of pale skirts.

"You'll start bleeding again."

Ren pulled a dagger from her corset, holding it out with a shaky hand. The girl halted. "Who are . . ." Nausea rammed into her again. She stumbled back a few steps, bracing her free hand on the wall. She sucked in a breath. "Who are you?"

"We met outside the White Raven," the girl said. "I'm Holland. Don't you remember?"

Ren thought back. She remembered meeting Darek's friends and the confrontation that followed, remembered leaving the warmth of the tavern for the snow-covered streets of Denfell. And then she remembered the girl who had been standing outside, waiting for her. Her skull gave a sharp throb.

"An explosion," Ren said, the details filling themselves in. "What happened? Where am I?"

"My house," Holland said. Her bright curls were in a messy disarray, a small scratch on her eyebrow was wet with blood, and there was a good deal of dust on her dress. "King's Children raided the White Raven. I paid a coach a fortune to bring us back here and keep quiet about it. I have to say, for someone so tall you're frightfully light."

"I'll tell my chef to increase his portion sizes," Ren said, her sarcasm less biting than usual, due to the head wound. "Why did you bring me here?"

"Should I have left you unconscious on the street?"

"It depends on what you want."

"I only wanted to meet the girl Darek and Markus are so certain is the key to our success," Holland told her. "But if you ask me, you're more trouble than you're worth."

The knife grew steadier in Ren's hand as the nausea began to ease. "Good thing I didn't ask you." Holland gave a soft laugh, and Ren straightened up from the wall, her fingers flexing on the hilt of her blade. "Something funny?"

Holland tilted her head, a smile playing on her lips. "How have you and Darek not killed each other yet?"

"Inhuman willpower on my end."

She chuckled again and crossed her arms over her stomach. She eyed Ren's knife like it was a curious oddity, not a weapon. "Can I ask you something?"

"I'd prefer if you didn't," Ren said.

"I know you don't care about the rebellion, so I'm curious, what do you care about?"

"Money."

"Besides that."

Ren's eyes narrowed in irritation. She lowered her knife to her side. "I'm going to save us both a lot of time. Decency doesn't keep me warm at night." Right and wrong, black and white, none of it mattered. Ren was on whichever side granted her the most fortune. "I've never claimed to be a good person."

Holland sighed dramatically. "None of us are *good people*. We've all done things we're not proud of. We've all made mistakes. Your demons might be louder than mine, but we each have one or two hanging around. We're all just people, Ren. We're doing our best."

Ren studied her. "I'm not sure what you want from me."

"I'm not entirely sure what I want from you, either," Holland admitted.

"Glad that's settled then." As Ren tucked her knife into her corset, she glanced around the room. Clawed chairs were upholstered in dusty rose, and matching curtains brushed the hardwood floors. Two windows stretched up to the ceiling and looked out on an empty, snow-covered road scattered with glowing streetlamps, the river twinkling beyond. Gold leaf decorated the walls, a vase of eucalyptus leaves sat on an end table, and a fire burned in a white mantelpiece. Holland clearly had money, but at least her house seemed to be a reasonable size.

It actually reminded Ren a bit of the home she'd grown up in, all wide windows and soft colors. It was more opulent than her old yellow house, but Ren's parents had been fortunate enough to afford something similar, thanks to her mother's business venture—whatever that had been. The fact that Ren couldn't remember much about it made her wish she'd asked more questions, figured out who her parents were when she had the chance. Instead, she'd always see them through the eyes of the girl she used to be. Though maybe it was better that way. They'd been a compass, showing kindness and compassion, teaching Ren right from wrong. But she'd disregarded the lessons long ago, and she didn't think they would have liked the person she'd become.

"I was the one who found you, you know," Holland said.

Ren flicked her eyes back to the redhead. "How'd you figure it out?"

"I've seen silver up close. It was the way you move when you fight. Your hands are very expressive. I noticed you twisting your wrists, as if you wanted to use silver." She shrugged. "It was just a hunch."

A knock came at the front door, and Holland mumbled a series of unladylike words under her breath as she went to answer. Her heels clicked, the door groaned softly, and she exclaimed, "Jaston!"

Ren wandered into the modest foyer just as the door clicked shut. She propped one shoulder against the sitting room doorframe and crossed her arms over her chest, skimming Jaston's skinny form. His sandy hair was askew, his hands badly scraped and covered in dried blood the color of rust, and he didn't have a coat or even a sweater on over his shirt. His wide eyes met hers. "Ren?"

Ren glanced at Holland. "Should I say your name now?"

Holland huffed a laugh. To Jaston, she said, "You got out."

"I was lucky," he replied. "A few of us were able to crawl through a hole in the wall before the King's Children came in." His gaze roamed over Ren for a moment, then his attention went back to Holland. "Darek and Riko aren't home. Have you heard anything?"

"Not yet. If I do, you'll be the first to know."

Jaston ran a scratched hand over his face. He nodded. "If either of you see Darek, let him know I'm fine."

"We will," Holland promised.

He took a step toward the door, but paused. He looked over at Ren. "I'm glad you're okay."

"Are you?" she asked.

When he started forward, lifting a hand as if to touch her, Ren glared at him so severely that he froze. His arm dropped back to his side. "Yes."

She studied him through a piercing gaze. It was a few long seconds before she decided he seemed sincere enough. "This doesn't mean I like you."

"Fair enough." With a dip of his chin, Jaston pulled open the front door and left.

Ren pushed herself off the doorframe. "Where's my coat?"

"You should stay for a while," Holland said. "That gash

on your head is pretty severe. You might pass out before you make it home."

"I'll manage."

"I have cherry tarts from Noble Finch."

Ren stopped. Katarine Vespar's cherry tarts were something of a legend. She made three hundred every day, no more and no less, and when her doors opened at precisely six in the morning, the tarts sold out in less than ten minutes. All the begging in the world couldn't convince her to make another batch. Cherry tarts had never been high on Ren's list of priorities, but she couldn't deny that she was curious.

"How'd you get your hands on them?" Ren asked.

"Perks of being the owner's daughter."

Ren snorted. She should have guessed—Holland's bright hair was the same shade of red as Katarine's. "Well, I am quite famished, now that you mention it."

Holland ushered her to a kitchen filled with so many sweets that it was as if she expected Denfell to run out of sugar. It was as colorful a room as Ren had seen, with pastel delicacies displayed under glass trays and domes, the hues offset by white countertops. The entire room smelled like warm cake, and Ren's mouth immediately set to watering.

Holland placed a blue macaroon in her hand, directing her to sit while she went upstairs to change out of her dirty skirts. When she returned, she retrieved a white box from a glass cabinet. "Noble Finch" was written in an elegant golden scroll across the top, and the inside was lined with powder-pink tissue paper. She gave Ren a round tart the size of her palm, the top loaded with bright-red cherries that looked too perfect to be real. Ren took a bite and fought back a sigh of pleasure.

"Good, right?" Holland asked, licking cherry sauce off her fingers.

Ren made an inelegant noise and shoved the pastry into her mouth. She held out her hand for another. Holland laughed through a full mouth, handing over a second tart as perfect as the first.

After three cherry tarts and a couple admittedly incredible cakes, Ren was steadier on her feet and feeling a little less like someone was using her skull for drum practice. Licking icing off her fingers, she ventured back to the sitting room and scooped up her coat. She'd gotten one arm into a sleeve when a banging came at the door, loud enough to raise the dead.

"Holland!"

The voice was deep and angry. Whoever it was, he wanted in—badly. And the next series of knocks made it clear he wasn't leaving until he got what he wanted.

CHAPTER
TWENTY-TWO

"Holland!" Kellen shouted. He slammed a fist against her front door. "Holland, open up! I know you're home!"

Having run most of the way here, Kellen was out of breath, with a seriously painful stitch in his side. He'd wanted to take a horse, but the tunnel was the only way to slip out of the castle unfollowed, so he'd pulled his hood up high, shoved his mask on his face, and hurtled through the city like a messenger relaying news of war on the horizon.

"Holland! Open your godsdamned door!" Kellen banged and banged until his fist was sore.

The door jerked open. "*What?!*" Holland all but screamed in his face. She'd changed into clean pants and a shirt, an outfit Kellen never would have guessed she'd own, let alone wear, and she'd tied up her curls. The slice above her eye had been cleaned, but it was still unbandaged.

"How did you get that cut on your eyebrow?" Kellen asked.

"Are you drunk?"

"Where were you tonight?"

Holland gave him a look like he'd lost his mind. "I was out."

"Where?"

"Where I go is none of your concern."

"I command you to tell me where you were," Kellen said. The words sounded forced and strange coming out of his mouth—he tasted the wrongness of them—but he remained firm before her.

"You *command* me?"

"Yes."

"Well, I command you to go fuck yourself."

She started to swing the door closed, but Kellen put a hand out to stop it. "Let me in. You don't want to do this out here."

"Let the man inside," came a girl's voice. "Gods, just make the yelling stop."

"Who is that?" Kellen asked, craning his neck to see around her. The foyer was low-lit and empty.

"Fine," Holland said. She jerked the door open and waved him through, performing a dramatic curtsy as she did. "Fine."

Adjusting his mask, Kellen stepped into her house and passed through the entryway. The green-eyed pit fighter from two weeks ago was quite possibly the last person he had expected to see resting against the back of Holland's sitting room couch.

"It's you," he said. She looked almost exactly as she did then, leather corset very much included. There was a fresh gash on the left side of her temple that disappeared under a long tangle of black hair, and the dark slash of cosmetics around her eyes was a smeared mess. Her red coat was slung over the couch beside her.

"Have we met?" she asked warily. "Wait, aren't you . . ." She turned her eyes to Holland. "You know the South Terth pit lord?"

"Don't ask," Holland said.

The girl—Ren, her name was Ren, he hadn't forgotten—looked back at him. "Interesting." She cocked her head and drummed her fingers against the pink upholstery. "Why the mask?"

"Women like a sense of mystery," Kellen said. "Or so I've been told."

"Perhaps you're being too literal."

"You think so?"

"Just a tad." Ren grabbed her jacket and draped it over an arm, straightening off the couch. She approached him, leaned in close, and hooked a finger around a string on his shirt. Her breath hot on his skin, Kellen's only thought was that beneath a chalky layer of dust, she smelled of vanilla and cedarwood. "The mask has its appeal, but personally, I think it's what's underneath"—she tugged on his shirt string, her eyes darting down and back up again—"that counts."

Kellen's heart was galloping in his chest, and his ears were a little warm. He should have had a hundred responses ready, but he searched and came up empty.

Ren released him. She turned to Holland. "I'd better go."

Without a proper parting word, she left them both in the sitting room. Just before she stepped through the front door and out of his life for a second time, Kellen asked, "Will you come back to my pit?"

"We'll see," she replied.

And then she was gone.

Kellen rounded on Holland. "I thought you didn't know her."

"We're newly acquainted."

He narrowed his eyes. Honestly, she couldn't possibly expect him to believe all of this was a *coincidence*. "Why was she here?"

"It doesn't matter."

Holland turned on her heel, clicked out of the room and across the foyer, and bounded up the curving staircase. Kellen followed her to her bedroom, where a fire flickered in the mouth of a marble mantelpiece. Standing in the doorframe, he watched as she stationed herself at her vanity table and let down her long red hair. Firelight glinted off the curls.

"The White Raven was attacked tonight," he said.

"Is that what all the commotion was about?" she asked, picking up a brush from among a crowd of cosmetics and bottled floral scents. She dragged it through her knotted strands with a grimace.

"Please don't play dumb, Holland. It's insulting."

"I'm really not sure how I'm expected to have known a tavern was attacked."

"You were there."

The brush stilled. She stared at his reflection in the mirror. "Have you gone completely mad?"

Kellen yanked his mask from his face and stuffed it into his pocket like the black silk had mortally offended him. "Are you working with the rebels?"

Setting her brush aside, she swiveled around on her stool to meet his eye directly. Her face betrayed nothing. In fact, she looked offended. "What is wrong with you? Why would you even ask that?"

"You live blocks from the White Raven, which, by the way, is where rebels have been meeting. On the same night it's attacked, I come here to find you covered in dust, looking like the hells, with some girl you said you didn't know. And what about that boy who was here last week? He asked if you still wanted to help. Help with what?"

She was looking at him as if she thought a stint in the hospital's madhouse might do him some good. "Do you hear yourself right now?"

"Cut the shit, Holland," Kellen snapped, sounding so unlike himself and so like his father.

Holland stood from her stool and shoved her arms across her chest. "I just met Ren tonight. I was curious about her, so I went to a fighting pit and I got caught up in a brawl there. I'm fine, though, thank you for asking. As for the boy, it's a personal matter, one that I do not wish to discuss."

"If that's true, why did you refuse to tell me where you were?"

She stalked forward. "You cannot come in here and

demand answers of me like I am a pupil to command. You may be a prince, but I will not tolerate being treated as an inferior. I am your *equal*." She emphasized the last word with the jab of a manicured finger to his chest.

Kellen stared down into her hazel eyes, which might as well have been as blazing as her hair, and heard his brother's words. They sounded in his ear. He felt the heat of them as close as a whisper. *Stop being so soft.* Then his father's voice was there, too, seething with contempt. Nineteen years of criticism. Two decades of failure. Their voices bled together, pouring into his head like a vein that had been ripped open, and there was no staunching the flow. It kept coming, and it seemed like it was never going to stop, and Kellen just wanted peace. That was all. Just a little peace.

He wrapped his hand around Holland's finger. "I could turn you in to the King's Children. They'd torture you if they thought you knew something."

Hurt skittered across her face, hurt and fear and something else, something Kellen couldn't name—or maybe he just didn't want to recognize it for what it was. It occurred to him this may have been the first time he'd seen real emotion on her round features.

She yanked her hand from his grasp and backed away. "Kellen," she said quietly. "You wouldn't."

Of course he wouldn't. He couldn't possibly. He'd only thought . . . He didn't know what he'd thought, but watching Holland now, how truly afraid she was, he knew Heath and his father would be so proud.

Kellen's chest was tight.

"I'm sorry," he said. "You're in no danger from me. I swear it." When Holland didn't say anything, when that horrible expression didn't fall from her face, he began to back out of the room. "I . . . I'll just go."

He started to turn away.

"You don't need to be like them," Holland said suddenly, quietly. "I know why you run that pit, why you come here every night instead of going home, but you should stop trying to be someone you're not. You're better than your family." She paused. "At least, I hoped you were."

Kellen swallowed down a lump in his throat. He had no idea how to respond to that, so all he said was, "Please be careful, Holland. Whatever you're involved in, I don't want to see you get hurt."

He turned for the door.

"When will you learn?" she said to his back. "Some things are worth the pain."

Kellen walked out of her house and into a pub, where he drank away the memory of what he had said, if only for a few hours.

CHAPTER
TWENTY-THREE

The Hessler District looked like it had been built by men who'd forgotten half their supplies and hadn't particularly felt like going back for more. No two buildings were even. A three-story home stood next to a squat sprawling structure. The few places that may have been intended to complement one another were lopsided, their walls and windows glaringly crooked. A few blocks east and a walk over the Battgandon River, the houses were as bright as garden roses, but here, the colors had faded until they were nothing but an indistinguishable mass of gray. Rooftops jagged across the skyline like a pattern that had given up.

And Hessler was the nicest of the slums. The Terth didn't have enough rooftops for there to be a pattern in the first place.

"This is safe?" Markus asked when they arrived at the Hessler Compound.

"Safer than our house," Darek said.

This wasn't the first time Darek had seen Ren's home—if it could properly be called a home—but it was the first time he'd gotten so close. The building was made of drab gray stone, cracks running through the facade like a chaotic city map. Though most windows still contained glass, a few were boarded over with thick slabs of wood, and the shingled roof was patched more heavily than a ship returning from battle. It might have been more run-down than any place in Atterton, but in Hessler, the Compound fit right in.

They stopped in front of a set of double doors that were weatherworn but appeared secure enough. Markus inspected the building, his gaze lingering on some wooden support beams that may have been rotting. "This place looks like it's going to fall apart the moment the door opens."

Darek made a sound of agreement as he rapped his knuckles against the wood. "We'll have to hope it doesn't."

One of the doors opened a crack, and Darek could just make out the eye of a small boy. "What do you want?" the kid asked, keeping the door nearly shut.

He sounded more terrified than defiant, and Darek remembered he was covered in blood, his own and the guard's, with a broken nose and a seriously battered face. He probably looked like something that had crawled out of the Desert of Lost Souls.

"I'm looking for Ren," Darek said as pleasantly as he could manage.

"She's not here."

"What about Freya?"

The boy gave him a half-skeptical, half-frightened look through the sliver of open doorway and said nothing.

"You don't need to let us in," Darek assured him. "Will you please tell Freya that Darek is here? I'm a friend."

"Okay," the kid said and shoved the door closed.

Barely a minute passed before a curly haired girl was pulling it open again. Freya was dressed in the same rusty-orange skirt she'd been wearing earlier that day, a huge worn sweater swallowing her frame, and silver jewelry crowding her fingers and neck. Her eyes grew round. "What in all nine hells happened to you?" she asked Darek.

"The White Raven was attacked by King's Children. We need a place to stay. Just for a little while."

"Of course." She ushered them inside. "Ren isn't with you?"

"I was hoping she would be here," Darek confessed as she shoved the door shut. "Have you seen her since you left the tavern?"

"No. I've been reading at a party all night. I just got back ten minutes ago."

She led them out of the small entryway and down a hall. They passed a living space cluttered with sagging couches and mismatched furniture, then a kitchen and dining area containing three tables—each a different size and shape—and dozens of shabby chairs, none of which seemed to have a mate. The inside of the Hessler Compound would have been as lifeless and dank as the gray stone outside if it weren't for all the kids. They were huddled on the couches, eating at the tables, running up and down the stairs at the end of the hall. They yelled back and forth, chattered like excitable birds, and generally created a din of noise to compete with Traders' Hall. Based on the size of the Compound, Darek had previously estimated that around twenty kids lived here. It now appeared to be at least double that.

"When was the last time you saw her?" Freya asked. As they ascended the staircase, they nearly collided with a couple kids skipping down it. "Careful!" she shouted after them.

"Maybe two hours ago," Darek guessed. "My friend pissed her off, and she left. You'll be unsurprised to hear that she didn't tell me where she was going."

They came to the second floor, which was comprised of a long, narrow hallway lined with doors—some closed, and others standing ajar. A few kids were huddled in blankets on the floor. Freya continued up. "That sounds like Ren," she said.

"Are you not concerned about her?" Markus asked.

"I'm always concerned about Ren. It's a natural state of existence when you're friends with her."

The third floor was calm and deserted, with only two doors standing opposite one another. Freya slipped a key into the door on the left, pushing it open, and Darek followed her into a room that could have been mistaken for a fortune-teller's tent. The floor was covered in so many carpets and pillows that he could hardly make out the wooden boards beneath. Layers of sheer fabrics and silks adorned the walls, beaded curtains hanging before the entrances to what must have been a washroom and bedroom. In the small sitting area, a deck of tarot cards was scattered across a squat table. The place looked pretty much exactly how Freya dressed, and a strong aroma of amber incense lingered in the air.

After directing them to a worn couch, Freya disappeared through one of the curtains, its beads tinkling in her wake. While Markus slumped forward to brace his elbows on his knees, Darek let his head fall back. He found himself staring up at a painting of the night sky, bronze stars dotted against a swirling blue backdrop, thin lines forming the constellations. In the direct center of the ceiling was an image of the moon in all its phases, circular like a clock with too many hours. The detail involved was impressive. If Ren hadn't told him Freya knew how to read the stars about as well as a sheep could sing the Erdis anthem, Darek might have believed the girl was the real thing.

Freya returned with healing supplies. Moving aside her tarot cards, she perched on the edge of the squat table and piled the medicines and bandages beside her. Then she pushed up her sleeves, bracelets jangling on her thin wrists, and began to dig dirt from Darek's face. He winced, swallowing back fresh pain as she cleaned his wounds with alcohol, yanked a needle through the gouge in his leg, and made a sling for his arm from a long strip of cloth. When she set his broken nose, his vision went white. By the time she was finished, exhaustion clung to his body, his bones heavy, muscles tight. Darek felt like he'd gotten into a fight with a battering ram.

Freya tossed him a jar of transparent cream. "Put a bit of that on your worst cuts. It'll help with the scarring."

She took her supplies to the kitchen, which was really only an extension of the living room with a sink and some counter space.

Darek dabbed cream over the scrapes on his face, and the raw skin went blissfully numb. "You work like a trained healer," he commented, covering the stitches on his thigh. "Did you study somewhere?"

He was setting the jar on the table when Freya dropped onto one of the many floor cushions beside the couch. "I taught myself," she said. "Around here, we can't really afford the hospital."

Darek nodded, though he didn't understand what that was like, couldn't imagine what it might be like, not when his family was wealthy enough to skip the hospital entirely and have a healer come to them.

"What happened?" Freya asked after the silence had gone on a little too long.

Darek glanced at his brother, who was staring at the floor. "King's Children raided the White Raven. I got out, but I was stopped by a guard. That's how this happened." He waved a hand over himself. "I thought I was screwed, but Markus showed up and he—well, he . . ."

"I killed him." Markus's voice was raw. He tore his eyes from the rugs and turned them on Freya. "He was going to stab Darek."

She didn't hesitate or shy away, but held his gaze. "The gods forgive," she said. "So should you."

There was a steadiness about Freya, something in her that a drowning person could grab on to and stay afloat.

Darek had the thought that she was much too decent to be friends with someone like Ren. Then he felt a bit guilty. Hadn't he promised himself he would be kinder to her?

"Where does Ren go when she's upset?" Darek asked.

"The fighting pits. A tavern to play a game of cards. The Golden Strait. Sometimes, the Sollertie."

"The art museum? Why?"

"Why does anyone look at art? Perhaps it makes her feel a little less alone."

It was as good an explanation as any, though Darek really couldn't see Ren wandering the echoing halls of the Sollertie, quiet and contemplative. She was not a delicate cherry blossom drifting down from the trees on a spring breeze. She was more like the storm that upended the cherry tree, the kind of person who wasn't satisfied unless she was putting her fist through something.

Darek stood. "We should look for her."

Right then, the muffled sound of boots came from outside the door. Freya listened. "No need," she told him. "Ren!"

The door popped open. Ren's hair was a disheveled mess, there was a fresh gash at her temple, and she had one hell of a bruised eye, but she looked fine otherwise. Darek let out a deep breath, releasing tension he hadn't even realized was there, surprised at just how relieved he was to see her.

"Your face looks like a dog chewed on it," Ren said to him in lieu of a greeting.

"The White Raven was—"

"Attacked, I know," she said, stepping into Freya's suite and swinging the door shut. She pointed at the wound on her head. "I didn't do this to myself."

Darek started toward her—to do what, he didn't know. "You were still there when they blew out the front doors? Are you all right?"

Before he was close enough to touch her, she jerked away. "I'm fine." She headed for the kitchen and began pulling open the cabinets. "Freya, why don't you ever have anything stronger than tea around here?"

"You don't need a drink," Freya said, rising from the floor. "Let me see your head."

"I'm fine," she said again.

"Ren, come on."

Ren heaved a sigh. She sunk to the floor and tipped her head back against the wall, draping her forearms over her bent knees. Freya kneeled beside her to inspect the cut. "You need a few stitches," she said. She unscrewed the small bottle of liquor she'd used on Darek's leg, which he assumed Ren wasn't allowed to drink, and washed out the wound. Then she shoved a needle into Ren's forehead. Ren hardly flinched—she looked bored, even—and Darek couldn't help but admire her high pain tolerance.

"Someone's already cleaned this," Freya said, sewing the skin shut. "Though they did a poor job of it." She tied off her work, snipped the string, and dropped the needle into her pile of used supplies.

"Yes," Ren said. To Darek, she added, "Holland sends her regards."

"You were with Holland?" he asked.

"She surprised me outside the tavern. You didn't know she was there?"

"Um," Markus said. They all looked to where he was seated on the couch. "Did I forget to mention Holland wanted to meet Ren?"

"Yes, I think you did," Darek said.

Markus mumbled something that sounded like, "Sorry," and ran a hand over his face.

Darek watched his brother for a moment longer before turning back to Ren. "It doesn't matter. She was going to meet you eventually."

He and Holland may have had their personal issues, but she was one of only a few people who knew the full extent of their plans. While Darek had trouble tolerating her presence, he did trust her with his life. He'd known her since they were kids, had grown up attending school with her, and had fallen into the rebellion alongside her. Holland's father, also a rebel, had died in the same raid that had killed Darek's mother, and even though Katarine Vespar had forbidden Holland from following in her father's footsteps, she'd joined up with the rebels anyway.

"I like her," Ren said.

Of course she did. And that's what Darek had been afraid of. Alone, both girls were their own forces of nature. Together, they might very well be cataclysmic. "What did you two talk about?" he asked.

"A little of this, a little of that," Ren said mildly, eyeing Markus on the couch. "What's wrong with him?"

Freya leaned in to explain what had happened. "The guard who attacked Darek died."

"So?"

"Markus has never killed anyone before," Freya added in a hushed tone.

"People die every day. He might as well get used to it."

Darek went tense, but before he could spout off anything harsh, Freya snapped, "Ren!"

The girls stared at each other, Freya's stern expression resolute as they held some kind of silent conversation, until finally Ren sighed again. She pushed herself off the kitchen floor, the carpets muffling her steps as she went to stand in front of Markus. She stared down at him and said, "Let yourself feel it."

Markus lifted his head, brow wrinkling. "What?"

"The pain. You need to let yourself feel it. If you don't, you'll never let it go. If you shove the pain away, if you ignore it, you won't move past it." He was quiet, his eyes uneasy, and Ren added, "Feel it. Don't make yourself numb. Don't— Never mind. Just . . . just get some rest. There's another couch in my suite. One of you can sleep there." She pulled out a watch to check the time. "I'm going to lock the front doors."

And with that, Ren departed the room.

The door clicked shut, and Darek thought he knew what she had been about to say.

Don't make yourself numb. Don't be like me.

CHAPTER
TWENTY-FOUR

Ren couldn't sleep. Maybe it was because a tavern full of rebels had been attacked, or maybe it was that Markus had killed a man and was sitting on Freya's couch doing an impressive imitation of a statue in Keepler's Prospect, or possibly it was the knowledge that Darek was just a door away, asleep in her own sitting room.

But it was most likely her pounding skull. Ren was really starting to regret agreeing to take part in a revolution. She hadn't realized being a rebel would come with so many head injuries. In the past two weeks, she'd been knocked unconscious twice, which was almost as many times as she'd been decked into oblivion in four years' worth of pit fights.

Seven hundred thousand gold pieces.

She stared up at the bare ceiling beams and ran through the night's events, from the blasted tavern doors to her encounter with the South Terth pit lord. Ren had forgotten about him the second she'd left his pit, but he clearly couldn't say the same about her. His smile was the playful kind that had gotten Ren into bed before, and though half his face was hidden by a mask, he clearly had a handsome one. He'd been simple enough to ruffle. A suggestive line here, a look through the lashes there. Men. They made it too easy.

Ren felt a familiar itch, a desire to release a bit of whatever was swirling around inside her. She slipped from bed, changed quickly, and stepped out into the sitting room. Darek's prone body sprawled across her couch pulled her up short. He'd removed his sling and had a palm resting on his stomach, while his other arm was raised around the back of his head. His legs hung off the end, feet bare, chest rising and falling in a steady rhythm like waves rolling into shore on a cold, clear night. He looked so . . . Ren didn't know what he looked like, but she didn't hate it. Even in sleep, his face was comprised of lines and angles, and a chunk of hair had come free of his knot to brush his cheek. He was so broad, lying there on her tiny couch, and for just a moment Ren considered his chest, how it would feel against hers.

A shudder went over her, and she unstuck herself from the floorboards, dashing across the room and out her door as if fleeing a vengeful ghost.

The basement was as cold and dark as a graveyard under a moonless winter sky. Gooseflesh covered Ren's arms, her breath puffing in the dry air. There were no candles or lamps, no windows to let in a glow from the moon, but Ren didn't need the real starlit sky. She could create one of her own.

Standing in the middle of the room with lifted palms, her silver swirled upward and pooled overhead. The shadows pulled back, the bare basement walls revealing themselves as she moved her fingers and wrists, directing the magic into shape. When she was finished, a replica of the painting on Freya's ceiling floated overhead: the phases of the moon, every constellation and stray star, the faint lines connecting each tiny dot. Her silver bathed the room in a cool, bright glow.

Ren tasked a piece of her mind with ensuring the magic didn't falter and turned the rest of her focus to a sand-filled leather sack chained to the ceiling. Standing before it, she stripped off her top and tossed it aside, then tied back her hair. Once the braid was done, she wrapped long scraps of white fabric around her wrists and knuckles, pulling them tight in the way Aidann had taught her five years ago. She flexed her wrapped hands, thinking of him. *I hope you're happy, you horrible idiot.*

Ren threw her first punch, and a second followed, then a third. It didn't take long to fall into a rhythm, the steady sound of her fists striking leather driving out the noise in her head. The silver scene up above never flickered or faded, but it had taken years to reach this point; while Ren may have been born with magic, controlling it was not like breathing or blinking or self-loathing. She actually had to work at it.

Ren hit the bag wrong, and pain shot up her wrist, a hiss escaping through her teeth. When a voice came at her back, her heart gave a startled jerk. Instinct spurred her into motion, she pivoted, and before she knew what was happening, her fist was swinging at Darek's face. He ducked just in time, and her arm soared over his head.

Breathing hard, skin warm and slick with sweat, Ren braced her hands against her thighs and tried to calm her heart's erratic hammering. She narrowed her eyes at Darek. "Don't sneak up on people like that! What is wrong with you?"

He straightened out of his crouch. "You almost punched me in the face, and you're the one complaining?"

"Maybe your face shouldn't get in the way of my fist."

Ren suddenly remembered that she wasn't wearing anything but a band across her chest and a pair of pants. She whirled around, curving her right shoulder into her body as she scanned the room for her shirt.

"Ren . . ." Darek said.

She ignored whatever comment he wanted to make and located her top at the edge of the room. After she'd tugged her shirt on, she undid her braid and shook out her hair, taking the time to get her bearings. Ren had never cared for propriety. It wasn't about that. It was the scarring across her right shoulder, the reminder of nine years ago. All of Ren's clothing covered her shoulders. No one saw the scars. She didn't even want to look at them herself.

She took in a breath and faced Darek. He was dressed in a simple white tunic that Freya had scrounged up to replace his blood-stained one, his injured arm once again held in place by a piece of fabric acting as a sling. Dark bruises blackened the skin around his nose and beneath his eyes. He was watching her carefully, his messy hair tinted gray in the light of her silver. And, gods, why was she still thinking about his chest?

"Stop it," Ren said.

"Stop what?"

"Looking at me like that."

"How am I looking at you?"

"Like . . . I don't know . . . like you don't completely hate me."

He cracked the smallest hint of a smile, something tentatively amused. "You would prefer if I glowered at you?"

"I'd prefer if you'd stop looking at me altogether."

"What if I can't?"

Ren stilled, her stomach going tight and dipping strangely. Had he really just said that?

Her eyes flitted around the room, first to the sand-filled bag, then up to the stars overhead, and then back to him. They needed a change of subject. "What are you doing down here?" she asked.

"I heard you leave your suite." He shrugged. "Light sleeper."

Her brows rose. "You followed me?"

"Not exactly." Darek rubbed at his shadowed jaw. "I couldn't sleep, so I was wandering around. I was in the kitchen when I heard you down here." He placed a palm on the punching bag. "Where did you learn to fight? I never asked."

"Nowhere." Ren yanked the wraps from her hands, grimacing as she freed the wrist she'd tweaked. It wasn't sprained, just sore.

She hadn't noticed Darek approaching, but suddenly he was there in front of her, close enough to see that beneath the bruising, there was a dark freckle at the edge of his nose. Ren's breath caught in her throat.

"Are you all right?" he asked.

He was so near, the heat of him dancing over her flushed skin, and she worried her body was going to betray her. She worried she'd lean into him, just to see if he'd lean back. She swallowed, unsticking her throat. "I don't know why you care."

"What's that supposed to mean?

"It means you can't stand me, Darek. You've made that clear, so whatever you're doing, just stop."

Emotion flickered across his face, there and gone. "I'm not *doing* anything. I wanted to know if your hand was okay. That's all."

"Don't worry. I can still be part of your revolution with a tender wrist."

"Is that all you think I care about?"

"Isn't it?"

Darek frowned down at her, and she swore his eyes flickered to her lips, as if she weren't the only one thinking about doing things they shouldn't. He turned and stalked toward the middle of the room, a limp to his walk. He stopped by the punching bag, tipping his head back to study her silver. An hour seemed to pass before he spoke. "This is beautiful, Ren."

"I thought my *tricks* didn't impress you," she replied.

"Does this mean you finally regard me as highly as you would a dog?"

He dropped his chin to look over at her. "Only you would find a way to turn a compliment into an insult."

"One of my many charms."

"Why are you so difficult?"

"Probably because you haven't taken my advice to run in front of a carriage."

At that, Derek's glower finally decided to show up. "Have you ever had a civil conversation in your life?"

Ren pretended to think for a moment. "Not that I can recall."

He stared at her with that unreadable expression of his, face shuttered like a window in anticipation of a storm. "Fine. But if you think you can tolerate my presence for a little while longer, we should discuss the Royal Carnival. It's coming up in a few days, and I want you to make an appearance."

"Fine. Upstairs, though. It's freezing down here."

As Ren yanked open the basement door and began to ascend the creaking steps, she released the hold on her magic. The moons and stars lost their shape, her silver swirling in a thin layer, like early morning fog creeping over the Battgandon River, before it disappeared completely.

It was just before sunrise, that time of day that seemed to rest on the other side of stained glass, and the peeling kitchen walls were tinted blue. A long, scarred table sat in the middle of the crowded room, rickety and mismatched chairs jutting out around it. During the day, the kitchen was filled with so much screeching that Ren could hardly hear herself think. Now, silence clung like a wet blanket, flames burning low in a brick fireplace. With the arm that wasn't in a sling, Darek threw two pieces of wood in and stirred the embers until they caught.

Ren held her hands out, warming her reddened fingers. "So what do you want me to do now?" she asked.

Over the past two weeks, Ren and her silver had paid frequent visits to the slums and back alleys of Denfell. It was all going according to Darek's plan. Ever since that first day in the Underground, the illegal marketplace had been awash with whispers about a silver wielder living in the city, someone who posed a threat to the king. Ren never thought she'd see the day that anything but criminals and bad smells came out of the Underground, but some of those whispers were beginning to sound a bit like hope.

Darek straightened up and regarded her carefully. "You're not going to like it."

Ren sighed. "Just tell me."

He ran his free hand over the back of his neck. "We've gained traction, but a lot of people seem to believe that the silver wielder they've been seeing is just Prince Kellen."

"And?" Ren cut him a look from the corner of her eye. His bronze skin glowed in the light of the fire, the edges of his jaw sharp as a butcher's knife.

"We need to dispel that rumor."

Dropping her hands to her side, Ren tipped her head back and groaned. "You want people to know I'm a girl."

"Yes. I know you can't show your face yet. Keep

wearing the mask, but we need to make it obvious that you're not the prince."

She glared at the fire flicking in front of her and said nothing.

"You know I'm right," Darek added.

Of course he was right. Ren hated his plan, but that didn't mean it was a bad one. "I have half a mind to ask you for more money."

"We are giving you plenty of money."

She grumbled a rude comment under her breath. "Where do you want me this time? The Terth? Here in Hessler?"

Darek shifted his weight. "That's the other thing."

"Oh gods. What *other thing*?"

"I want you to move aboveground. I'm thinking the docks south of the river would be a good place to start. They're far enough out of the way that there's less risk of attracting the wrong attention, but busy enough to spark more rumors."

Slowly, Ren faced him. He stared down at her, and there it was again, that same expression he'd had in the basement. She couldn't put her finger on it, but his eyes were softer somehow, and it did strange things to her stomach. "Darek, no. I can't."

"Please, Ren," he said. "I know it's a huge risk, but we'll do it on the first day of the carnival. With the events going on around the city, the king and his men won't be paying attention to the docks."

"If I didn't know any better, I'd think you were trying to get me killed."

"I wish there were another way, but right now the only people who know about you are people who visit places like the Underground. It's not enough." She didn't speak, and he drew nearer. "We need you, Ren. We're so close."

"Showing my silver in the slums was bad enough. This is so much worse."

"I'll be there the whole time. Nothing will happen to you."

Like his eyes, his voice was softer, too, at odds with the man she had come to know over the past two weeks. She wasn't sure what to make of it. She preferred Darek rude and harsh. At least then it was easier to hate him.

Ren stepped away from the fire. "I don't care about your promises. Especially ones you can't keep."

The kitchen window had a view of the building next door: a gray, empty shell with boarded-up windows and a crumbling brick facade. Staring at it, she reminded herself just how rich she would be when this was over. Maybe *she* would buy a home in Lan Covve—as long as it was far away from Darek's.

She rotated around and looked him over, flames dancing at his back. Her mouth ticked down, and she thought, *I must be out of my damn mind.*

"Fine," she said.

"You'll do it?"

"I just said I would, didn't I?"

His chest deflated, shoulders relaxing as if he'd been holding his breath. "Thank you."

"Just so you know, if I die, your stupid mansion is the first place I'm haunting."

She left the kitchen, and Darek trailed her to a staircase that groaned under their weight. When they came to the second floor, a little girl with a head of dull copper curls appeared from a nearby door, inching out into the hall and shutting it behind her. Ren stopped. The girl hovered silently in front of her.

"What is it, Isa?" Ren asked.

"I . . ." Her eyes darted to Darek.

"Ignore him. Heavens know I wish I could."

"I . . . Ren . . ." The girl's chin trembled. Tears crested, rolling down blotchy cheeks. Isa's mumbling was wet and incoherent.

Ren cast her eyes toward the ceiling. "I can't under-stand you if you're crying."

"I don't . . . I don't have—" And then she was incom-prehensible once more.

"Isa," Ren snapped. "Stop. Crying."

The girl swallowed. She wiped her wet cheeks and looked up at Ren, her eyes much larger than was fair. "I don't have any money," Isa said, lip wobbling again.

So that was what this was about. Although Freya owned the place, she was too kindhearted to do what needed to be done. The kids knew Ren was the one who enforced the boarding fees, and if they didn't pay up, they'd be on the street. Ren had cast kids out before, and she hadn't been quiet about it. They weren't running a charity.

But Isa was so young—not even nine—and she'd been living at the Compound since Freya had bought it. She was one of the last orphans Aidann had taken in.

"You don't have any money?" Ren repeated, and Isa shook her head. "None at all?"

The girl was close to tears again. "I have a few copper coins, but—"

Ren raised a hand. "Isa, I'm going to give you another week to find the silver. All right?"

"Really?"

"Yes, but only one week. If you don't have it by then, you'll have to go."

Isa bobbed her head, her limp curls bouncing. "I promise I'll get it." She slipped past Ren, gave Darek a wide berth, and rushed down the stairs.

"And Isa?" Ren called after her. "The Royal Carnival is next week. See what those fingers might find in the crowds."

She and Darek continued up to the third floor. While they walked down the short hallway that led to her suite, Ren glanced over and caught him watching her again. She stopped in front of her door, turning to face him. He was just a handbreadth away, and it made her wonder, what would she do if he pushed her up against the door and brought his mouth down on hers? All it would take was one step.

Ignoring the way her pulse fluttered in her neck, she said, "I thought I told you to stop looking at me like that."

"That was decent of you," was his response.

It wasn't what Ren had been expecting him to say. She'd threatened to throw a little girl out onto the street in the middle of winter. She would do it, too, if Isa didn't get the money. Ren had some words for what that was. *Decent* was not one of them. But she supposed it could have been worse. She could have given Isa no time at all. Maybe decency was relative.

"Don't get used to it," Ren said. She opened her door and strode inside. "And quit looking at me like that."

CHAPTER
TWENTY-FIVE

Lesa burst into Adley's room at an ungodly hour, even for the King's Children, her voice startling Adley awake. She yanked the covers back, mumbling under her breath. "That mother . . . son of a . . . going to throw him in the Iron Sea. Wake *up*, Adley!"

"What, Lesa—gods, what time is it?" Adley sputtered, her eyes bleary.

"Too early for this shit. Ethen killed one of your prisoners."

Adley snapped to clarity, springing out of bed and fumbling for something to pull on over her nightdress. "What happened?" she asked, groping for her black overcoat. She tugged it on and yanked her hair out of the collar.

"I don't know," Lesa said. "Rakel told Tarrus, who told me. The rebel is still in the dungeon."

After Adley shoved her feet into her boots, the two of them rushed out of her room and down the darkened hall, taking the stairs two at a time on their descent to the dungeons. The guard stationed outside the door pulled it open, and Adley pushed through, her feet thudding against the dank stone steps, Lesa on her heels. They entered the dim corridor of cells, dozens of iron bars and a dirty stone floor, the stink of rot and death swarming the air like an infestation. Adley's eyes scanned the prisoners as she paced the row until she spotted the young barmaiden from the White Raven, her coppery hair streaked with grime. She'd been dumped unceremoniously in her cell, her body mangled in such a way that Adley didn't want to examine it too closely. Her wounds were still raw. The salty tang of fresh blood tickled Adley's nose.

"I'm going to kill him," she said.

She turned on her heel and barreled past Lesa. The trip back to her room was a blur. One minute Adley was in the dungeons, and the next she was pulling her bow off the wall and grabbing an arrow. She stomped down the hall, shoved open Ethen's door, strung her bow, and let her arrow fly.

She missed on purpose. He was sitting in bed, sharpening a knife in the light of a burning lamp, and her arrow slammed into his wooden headboard, an inch between it and the side of his head. He jerked in alarm and shot up from the mattress, knuckles going white around his dagger.

"*What the fuck?!*" he shouted. There was murder in his expression as he stood barefoot on the cold stone floor, wearing his black uniform pants and a wool sweater. Dark-blond hair obscured one eye, and the sheets were a rumpled mess behind him.

At some point, Lesa had shown up with more arrows in hand, and Adley took one. "You killed one of my prisoners, you lunatic. You're lucky I didn't put that arrow in your neck."

"What does it matter?" Ethen asked, his stare flickering to the tip of her arrow.

She saw the calculation there, knew he was weighing his next move. Could he throw his knife before she fired off another shot? Unlikely. He was good with a blade, but Adley reckoned she was better with her bow.

"You weren't getting anything out of her anyway."

"She was *my prisoner*. She wasn't yours to interrogate. Why don't you go torture your own rebels? Oh, that's right, you don't have any!"

Adley was livid. She thought her anger might catch the night on fire. Ethen had *no right*. He wouldn't take this from her. She wasn't going to let him steal her one chance at freedom, at happiness, at righting all the wrong she'd done.

A few doors popped open along the corridor, and more Children entered the hall, wearing nightclothes and mussed hair.

"What do you think you're doing?" demanded Lyle Mcillen, a boy a couple years younger than Adley and one of Ethen's lackeys. With large muscles to compensate for the size of his brain, he worshipped Ethen like a god and not the persistent thorn in Adley's side.

"Shut it, Mcillen," Lesa snapped. Her withdrawn blade winked in the faint light, and Lyle froze in the middle of the corridor.

"What are you going to do, Adley? Shoot me?" Ethen asked.

"Don't think I haven't considered it."

Adopting a cocky tilt to his chin, Ethen took a step forward, and if he thought Adley missed the way he angled his blade toward her, he was mistaken. Her grip tightened on her bow.

"You don't have the guts. It's why you'll never be Fang."

Adley narrowed her eyes. That was the problem with Ethen and all the men like him. He thought because she was quiet, because she liked books and the way flowers blossomed on the hills in spring, because she was a *girl*, he could dismiss her as frivolous and unimportant. Weak. He was wrong.

Before Ethen could take his next breath, Adley released her arrow. It cut through fabric to slice the side of his thigh, and his leg buckled, a hand going behind him to catch on the bed before he dropped to the floor. A string of obscenities spilled from his mouth, profane enough that he'd surely need a confessional tomorrow.

"Stop being so dramatic. I barely grazed you." Adley could have killed him. She was ready to raise at least a few of the hells. But unfortunately, King's Children were allowed to kill everyone but each other. Something about *wasting valuable assets*. So Adley would have to settle on making Ethen squirm. She took another arrow from Lesa and loaded her bow. "What did the rebel tell you?"

Ethen only glared at her, his breathing heavy.

Adley lifted her bow and settled it on him. "Whatever you learned, it's my information. I want it."

He threw his blade. She pivoted, but it caught her shoulder, ripping her coat and the cotton nightdress underneath, the metal eating into skin. She hissed through her teeth as a hot shot of pain coursed down her back. The knife dropped to the stones with a clatter, breaking the silence in the corridor. King's Children erupted into a garble of shouts, Lyle charged, Lesa punched him in the nose, someone laughed manically. Noise echoed off the walls and rolled down the stairs, every door gaping wide, candlelight spilling out of rooms to throw shadows across the walls.

Gritting her teeth, Adley dropped her bow, palmed her arrow, and stormed into Ethen's room to grab him by the front of his sweater. He may have wounded her, but he'd also sacrificed his only weapon. Big mistake. She slammed him into the wall, hating the conceited smile that remained on his face even as he winced in pain. It only disappeared when she put her arrow to the inside of his thigh.

"You wouldn't dare," Ethen said, but his face had gone very, very white.

"Haven't you tested me enough for one night?" Adley said quietly, so only he could hear.

He swallowed, his neck bobbing.

She increased pressure on her arrow. "What," she said slowly, "did you learn?"

Holding Ethen's gaze the entire time, she inched the

arrowhead upward, pressing harder against the major artery inside his leg until he cracked. "Fine," he snarled. "The girl didn't tell us anything. It was that Sirican man. He kept begging us to spare her. He gave up a rebel safe house: Rosewater Inn." There was that smile again, inching back in place like a skin disease that wouldn't go away. "We thanked him for his confession by killing the girl."

Smug bastard. He just couldn't help himself, could he? Even with her hand at his throat and an arrow at his most vulnerable point, he had to throw it in her face. She could see it in his eyes, staring down at her: *I win.*

Adley's grip tightened on her arrow. Maybe she should kill him and deal with the consequences later. She'd never enjoyed inflicting pain, enjoyed carrying that pain to a final, irreversible end even less. Every time she did it, she wished she could take it back. But she suspected there would be something perversely satisfying about shoving her arrow into Ethen's artery. She could do it. It wouldn't take much pressure at all.

"What is the meaning of this?" demanded the voice of the crown prince. It was only then that Adley realized the corridor outside had gone still.

She immediately released Ethen and stepped back, turning to the open doorway. Heath Lyandor stood there in a set of rumpled clothes, looking less than his usual pristine self. The ties on his cotton shirt were hanging open, his golden hair flattened from sleep, circles beginning to darken the skin beneath his eyes. Jaw clenched tight, his stare was hard as it darted between Adley and

Ethen. The lamplight flickered in his blue eyes, shadows slithering across his face. No one spoke, waiting to see what the crown prince would do next.

When his attention finally settled wholly on Adley, she tried not to recoil. There was something dark and dangerous and *wrong* in Heath. He was so cold and calculating, careful never to betray his true emotions, but beneath the surface sat something a little bit deranged. She wondered if she was the only one who saw it.

"Farre, come here," he said calmly.

Holding her breath, Adley stepped forward, the cut on her shoulder throbbing. He held up his palm, and she laid her arrow in his waiting hand, instructing herself not to shake.

"Do you find the bow and arrow to be an effective weapon?" he inquired, examining the tip.

"Yes, Your Highness."

He gave a hum of approval, rolling the black wood between long, elegant fingers. He placed the arrow to her throat, the cold metal kissing her skin like a deadly snake poised to bite. A hundred thoughts flooded her mind at once: *Don't flinch, keep breathing, hide the fear, don't grab the arrow, don't shove it through his throat instead. You could, but don't.*

He stared into her eyes and pressed down on the arrowhead. There was a sharp sting of pain, and then warm blood dripped down her neck as he dragged the tip across her throat. It was a shallow cut, superficial. She'd heal so long as he didn't dig deeper. After a few painful seconds, he paused, but he didn't remove the arrow from her skin, as if considering how much further to go, if he shouldn't stop at a small cut.

Don't flinch, don't flinch, don't flinch.

She only started breathing again once he pulled back, lowering the arrow to his side. "Let this be your one warning. Do not attempt to harm another King's Child again. Have I made myself clear?"

"Yes, Your Highness."

"Good. Now leave. I have some business to discuss with Delano." Adley squeezed past him into the hall, and he tossed an icy-blue glance over his shoulder at the King's Children still gathered outside their rooms. "That goes for all of you. If I hear from any of you before morning, you'll be using one another for target practice tomorrow." Feet shuffled across the stone floor, doors creaking and groaning as they were pulled shut. Before Lesa could get to her room, Heath called, "Except for you, Lesa! Wait for me out here."

The crown prince stepped into Ethen's room and shut the door, Lesa glaring after him. Adley grabbed her hand and squeezed, soft and quick. "I think I'll go for a walk. I can't sleep after that."

Lesa assessed her neck, her shoulder, all the blood. Her brow crinkled in worry. "You should be going to the infirmary."

"I've had worse."

"I know. I still don't like seeing you hurt."

Her concern made Adley's chest ache. What the two

of them had, no matter how dangerous, was the best thing in her miserable life. It made up for the bad, Lesa's violent streak and the knives she didn't mind getting bloody. Those things didn't matter so much when she looked at Adley the way she did, when she cared, more than anyone ever had or would. The words almost slipped from Adley's lips then, like a reflex. Three words that neither of them could ever say, not while they belonged to the throne. Adley knew that, but her heart was heavy with the unsung confession.

"Let's go to Rosewater Inn first thing in the morning?" Adley asked instead.

Lesa nodded. Adley wanted to lean in and kiss her, smooth her brow and twist her fingers in Lesa's blonde hair. But Heath was too close, and her heart was too fragile, so she did what she had to and turned away from Lesa, leaving her alone in the hall.

Adley usually ended up in the library when she couldn't sleep, with its high ceilings and arched windows made of stained glass that glimmered like promises in the sunlight. It was quiet and serene in there, especially when the sun faded and the rest of the castle went to bed. It smelled of oak and parchment paper and nonthreatening things. Adley felt at peace in the library. She felt . . . not like her true self, but maybe something close to it.

But tonight, she didn't make it to the library. As she rounded the bottom of a staircase onto the second floor, she ran straight into the youngest Prince of Erdis.

Kellen grunted and stumbled back, his hand flying out of his pocket, a piece of black silk with it. The fabric

fluttered to the floor, two holes cut into the middle—was
that a mask? He snatched it up, shoving it back into his
long, black coat, the buttons open to show off an ivory-
and-gold vest.

Adley eyed his pocket. She still had no idea where the
prince made off to every night, why he always came home
at an hour belonging to the god of mischief, and how in
the hells he managed to escape the castle undetected. And
what did he need a mask for? It drove Adley a little mad,
not being able to figure him out. Kellen was supposed to
be a wastrel and a drunk, but if that were true, he was an
extremely coherent one.

"Adley!" he said a little too loudly, running a hand
through his blond hair. He smiled, a genuine, bright smile,
so different from his brother. But then he took in the cuts
and the blood, her mess of waving hair, the coat tossed
over a nightdress, and his expression faded. "What happened to you?"

"It's nothing."

"You're injured."

"I'm fine." She attempted to step past him, but he
moved into her path.

"Can I look?" he asked, gesturing at the bloody rip
on her shoulder.

"Are you a healer now?"

"Not yet, but maybe one day." He cocked a grin. "I've
been told I'm good with my hands."

She sighed. "You're not going to let me by until you
assess my injuries, are you?"

His lips lifted higher. "No. Now sit."

He directed her back toward the staircase, and she took a seat on the second step from the bottom, grimacing as she pulled off one sleeve and peeled the torn nightdress from her sticky skin. She rolled it down her shoulder, aching so much she could hardly stand it. Leaning her head against the pale stone railing, she closed her eyes and took a full breath.

Kellen whistled low. "Looks like it hurts."

Adley huffed a laugh and peeled her eyes open. He was crouched beside her, concern in his blue eyes. "Is that your professional medical opinion?"

"My professional medical opinion is that you should see a medical professional," Kellen replied as he took a seat next to her on the stairs.

"Were you visiting your friend? The baker's daughter?" Adley asked him. Was that what the mask was about, some strange sex thing?

"I . . . ah." He fidgeted, ran his fingers through his hair again, the curling strands shining in the light from the low-burning sconces. "No, I haven't seen her in a few days. I . . . I did something stupid." He tugged at his sleeves. "I'm not sure she'll forgive me, and she would be well within her rights not to."

Adley didn't ask him what he'd done, and he didn't share. She wondered how Kellen had turned out the way he did, warm when his brother was not, kind when he had no reason to be. Was he really out every night, drinking himself into a stupor, visiting brothels, and gambling away the crown's money? Sitting here on the stairs with the prince, Adley doubted it. He didn't smell of liquor, he didn't leer, he wasn't crude. She thought this was closer to who Kellen really was, the Kellen he could be when no one was looking.

Neither of them spoke for a while, and it was nice, just to have some company in the silence. It was a comfort Adley hadn't realized she'd needed. "I got into it with one of the other King's Children," she confessed. "Ethen Delano."

Kellen shuddered. "That guy gives me the creeps."

Adley smiled softly in response.

Kellen watched her for a while, his blue eyes a little too keen, like they saw more than they should have.

"What?" she asked.

"Do you really want to be King's Fang? I heard about my father's competition, and I know you've been looking for the rebel leader."

That was when Adley should have gotten up and left. She'd already revealed too much. Kellen was unearthing parts of her she needed to keep hidden. But instead, she closed her eyes once again and inhaled deeply. Her shoulder hurt, and her neck hurt, and her heart hurt, and they would keep on hurting until she escaped this place. She didn't see another way. She had to become Fang.

"I'm so tired." The words spilled out of her mouth like a sin that needed confessing.

Kellen was quiet. "Of what?" he eventually asked.

Adley took one more breath, and then she opened her

eyes and pushed up from the stairs, wincing as she tugged up her nightdress and coat. "I should go."

He quickly stood, too, looking almost disappointed to see her leave. "Please tell me you'll visit the infirmary so that I might sleep soundly tonight. It takes quite a lot of beauty rest to look this good, I'll have you know."

Her laugh was short and soft. "Good night, Prince Kellen."

"Good night, Adley."

Adley turned and began to make her way down the arched hall, the walls low-lit and covered in shadows.

"Oh, and Adley!" Kellen called after her.

She looked back over her shoulder.

"Please call me Kellen."

She tipped him a weary smile and continued through the castle. It was a shame Kellen wasn't set to inherit the throne. This country would be a better place with him as king. Maybe if more kings were a little more like Kellen and a little less like his father, there wouldn't be a need for King's Children at all.

But it was just a wish, a fruitless dream. There would always be King's Children, but she didn't always have to be one. She'd find the rebel leader. She'd hand them over to the king. Whatever it took, she would do it.

CHAPTER
TWENTY-SIX

E arly on the first day of the Royal Carnival, hours before the sun had graced the sky, Darek was awake and standing outside Ren's bedroom door. He knocked, but no response came.

"Ren?" he called. There was a faint rustling, like she was getting up, but another half a minute went by, and the door remained firmly closed. He set a hand on the doorknob and hesitated. Entering Ren's room without her permission wasn't the very last thing he wanted to do, but it was close. He didn't relish the idea of getting punched in the face under any circumstances, but especially not now that his nose was starting to show signs of healing and he was able to move about without a sling around his shoulder. However, Darek really needed to be somewhere, and the Compound doors were locked.

When he pushed in her plain wooden door, he repeated Ren's name, but still she didn't wake. By the faint light filtering in through a partially curtained window, Darek saw that she was lying in the middle of her bed, tangled plum-colored sheets twisted around her long legs, which were bare beneath an oversized shirt. Old and new bruises dotted her skin, splotches of blue and green and purple that reminded Darek of one of Markus's paintings. A pile of blankets was on the floor, as if she'd kicked them off in her sleep.

She looked so vulnerable. Darek remembered three nights ago and the way she had hunched in on herself when she'd realized her scars were visible, how she'd tried to conceal them. But Darek had seen. The scarring was about as large as the expanse of his hand, covering the top of her right shoulder, licking at the base of her neck and collarbone. When she'd been burned, the pain must have been excruciating. Ren was lucky she hadn't died from infection.

Slowly, Darek was figuring her out, and he didn't know how to show her that she didn't need to blame herself for the things that had happened in her past. It wasn't even his job to show her. He may have stopped hating her— however that had happened—but he absolutely did not *like* her. If he sometimes thought about her legs wrapped around his hips, it was only because she looked so good in that damned corset and he was only human. It didn't mean anything.

But he did wish she wouldn't hide the scars. He wished she weren't ashamed of them.

Ren's chest was rising and falling rapidly, a sheen of sweat visible on her knit brow. She made a noise that was half gasp, half cry, and jerked her head to the side. Her hair shifted away from her forehead, exposing a red line at her temple, her souvenir from the White Raven. She'd been able to remove her stitches just two days after Freya had put them in, and now, a day later, the cut looked like an angry scratch.

"Ren," Darek said. He approached her bed, which was nothing more than a mattress elevated on wooden crates, the wall serving as a headboard. A lamp sat atop her bedside table, and next to it, the book she'd stolen—excuse him, *borrowed*—from his library. He wondered if she'd started it yet.

Ren's breath hitched, her legs kicked, tugging the knotted sheets tighter. Darek placed the back of his fingers to her cheek and found her skin clammy. "Wake up," he said softly. "Ren, wake up. You're having a nightmare."

She jolted upright with a gasp, her fingers clenching the dark sheets. Air hitched in and out of her lungs as her bleary green eyes found his. "Darek?" She sounded confused and uncertain and not at all like the girl he knew. "The crown prince—he was . . . he was in my head."

"You're okay," he soothed. "It was only a dream."

She ran a hand over her face and through her hair, pushing the strands away from her sweat-soaked forehead. Her unkempt hair, her bare legs, her bed—it all stirred something in Darek's chest that he refused to examine.

Once her breathing had settled, she kicked free of the tangled sheets and sagged back against the wall. "I know it was only a dream. I'm not five."

There she is, he thought, nearly smiling. He realized he didn't much mind her sharp tongue anymore. In fact, sometimes he kind of liked it. It was a bit unsettling, just like the other night when he'd confessed that he couldn't stop looking at her. *What if I can't?* The words had slipped out entirely of their own volition. He didn't know where they'd come from or why he'd said them, but they were out there, and he couldn't take them back. Besides, he'd been a little curious how she'd react, what she would say, if she thought about him when he wasn't around. Maybe he didn't want to take them back.

Ren twisted her mess of hair over one shoulder. "What are you doing in my bedroom? Watching me sleep?"

"I need you to let me out. I have an errand to run."

With a questioning frown, she stretched across the mattresses and plucked a watch from her side table to check the time. "Who runs errands at three-thirty in the morning?"

"Clearly, I do."

"Where are you going?"

"I have to talk to a man about some tea."

Ren gave him a flat look, like she thought he was trying to play her for a fool and doing a poor job of it. "You have to talk to a man about tea. In the middle of the night."

"That's right."

She eyed him for the length of three seconds, then shrugged. "Far be it from me to keep a man from his tea." Stretching over, she rattled open the side table drawer, pulled out a heavy brass key, and tossed it to him.

Darek caught it. "You're giving me the key?"

"Well, I'm certainly not getting out of bed and walking down two flights of stairs for your sorry ass. It's freezing, and I want to go back to sleep. Just hold on to it." She retrieved her blankets from the floor and pulled them over her legs. "And if you don't lock the doors behind you, I'm leaving you outside tomorrow night and praying you get frostbite."

Darek curled his fingers around the cool brass. It was a meaningful gesture, even if it hadn't been her intention, that she trusted him enough to hand over a key to the building. As far as he knew, only she and Freya had them. "I didn't think you believed in prayer."

"I don't. But for you, I'll make an exception."

Darek raised a hand to his lips and rubbed away what might have been a grin. He started toward the door, but paused. "How are you feeling?" he asked. "About tonight, I mean?"

Ren tugged her blankets up to her chest. "You mean how am I feeling about heading to the docks and risking my life for your moronic rebellion? You know, not great."

"Ren—"

"I'm ready, Darek. I might not be looking forward to it, but I'll be there."

He stared at her for another moment, then dipped his chin and departed the room.

Outside, after he'd double-checked that the doors were indeed locked, as he was making his way down the skinny, crooked street, Darek glanced back at the Hessler Compound. A third-story window was glowing yellow. Its occupant had recently lit a lamp.

Darek sat on the steps of an empty stoop, reading. Curved forward with elbows braced on his knees, his gloved fingers flipped the page. It had begun snowing on his walk across the city, and the sleeves of his black coat, which Holland had delivered to the Compound the day after the raid, were sprinkled with white. The street was empty at four in the morning, but it wouldn't be for long, not here in the Garley District. A block away was Garley's main plaza, where early each morning, merchants opened their stalls for business. Beneath bright swatches of fabric strung up on rope, they sold grains, produce, spices, meats, and countless other goods to everyone from dock workers to castle staff.

Boots thudded down the street. Darek glanced up, caught sight of the tea merchant, and rose to his feet, stowing his book in his jacket pocket. As the two embraced hands, Darek nodded to a thin alley beside the building. Once they were deep enough into the alleyway that Darek was sure they wouldn't be overheard, he undid the top three buttons of his wool overcoat and slipped a hand inside, withdrawing a purse of gold. He gave it to the man.

The merchant counted the coins, then cinched the purse strings closed and stowed the gold in his own far shabbier pocket. "All right," he said. "Give it to me."

Darek produced a small glass jar filled with crushed hycanthian flowers and handed them over. The man peered at the dried pale-blue leaves. "This poison?"

"No."

"Because the princes have food testers. If they think I did something to their tea, it'll be my head."

"They're not poisonous, and they won't affect the testers. I just need you to make sure they're mixed in with Heath and Kellen's tea blends."

"I'll do what I can, but like I told you: once the castle maids purchase the tea, it's out of my hands. I can't guarantee they'll drink it. You'd need someone in the castle for that."

Darek needed someone in the castle for so many reasons he'd lost track of them all. But it had proven impossible to place a spy inside. He was done wasting lives. "Let me worry about that," he said, knowing worry was all he could do. Unless he thought of something better, he would have to pray the princes drank the flower-seeped tea and that they consumed enough of it. "You think the maids will purchase the tea today?"

"If not today, soon. They haven't been to my stall in a couple weeks."

"I'll stop by the market next week to check."

The tea merchant nodded and tucked the jar away. "Carnival's tidings," he said with a tip of his chin.

After the man left, Darek waited five minutes before emerging from the gap between the buildings. The Garley marketplace was east, so he went west.

Denfell was still asleep. Streetlamps cast a hazy glow while snow gradually coated the city, ensuring everyone would be bundled tight for the carnival's opening day. Darek remembered the last time he'd attended the event with his mother. He'd been twelve, and it had snowed then, too. It was one of the last solid memories he had of her, so while he knew he should have hated the spectacle and everything it stood for, he couldn't find it in himself. The Royal Carnival always reminded him of Alyah Hollistair.

Lost in thought, Darek was walking along the Battgandon River when he heard a burst of commotion. His head snapped up. Outside a bed and breakfast down the road, a half dozen members of the Royal Guard were corralling a group of people dressed in nightclothes, as if the whole inn had been roused from sleep. Darek forced himself steadily forward, allowing a cursory glance at the crowd—just a curious Denfell citizen out for an early morning stroll.

A blonde-haired girl pounded out of the building, followed closely by another girl with Sirican features and a thick braid trailing over one shoulder. They wore black double-breasted trench coats buttoned to their chins, lion heads stitched on the chests. King's Children.

The blonde one latched on to the robe of an older man and yanked him close. When she spoke, the warning in her voice was thick with the promise of violence. "If there are any hidden rooms you haven't told us about, now would be the time."

The man tried to respond, but all that came out was unintelligible stammering.

"Speak. Clearly."

"N-n-no," the innkeeper managed. "Th-there are no rebels here, I-I swear it."

She glanced over her shoulder at the other King's Child, her brows raised in silent question.

"Let him go," the Sirican girl said indifferently. "We tore the place apart. It's another false lead."

The blonde returned her stare to the innkeeper, her fingers drifting toward her thigh. She shoved him away, and as he stumbled back into the small crowd, she and the other girl detached themselves from the royal guards. They bent their heads together, speaking too quietly for Darek to overhear.

The walkway by the river was narrow, and he had to push his way through the terrified group as he passed the inn, but he wasn't stopped. No one suspected he was the person these girls were searching for. He hoped it would stay that way for a while yet.

He was twenty feet away when a voice called out to him. "You there!"

Darek froze. It was an effort to force himself to turn back, and when he did, he found the King's Child with the braided hair walking after him. He stopped breathing, his heart pounding against his ribcage like a toll-bell gone rogue. Her trench coat swayed around her heavy boots.

She stopped and held out a book. "You dropped this. Fell from your pocket back there."

Biting back his relief, Darek took it. "Thank you."

She smiled, a slight, little thing that was barely a smile at all. "I hope you're enjoying it. The story is one of my favorites."

He blinked in surprise. "I . . . Yes, mine, too."

There was that hint of a smile again, then she dipped her chin and began to turn away.

"Are you going to hurt them?" Darek couldn't stop from asking.

She looked back at him, and a flash of something so sad passed over her face, Darek almost believed her when she said, "Not if I don't have to."

As she returned to the crowd huddled outside the inn, he studied the book in his gloved hand. He'd never have thought a King's Child would enjoy literature, let alone something so sentimental and romantic. Soldiers like her belonged in battlefields and torture chambers, not libraries.

He took a moment to watch the girl stroke her horse's neck before shoving the book into his coat and continuing along the river's edge. While he walked, he willed a sense of calm and forced himself to think. The rebellion had safeguards in place for if they were caught. The inn was one of a couple dozen venues around Denfell they'd agreed to name in place of true information. Since last week's attack on the White Raven, at least ten similar locations had been raided—the defunct candle factory with broken windows looming along a mostly abandoned Hiatt Street, a warehouse not far from the Royal Opera House where props were stored. Just over half were left, and Darek knew what that meant: Riko wasn't going to last much longer.

His friend was breaking.

"We need to go tonight, while the Royal Carnival is happening," Darek said, standing before an empty fireplace in his drawing room. Outside the windows, the quiet neighborhood was soaked in an early morning gray tinge, the sky a shapeless mass of clouds.

"I agree that we can't let Riko rot in there, but we don't even have a plan," Jaston protested. "Don't you think we should wait? We could try and get someone in the castle."

"That'll take too long," Darek said. "It's the first night of the carnival. The castle will be deserted. We won't get another chance like this. And I do have a plan."

"'I'll figure it out' is not a plan. Riko is my friend, too, but Darek—"

"This isn't just about our friend. It's about all of us. Riko knows too much. He's given up half our false locations, and soon, he won't have any choice but to start giving up real information. We have to get him out of the castle now."

Darek wanted to believe that Riko would never turn them over, but it was easy to think that from a spacious living room in Denfell's wealthiest district. His friend was stuck in the castle dungeons. He was being interrogated by the king's most brutal weapons. Darek hoped Riko would keep quiet, but he wouldn't level blame if he didn't.

"I want you in a prison guard uniform," he told Jaston. "You're coming with me."

With stolen uniforms stockpiled, they could pose as anything in the city, from hospital healers to members of the Royal Navy. But they'd never tried to infiltrate the castle before, not like this. They'd never attempted to get anyone out.

Darek pushed the thought away. "You have until dusk to fabricate the papers. I want us listed as prison guards with orders to transfer a man fitting Riko's description from the castle dungeons to the city prison."

Darek didn't know what he would have done without Jaston, whose skill at faking any number of documents saved them both headaches and execution sentences. He'd even managed to get his hands on the royal seal. Not a fake or a copy, but the real thing: a heavy bronze stamp with a lion's head carved into the surface. When Darek had visited Lan Covve two weeks ago for his business meeting with the Queen of Erdis, her guards had hardly looked twice at his forged papers.

"What about the others?" Jaston asked.

"It'll be too suspicious if we try to empty the dungeon. Riko is the priority. I'll track down a prison wagon and meet you outside Bell's Bonnets at six," Darek said, naming a recently shuttered hatter's shop a couple blocks from the road that led up to the castle.

"I'm coming, too," Markus said.

Darek hadn't explicitly invited his brother to take part in this conversation, but he'd wandered into the room when Jaston showed up, and Darek knew how well it would go over if he tried to make Markus leave. "No," he said.

"Please, Darek. I want to help."

"I don't care what you want. It's too dangerous."

Markus's mouth pressed into a stubborn line.

"Everything we do is dangerous. I'm not a little kid anymore. Let me help. Please." His eyes drifted to a painting on the wall. It was one he'd done himself, an image of a couple embracing atop a bridge spanning the river, the twilit sky above them a smudge of purple and orange. He'd made it for their mother. "I can't do nothing."

Everything inside Darek wanted to refuse and then lock Markus in his room for good measure. He heard his last words to his mother; they pulsed in his head like a heartbeat. *I promise, I promise, I promise.* She'd asked him to take care of Markus, and it was a vow he couldn't possibly break. If he did, he would never forgive himself. He didn't think he would be able to live with himself at all. Since that night in the tunnels, whenever he looked at Ren, he saw what it was like to carry around that kind of guilt. Sometimes, it was as if he could feel her pain, like it was too large for her to shoulder alone. He didn't know why, gods help him, but there were times when he wanted to help her bear the weight.

But Ren might have been stronger than he could hope to be. She had gone on living after the fire, in her own screwed-up way. If Markus died, Darek didn't think he could take the pain. But he knew what it was like—heavens, he knew so well—to want to continue on because their mother couldn't, because the king had put her in the ground nine years ago.

"Fine," Darek relented. "You can come. Jas, get papers for Markus."

Jaston bobbed his head and left the house, Markus

and Darek watching him go. If it had been any other day, this plan would have been nothing short of suicide. It still might be. But Darek was counting on the Royal Carnival. He knew the Royal Guard was working on a skeleton crew, while the royal family and every visiting courtier would be at the carnival for hours. Most of the King's Children had the night off. Tonight should go smoothly. In and out. Easy.

"You think this'll work?" Markus asked.

We're about to find out, Darek thought. "Yes," he said.

CHAPTER
TWENTY-SEVEN

On the afternoon of the first day of the Royal Carnival, Denfell was filled with far too much cheer. Despite the cold front that had moved in, groups walked arm in arm toward the festivities, greeting one another as if every person in the city was a dear friend. Shop carts lined the streets, steaming cups of tea and cider passing from one gloved hand to another. When Ren walked by a flower stand, a woman offered a sprig of holly for her hair. Ren narrowed her eyes at the bright-red berries.

The energy was infectious, like the plague, and she refused to fall victim to it. Even the Atterton District, with its unreasonably bright buildings and litter-free streets, was less subdued than usual. As Ren arrived at the gate outside the Hollistair's blue mansion, the neighborhood's residents were all headed in one direction or another. Wrapped in expensive coats and scarves, some were returning from a morning of shopping, while others made their way to a performance by the Orian Circus. Very few people were in sour enough moods to give Ren the distrustful glances she usually received on this side of the river.

It was a little disappointing. She was getting kind of

tired of glaring at Darek, and his neighbors made for a nice change of pace.

Passing through the gate, she bounded up his front walk and took the porch steps two at a time. His front door was unlocked, so Ren stepped into the tall foyer, swinging the door shut behind her and letting the bang announce her presence. The mansion was quiet, muted-gray light filtering in through the windows. It had only been a few days since the raid on the White Raven, and Darek and his brother were still staying at the Compound. Their home was cold and dim, as if no hearths or lamps had been lit for a while.

Holland and her head of styled red hair appeared in a doorway to the right. Her pale-pink dress shimmered like gossamer, with layers of draped silk, chiffon, and intricate beading. It was completely impractical, and Ren doubted Holland's ability to do much more than walk in the thing, but she had to admit, the gown was gorgeous. Ren could easily have gotten one hundred gold pieces for it at the Underground.

Holland's heels clacked on the marble floor as she glided over to Ren. "Thank the gods you're here," she said, latching on to Ren's arm. Holland towed her into a drawing room that was as large as the rest of the house, with couches and chairs covered in white fabric, thick curtains to match, and mahogany shelves. A painting of a smudged couple on a bridge hung above the hearth. The fact that the décor was tasteful and elegant irritated Ren more than it probably should have.

Darek was on the opposite side of the room, as far away as he could be without opening a window and jumping out. With his arms shoved over his chest, his ever-present glower was in full force, but today it seemed to be directed at Holland, rather than Ren. His hair was pulled back from his face, and while his nose looked better than it had two days ago, the bruising was still obvious, the skin beneath his eyes a swirl of purple.

"You requested my presence?" Ren asked him. She trailed a hand over the back of a couch, her eyes tracking the space like she planned to rob it. Earlier that day, Markus had shown up at the Compound and said Darek wanted to see her, then immediately left. He had been uncharacteristically nervous, his hands flapping about as if itching to pick up a paintbrush. "What's this about? Your brother was awfully cryptic."

"We're breaking Riko out of the castle dungeons tonight," Darek said.

Ren blinked at him. "Has anyone ever told you that you have a terrible sense of humor?"

"I want you to go ahead with our plan for this evening. Holland will be at the docks instead of me."

No one spoke for several seconds. "You're serious?" Ren asked.

"I am," he said, as if he weren't about to serve himself up like an animal arriving early for its own slaughter.

She ran her gaze over his long body, from brown boots up to a black shirt tucked neatly into trousers. "I always knew you had a death wish. You and your brother and all you damn rebels." She turned to face Holland, who was hovering by the open doorway. "Tell Darek he's an idiot, will you?"

"He's right, Ren. Riko can't stay there any longer," she said, and before Ren could deliver a retort, she added, "He knows about you. You really think it's a good idea we just let them continue to interrogate him?"

Ren glared at her because she couldn't think of anything better to do. She let out a curse and looked back to Darek. "You're going to get yourself killed."

The idea distressed her more than she thought it would.

"I won't." He took a couple steps toward her, seemed to think better of whatever he was going to do, and stopped before he got close. "The castle will be empty tonight. We'll be in and out before anyone knows a thing. But it would be helpful if you created some kind of distraction."

"A *distraction.*"

"Don't do anything stupid, like get yourself caught, but keep the attention away from the castle. You should make a statement. Show we're willing to defy the throne."

Ren thought on it for a moment. "I'm taking this as permission to blow something up."

Darek's typical stony look cracked, his lips twitching up. But the hint of humor faded faster than it had come, and his dark eyes were entirely hard once more. "Ren, I mean it. Do not get caught."

His sincerity caught her off guard, just as it had in the basement the other night when he wouldn't stop looking at her with that stupid expression. It made her feel unprepared. She really didn't like it. "If you're beheaded . . ."

"You'll what?"

She didn't say anything, mostly because she wasn't sure where she had even been going with that threat. His heavy stare seemed to bore into her, as if there were more he wanted her to know, like he was waiting for something. Her eyes held his, her heart picking up a beat. She didn't know why, but her feet might have wanted to take a step forward.

"Don't worry," he said. "I'll be fine. You'll still get your money."

Ren's mouth popped open, and she snapped it shut. She hadn't been thinking about gold at all, and she really should have been. Izram Nevskov certainly was. "I'll expect you back at the Compound when you're done," she said.

"I'll be there."

Ren took another second to eye him, lips pursed, then left the drawing room. Holland followed her into the foyer, where she grabbed a long, cream-colored coat from the rack by the door. Ren watched her, a brow lifted.

"There is absolutely no way I'm going into this thing blind," Holland said, producing gloves from her pocket and tugging them on. "So what are we blowing up?"

Ren let out an amused noise through her nose. She popped open the front door. "Come on. I'll tell you on the way there."

"Where are we going?"

"The Underground." Holland's face contorted into a

look of disgust, and Ren gave a short laugh. "I agree. But what's a girl in need of highly illegal substances to do?"

The two departed the Hollistair mansion. Once they were walking beneath a sky heavy with clouds and the blue facade began to fade into a sea of paint, Holland commented, "It's okay to be worried about Darek."

"I'm not," Ren replied. The only person she worried about was herself . . . and Freya from time to time. That was how it had always been. She was determined to keep it that way.

As they traveled over the Battgandon River and wound their way south, the city transformed. Vivid paint gave way to cracked brick and buildings the color of storm clouds. Wide streets lined with trees and lamps dwindled down to skinny roads unsuitable for a carriage. Fine fabrics were traded for rough wool and used clothing. The crisp air of the north became a swirl of salt, soot, and ale. Holland's eyes darted into every dark corner, and when a group of men came thundering by, their laughter ringing around the dirty street, she leaned in close to Ren.

"Relax," Ren said. "They're harmless."

"How do you know?" Holland whispered.

"I've met enough people who aren't."

They were nearing the Underground when the back of Ren's neck prickled, and her ears picked up on the soft fall of shoes in the street behind them. She slowed, grabbing on to Holland's arm to stop her. Ren's hand went to her corset. Her fingers closed on metal, and she rotated, sliding the blade free.

The first thing she saw was a once-broken nose that had healed wrong. Then the rest of Izram Nevskov came into focus. His hair was slicked back, and his black coat hung open over a blood-red vest made of silk. Four men were at his back.

"Good afternoon, Ren," he said, drifting forward on long, lean legs.

Ren dropped her hand to her side and slid the knife up her sleeve, curling her wrist so she could flick it out quickly if needed. Nevskov had never tracked her down before. Once a month, she delivered a pouch of gold to his mansion, and that was that. Ren's throat was dry. Her heart thundered under skin and bone.

"Who's your friend?" Nevskov asked. "And more importantly, where did she get that delightful coat? The fur is exquisite."

Ren stepped in front of Holland. "What do you want, Nevskov?"

The gang leader tore his blue eyes from Holland and focused them on Ren. The weight of his stare made her skin itch. "You're a beautiful girl, Ren. So full of potential."

"What do you *want*?" she repeated, fingers inching toward her coat pocket, where she kept a neck dagger.

He stepped so close that Ren could see the exact spot where the bones in his nose had cracked. It took a serious effort of will to keep from flicking out her knife and shoving it into his neck. He leaned in and said softly, as if whispering into a lover's ear, "I want my money."

A cold shiver ran over Ren's back. She stared into

Nevskov's bright-blue eyes, every muscle in her body coiled tight. "You want more money? I can make bigger payments—"

Nevskov's smile was edged like a blade. "While I appreciate the offer, I'm not here to negotiate. This city is headed for war faster than even I had realized. I intend to collect what's mine before the hells break loose." His eyes scanned her face, his gaze calm but hungry.

Ren didn't dare breathe.

There was movement at the edge of her vision, followed by a loud gasp, and Ren whipped her head toward the noise. One of Nevskov's thugs had a hand wrapped around Holland's arm, and another had a knife at her jaw. Ren assessed the scene for two seconds, then looked back to Nevskov. "I met that girl three days ago," she told him. Her hand entered her pocket, finding the handle of the neck dagger. "If you think threatening her is going to accomplish anything, you don't know me very well."

Ren wasn't entirely sure how much of that statement was a bluff and how much was the gods-honest truth.

Nevskov stared down at her. His hand shot forward, latching on to her wrist, and he dragged it out of her pocket and into the space between them. He twisted it back. Ren hissed as pain lanced through her hand. The knife fell from her grip, clattering onto the stones at their feet.

"Perhaps this will be motivation enough," Nevskov said, his grip so tight he was seconds from breaking bone. "You have one week to pay off your debt. After that, you'll be fighting in the pits for me until I have every last piece of gold you owe me." He yanked her into his body, and the hand that wasn't squeezing her wrist brushed the hair from her cheek.

Ren swallowed down the urge to spit in his eyes.

"And then, darling, you'll belong to me."

Nevskov released her. Ren stumbled away, cradling her aching wrist to her chest as his men let Holland go and drifted to his side. The gang retreated, melting into shadows like wraiths, disappearing as swift and silent as they had come. Quiet fell on the street and settled like dead leaves.

Ren's hands couldn't seem to stop shaking. She took in a breath to steady herself and retrieved her dagger from the ground. Once she'd dropped it into her pocket, she glanced at Holland. "You all right?"

Holland smoothed down her fur collar. "I should be asking you that." She nodded at Ren's wrist. "Is it broken?"

"It's fine." She lowered her arm to her side and tried not to wince when it gave a sharp throb.

Neither of them spoke for a while, until Holland finally said, "How much do you owe him? I might be able to—"

"No."

"I only thought—"

"It's none of your business, Holland. Stay out of it." Ren freed the blade she'd shoved up her coat sleeve and returned it to its place in her corset.

"Everyone needs help sometimes," Holland told her.

Ren looked back down the street, at the gray buildings reaching for a cloudy sky, dirty windows and crooked doors and barren stoops scattered along the walls. Snow gathered on awnings and melted into dark puddles on the ground. It was so empty Ren could almost fool herself into believing it always had been. "I can help myself."

Ren tightened her black mask around her head and pulled up the hood of the form-fitting coat she'd snagged when she and Holland had stopped by the Underground earlier that day. It wasn't as nice as her red jacket, but it had a similar shape—a cropped front and trailing coattails to show off her figure—ensuring there would be no mistaking her for one of the princes tonight. Under leather gloves, her palms were sweaty. She ran her hands over her corset.

Seven hundred thousand gold coins, she thought. The number had begun to lose meaning, but then Nevskov had nearly snapped her hand in half. Her wrist was currently a deep shade of purple. It ached like all nine hells.

It was just after dusk, and the last dregs of sunset were fighting a losing battle against the night. Here on the far southeastern edge of Denfell, where the city met the water, the Iron Sea was as black as tar. Most weeks, the Royal Navy dominated Denfell's ports, but with the Royal Carnival in full swing, vessels from across the world were docked at the edge of the city, traders and merchants and performers all here to celebrate the Erdis kingdom.

What a colossal waste of time.

Ignoring the pain radiating from her wrist, Ren shook

out her hands and turned her gaze from the sea to the city. Thanks to the start of the carnival, it was fairly busy as far as nights at the docks went, but Holland was easy enough to spot in the crowd, with hair so vibrant it was fair competition for the building at Ren's back. When Ren caught her eye, Holland nodded.

Heart hammering like a racehorse, Ren headed for a stone wall running along the water, deliberately barging into a group of bystanders as she went, and jumped onto the ledge. Before anyone could turn their looks of annoyance elsewhere, Ren lifted her palms and called her silver. She sent it up over her head, gathering it there until the entire stretch of road and the buildings beyond were glowing as brightly as if a bolt of lightning had stuck but never dissipated, until every eye was turned toward her. Shocked silence met her ears.

Ren's throat was dry. She swallowed, steadying herself. Stretching her hands and twisting her wrists, she urged her silver into motion. It rolled and swirled as she called up more, tumbling like waves crashing in a violent storm. She paused, giving her audience time for their heads to catch up to their eyes, then turned to face the sea and a dozen Royal Navy ships. Ren shoved her hands forward. Her silver raced across the water and slammed into the bottom of the nearest ship. Wood splintered and shrieked, water gurgling as it rushed into a hole now gaping in the hull. At Ren's back, the crowd collectively gasped.

Ren watched the naval ship descend into the inky sea, water creeping up its side inch by inch. Her lips tugged up. After so many years of fear and pain, of nightmares and anger, Ren was finally extracting some revenge. She didn't know why she hadn't thought to do this years ago.

When she faced the street once again, the whispering had already started. Dozens of hushed voices bled together like white noise, the promise of more rumors to come, at last with a woman attached to them. Her remaining hesitation dripped away. There really wasn't any point in quitting now, and frankly, Ren didn't want to.

She'd raised her hands to start again when a shout made her pause. "Stop right there!" Two men in red Royal Guard uniforms were sprinting toward her with swords drawn. They must have been stationed at the docks.

"In the name of King Mattheus—"

Ren swung her arms around and stretched her fingers. Two rivulets of silver shot from her hands. The guards tried to dodge them, but weren't quick enough. The magic lifted the guards into the air. Ren turned, and in one swift motion, she flung them at the next ship over. The hull blew apart in a burst of wood, silver, and red uniforms. The once-calm water splashed and churned as a second ship started going down. At her back, the whispering grew louder.

She went again and again, tearing holes in ships and drawing the city to her.

CHAPTER
TWENTY-EIGHT

As the sky grew dark, the streetlamps were lit one by one. The Battgandon River was calm, gondolas and little boats drifting through the dark water, small wakes lapping gently at the river's stone walls. A railing ran above the water's edge, and Lesa and Adley walked beside it, their fingers interlinked.

"I'm serious!" Lesa said. "Pickled fish is amazing."

"It sounds vile," Adley said, wrinkling her nose.

Lesa gave a mock gasp and abruptly stopped, pulling Adley up short with her. Narrowing her black eyes, she glanced around at the stalls scattering the street, found one lined with ten different species of fish, and smiled.

"No," Adley said as Lesa began to tow her toward the fishmonger. "No way."

Lesa tugged her up to the stall, where she ordered a bowl of pickled fish from a salty-haired man with skin weathered and tanned like old leather. She exchanged a silver coin for the wet, pinkish strips, and when she faced Adley again, the expression on her face could have been gifted by the god of mischief himself.

Adley backed away from the stench of vinegar. "I'm not eating that."

"Come on." Lesa dangled a piece between two gloved fingers as she stepped forward, matching Adley's pace. "Just try it."

"Not going to happen." Adley's hips hit the railing. "It looks like a bloated worm."

Lesa stopped in front of her, fish pinched in her fingers. "Eat it."

The sharp tang bit at Adley's nose, and she shook her head, trying not to smile. She shifted forward, bringing her lips to Lesa's, the bowl of fish trapped between their chests. For one second, she only kissed Lesa, and then she snatched the bowl, flung out her arm, and sent the fish flying into the river.

Lesa pulled back. "Adley!" she exclaimed, gaping at the wooden bowl and strips of pickled fish floating in the water. Laughter burst from her like sunlight breaking through clouds. She scooped Adley's face between her hands and kissed her.

Adley tasted her laughter, clear as spring water. It spilled into her, filling her to the brim, overflowing and uncontainable, until she was laughing, too.

"You'll have to pay for that bowl, you know!" the fishmonger called from his stall, a chuckle bouncing through his voice.

Adley wondered what he saw. Not two King's Children—he wouldn't have made them pay if he'd known what they were. But they wore no leather, save for their boots. The Lyandor lion head was stitched on neither Lesa's cobalt jacket, nor Adley's lilac dress and gray cloak.

Every year, the King's Children were given the first day of the Royal Carnival to do with it what they would. It was the only full day of freedom they were granted, the one day they were permitted to walk about the city out of uniform. The chances of being spotted were low, low enough to risk kissing by the water, and even if someone from the castle did happen by, it was unlikely they would be recognized. They were just another couple enjoying the festivities.

In Lesa's embrace, Adley let herself believe it. They weren't King's Children, only two people who could be together without fear. It was nice, pretending for a day.

Adley gave the fishmonger more silver, apologizing for the loss of his bowl, then she and Lesa began to wander. Without a destination in mind, they followed whatever caught their attention. A flash of bright color, the waft of warm food, a plucked guitar string. It was properly dark by the time they stopped to purchase cups of mulled cider and watch gondolas glide down the river, carrying occupants huddled beneath piles of furs. Lamps bobbed at every bow, drifting over the water like fireflies.

"What's that?" Lesa asked, standing up straight and staring off in the direction of the docks, where an unnatural silver light was spilling over the rooftops. It looked an awful lot like magic.

"Let's check it out," Adley said.

They left the river's edge and wound their way through

the lamplit city streets, passing by buildings that weren't quite as vivid here on the south side of the Battgandon, but were putting up an effort to show off their colors nonetheless. They slipped into a narrow alley that led to a wide expanse of street bordering the sea. The road ahead was crammed with bodies angling for a better view—of what, Adley still wasn't sure—and the bright light set the edges of the buildings aglow. Adley and Lesa joined the crowd and stopped dead.

Standing atop a stone wall, bobbing ships at her back, was a girl. She was very tall and very thin, a hood drawn up and a mask in place over her face. Her hands were raised above her head, and silver was swirling in the air.

Adley stared, slack-jawed. It had to be a trick, a daft idea of Prince Kellen's. It seemed like something he would find funny for some inane reason. This couldn't be what it looked like. Surely someone at the castle would have heard about a silver wielder in Denfell.

But then the girl moved her hands, and the magic moved with her, and Adley didn't think this was the prince's doing after all. The girl pivoted, her arms flinging forward, and silver shot out over the water.

Oh, dear gods.

Wood cracked and splintered as the silver punched through the hull of a ship. But it wasn't just any ship—it was part of the naval fleet. About ten other vessels were slowly slipping beneath the water, each of them belonging to the Royal Navy. And it looked like the girl was only getting started, because her hands were glowing silver again. The sea slapped against the docks, chunks of wood bobbing along the black surface.

This was no trick. The girl had silver, silver that was only supposed to belong to the Lyandors. The king couldn't know. He would be furious. He'd have killed her long ago. She had to know that, which meant one thing: she was showing herself for a reason.

Adley's lips ticked up. "Come on," she said to Lesa, pulling her into the enraptured audience.

As they snaked through, bits of conversation floated by, questions tossed out to everyone and no one.

"Who do you think she is?"

"A fraud is all. I bet she's setting off fragor explosions."

"No way. Do you see her?"

Out on the water, another hull broke apart. Wood snapped, and the sea swirled.

"I heard she's King Mattheus's daughter."

Adley shook her head. Denfell liked the sound of its own voice too much. The people of this city would believe a colony of dragons lived in the sewer system if there was enough talk about it. As if the king were careless enough to father an illegitimate child, *a silver wielder*, and let her live.

There were too many bodies to shove past without making a scene, and the girl was too close to risk losing now, so Adley stopped in the middle of the crowd. She turned to Lesa. "Can you get me a look at her face?"

Lesa studied the wielder, fingering one of the knives strapped to her thigh. "You think that's the girl the rebel was talking about? The pit fighter?"

"I'd place gold on it," Adley said. "It's too much of a coincidence. First, she's destroying the king's ships. And second, why would a silver wielder show herself now if she's not working with the rebellion? Why would that rebel have mentioned a girl at all, if she weren't someone important?"

Adley wondered how long they had been at this. They must have been sticking to the slums until now, since that was about the only place in Denfell they could have gotten away with it. The seedier parts of the city had never been a priority, and ever since they'd learned about the White Raven, the castle had had all eyes focused on the Atterton District.

"I don't think there's anyone more important than a silver wielder," Lesa agreed, "considering they're supposed to be extinct."

Lesa began to slide a blade from its sheath, but Adley put a hand over hers before it came all the way out. "Don't kill her. We have nothing if she's dead."

"You're no fun," Lesa said.

"Lesa, I'm serious."

She sighed, like she had faced no greater inconvenience. "Yes, all right, fine. I'll let her live if I must."

Adley removed her hand, and Lesa freed the dagger. She kept it at her side while she sighted the silver wielder, who seemed to be watching them as much as they were watching her. As the girl's magic undulated overhead, Lesa marked her target, raised her arm, and threw.

The blade whirled through the air, catching on the

edge of the wielder's hood and tearing it from her face. Lesa quickly flung another dagger. It sliced the side of her mask, cutting both fabric and pale skin. The mask dropped away, and black hair tumbled to her waist, blood sliding down her cheek, her face entirely exposed. Adley spent the following second committing the wielder's features to memory. With a heart-shaped face, full lips, and darkly lined eyes that were probably green—though it was hard to tell in the harsh light—she was the kind of girl who would stand out at a fighting pit.

"Got you," Adley whispered.

The wielder was quite a bit younger than she had expected. She could have been twenty, but Adley guessed the girl was about her age: eighteen or so. She would make a fine martyr, and now that people knew about her, the king would have to play this one carefully. The rebellion was already a serious problem. The last thing they needed was a citywide uprising over the death of a beautiful girl.

The wielder's magic blinked out, and the street went dim. The crowd swiftly descended into an upheaval of shoving arms and stomping feet, shouts coming from all directions. The girl jumped down from the wall and raised her hood, slipping through the commotion and breaking out of the riot long before Adley had any hope of reaching her.

The girl didn't take off right away, but paused in front of a streetlamp with silver glowing in her hands. The magic shot up, breaking the lamp from its pole, and she turned to launch it out to sea. It soared through the air in a binding arc and disappeared onto the deck of the closest ship, the last naval vessel still floating at this particular dock.

The silver wielder turned and ran.

A boom like a fragor explosion rang through the cold night air. The ship's deck burst apart. The crowd screamed. Someone rammed into Adley's side, and she staggered back. She shielded her eyes as broken wood splashed into the water and fire overtook the deck, racing up the mast, eating the thing alive. A second explosion went off, and the hull splintered outward. Within seconds, the entire vessel was consumed by flames.

"What do we do?!" Lesa shouted over the din of panic. Fire raged, and ships rocked on their way down, and everyone who had been witness to the display of treason fled in five different directions. "Do we tell the king?"

Adley considered it. She knew what she was supposed to do. She was supposed to go straight back to the castle and report to the king, tell him everything she knew about the girl so he could enact a citywide manhunt to find her. And then Adley would be stuck in the castle for the rest of her life. They'd burn her bones and scatter the ashes in the Iron Sea, and she'd never know peace. Her dirty soul would crash against the rocks, drown in the waters like a shipwrecked sailor.

She shook her head and leaned in to speak without yelling. "Not yet. If the king finds out about her, he'll send all his men after her, and I might never be made Fang. I want to bring her in."

Adley stared at the sinking naval ships, wondering

if she could get any more information out of the Sirican rebel. The sea splashed against the docks, the smoldering remains of the last vessel dancing over midnight waters. She just hoped word didn't get back to the castle before she could track the girl down.

CHAPTER
TWENTY-NINE

Dressed in prison guard uniforms, the small group of rebels rattled up to the castle, Jaston driving the horses and Darek beside him on the front seat. Markus walked alongside the barred wagon, its wooden wheels jostling on the uneven stones.

As they pulled to a stop, a castle guard detached himself from the front gate. "What's this?" he asked.

Darek pulled the freshly fabricated documents from his jacket and presented them. "We have transfer orders for a prisoner."

The guard thumbed through the papers, which bore the signatures and seals of both the prison warden and the captain of the Royal Guard. Darek happened to know that the captain was watching a performance in the Orian circus tents right now, and he wouldn't be back from the carnival until well into the night.

"I didn't hear anything about a transfer," the guard said.

Darek jumped down from the carriage. Habitually, he reached up to sweep his hair back, which he was letting hang over his bruised face in an attempt to obscure his features, but caught himself in time. "You're hearing it now," he replied.

The guard frowned, continuing to assess the transfer orders. His heart twice as heavy and beating out a hard rhythm, Darek crossed his arms and adopted an expression that said he'd rather be in the heart of the city celebrating with the rest of Denfell. Jaston ran a hand over the snout of one of the horses, while Markus heaved a sigh, dropping back against the wagon's bars. Miraculously, his brother wasn't fidgeting.

"What's the problem?" another guard asked, joining the group.

"Prisoner transfer," said the first as he handed over the papers.

The second guard shuffled through them, briefly scanning the rough parchment before passing them back. "Everything looks in order."

The first guard returned the documents to Darek. Tucking them away, he tamped down his swell of relief. There was time yet for everything to go wrong.

Three guards remained at their post outside the castle gates while the first led Darek, Markus, and Jaston into the inner courtyard. Up close, the castle was monstrous. It loomed over the yard, its spiked turrets silhouetted against the sky like jagged saws. They followed the guard down an arched corridor to a gated doorway. A large iron key opened the gate, and the guard ushered them into a stone stairwell, pulling a lit torch off the wall outside before stepping through himself. The door was locked behind them, and they were led down. Moisture clung to the walls, and by the time they reached another gate at the bottom of the stairs, the air had gone stale. The dank smell of mold crawled into Darek's lungs and burrowed deep. In the flickering torchlight, the stones seemed to be weeping.

"Hold this," the guard said, shoving the torch at Markus. He unlocked the second gate and shouldered the groaning metal inward, giving them access to a long corridor lined on both sides by iron bars. He took the torch back, and they trailed him into the dungeon.

Darek consulted the transfer papers. "Orders are for a man in his early twenties. Sirican, it looks like. He was brought in last week after a raid in Atterton."

Torch held aloft, the guard led them down the corridor. In the dull-orange light, through heavy cell bars, Darek could just make out filthy prisoners huddled on the dirt floors, and if he looked closely enough, he'd see their missing pieces, how broken they were. No one moved; no one spoke. Silent and still, to take a breath felt like an affront, an insult to the god of death. This place was a graveyard. These prisoners were skeletons buried in unconsecrated ground.

And there, three cells down, was Riko. Lying unconscious on his back, half of his hair was drenched in blood, and his mouth was puffed in the way of someone who had lost a number of teeth. Although Riko still wore the shirt he'd had on the night of the raid, it was caked so heavily in filth that no one would have guessed it had once been light blue. All the skin on his right forearm had been peeled away, leaving behind raw flesh and muscle. A metal pail was knocked over. Its contents soaked the dirt around his body.

Riko was so covered in bruises, open wounds, and his own blood, Darek almost hadn't realized it was him. He'd been about to turn his attention to the next cell when he peered closer at the man curled on his side and recognized the dark hair, the shape of his nose, the mouth that rarely curved down. Pain stabbed Darek like a knife wound, but worse—he would have preferred the knife.

"Here he is," Darek said. It was agony to act like he didn't care, like he'd never seen this man before, as if he hadn't been laughing with him over drinks five days ago.

The guard brought his torch closer and scrutinized Riko in the dim light. Darek held the papers up so the guard could read the prisoner's description. The man nodded. "That's him." He gave Darek the torch and stuck his key in the lock.

Darek trailed the guard inside, bent down and put his fingers to Riko's throat. He didn't find a pulse. He didn't find anything. There was only the silence of a heart that had given out, blood gone cold and stagnant in veins.

Darek went still. His bones locked up. The cell seemed to press into his spine, the top of his head, his eyelids and nails. The quiet was unbearable. With two fingers at his dead friend's neck, Darek suddenly no longer wanted to pretend. He couldn't. He would pull out his knife, and he would shove it into the guard kneeling beside him, find his heart, render it as still as Riko's.

And then, a beat. It flickered beneath Darek's fingers. His breath caught. He adjusted his touch, and the pulse came again, faint, but there. He slapped Riko's face and hated himself as he did it. His friend didn't wake.

"The reaper's coming for this one," the guard said. "Best leave him behind. He won't be of any use to the prison."

"No. The warden wants him. We have our orders." Darek gave the torch back to the guard and looked at Markus. "Get in here. We're going to have to carry him out."

They each placed one of Riko's arms over their shoulders and pulled him from the ground. Head hanging limp on his neck, Riko's bare feet dragged through the dirt as they carried him out of his cell and shuffled toward the stairwell. They were halfway there when another castle guard came pounding down the stone steps, this one a good decade older than the men stationed at the front gate. His feet slowed, brows lifting, but his surprise lasted no more than two heartbeats before it disappeared, a suspicious cast to his stare as his eyes carefully rolled over all of them. "What's the meaning of this?"

"Prison transfer," said the first guard.

The older guard dropped his hand to the pommel of his sword. "No one ordered a prison transfer."

"Captain Xanicks did. He signed the papers."

Shifting awkwardly so as not to drop Riko, Darek reached into his jacket and pulled out the forged documents. The older man came closer, holding up one palm, and Darek set the papers in his hand. The guard, who appeared to be the one in charge while the captain was away, scrutinized them with more care than the men at the gate. His lips hardened into a line, and Darek's heart froze mid-beat. Jaston hadn't had long to put the papers together. Maybe he'd made a mistake.

"Rebel scum," the guard spit. "I've seen Xanicks's signature a hundred times, and this isn't it." He threw the papers aside and unsheathed his sword in a sharp screech of metal.

Darek wasn't about to give the younger guard time to move for his own weapon. Dropping Riko's arm, he launched himself at the man and grabbed on to his head. With a harsh jerk, Darek broke his neck, and the torch tumbled down, the guard following. He hadn't hit the dirt before Darek was rushing the older guard. The man swung. Darek ducked the arc of his sword and slammed into his torso, using his shoulder like a battering ram. The force took them both down, and the guard's head cracked against the bottom step of the stairwell, Darek landing on top. He whipped out a knife and shoved the blade into the guard's chest.

Darek didn't move as the man registered what had happened. He blinked. His hand drifted to his chest, felt the knife stuck there. Fingers came away wet and red. His eyes shifted to Darek. He gave a shallow gasp and was gone.

After allowing himself a single deep breath, Darek yanked his knife from the dead guard's chest, wiped the blade on the lining of his own coat, and got to his feet. The knife went back in the sheath at his hip, and he retrieved the transfer orders from where they'd fallen. He searched the floor for the set of iron keys the younger guard had been carrying and found them pressed into the dirt beneath the man's body. "We'll lock them in empty cells," he said. "Make it look like they're prisoners. We should be far away by the time anyone finds them."

Jaston didn't blink. He only bent down and started to drag the younger guard toward an open cell. Looking faintly ill, Markus adjusted Riko on his shoulder and watched Darek do the same with the older man. Both guards were arranged with their backs to the corridor. Darek locked them inside, and to anyone passing by, they were just two more bodies rotting in the musky dungeon.

"Let's get out of here," Darek said, grabbing Riko's arm again.

Markus hesitated, staring around at all the cells and the people still trapped inside them.

"Markus," Darek said firmly.

His brother glanced at him over Riko's dangling head. Darek knew what he was thinking. Darek was thinking it, too. He wished they could rescue everyone now, but that was impossible. They'd never make it past the guards. The only way to help these people was to end the king's rule once and for all. "We need to go."

Markus swallowed. Finally, he nodded.

After they'd closed and locked the bottom gate, Darek and Markus carried their friend up the dark stairwell and out into fresh air. Jaston locked the top gate and pocketed the keys, then they shuffled through an arched walkway.

Out in the courtyard, a huge fountain sat quietly, the water inside partially frozen over. As they skirted around it and made their way down the stone path toward the castle gates, a small group of men dressed in maroon uniforms ran past, their swords clinking and boots thundering. Under the iron teeth of the front gates, the remaining three guards had their attention trained on the crowded city below. Darek caught the faint scent of smoke, and he glanced down the hill. A fire was raging at the docks.

"What's going on?" Darek asked.

"Someone destroyed a bunch of Royal Navy ships. Must have taken them down with fragor."

Godsdamn, Ren, Darek thought. If they hadn't been dead men walking, if Riko weren't unconscious and covered in his own blood, and if he hadn't just killed two men, he would have been amused. And a bit impressed.

"The rebellion?" Jaston asked.

One guard grunted, while another said, "Probably. They're getting out of control. King Mattheus has his hands full with that lot."

The third guard quickly assessed their group before looking back to the city. "Where's Grant?"

Darek assumed Grant was the guard whose neck he'd snapped. He wished he hadn't learned his name. "Don't know," he answered. "Said he had something to take care of."

The guards glanced at each other and shrugged, more concerned with the commotion at the docks than the transfer. "Need help with that prisoner?"

"We can handle it," Jaston said, removing an iron pad-lock from the door at the back of the wagon. He pulled it open, and Darek and Markus dumped Riko inside. Jaston banged the barred door shut, the padlock returning to its place.

Once he'd pulled himself up onto the bench and Jaston had taken his spot at the reins, Darek tipped his head to the guards. "Carnival's tidings."

Gathering the reins in his gloved hands, Jaston got the horses moving with a click of his tongue and a snap of his wrists. As the carriage turned and rolled down the hill, with every clipped horse hoof and rattling wheel, Darek expected the worst. He waited for the guards to realize that a group of rebels had willingly walked into their dun-geons—and walked out. He waited for disaster to strike.

They made it to the bottom of the hill and wound their way through the streets. Down an empty alley, they changed out of uniform, removed Riko's chains, swapped the prison carriage for a private coach with satin walls. They rode in silence to Darek's house, where they carried Riko inside and sent for a trusted healer. Riko would live, the man said, but another day in the castle dungeons and he might not have. He left them with medicines and orders for Riko to rest.

Darek paced, worry crawling like beetles under his skin.

Well into the night, when the fire had died down to embers, a croak fissured the silence. "Darek."

He rushed to Riko, kneeling beside the guest bed they'd laid him in. "I'm here."

Riko blinked drowsily up at the red silk canopy. "Where . . ." He trailed off, eyes drifting closed.

"You're okay. You're safe."

"Darek . . . Ren . . ."

Darek frowned. "Ren isn't here, Riko."

His eyes fluttered open, but immediately drooped again. He murmured something that sounded like, "Made . . . a mistake . . ." But it was so quiet that Darek wasn't entirely sure. They were Riko's last words before he faded into unconsciousness once again.

CHAPTER
THIRTY

The last day of the Royal Carnival dawned cold and white. A heavy covering of snow lay atop the castle's parapets and turrets, and the servants had spent all morning entangled in a battle to clear pathways both inside and outside the castle walls. But though the gray clouds were thick, the snow and wind were showing mercy. All said, it was as lovely as a winter day could be, and Kellen would have been glad for it on any other occasion. But today, as he rode into the city in a carriage with his father, the crown prince and queen settled in their own carriage ahead, the Royal Guard and King's Children marching around them like a human fortification wall, Kellen would rather have been anywhere else.

Bundled in a thick maroon cloak, a pelt of fur at his shoulders, he dipped a hand into his vest pocket and fingered the silk mask he'd stowed there, contemplating the escape he had planned. Every year, Kellen usually managed to slip away from his princely duties for at least one day of the carnival, but the guards were becoming too good at their job, and he was having a hell of a time shrugging them off. All week, he'd been stuck on the stage in

Talmarquin Square, seated in a garish chair beside the rest of his family and forced to watch the festivities from afar. Today, that was going to change. He wanted to visit the dessert stalls and the street performers, watch the Ticharran fire-breathers and the acrobats from the Orian Circus. He wanted to breathe in the joyous air.

As a prince, Kellen despised the Royal Carnival. It was a blaring reminder of everything he spent his nights trying to escape. When he sat above the city, he couldn't run away from the fact that no matter how hard he tried, he'd always have a crown, always be a Lyandor. His title tainted the carnival. But as a commoner, he adored the celebrations. So a commoner he would become. As long as he made it back in time for the Crown's Demonstration, which would mark the end of the carnival, his father's complaints should be minimal.

"Don't look so glum, son," the king said. "Your suffering is almost through."

"Brooding suits me. I have the jawline for it," he replied, staring out his curtained window at the colorless sky.

"But not the humility."

Kellen glanced at his father, who sat stiffly in his seat, a crown encrusted with rubies on his head and a golden cloak pooling around his slim frame. At every bump and jostle, his glare hardened, and by the time they made it down into the city, Kellen half expected silver to shoot from his father's eyes. He'd been in a horrific mood since the first night of the carnival, when rebels had broken into the castle dungeons, killed a couple guards, escaped with a prisoner, and sunk a bunch of naval ships—all in under an hour. And they'd miraculously found a silver wielder to work with, some insane girl with a death wish. The king had ordered his soldiers to bring her in, but seeing as no one had any idea what she looked like, it was a bit of a lost cause. When Kellen heard about what had happened, he hadn't been able to help his bubble of laughter. The rebels had to be the bravest bastards he'd ever seen. It was damn impressive, if you asked him, which no one ever did.

"Do you think Heath is nervous?" Kellen asked.

His father grunted in response.

Kellen resumed watching the clouds, the carriage rattling down the road. With so many guards surrounding them, he couldn't see when they entered the heart of the city, but he could hear it. The streets were flooded with people, excitement swirling in the air, thick like the tang of salt at the docks, and the procession was forced to slow its pace to a crawl. Kellen caught a whiff of sweet rolls, the scent striking a balance between syrupy sweet and richly buttered in that way no one but Katarine Vespar could achieve, which meant they were passing Noble Finch. He hadn't seen Holland since last week, when he'd lost his mind and threatened to turn her over as a rebel sympathizer. He'd regretted it every day since, but he couldn't bring himself to face her. He didn't know what he would say even if he did pluck up the courage.

I'm sorry.

Will you forgive me?

I may be dreadful and horrible, but I'm nothing like my brother.

And maybe you're right. Maybe I should stop trying to be like him.

I miss your red hair.

I miss you.

None of it was right. Words had never been so elusive.

They clopped into Talmarquin Square, a flat expanse of gray stones surrounded on four sides by buildings of all different shapes, sizes, and bright hues. The carriages pulled to a stop next to the elevated stage, the area cordoned off with gold rope. A guard popped open the door, and the king stepped out to thunderous cheers. Kellen got his eye rolls out of the way inside the safety of the satin walls, then hopped out himself. With a beaming smile, he waved to the gathered crowd and continued to wave as his family ascended the steps to the stage and settled into their seats. From the corner of his eye, he caught his father's annoyed stare, but Kellen only kept waving.

Any minute now.

Right on time, a group of men barreled through the crowd, fists flailing. They punched out into the empty space around the stage, breaking the line of guards tasked with keeping the area clear. It was all the fuel the crowd needed, and suddenly, two dozen people were brawling.

Swallowed up in the fray, Kellen was cut off from his guards. He only had a moment, but a moment was enough.

He removed his cloak, tossing it over the nearest body, and pulled up the high collar of the nondescript and rather shabby jacket he was wearing beneath. He swerved through the fists and stumbling bodies, past the men he'd paid to cause the scene, and lurched out into the sea of people like he'd been shoved. Keeping a hand pressed to his face as if protecting a broken nose, Kellen pushed his way through the captive audience. When he was far enough from the action, he hunched over and tied his mask on, then continued to shoulder forward until he broke through the crowd and into open air.

He stood up straight. Before him were rows of candy-colored stalls, painted as if in defiance of the gloomy sky. To his right, a toothy boy was bouncing on the balls of his feet while his father purchased a pink puff of spun sugar. At the next stall over, a man clipped a bracelet on his companion's wrist, and she smiled, leaning in to kiss his cheek. Just down the road, a group of delighted kids were gathered around a jester, shrieking with laughter. Off in the distance, Kellen caught the lilt of a fiddle.

He grinned. He was free.

After purchasing a bag of salted caramels from a nearby stall, Kellen began to drift. While the Royal Carnival's main events were a constant, everything else changed from year to year, and you never knew what you might find down a random side street. He meandered past men, women, and children selling everything from fish sandwiches to healing crystals, and he stopped to chat with traders who had sailed across the Iron Sea. They brought Orian silk scarves and shawls, jewelry made of gemstones from the clear blue waters of Sirica, teas from Brede. To Kellen's surprise, goods from Glynn were also available—furs and thick hats and gloves, along with scrying boards and rune stones. The merchant must have had to jump through a hundred hoops just to enter Erdis. Travel to and from Glynn had been outlawed ever since the Silver Purge, when the frozen northern country took in magic wielders fleeing the genocide. Today, the last of the wielders lived in Glynn, barricaded behind snow and mountains and fear. According to his father's spies, they were in no position to pose a threat, but the crown wasn't taking chances.

Kellen bought a pendulum necklace from the Glynn merchant just to reward the man for having the guts to come here at all. He chose a blood-red crystal attached to a thin silver chain and slipped it into his pocket with a thank-you. Then he went in search of the performers.

He found the Orian Circus in East Welsley Park, where they'd pitched huge tents the color of orange peels and lemon rinds. Kellen spent an hour there, watching aerialists twist and turn high above the audience, more fluid than water in a stream. Contortionists folded themselves into impossible shapes, acrobats tumbled and swung across stage, and illusionists conjured birds from thin air.

Another hour of his time went to a stretch of the Battgandon River and the Ticharran fire-breathers gathered there. After that, Kellen was off to Keepler's Prospect, where actors from the Royal Theatre were putting on a production of *The Knave's Heart*. Leaning one shoulder against a marble statue, Kellen settled in to watch the play. When a wave of laughter rolled through the audience, uninhibited and raw, some of the tightness in his chest eased. There was beauty in this ugly city. There was culture and art and innovation, architecture and music. These people had stories on their tongues and spirit in their hearts. Imagine what this place could be, imagine how it could thrive, if only the king would let it.

When the play broke for intermission and the crowd got up to stretch their legs, he spotted her: a girl with raven hair cascading down her back in a messy curtain. He almost didn't recognize Ren without the leather corset. Standing beside a statue of the goddess of spring, she'd traded her dark-red coat for a long white one with a large collar of fur that hung open over a green silk dress. She reached into her pocket and pulled out a silver watch, flipping the front open to check the time. It went back into her pocket, and Ren turned away from the plaza, taking the steps down toward a bridge.

Kellen couldn't help himself. He followed her out of Keepler's Prospect, over the bridge to the southern side of the river and into an alleyway, losing sight of her as she swept through an archway up ahead. He passed through the curving limestone walls she'd disappeared around and emerged in a small courtyard packed with dancers. Beneath a row of arches at the edge of the yard, a group of musicians played their instruments with enough zeal to snap the strings. Above the revelry, people leaned out of windows and clapped along to the music. It was nothing like balls at the castle, where guests moved in carefully choreographed steps. There was no conductor or orchestra here, no bows or curtsies. This was pure, unadulterated dancing, without rhyme or reason, without direction or purpose.

Kellen tipped his head back and laughed.

Stepping away from the wall, he let the music sweep him up. He hooked on to the end of a snaking chain, allowing himself to be tugged by the elbow around the courtyard, and when he caught sight of four little girls wiggling out of rhythm, he asked them to dance. They screeched in response, latching on to his hands and pulling his arms like unskilled puppeteers. Kellen was glad to let them lead.

As he twirled one of the girls around on his finger, he scanned the courtyard for Ren, finding her in the mouth of an arch across the way. "Excuse me, ladies," he said, bowing to the girls gathered around his legs. Their disappointed *awws* sounded in high-pitched unison.

Kellen swerved through the dancers and approached Ren. Up close, he could tell that her dress was two shades darker than her eyes, which, in the light of day, Kellen decided were like a forest during sunset. The fitted bodice had a heart-shaped neckline dipping low, the skirt fell in one clean, silken line down to the cobbled street, and she wore thick white gloves. Simple and elegant. If he didn't already know her, no one could have possibly convinced Kellen that this girl was an orphan living in Hessler or that she'd won a pit fight in south Terth three weeks ago.

"Fancy running into you here," he said.

"I knew you were following me," Ren replied, indifferent.

She tossed a glance at him, then looked back to the dancers. "This isn't a masquerade."

"And thank the gods for that." Her lips were painted a dark-plum color. Would they be as sweet as the fruit, Kellen wondered, if she let him have a taste? "You're too beautiful to hide behind a mask."

Ren's eyes flicked to him and stayed there this time. She visibly assessed him, from the locks of his fashionably cut hair—carefully messy strands on top, shorter on the sides—down to the soles of his black boots, and back up again. The way she lingered on his mouth was too obvious to be unintentional, and his heart picked up a notch as he sidled closer. "Like what you see?"

Kellen wasn't short, but Ren barely had to lift her chin in order to meet his stare. "I'm still deciding."

"Is there anything I can do to sway the verdict?"

She tilted her head. There was a cut on one side of her temple, a red line in the process of healing. "Quite possibly," she said.

Kellen slipped a hand beneath her coat and cradled the dip of her waist. She leaned into his touch, her green irises unwavering. Gods, she could murder someone with those eyes. It really wouldn't be a terrible way to go. "Dance with me?"

For a moment so brief he thought he might have imagined it, her attention flickered to something over his shoulder. "Yes, all right."

Releasing her waist, Kellen gripped her hand instead and led her into the center of the little courtyard. She placed a palm on his upper arm at the same moment that he pressed one to her back, and with a grin, he tugged her close. When they began to dance, Ren allowed Kellen to lead, but if she'd felt like it, she could have dragged him around the courtyard by the lapels of his jacket and he would have been grateful just to be in her clutches.

"You dance very well for a pit lord," she said as they skipped in a wide arc.

"Oh yes. I'm the undisputed victor of the yearly dance competition. All the other pit lords are positively green with envy."

Kellen lifted an arm to spin her in a quick circle, his hand never leaving her waist. She wasn't as good a dancer as him, but she wasn't bad, either. It was probably all that pit fighting. The girl had to be quick on her feet.

"There's a dance competition?" she asked.

"Indeed there is. But don't tell. It's meant to be a secret."

Kellen twisted his hands, flipping Ren around so that her back was pressed to his front. One of his arms hugged her to his body; the other gripped her hip.

She was a little breathless when she spoke. "I'd like to be invited next year."

"Perhaps we could compete in the couples category." Kellen leaned down to her ear. "It would require hours of rehearsal," he said softly, his lips against her hair. "We'd get hot. And very sweaty. I hope you don't mind."

He guided her to face him again and pulled her flush against his chest. Their form was a disaster, with Ren's arm flung around his neck and Kellen's hand down at the small of her back. Her cheeks were reddened.

"Think you can keep up?" Ren asked, brushing her fingers over the bare skin at the back of his neck.

He tightened his hold on her. "I know I can."

Ren took in a breath, eyes flicking down to his mouth. Kellen returned the look and leaned in.

Then Ren's hand was spidered over his mask, trapping his nose and mouth like a muzzle. "I don't even know your name," she said with obviously feigned indignation. "What kind of a girl do you think I am?"

She removed her palm from his face and slipped out of the hand he had pressed to her back, but he didn't let go of her fingers. "Wait."

Her dark brows arched in question, but Kellen said nothing more. As the dancing continued around them, they were bumped and jostled, apologies tossed their way like bouquets at a wedding, but their gazes held. Ren seemed to be deciding what to say. Maybe she would ask him to dance another song or go for spiced elderberry tea, then walk down the Battgandon River side by side, their breath warming the winter air like puffs of thick smoke. Kellen really wanted a peek inside that head of hers.

In the distance, over the stomping feet and plucked strings, Kellen heard the faint tolling of a bell. He silently cursed. "I have to go," he said, even though all he wanted was to dance with Ren all night, to trade suggestive lines and learn exactly what made her laugh. He still hadn't seen her smile. "Come back to my pit. You don't have to fight. I just want to see you."

"Why?" she asked.

"Perhaps I'd like to get to know you."

"There's not much to know."

He gave her the type of smirk women liked to gossip about. "I doubt that."

Without breaking her stare, he lifted her hand to his lips and placed a kiss on the soft leather of her glove. Though she looked faintly amused, a slight twitch to her dark mouth and a glint in her eye, she was otherwise impassive. But Kellen had to wonder, if he moved his fingers a couple inches and felt her pulse, would it be pounding like his?

Kellen dropped Ren's hand, and however much he didn't want to, he turned his back on her, weaved through the dancers, and left the courtyard behind. As he crossed the Battgandon River and made his way north, he covered up the parts of himself that had been stripped bare for the day. By the time he arrived back at the stage in Talmarquin Square, Kellen was a prince once more.

CHAPTER
THIRTY-ONE

He didn't like watching her with someone else.

Of course, Darek would never admit that to anyone, himself included. He only stood at the edge of the tiny courtyard, shoulder propped against an arch, and tracked Ren as she twirled like a figurine in a jewelry box. Her partner was skilled, and he knew it. It was in his grin, in the way he held his shoulders as if no weight could bow them. Like he was used to people listening when he spoke. The man could have at least shown a little humility. He didn't have to be so cocky.

Darek was really starting to regret telling Ren to meet him here.

"You could have asked her to dance," said a voice at his shoulder.

Darek didn't glance at his brother. Out in the crowd, the man dipped Ren and pulled her swiftly upright. At least she wasn't smiling. Darek didn't think he'd ever seen a genuine smile from her. Her lips were just another set of blades, and she only lifted them when it served her purposes. To charm or bribe or distract. To deliver a killing blow. Darek was satisfied to see that he wasn't the only one who had difficulty winning something real.

"I don't want to dance with her," he said.

"Then why can't you take your eyes off her?"

At that, Darek turned his head and glowered at his brother.

Markus laughed. "Maybe I'll ask her to dance," he mused.

"Go ahead," Darek said, looking back at the dancing and trying to pretend like he wasn't looking back at her.

"She dances well."

"I hadn't noticed."

"I suppose you hadn't noticed her dress, either."

Oh, Darek had noticed it. Noticed the way the dark-green fabric brought out the color in her eyes and set her pale skin glowing, how it dipped and glided, smooth as a lake on a particularly calm day. How she looked so different in it, compared to the hard lines of her usual attire. Yet Ren still looked like herself, the same annoying, devious girl Darek had come to know over the past three weeks. He had always suspected she'd been blessed by the god of deception. The dress only confirmed it.

"What does it matter if I noticed her dress?"

Markus cocked a smile. "So you admit it?"

"It's a dress. It's green. You noticed it, too."

"Whatever helps you sleep at night, big brother," Markus said, clapping Darek on the shoulder and setting his sights on a boy across the yard. Darek watched as

Markus introduced himself. The boy blushed, then nodded, agreeing to join his brother in a dance.

When he turned his gaze forward once again, Ren and the masked man had stopped dancing and now stood in the middle of the lively crowd, completely still. The man leaned in, and Darek's brows pulled down. He was going to kiss Ren. Darek didn't know why he cared. Ren had surely kissed men before. She didn't belong to Darek. She didn't even *like* Darek, never mind that he swore her eyes had flashed to him when the man had first approached her. She could do as she pleased.

But then Ren shoved a hand to his face, and Darek's shoulders let go of the tension he hadn't realized he'd been wearing like a heavy woolen cloak. The two exchanged words, their fingers intertwined, until finally he left her in the middle of the courtyard.

Without giving indecision time to set in, Darek pushed off from the arch and maneuvered through the crowd. When he got to her side, Ren lifted her brows, the action pulling at a healing cut on her temple. Something had happened the first day of the carnival—that much, Darek knew—but whenever he asked for the details, Ren brushed him off or told him not to worry, then went about glaring at him like she'd never met anyone more annoying. Still, she'd been a little wary the past few days. She kept her chin down whenever she left the Compound, her hair obscuring her face and eyes darting around as if she excepted a knife to come flying for her head.

He glowered at the red mark. Did she really have to

be so bleeding stubborn all the time? He just wanted to know where the damn cut had come from.

She'd gone lighter on the cosmetics around her eyes, a simple line of black, rather than her usual angry smudge. She was no less striking today than she had been yesterday or the night he'd woken her from the throes of a nightmare, bare-faced and perspiring. Why did that bother him so much, that he found her attractive?

Why did everything about her *bother him so much*?

Even in his own head—even just the thought of her— Ren was somehow managing to irritate him. How very typical.

"Yes?" she asked off his silence.

He still didn't say anything. He wasn't sure what to say. Why had he come out here? To ask her to dance with him? Maybe he wanted to ask her not to dance with another man tonight—any other night, for that matter. Not that it was something he had any right to ask. He didn't know why he even cared at all.

The music came to a halt, the dancing stopped, and the revelers burst into applause. Under the archways they'd claimed as a stage, the musicians performed little bows. The flux shook sense back into Darek's head. "The Crown's Demonstration will be starting soon," he said. "We should head over to Talmarquin Square."

Attendance was mandatory—or as mandatory as these things could be. Those on the streets were ushered toward the massive square by the Royal Guard, anyone caught dallying was personally escorted there, and shops and cafés along the main roads were cleared out. The only way to skip the spectacle was to hole up in a private residence or someplace else off the beaten path. Guards simply didn't have enough time to knock on every door and drag people across the city, though Darek suspected each year the king considered making them do it anyway.

But even if viewing the demonstration had been on a volunteer basis, Darek still would have gone. He'd been studying the Lyandors for years, and he never missed an opportunity to get to know them a little better.

Ren did not seem to share his interest in the royal family. When she frowned, he thought she was going to refuse to go, but she only buttoned her coat over her dress and nodded.

Darek grabbed Markus on the way out of the courtyard, and as they traipsed north, he made sure to stay in the thick of the crowd, out of sight of any guards on the off chance they might be recognized. At his right, Ren had suddenly become the least graceful person he'd ever known. She bumped and jostled her way through the crowd, apologizing again and again. Darek resisted the urge to roll his eyes. If she had ever uttered an authentic apology in her life, he'd grant her wish and toss himself headfirst into the Battgandon.

The city was pouring into Talmarquin Square. From above, it must have looked like floodgates opening and a sea of heads rushing through. At the edge of the square, Darek, Markus, and Ren took up a spot in front of a yellow building with white trim, in view of the elevated stage some couple hundred feet away but far enough to the side to avoid the press of bodies. Darek pulled out a gold pocket watch and checked the time. The demonstration would start in about five minutes. The streetlamps winked to life one by one.

Ren held out a bracelet made of small amethyst gems connected by a silver chain and showed Darek her wrist. "Help me put it on?"

He glowered at the purple stones. "What is wrong with you?"

"Would you like a list?" She curled her fingers in and tucked the bracelet away. Toying absently with the newly stolen goods in her pocket, her attention drifted to the crowd before them.

The light was quickly fading. If the clouds hadn't been so thick, Talmarquin Square would have been bathed in a brilliant gold hovering on the cusp of sunset. The stage stood empty at the front of the square, maroon curtains embroidered with two gold lion heads on full display. In a makeshift orchestral pit, a group of musicians from the Royal Symphony were setting up. Ren blew out an impatient breath and began to pick at the ends of her dark hair.

Darek didn't know what compelled him to say the next thing that came out of his mouth. "Who was that man you were dancing with?"

Ren went still. She glanced up at him. "Why do you want to know?"

He was asking himself the same question.

But Darek didn't have much time to contemplate the

answer, because the orchestra was playing their opening notes, a hush settling over the crowd. "Forget it."

The music grew louder as four Ticharran fire-breathers treaded up the steps and spread themselves out on stage. They held lit batons, their oiled chests gleaming.

"No, Darek, do tell," Ren pressed. "Why are you so curious about the men I dance with?"

Darek clenched his teeth. Instead of responding to her query, he added another of his own. "Are you interested in him?"

"You are as tall as a tree and as dumb as one, you know that?"

The music picked up pace, and the fire-breathers twirled their batons. Flames dancing, they glided to the corners of the stage while notes dipped and swayed in a melodic rhythm. As one, the Ticharran men breathed clouds of flame. Every torch on the stage burst to life. Fires burned high on the right and left, and two dozen small flames dotted the front of the stage. The shadows drew back, the curtains shimmering like wet blood.

"You didn't answer my question," Darek said.

The audience clapped as the fire-breathers departed the stage.

"Heavens, Darek, so what if I am interested in him? Is it any of your business who I let into my bed?"

No, it certainly wasn't. Maybe if they were together. Then he wouldn't want anyone in Ren's bed but himself.

Gods, what was wrong with him? Why did he keep

finding himself here, thinking about Ren and her damn purple bedsheets?

The orchestra beat their drums in a frenzy, and the curtains drew open to reveal King Mattheus, a ruby-studded crown atop his dark hair, and a cloak of pure gold gently swaying at his back. He stood alone at center stage.

"It's not as if anyone else had asked me to dance," Ren said, more distracted now. She eyed the king, her shoulders stiff under a white fur collar.

King Mattheus held his hands out to his sides, silver licking at his palms.

Darek steeled himself, and his attention shifted from the stage down to Ren. He couldn't believe he was about to utter the next nine words. "If I had asked, would you have said yes?"

Markus sucked in a sharp breath. "Darek," he breathed, his voice low and horrified.

Darek whipped his head toward the king, and his heart nearly stopped. Two men and one woman with shackled wrists were shuffling onto the stage. They were badly beaten, but the blood and dirt had been washed away so their faces were recognizable to those who knew them—like Darek and his brother and anyone else who frequented the White Raven. All three rebels had been captured in the raid last week.

Before Darek knew what he was doing, before he could even think to stop himself, he took a step forward. A hand clamped down on his collar. "Don't," his brother whispered. "Please."

He came to his senses and fell back into line beside Ren. Markus dropped his arm, but no matter how hard he tried, Darek couldn't uncurl his fists. He shoved them into his pockets.

The rebels halted directly in front of King Mattheus. Silver swirled behind their backs, creeping forward to wrap itself around their legs, sliding up their arms and chests. The music was still playing, but it was fuzzy background noise to the one thought racing through Darek's mind: he could do nothing to stop this.

King Mattheus raised his arms, and his silver lifted the rebels into the air. They floated five, ten, fifteen feet above the stage, hanging suspended before the crowd. No one moved. Torches flickered. Then the king rotated his wrists, and the silver twisted. The rebels spasmed, their screams mixing with the music. Darek closed his eyes and said a prayer.

When the orchestra abruptly stopped playing, he forced himself to look. King Mattheus jerked his arms, and the rebels' screams ricocheted off the buildings as their bodies contorted, folding in on themselves in sickening ways. Darek didn't know if he imagined the sound of cracking bone or if he heard it, but either way, it didn't really matter. In the corner of his vision, he saw Markus shove a hand to his mouth, his eyes squeezed shut. Ren's face was cold and blank. She was so still she could have been a statue.

She wasn't the only one. Quiet and tense, it was as if Talmarquin Square had frozen over.

The king lowered his arms and brought the rebels

down, their bodies thumping loudly onto the stage. The silver glow faded, and then it was only the king of Erdis and three dead rebels at his feet. Not one person in the square spoke. No one shifted a foot as the slow hum of music started up again and the curtains closed on the scene.

"Is that it?" Ren asked, her voice hard. "Is it over?"

Darek shook his head. It wasn't the first time the Crown's Demonstration had included something sadistic. Last year, the king and his sons had fancied themselves puppeteers, using their silver to push some poor souls around stage. By the end of it, when the Lyandors had lowered their arms, a few people had collapsed from exhaustion. But this year's demonstration was supposed to last quite a bit longer, and the princes should have been present.

"The choreography didn't look anything like this," he said. His voice was deep and rough, as if he hadn't spoken in months. He couldn't stop picturing snapped spines. Screams echoed in his head. He held on to the promise he'd made his mother. This wouldn't be for nothing. In the end, the torture and violence and death would mean something.

The orchestra started up again. Darek wanted to hate the musicians, and part of him did, but another part of him recognized that the king's grip on the city was so strong, his wrath so fierce, most of them were likely there by force. Darek wouldn't be surprised if they only played because they had families to protect.

It was inching past dusk, and the cloudy sky was fading

from gray to black. In the torchlight, the curtains shifted between shades of crimson, and for the second time that evening, they pulled apart. The rebels' bodies were gone, and the king had returned, now with the princes flanking him. Where King Mattheus wore gold, the two youngest Lyandors were dressed in maroon cloaks. Darek assessed them through narrowed eyes, his jaw clenched.

At twenty-two years old, Crown Prince Heath made regular public appearances. He attended trials and executions, visited the Royal Theatre and Opera House, greeted emissaries when their ships docked at the harbor. His smile was charming, and his manner was easy. Both did his bidding as effectively as a royal decree, and Darek didn't trust him.

Prince Kellen was three years younger and more likely to be spotted in a tavern than involved in any political affair. The city ran rampant with rumors. By this point, Darek had heard of one hundred illegitimate children and even more illicit affairs, and though he doubted the former, there was likely some truth to the latter. But Kellen still had a claim to the Erdis throne, which made him a problem.

Heath and Kellen were rarely spotted together, so Darek often forgot how much they looked alike: tall and lean, a light tan to their skin, and hair like burnished gold, their fine features a little too attractive. They both might have been described as pretty—elegant, even.

The three Lyandor men turned their palms out at their sides, fingertips touching. They formed one long line, from hand to hand to hand. The king called up his silver first. It formed in his palms like flickering flames, growing larger and larger, then jumped to his sons. The princes added their own magic, stoking the silver flames into two bonfires hovering on either side of the king. The silver arced over the princes' heads and landed in their outstretched hands on either end of the line. Four fires swirled and snapped.

In synchronization, the king and his sons lifted their arms over their heads, and their silver fire collapsed into a blinding orb that must have been twenty feet wide. They pivoted to face each other, twisting their wrists. The silver morphed in the air, spreading and thinning like saltwater taffy pulled by a confectioner.

The music reached its dramatic crescendo, and a massive silver lion swirled into shape. The Lyandors stepped into a line and brought the lion down in front of them. It prowled from one side of the stage to the other, mane as wide as the sails of a ship and paws the size of carriages. When its mouth opened in a silent roar, the orchestra pounded their drums and clashed their symbols. Those closest to the stage would have ringing ears for an hour.

"This is such bullshit," Markus muttered.

Darek cut his eyes to his brother, who had on the deepest frown he'd ever seen. Between the two of them, Ren was staring at the stage with a look on her face Darek couldn't place. Disbelief, maybe? Shock?

"Ren?"

The king and his sons lifted their silver lion off the stage, pausing while it rotated in the air. Then they flung out their arms, and the animal sailed into the crowd, teeth bared, claws out. Just before colliding with the screaming audience, it exploded in a swirl of mist.

"What is it?" Darek asked.

Slowly, Ren tore her gaze from the demonstration. She turned toward him, wide-eyed. Silver fell over the square like glittering rain.

"Ren?" Darek tried again, exchanging a worried glance with Markus. The crowd burst into applause as the silver drew together and became a flurry of birds, swooping and diving over their heads.

Ren glanced at the stage. She looked back to Darek and said, "I don't think the crown prince has magic."

PART THREE

CHAPTER
THIRTY-TWO

"In here," Ren said, standing before a locked door.

While the silver birds were fluttering through the air, Darek had nodded toward a side street. He, Markus, and Ren slipped out of the square to find the closest place they could talk without being observed or overheard, which happened to be a deserted tea shop. Ren summoned a thread of silver, goaded it through the gap between the bottom of the door and the ground, and unlocked the shop from the inside. A bell at the top of the door tinkled as she popped it open and stepped through, Darek and Markus close behind.

After he'd reengaged the lock, Darek asked, "Are you sure about Heath?"

"Positive," Ren said as they moved away from the windows and into the darkness of the shop, skirting around mismatched chairs and low-sitting tables wiped clean. "The way Heath was moving his hands wasn't right. If he'd been wielding, he'd have taken out the entire orchestra and a good portion of the crowd up front. I wasn't sure at first, but then he twisted his wrist in the wrong direction, and his silver didn't smash into the string section like it should have."

Darek hadn't noticed a thing, but then again, Ren was the one with silver. "What about Kellen?" he asked.

"I'm pretty sure he has magic. I think he and the king were sending their silver to Heath, and he mimicked them to make it look like he had his own."

"It makes sense," Markus said. "They always start the same way: the king's magic appears first and moves to the princes' hands."

Darek nodded. "This explains the choreography from the Royal Theatre. I've always felt like there was something off about it, but I could never figure out what it was. Someone there must know."

"How it possible for Kellen to have silver, but not Heath?" Markus wondered out loud.

"Same way I was born with silver," Ren said. She wiggled her brows at Darek. "A gift from the gods."

Darek gave her his flattest look. "You think you're really funny, don't you?"

"Not *really* funny. Mildly amusing, perhaps."

"Ren," Markus said, "how have you never noticed this before?"

"I've never seen the Crown's Demonstration before."

Both brothers just stared at her.

"Why is that surprising?" she asked.

"You've lived here your entire life," Markus pointed out. "Weren't you ever curious?"

"Not even a little bit," she replied.

Darek thought he understood. The demonstration was probably harder for Ren to watch than most people, because for her it wasn't just an obvious attempt at intimidation. It was an insult, a reminder that the Lyandor family had condemned thousands to death—Ren's parents, included—for the very thing they paraded around each year. Except, as it turned out, it was a lie. The crown prince couldn't wield magic.

But Ren could.

"Wait . . ." Darek said, a realization dawning. "Ren, the other night, when you were having that nightmare, you said the crown prince was in your head."

"So?"

"That wasn't the first time you've dreamed about Heath, was it?"

She shifted, tossing her messy hair over one shoulder. "So what if it wasn't?"

Markus gave her a look. "You dream about the crown prince?"

"It's not like that," Ren snapped. "He just shows up. It's not like I can control it. It doesn't ever really feel like a dream, though. It's almost like I'm seeing him. He looks so *angry*—all the time. And I thought *I* had problems."

"You didn't think that was strange?" Darek asked.

"Not really. The man is a monster. His family killed mine. It's called a reoccurring nightmare."

"No, it's not." Darek shook his head. "Ren, you're a shadow."

"Excuse me?"

"A shadow. It's something I read about a long time ago—this really obscure piece of silver lore. There are wielders known as shadows, someone who possesses magic when they shouldn't, born into the same generation as someone who doesn't have magic but should. I'd considered it before, but never seriously.

"The king has done a great job convincing the city Heath is a wielder. I'd never understood where your magic came from, but it makes so much sense now. You're Heath's shadow. That's why you've been seeing him in your dreams. There's this theory that people and their shadows are bridged in some way. The book I read didn't specify through *dreams*, but that must be it. Heath has probably been seeing you, too."

"Well, that's a comforting thought," Ren muttered. "So what does this mean for your revolution?"

Markus looked like he was about to say something, but Darek got there first. "It changes nothing."

"Really?" Ren asked. "Because if I were you—"

"Well, you're not me," Darek interjected, knowing he sounded harsh but not being able to stop. "So why don't you leave the rebellion to the people who actually care about it?"

Ren's eyes went cold. "Look how well that worked out for your mother." She turned on her heel, shoes clicking and green silk swirling around her ankles.

Darek and Markus stood in silence while she yanked open the door, the bell chiming softly as she strode out of the dark tea shop. It remained ajar behind her, the empty road in view.

Like locating the gaps in a suit of armor, she'd known just the place to strike Darek, just the spot that would make him bleed, but he was determined not to feel the pain. That was what Ren wanted, after all: for someone to ache as deeply as she did. She spewed her venom, thinking he'd swallow some and keep his distance. Darek wouldn't give her that. She could push him away, but he was going to keep coming back again and again, and she'd just have to deal with it.

"We need to start trusting her," Markus said. "We need to tell her."

"We will."

"When?"

Darek hesitated. He didn't have an answer. "I don't know. Soon."

"If we keep this from her—"

"I *know*, Markus. Let me deal with it."

Darek headed for the door, Markus following him out into the cold. The clouds were thinning, and pale moonlight brushed the little shopping district they'd wandered into, feathering over bricks painted in shades of green and yellow and pink. Two mugs sat abandoned on a round table outside the tea shop. On a bench across the street, someone had forgotten their hat.

"You don't know how to deal with Ren," Markus said.

"Does anyone?"

They set out for the Compound, having decided the

Atterton District still wasn't safe, especially not now that they'd broken Riko out of the castle dungeons and a handful of guards had seen their faces. It did help that the swelling was gone from Darek's nose and the bruising was lighter than it had been five days ago, but it was a feeble comfort. Jaston was lying low, too.

It took the better part of a half hour to trudge across the river and down to Hessler, and when they stepped through the doors of the cracked-and-graying building, they found everything much quieter than usual. No kids spilling over the arms of worn chairs; no shoes smacking across the dull floorboards or voices echoing down the halls. Markus eased the creaking door shut, and they headed for the stairs. As they passed the kitchen, Darek caught sight of a kid with rusty-orange hair sitting at the long wooden dining table by himself.

"Is Ren around?" Darek asked. He hoped she was—he wanted to make peace with her sooner rather than later.

"No," the kid said. He took a bite of bread that didn't look all that fresh. "She went to that pit near the Underground. Freya, too."

Darek suspected that might have been his doing. He'd obviously ticked her off earlier, and when she got angry, she hit things until they broke, probably hoping that somewhere along the way she would start to feel better. He doubted it ever worked. What Ren needed couldn't be found in the bloodstained sand of a fighting pit.

He checked his pocket watch. It was early enough that the city would still be wrapped up in the carnival festivities. "I'm going to stop by the house and check on Riko," he told Markus. Although it was a risk to venture toward their home, Riko had mostly been unconscious since they'd gotten him out of the castle, and Darek was hoping he might finally be able to speak with him.

"I'll stay here. I want to draw for a while," Markus said, to Darek's surprise.

His brother hadn't been creating much since killing the guard, and Darek hoped his work would still be romantic and soft, brimming with optimism. He'd always marveled at that—how Markus could breathe life into brushstrokes and smudges of charcoal, his ability to stir emotion with nothing but canvas and paint. It was its own kind of magic.

Darek clapped his brother on the shoulder and departed the Compound.

CHAPTER
THIRTY-THREE

No one spoke on the way back from the carnival. Not Kellen, and not his father. The king was in an even worse mood than he'd been on the way into the city, his distain hanging in the air like humidity. Kellen had expected some kind of reprimand or at least a demeaning comment about his earlier disappearance, but it seemed his father was taking the route of pretending he didn't exist. Kellen thought he might have preferred verbal debasement. The silence was heavy and uncomfortable; it made him feel as if a punishment were coming.

When their carriage came to a stop inside the castle walls, Kellen was in such a haste to escape he practically tumbled out onto the stones. As he righted himself, he caught a glimpse of his brother striding inside, maroon cloak flapping furiously at his heels. Before heading in, as well, Kellen undid the gold buckles on his own showy cloak and handed it off to the nearest guard.

With his hands shoved into his coat pockets, Kellen meandered through the towering doors, offering a nod to the guards who held them open. The entryway was aglow. Candles slowly melted in the chandeliers high above, and lamps burned bright, their light washing over a set of pale stone staircases, intricately carved banisters and walls, and tapestries threaded with rich gold string. As Kellen made his way to his chambers, the tap of his shoes filling the empty halls was the only sound to keep him company.

A long hallway greeted him at the top of one staircase, a row of arching windows set into the wall. He decided to go left instead of right, toward his brother's chambers instead of away, because even though Heath didn't need his concern, nor did he much deserve it, Kellen couldn't help the small part of himself that wished they could find their way to a better place. Heath was a pretty terrible brother, this was true, but it wasn't as if Kellen was winning many awards for his own brotherly behavior.

At the end of the hall, Heath's door was cracked, yellow rimming the edges and leaking out to cast a solitary beam of light on the floor. Kellen stopped and listened. It was quiet on the other side. He rapped his knuckles against the wood. "Heath?" Slowly, he pushed the door open to reveal the inside of his brother's massive bedchamber, where a fire was roaring in its hearth. Shadows danced over a plush rug and a canopied bed. A red velvet settee with clawed feet was stationed before the fireplace, a maroon cloak and leather jacket thrown in a lump on top.

His back to Kellen, Heath stood beside the hearth and stared into a large mirror propped against the wall. His palms were faceup in front of his chest, blue eyes as sharp as the edges of raw sapphire. He curled his fingers in and unfurled them. Nothing happened.

Kellen shoved his hair out of his face as he stepped fully into the room. "Heath . . ."

"It's not fair," Heath said, watching his hands.

"I know."

Heath looked up and met Kellen's gaze in the mirror. His eyes flashed. "You don't even want silver. I hate that you don't appreciate it. You only use it because if you don't, it'll explode."

"I would give you mine if I could," Kellen lied. He didn't want his silver or the violent Lyandor legacy attached to it, but he didn't want Heath to have it, either. He'd never admit it to anyone, but he thought they were all lucky his brother had no silver of his own. Kellen suspected the way his father had opened today's demonstration was child's play compared to what Heath would do with that kind of power.

Then again, Kellen had to wonder if things would be different had Heath been born with silver. He'd always known his brother was poisoned by his lust for power. It ate away at him like rot consuming a felled tree.

Heath had also once had a shadow running around, that little girl he'd said he dreamed about, which didn't help things. There was an old belief, back from when silver wielders were still plentiful, that shadows were the result of inadequacy. It was thought that a person born without silver wound up that way because they weren't worthy to wield it, and though no one talked about it, Heath and the king both seemed to subscribe to this idea. Kellen wasn't sure what he believed. He thought maybe the gods were just sparing them from his brother.

It did make him wonder, though: what if the girl hadn't died like she was supposed to? What if, like her silver, she'd existed when she shouldn't have?

"Do you think that wielder who sunk our ships could be your shadow?" Kellen asked.

Heath's expression iced over. A muscle twitched in his jaw. "She's dead. Father saw to that." He pivoted, tearing open the top buttons on his shirt. "I'm sick of this." He pulled his belt and sword off, stalked forward and tossed them on top of his cloak, then dropped onto the settee.

"Sick of what?" Kellen asked.

"All of it." Heath ran a hand through his hair and braced his elbows on his knees. "The demonstration. Pretending like I have silver while you and Father cover for me. For the gods' sakes, Kell, the Royal Theatre has to come up with our choreography because I can't wield."

Kellen opened his mouth, but stopped when Heath looked up. The lines of his brother's face were severe.

"Don't lie to me like you do every year and say that we'd need choreography no matter what. I know you and Father could do what we did today without *help*." The word sounded bitter on his tongue. "I can tell Father is sick of it, too. I've done everything I can to please him. This kingdom matters to me. The crown matters to me. I've been trying to show him that, but nothing is ever enough. I'm not enough for him. And Mother ignores me entirely. It's like I don't exist."

Kellen fought a sigh. The demonstration never failed to put his brother in a mood, and after nearly two decades of this, Kellen's patience was wearing a little thin. Maybe coming in here had been a bad idea. "Welcome to the club, Heath."

"At least Mother spoiled you when you were a kid. I never even had that." Heath gave a strange, cold laugh. "You know what the worst part is? You don't care about any of it. You are the worst prince that Erdis has ever seen. Everyone knows it. Father once told me he wished he could be rid of you, but he needs your silver."

Kellen looked down, tugging at his sleeves. It wasn't like the confession surprised him. Once, their father had informed Kellen that the only reason he kept him around was because Kellen might one day need to produce heirs for Heath, if his brother couldn't bear silver wielders. It was just another harsh comment in a long litany of them, but Kellen didn't exactly enjoy verbal abuse. He wasn't about to ask it to bed with him.

"And yet," Heath went on, "sometimes I think you and I are in competition for biggest family disappointment."

"I promise you I am the reigning champion when it comes to disappointing our father."

The king's voice came from the open doorway. "I don't know about that."

Kellen started, his spine automatically pulling straighter, and Heath jumped up from the settee as the king of Erdis entered the room, still donning his golden cloak and matching crown. The space seemed to shrink and grow cold, as if a window had popped open.

"Father," Kellen said, stepping forward. He put on his easiest smile. "I was just telling Heath that the demonstration went rather well this year, don't you think?"

"Do shut up, son. Your charm may work on the whores in the city, but it won't work on me."

Kellen let the smile fall from his face. He threw a look at his brother, but Heath only watched the king.

"As for the demonstration"—despite the fact that Heath had an inch on their father, he somehow still managed to stare down at his eldest son—"you were adequate."

"*Adequate?*" Heath said, nose flaring. "That's it?"

The king met Heath's indignant expression with one of his own. "Well, surely you don't expect me to shower you with praise. Call up some silver, then maybe I'll pay you a godsdamn compliment."

A muscle feathered in Heath's jaw. Kellen noticed, but he wasn't sure their father did.

"There is a council meeting tomorrow morning, and I expect you both to be there." His eyes shifted to Kellen. "That includes you, Kellen. Stop sneaking away, and act like a prince for once in your life."

"Father," Heath interjected, "I actually wanted to speak with you about some ideas I have in regard to the treaty. Perhaps I could present them at the meeting?"

If Heath's eyes were cold, the king's were a frozen tundra. "Have you not wasted enough of my time? Now you want to waste my council's time as well?"

Heath snapped his mouth shut. It was quiet for far too long, until finally he said, "No, Father. My apologies."

He didn't really sound sorry at all.

The king spent another moment looking over his sons, then he turned and left, golden cloak fluttering behind him as he swept down the low-lit hall, heading for the stairs at a brisk pace. His footsteps could be heard long after he'd disappeared from sight.

And people wondered why Kellen wouldn't just stay in the castle.

Heath turned his back on both Kellen and the open door. He walked over to the fireplace, where he picked up an iron poker and began to prod at one of the already blazing logs.

"Heath—"

All of a sudden, Heath whirled toward his mirror, the poker raised above his head. He brought it down hard. Glass shrieked and fractured, cracks splintering like a spider web over the reflective surface. Kellen stood frozen as shards of mirror dropped from the golden frame and rained down to the floor, the jagged edges as sharp as a newly forged knife.

Heath was motionless before the broken mirror. Kellen stared at his brother with wide eyes, his mind gone blank. The sound of shattering glass rang and rang in his ears. He was sure he would hear it in his dreams tonight.

"I want you to go, Kellen," Heath said in a voice so low it was hard to make out the words.

Kellen went.

CHAPTER
THIRTY-FOUR

When Darek arrived at his house, he went straight to a guest bedroom on the second floor that overlooked a sparkling river and a city of lit windows. Riko was asleep in a heap of deep-blue fabric, not looking much better than he had when they'd first brought him here. The blood and filth had been cleaned away, but his entire face was swollen, like he'd been attacked by a swarm of bees. He was covered in more bruises than not, and though there was a thick bandage wrapped around his right forearm, Darek had seen what was underneath. Riko's arm would be scarred forever.

Darek went downstairs to thumb a book from the library shelves before settling into the chair beside Riko. He kicked his feet up on the duvet and flipped the novel open, reading by the light of a crackling fire in a hearth at the foot of the bed.

About ten minutes passed before Darek heard the distant sound of the front door clicking shut. Swinging his legs down, he set the book aside and slipped out of the room. The hall was shadowed, the lamps unlit, moonlight falling in squares across the pale floors and ivory walls.

Jaston appeared at the top of the staircase just as Darek was easing the guest bedroom door closed.

"How is he?" Jaston asked, tugging open the buttons of his overcoat.

"Still sleeping," Darek said. "Did you see the demonstration?"

Jaston was in the middle of unknotting his woolen scarf, and he finished the job with a terse yank. "Yes. I thought I was going to be sick. The night we overthrow that bastard, I'm getting piss-drunk and buying everyone we know a celebratory ale. I swear, if we don't get this done soon—"

"The crown prince doesn't have magic," Darek cut in.

Jaston's chin jerked up. "What?"

"Heath isn't a silver wielder. Ren figured it out. She says King Mattheus and Prince Kellen were only making it look like he is. And before you ask, yes, she's positive. Looks like you were right about her being a shadow."

Dropping his arms to his sides, Jaston fell back against the wall and stared down into the foyer. "Well, I'll be damned." He looked at Darek. "What can we do with this?"

"I was thinking about that," Darek said, leaning against the railing opposite Jaston. "We always knew the hycanthian flowers were a risk. There was never any guarantee they would work, but now that we don't need Heath to drink them . . ."

"We could kill Kellen," Jaston finished. "But how? We both know killing the Lyandors is impossible; otherwise, someone would have done it by now."

"It'll be tricky, but if we can get to any of them, it'll be Kellen. You've heard the rumors. He sneaks away from the castle without his guards. We just have to figure out where he goes."

A pained groan came from behind the guest bedroom door, followed by a mumbled, "Darek?"

They both bolted upright. Darek made it to the door first and pushed into the room, Jaston close behind. Riko was blinking blearily, and for the first time since the beginning of the Crown's Demonstration, the pressure in Darek's chest lightened. "It's good to see you awake," he said softly, coming up to the side of the bed.

Riko gave another groan. "Hurts."

"I know. I'm sorry."

He shifted his head toward Darek, blinking once. His eyes went wide, and he pushed up onto his elbows, a grimace twisting his face. "Where is Ren? Is she okay?" His voice was rough from disuse and laced with panic.

Darek placed a hand on Riko's shoulder, gently urging him down. He felt his forehead, but his friend didn't have a fever. "Shh, Riko, it's okay. Ren is fine."

He collapsed back, eyes drifting shut. "No, you don't understand. I messed up. Oh gods, I messed up."

Darek glanced over his shoulder at Jaston. There was a deep frown line above his nose. "What is it?" Darek asked Riko, but he didn't reply. His chest only rose and fell in pained shudders. "What happened?"

At last, Riko peeled his eyes open. "I told a King's Child about Ren. She's looking for her."

Darek went still. It was as if a brick had been dropped into the pit of his stomach, and the weight only got heavier as Riko tried to explain. His memory was hazy at best, but it sounded like he'd been disoriented after hours of torture. He didn't know how the slip had happened, but he'd told a King's Child about a girl they were working with, a pit fighter.

Tension clung to every muscle in Darek's body. He was a statue made of it, so stiff that if he moved, he might break.

Behind his back, Jaston asked, "Darek, where's Ren?"

Darek wasn't prone to violence, but right now he thought putting his fist through the guest bedroom wall might make him feel better. It might turn him from stone into something human again. Ren's perpetually narrowed stare flashed through his mind.

"I have to go," he said, pulling his coat off the back of the chair. He dashed out of the room, tugging on a sleeve as he ran.

"Where is she?!" Jaston yelled from the doorway.

Darek sprinted down the stairs three at a time, thanking the gods that the boy at the Compound had told him where Ren had gone. "She's at a fighting pit!" He wrenched open his door and took off down the front walk. Streetlamps lit his path as he raced in the direction of the Underground, praying he wouldn't be too late.

CHAPTER
THIRTY-FIVE

It was hours past the official end of the Royal Carnival, and Adley was performing a sweep through a seedier part of the city, where lamps were rarely lit and no one was out unless they had a nefarious reason to be roaming the darkened streets like a wraith. She was more determined than ever to find the silver wielder who had sunk thirteen ships on the first night of the carnival. As it turned out, the girl's little stunt had been something of a diversion. At the same moment Adley and Lesa had been watching her wield silver, a group of rebels had been breaking a prisoner out of the dungeons—one of Adley's prisoners, the same man who'd let slip that the rebels had a female pit fighter in their midst. It only confirmed Adley's suspicions that the wielder was the girl she was after.

Adley passed between tall, thin buildings, many of which were abandoned, their windows broken and boarded up. The construction didn't seem to have any rhyme or reason—dead ends randomly appearing, and corners forcing her to alter her path—but after a while, she caught the unmistakable screams of a fighting pit nearby.

Adley had always let pit fighters be. Though she had

a vague idea of where the city's pits were located, she never visited. Pit fighting wasn't illegal, even if it should have been. Most investors had a roster of fighters they provided with room and board, but only for a hefty fee and an even larger interest rate. Then they shoved their fighters into the sand and took their winnings when it was through. It was slavery, pure and simple, but that wasn't really illegal, either.

Following the raised voices, she eventually came upon a set of rusted steel doors. She pulled them open, and the smell of blood and sweat assaulted her nose. When she went to step inside, a beefy hand slapped into her chest. The bouncer didn't spare her a glance. "Two silvers."

Adley snatched his fingers and jerked them back, the bones snapping. He spit a curse, but it was drowned out by the feverish roar spilling from the room. "Do not touch me," she said, dropping his broken hand.

Teeth gritted and nostrils flaring, the bouncer looked one second from striking her, but then his eyes flitted to the lion stitched on her chest, the leather uniform, the bow and arrows slung over her back. He dropped his chin and mumbled, "Apologies." Damaged hand cradled to his chest, he stepped aside and held the door open.

The room was large, square, and covered in flickering shades of orange, with sconces lining the stone walls and three iron chandeliers dangling from the ceiling. Adley scanned dozens of heads, all eyes trained on the circular pit. Moments after the door clanged shut, fists shot into the air, groans intermixed with thunderous cheering.

Adley plunged into the crowd and pushed forward until she came to the wooden divide between the observers and participants, the few people who had noticed her leather uniform backing up a step to give her a wide berth. Two fighters were facing off in the sand. One was a man with a bare chest, tanned and taut, his hair a sun-bleached blond, and though he wasn't particularly muscular, what muscle he did have was hard as stone. The other fighter was a tall girl, a long braid of messy black hair trailing down her back. Her bodice was crafted from leather, and the gold buckles on her knee-high boots glinted in the torchlight. She had one hip jutted, hands on her thin waist, lips pursed in a smirk.

Although she may have been slight enough to snap in half under a strong breeze, it looked like the silver wielder from the docks was winning. The man was crunched forward, hands braced on his thighs while he sucked in ragged breaths. He sneered at her, his frustration obvious, and pushed up straight to stalk forward. The girl dragged her green eyes over his body, from the ragged ends of his hair to the worn soles of his boots, as if she had never been less impressed in her life.

Her opponent pulled his fist back and rounded a punch, but he didn't land it. The girl dropped to the sand and rolled, springing to her feet a yard away. When he went after her again, she bounced out of reach. Over and over it went, and the silver wielder never threw a single punch of her own. Adley could see why. The other fighter outweighed her by at least fifty pounds, and while she was quick as a whip, she couldn't win with her own strength, so she used her opponent's instead. What had once been an asset to this man was now working against him. The girl was wearing him out, both physically and mentally, and she would keep at it until what strength she did possess was enough to win.

Despite herself, Adley was impressed. It really was clever.

When the man came for her once more, he was so sluggish that the girl was able to latch on to his arm and bend it into a painful angle behind his back. As she lifted his elbow, she pushed his neck down, forcing him into a hunch. She whispered in his ear, and he sneered, kicking out in an attempt to knock her off balance. Twisting his arm, she maneuvered him around, swept his feet out from beneath him, and shoved him onto his back in the sand. Then she was straddling him, and before a blink had passed, she jabbed him in the nose. The hit was hard enough to break bone, causing blood to flow over his face. The audience roared, fists pumping and bodies jostling as the girl attacked again, this time with a punch to the throat. The man writhed beneath her. She readied her arm a third time, and that was when he found her thigh and slapped his palm against it in surrender.

The girl stared down at him, fist still drawn back. It was a few seconds before she dropped her arm. She placed her hands on his chest and shoved to her feet, the swollen knuckles on her right hand and a messy braid the only indication she'd been in a fight. She didn't offer a hand to the man, nor did she spare a glance back at him as she walked away.

Adley knew her brows were lifted so high they were in danger of disappearing off her face. Wherever this girl had learned to fight, she would have made an excellent King's Child.

Grinning from ear to ear, the pit lord—who wasn't a lord at all, but a lady—jumped off the rail and met the wielder in the sand. She assessed the girl approvingly before turning toward the crowd. "Victor!"

As jeers and shouts rumbled through the fighting pit and the silver wielder held out a hand to accept her winnings, Adley reached for an arrow.

CHAPTER
THIRTY-SIX

The pit lord was placing two gold coins in Ren's palm when instinct tugged at her spine. She pulled her arm away, the gold coins tumbling down to the red-stained sand, and a moment later, an arrow pierced through the pit lord's hand. If Ren hadn't moved, it would have shoved through hers, too. As the arrow's momentum wrenched the woman's arm back, Ren sprung away, her hands automatically going to the slits in her corset before remembering she'd emptied them for the fight. Fortunately, Ren wasn't one to play by the rules, and she had a dagger stashed in her right boot, one she never gave up, pit regulations be damned. Thumbing it free, she turned to find the arrow's origin, certain it had been intended for her.

The crowd was a tumultuous mess, with people pushing for the steel doors, arms and fists flailing, shouts resounding around the stone walls. Amid the chaos, a King's Child stood at the edge of the pit, a bow in hand. In a leather uniform with a gold lion head on the chest, there was no mistaking her. There was something about her face, the dark hair that fell from her braid and waved against warm-brown skin, that looked familiar.

Oh, bleeding hells.

The King's Child had been at the docks the first night of the carnival, with the blonde girl who'd flung a knife at Ren's head and unmasked her in front of a good portion of Denfell. Ren still had a bright-red line on her temple to show for it.

Ren searched the chaos for Freya and found her weighted down with Ren's coat and knives. She wasn't running for the doors, but was shouldering her way toward the sandy pit—toward Ren. When they locked eyes, Ren shouted, "Go!"

Freya shook her head, still shoving forward. A man rammed into her side, and she was swept back in a rush of people. Ren feared someone was going to knock her unconscious and trample over her small body.

When the King's Child released another arrow, Ren didn't think. She threw up a hand, and a stream of silver light met the arrow in midair, knocking it aside. It looked like this was going to be her official coming-out party, whether she liked it or not, and anyone paying attention was an honored guest.

She turned back to Freya and screamed, "Get out of here!"

Freya paused, her face frozen in terror.

Please, Ren mouthed.

For one gut-wrenching second, Freya didn't move. Then she turned her back on the pit. Within moments, her dark curls were lost in the crowd.

Bow in one hand, the King's Child vaulted over the

railing. Her boots hit the sand, and she was running for Ren, never slowing as she nocked another arrow and pulled the string taut. Ren had only an instant to get a hand up. Silver burst from her palm, forming a wall of light in front of her, and the girl's arrow splintered on impact.

Ren drew her elbow back and shoved. Her silver slammed against the girl, knocking her to the sand. She rolled into the fall and sprang up half a second later, an arrow already in hand. Ren lashed a silver rope around her boots, the girl pulled her bowstring back, and Ren yanked her feet out from beneath her. The arrow went wide, but only just, the steel head tearing through cotton to slice the edge of Ren's bicep. She nearly dropped her knife as a hot stab of pain surged up her arm and blood blossomed along her sleeve.

Biting back a grimace, Ren faced the girl, who was lying on her back and struggling to kick free of the silver around her legs. "Look at you," Ren said, forcing nonchalance. "Can't even shoot me properly. Frankly, I'm insulted. Did the king not think me worthy of his best Child?"

The girl snatched a knife from her weapons belt and flung it. Ren threw herself to the sand, and the blade drove into the sole of her boot, a near hit, the impact reverberating up her leg. She yanked the blade free, then jumped to her feet, but she'd lost her hold on her silver, and the girl was up, too.

"Thanks for the knife." Ren rushed forward to meet the King's Child. She threw the weapon, wrapping it in silver to drive it through the air. The girl ducked, the knife shooting over her shoulder, and pivoted. Suddenly, she wasn't in front of Ren, but at her side. Ren called up her silver, but it was too late.

The King's Child drew a fist back and decked Ren in the face. She went down. Black erupted across her vision, pain blooming through her head. Warm, salty blood swirled in her mouth, a sudden pressure pushing on her chest. Ren blinked away the hazy darkness enough to register the boot planted on her ribcage.

"You talk too much," the girl said.

"If you're going to kill me, just do it," Ren gasped out. She didn't particularly want to die, but she wouldn't be surprised if she did. It was a miracle she had made it to eighteen. She'd escaped death nine years ago, and she'd been living on borrowed time ever since.

"Unfortunately for both of us, my orders are to bring you in alive."

Fuck that.

Ren had one knife left, and by some stroke of luck, it was still in her hand. She squeezed her fingers around the handle, lifted her arm, and shoved it into the King's Child's ankle.

The girl screamed. She stumbled back, her injured leg giving out, and Ren surged up. The sudden motion sent her head spinning, nausea threatening to take her down. She staggered back. Sucking in a deep breath through her nose, she called up silver and struck out, knocking the bow away from the King's Child before she could shoot again.

Ren was about to go for the girl's throat, but froze

when a slim figure with a crooked nose emerged from what remained of the crowd. He stepped up to the side of the pit, two men with biceps as large as her head flanking him.

She spit blood on the sand. "Nevskov?"

With styled black hair and a silk-lined overcoat, he was impeccable as always, dressed more for the opera house than a fighting pit. "So you're the mysterious silver wielder this city is losing their heads over," he said, voice as docile as ever. "My, my, my. Ren, darling, what other secrets have you been keeping from me?"

Ren glanced from Nevskov to the King's Child, who had gotten to her feet but was badly favoring one leg. She looked back to Nevskov. "What are you doing here?"

He cocked his head. "I know I gave you a week, but I'd grown tired of waiting. I had decided it was time for you to pay up." He paused. His eyes flickered to her hands, which were still glowing silver. "But considering recent revelations, I think you and I could come to an agreement."

Ren shifted, aligning herself with the open doors, calculating her route out. "I'm not interested."

Nevskov clasped his hands behind him. His thugs jumped into the pit, and she took two steps back. "You're a smart girl, Ren. I don't need to tell you what will happen if you refuse. So I'll make the offer one more time. Work for me. Give me use of those pretty silver hands of yours, and I'll forgive your debt. What do you say?"

Ren prepared to move. "Go to the hells and take the King's Child with you." She threw out her hands. Two rivers of silver surged, one toward Nevskov and his men, the other at the girl. The magic lifted them off their feet and threw them back. Ren didn't see where they landed. She was already running.

Outside the doors, she whirled around. Her palms went up, and silver slammed into the facade of the fighting pit. The stone groaned and cracked. Ren sent another pulse of silver at the building, and with one final shudder, the front of the pit collapsed in on itself with an echoing boom loud enough to wake the entire city.

A cloud of dust billowed out, engulfing Ren. Coughing, she careened back and smacked into a very hard chest. She twisted, silver fists ready to strike, but two large hands wrapped around her own, and a deep, familiar voice said, "Ren, it's me."

Her gaze flitted up to brown eyes, an angular nose, and a sharp, unshaven jaw. "Darek?"

"I'm here," he said. "We're here."

Ren glanced around his shoulder to see Freya standing a few feet away, clutching on to Ren's burgundy coat like a person lost at sea might cling to driftwood. She looked as if she were trying not to cry.

Ren met Darek's stare again. "Darek?" she repeated.

One of his hands went to her cheek, cradling her face. "Are you okay?"

She took in a shuddering breath. "I think . . ."

Another wave of nausea pummeled into her. Ren wrenched out of his grasp, fell to her knees, and was sick on the cobblestones.

CHAPTER
THIRTY-SEVEN

Darek had held her hair back, and she was too shaken up to speak, let alone punch him in the throat for doing it, even if it had been what she'd wanted to do. After what felt like at least ten minutes, Ren got unsteadily to her feet. He reached for her, and she cut him a glare. "If you so much as offer to carry me, I will stab you. I swear I will."

Freya handed over her jacket, and once she'd shrugged it on, they headed east. By the time they arrived at the Compound, Ren was a lot less shaky and a lot more pissed. While Freya stayed on the first floor to talk to the kids, Ren barreled up the stairs and swept down the hall to her suite, Darek on her heels the entire way. When she reached her rooms, she flung her door open, stormed inside, and kicked it shut. Only, it didn't close. Darek's palm slapped against the wood, and he pushed into the room, gently closing the door behind him. She had no idea why he'd followed her, and quite frankly, she didn't care.

She pulled a teeth-cleaning powder off a shelf in the bathroom and used a brush to scrub her mouth clean, assessing her face in the mirror. A red welt covered her left cheekbone and brow. It would be a nasty bruise tomorrow, but she'd seen worse. She rinsed her face with freezing water, rubbing off what remained of her cosmetics, and wiped the sweat from the back of her neck. Before exiting the cramped room, she rinsed away the blood drying on her arm and wrapped a bandage around her bicep, the cut giving a sharp throb as she used her teeth to pull the cloth tight.

Out in the main room, Darek was shoving kindling into the brick fireplace, but Ren didn't pause to offer a thank-you, even if she would have frozen in her sleep tonight without the warmth from a lit hearth. She only swept through the doorway and into her bedroom, where she yanked off her coat and kicked free of her tall boots.

"What do you need, Ren?" Darek asked as she lit the lamp on her side table.

She turned. He was standing in her open doorway, his overcoat gone, the sleeves of his dark shirt shoved up to the elbows. "What do I need?" Ren laughed, a cold and bitter thing, and repeated, "What do I need? Fuck, Darek, I don't know. How about those seven hundred thousand gold coins you owe me, for starters? And maybe after that you can bring my parents back from the grave, since you're here to grant my every desire."

Hurt passed over Darek's normally shuttered features. Good. Let him hurt.

"I'm only trying to help," he said. "I know it's not the same, but I also lost my mother when I was young. The king was to blame then, too."

"You think because your mother died tragically you

can relate to my pain? Save your empathy for someone who gives a shit."

Everything about Darek tensed—his jaw, his shoulders, the cut of his cheekbones—and his eyes flashed, but not in anger. It was something else. "You are impossible," he growled, stalking toward her.

She stepped back and promptly bumped into the wall. In the tiny room, he was a foot away, if that.

"Why do you refuse to let anyone help you?"

"I don't need help."

"Yes, you do. You need help more than any person I've ever met."

"So you're an expert on me now?"

"I see you better than you think."

Ren rolled her eyes and said, "Then, please, won't you enlighten me?"

"I know why Freya is your only friend. I know why you say every cruel, unforgivable thing that comes into your head."

"You don't know a damn thing."

"I know you want the whole world to hate you as much as you hate yourself. You drive everyone away because you think you don't deserve kindness—you don't think you're worthy of it." He came closer still, his chest nearly touching hers, and met her narrowed eyes. "Well, Ren, that's too bad, because I'm not going anywhere."

"Get. Out," she commanded, punctuating each word with all the force of a right hook.

"No," he returned in equal measure.

"What is your problem?"

"You are! Gods, Ren, *you* are my problem."

"Then leave!" She moved forward a half step, closing the negligent distance between them. Their chests were touching, and Darek had to crane his head down just to see her face as she told him, "The door is right there."

"I can't go. I wish I could, believe me, but I can't."

"Why the hells not?"

He clenched his jaw, his eyes flickering between hers. It was like he was on the edge of something, an edge he wasn't sure he should tumble over.

"Darek," Ren said slowly, voice as heated as his stare. "Why can't you leave?"

"Because I want you!" The words burst out of him as if he'd been fighting an uphill battle and finally given in to defeat.

Ren didn't know what she'd expected him to say, but it wasn't that. She was so stunned that for what was probably the first time in her life, she didn't have an immediate response.

"Heavens know why. You're bitter, angry, self-centered, sarcastic, mean—"

"If I'm so horrible, what are you still doing here?"

"I don't know. Gods help me, I don't know. I've tried not to—I've tried so hard—but, Ren, I want you." He placed his hands on either side of her head, pushing her to the wall and caging her in. "And I think you want me, too."

Ren's chin lifted, and her head fell back against the wall. She wasn't sure when her breathing had turned heavy, but she was acutely aware of the stubble shading the hard line of his jaw, his heavy brow and piercing gaze, the largeness of him compared to her. The top of her head barely passed his chin. Darek's body engulfed hers, his head curved down so that his lips were inches from her own, his breath hot on her skin. He smelled like a swirl of musk and warm spices. She'd never noticed before.

"Tell me I'm wrong," he said.

She wanted to. Oh, how she wanted to explain just how little he meant to her. He was about as important as the worms crawling in the dirt outside. Less than that, in fact. He was algae living on a sunken ship at the bottom of the Iron Sea—that was how much she cared about him.

But she wasn't able to say it, because the truth was, somewhere along the way, she'd stopped hating him.

Ren couldn't tell him that he was wrong.

He wasn't. Not even a little bit.

She couldn't bring herself to speak. Saying it out loud felt like losing, and she was not about to let him win. Instead, she latched her gaze on to his, and let that serve as an answer. She had never seen his eyes like they were now, liquid brown and molten hot.

He'd dropped over the edge, and he was taking her down with him.

Suddenly, Darek's hands were gripping Ren's thighs and he was lifting her to his waist as if she weighed nothing. He all but slammed her into the wall, every inch of his hard body pressing her to the fading paint. The cut on her arm throbbed, her eye stung, but she didn't care about the pain as her legs instinctively wrapped around his hips, her hands gripping on to the back of his neck. She didn't know who did it first—if she'd pulled his mouth to hers or if Darek had beaten her to it—but then his lips captured her own.

The kiss was heady and urgent and devoid of anything resembling tenderness. They kissed like they carried on a conversation, aggressive and angry and—gods, Darek was right: Ren wanted him, wanted him more than she'd ever wanted a person. Pinned to the wall, her legs tightened around his waist, and her lips opened, parting for him completely. He felt better than she'd imagined, all those nights she'd lay in her bed and stared at the ceiling, thinking about it, about him. As his mouth worked hers, he pulled the air from her lungs and the tension along with it, calming the caged thing inside her and replacing it with something just as wild, but not nearly as wretched.

They broke for breath, but not for rest. Ren's fingers went to the buttons on Darek's shirt and popped them open. She shoved the fabric from his chest, down his shoulders, his hips keeping her pressed to the wall as he shrugged out of the shirt and let it fall to the floor. Heat brewed low in her stomach as his lips returned to hers. She needed him, all of him. He eased off her body enough for his hands to find the back of her corset, his fingers making quick work of the leather bodice. He untied the strings, yanked them free, and tossed the whole thing to the floor, leaving Ren bare beneath a flowing white shirt.

Darek moved to the ties at her chest and tugged them

loose. She didn't want him to stop, she truly didn't, but when he neared the ruffled edge of her shirt, so dangerously close to her right shoulder, Ren froze.

"Darek," she said.

The hesitation and fear on her tongue made the syllables of his name dip and sway. He paused, lifted his chin—in this position, she was finally the taller of the two—and met her stare. "Is this okay?" he asked.

Heart thudding in her chest, she held his gaze for one moment, then two.

"Yes," she breathed.

He pulled aside the edge of her shirt and gently tugged it down, laying bare her right shoulder and the mess of scars there. And that was when Ren realized that Darek really did see more than she'd thought. Parts of her had slipped out, twisted bits and broken pieces, the sadness she'd dug a hole for and buried deep, a grave without a marker because she'd hoped no one would ever find it and one day she would lose track of it, too. But Darek saw it all. He saw her. And he was still here. For years, she'd wanted to run from herself, would have run and never looked back if given the chance. But he was *still here*.

"Darek," she said again.

His lips touched her rough skin, and she shuddered. Holding her tighter, Darek's mouth brushed over the past written on her shoulder, and she wasn't in pain, not like she thought she would be. She curved into him, her hands burying in his undone hair. His mouth pressed against her scars, more firmly than before, and a second shudder rolled through her. Something burned in her core, new and unfamiliar.

Skin on skin, every nerve threatened to spark and consume. And the most frightening part? Ren wanted to be consumed. She was begging for it, begging for him. Her previous experiences hadn't prepared her for how this would feel. When she'd been with men before, sometimes in misguided attempts to erase her aching and self-loathing, it was always dark, quick and messy and unimportant. It felt good for a night, and then she never saw them again. That wasn't Darek. She wanted more from him, and it terrified her.

She held on to him like he was the only thing keeping every one of her cracks together as he gripped her legs, backed the both of them away from the wall, and maneuvered toward the bed. After kicking off his shoes, he kneeled on her purple sheets, bringing Ren down on top of him to straddle his hips. And the way he looked at her . . . It was how she had never been able to look at herself. As if she were a person worth seeing, uncovered scars and all.

"I'm here, Ren," he told her, like he knew she needed to hear it. She could try to shove him back, she could be cruel and unkind, she could continue to tear herself apart if she really wanted to, but he wasn't going anywhere. She saw it in his eyes, felt it in his hands braced on her hips. This wasn't one night. It wasn't temporary. "And I'm staying. As long as you'll have me."

CHAPTER
THIRTY-EIGHT

While one of the king's advisors droned on about a subject as dull as his voice, Kellen doodled on a piece of parchment and fought a yawn, waiting for the council meeting to come to an end. Seated to his left, Heath shot annoyed looks in his direction every other second. Like the conversation, Kellen ignored those, too.

But he wasn't so absorbed in the shapeless lines he was drawing that he missed the moment the room went silent. He looked up to see a dozen pairs of eyes trained on him. "Sorry," he said, setting his quill down and sitting up straight. "What was the question?"

In his intricately carved chair at the head of the table, his father drummed his fingers against the polished wooden arm, the lion ring on his right forefinger flashing whenever it caught the light. The king didn't mask his annoyance as he told Kellen, "We were just discussing the treaty that Orian, Eslind, and Jareen have asked us to sign. Lord Bayllin was wondering if you had considered our counteroffer?"

"*Our counteroffer*," Kellen repeated, trying his best to

look knowledgeable. "Tricky business, that offer. I'm afraid I need more time to think on it."

"Prince Kellen," said Lord Bayllin, a man with a neatly trimmed peppery beard seated directly across the table, "the queen of Jareen will be patient for only so long. If you agree to marry her daughter, it could do wonders with easing tensions—"

"Wait," Kellen interrupted. "Marriage?"

"Yes, Kell, marriage," his brother stepped in. "Father would like to propose a marriage between you and Princess Tayliah Anejide, in lieu of signing the treaty."

Not wanting to give every man at the table another reason to find fault with him, Kellen said nothing, even though he was certain he would have remembered something like a marriage proposal.

"Perhaps if you bothered to attend council meetings, you would have known," Heath added.

Kellen recognized that he was a prince, and princes didn't have the luxury of love. He always knew one day it would likely come to this: a political marriage devoid of passion. But he'd thought he had more time to figure things out. He was only nineteen, for the gods' sakes, which may have been a suitable age for many people to marry, but not Kellen. He couldn't even seem to get his own head on straight, so how was he expected to maintain a healthy marriage? And besides, if he were being honest, he didn't want to wed someone he'd never even met. It felt like another way to trap him into a life he didn't want, a life he spent all his time trying to escape. The thought depressed the shit out of him.

Kellen cleared his throat. "I need a few more days."

"Prince Kellen—" Lord Bayllin began.

"A few more days," Kellen insisted.

Again, the table went quiet. After a pause, the king said, "Very well. What's next?"

"The rebellion, Your Majesty," provided one of the councilmen.

"Yes, of course. How could I forget?" the king said, like he was about as close to forgetting the rebellion as he was to forgetting his own name. He lifted his chin toward lacquered wooden doors carved with ridiculous lion heads. "Send them in."

The wide doors swung forward with a soft groan, and Lesa Ghan stepped into the room, dressed head to toe in black leather, chin held high and light-blonde hair swinging at her shoulders. She looked calm and deadly, every inch a King's Child. Stopping five feet shy of the table, she inclined her head. "Your Majesty."

"Why is Adley Farre not here?" King Mattheus asked. "I summoned you both."

"She's being tended to at the infirmary," Lesa said. "She was injured last night while attempting to bring in one of the rebels."

The king's lip curled. "Ah, yes. *That*."

Kellen had heard the details of what had happened, something about how Adley had found a rebel at a fighting pit, lost her five minutes later, and was nearly crushed to death when half the building came down in front of her. According to the pained report she'd given from her bed in the infirmary, many of the pit's patrons hadn't made it out. Kellen didn't know how a stone building had suddenly collapsed, but the entire south side of Denfell was one shaky foundation in serious need of repairs, so it was hardly a surprise.

"I understand you're assisting Farre in her search for the rebels," said the king.

"Yes, Your Majesty," Lesa confirmed.

A beat passed. "You two have grown quite close over the years. Don't think we haven't noticed."

Lesa's eyes shot to Heath, who sat like carved marble in his chair. "Yes. We're friends." There was a slight tremble to her voice, and it gave away more than it should.

Kellen swallowed a lump in his throat.

"I see," King Mattheus said, slowly folding his fingers over his stomach. Beneath his hands, his red vest shone like fresh blood in the light from the brass chandeliers high above. "So how close are you to finding the rebels?"

"We nearly have them. It won't be long now."

The king tilted his head, allowing silence to seep into the air. It was too long and too thick, as oppressing as rancid meat. Kellen pulled his shoulders back and shifted in his seat, glancing between his father and Lesa.

"You *nearly* have them, you say?"

"Yes." Lesa's eyes flickered from the king to Heath and back again.

"If you nearly have them, as you say, then why are they

sinking my ships and stealing my prisoners from beneath my nose?"

Heath stood, his hands going behind his back as he walked around the men gathered at the table. They were utterly quiet, observing the scene as if watching a theater performance. He approached Lesa, calm in the way snakes are before they attack.

"I apologize, Your Majesty, I—"

Quick as a viper, Heath smacked her across the face, hard enough to draw blood. She staggered back, the corner of her mouth tinged red. Kellen went stiff in his seat, torn between standing up to place himself in front of the girl and fleeing the room. Neither was a great option.

"I don't want apologies," the king said from his chair, but Lesa's dark eyes remained on Heath. "Tell me why you haven't found the rebels yet."

"We will—"

Another smack. It drove into Kellen's ears like a tuning fork struck too hard. Lesa's lip was split. Blood dripped onto her chin. Heath's voice was level as he took a step forward. "Try again."

"Why haven't you found the rebels yet?" the king asked. He sounded bored, and it made Kellen sick.

When she didn't immediately respond, Heath descended on her. "Answer your king."

"We'll find them," Lesa said weakly.

He grabbed her by the neck. "Wrong answer," he growled. He whirled her around and shoved until her lower back struck the gilded edge of the council table, her spine forced into an arch.

The council members closest to Lesa leaned away, as if she had a disease they didn't want to catch. A few men were beginning to look uncomfortable, and one said, "This hardly seems necessary, Your Majesty."

"When I want your opinion, Lord Martene," the king said, "I'll ask for it."

Heath's hand constricted. Lesa gave a choked gasp, her eyes going wide. Kellen gritted his teeth, his knuckles white on the arms of his chair. He couldn't take this anymore. "I think you've punished her enough, Heath," he said, doing his best to keep his voice even.

"Not quite," Heath said. He studied Lesa like she was an interesting painting, then leaned in, closing her throat entirely. She gagged, her hands clawing at his fingers, trying to pry them away.

Kellen surged to his feet. "Heath, that's enough."

"*Sit down*, Kellen," his father said. The expression on his face matched the fury in his voice—fury and disappointment—but what did he expect? This was who Kellen was. This was who he would always be.

Lesa scraped her fingers over the back of Heath's hand, nails tracking red lines down his skin, but he didn't so much as flinch. The king watched with an emotionless blue stare. At last, he said, "Kellen's right. I think we've punished Ghan enough. Release her, Heath."

At first, Heath didn't move. It took three seconds for him to relax his grip and step away. Lesa sucked in a ragged breath, a hand going to her reddened throat. Coughing and gasping, she slowly pushed herself up from the council table.

Before Kellen could properly sag his shoulders in relief, the king went on, "Adley Farre is at fault here. Once the healers release her, we'll distribute her punishment. I'm afraid I can no longer consider her for King's Fang."

"But, Father," Kellen objected, "she's not the only one searching for the rebels. Why should she be punished?"

"Her efforts have been a disaster," the king said. "The rebels freed her own prisoner, she has gleaned nothing useful from her interrogations, she has raided dozens of locations in my city to no success, and last night she let her one lead escape. She has been a failure since the beginning. In fact, she may no longer be fit to be a King's Child."

"No!" Lesa cried, looking more afraid now than she had when Heath was choking the air from her lungs.

"Is something the matter, Ghan?" the king inquired.

"Don't punish Farre," she said in a rush. "She's your best archer." Although her voice was rough, it was difficult to miss the strain there, the desperation hovering just beneath the surface.

Heath narrowed his eyes. "Why are you so worried about Farre?"

Lesa shook her head, but it looked more like a confession of guilt than denial. Kellen felt as if his throat was closing in on itself. He wanted to do something, anything, but how did you stop a runaway carriage?

The king stood from his carved seat, and there was

nothing easy about him. When he spoke, his voice was as cold as Denfell at midnight. "Do you care about Farre?"

"No, of course not."

Kellen saw through her. Everyone at the table did.

"Then it shouldn't make a difference to you if she's relieved of her duties as a King's Child," Heath said.

Relieved of her duties. What a pleasant way to put it. His brother's ability to turn a phrase had always amazed Kellen. As if Adley were merely being discharged from the army, not sentenced to death.

"Farre is too valuable," Lesa said. "You'll lose a talented warrior."

"Valuable to whom?" Heath demanded. "You?"

Lesa backed up, and her hips hit the edge of the table. "No—"

Heath took a step toward her. "You love her."

"I don't—"

"And she loves you. I've seen the way she looks at you."

Lesa shook her head. "She doesn't."

Heath snatched the lapels of her coat and yanked her close. "I don't believe you," he hissed into her face.

"Neither do I," the king said, still standing at the head of the table, a glowing hearth at his back. His presence loomed over the room, and Kellen half expected to look down and find his father's hands coated in the blood of everyone who had ever wronged him. "You and Farre have fallen in love. It is an act of treason. You both will be executed today at high noon."

Kellen's heart plummeted.

King Mattheus swept his eyes over the council members seated before him. Most men leaned back without a care, but the lord who had spoken out earlier was staring straight ahead, his profile hard. The king's gaze landed on Kellen. "You may leave, if you wish." His tone made it clear he was none too pleased with his youngest son.

Kellen shot one last look at Lesa. Her face was red, blood coated her lips, and the welt on her throat showed a clear handprint, the skin very nearly split where fingers had dug in. He pushed his chair back. It scraped across the floor, and if every eye wasn't already on him, that would have done the trick. He turned his back and left, his boots thudding against stone as the whole room watched him go.

After he'd stepped out into the hall, a crack fractured the quiet. When Kellen looked back, Lesa was on her knees and his father was standing over her, a thin stream of silver extended from his hand. The king pulled his arm back, raising the silver whip. A second crack came just as the door was drifting shut.

CHAPTER
THIRTY-NINE

Kellen burst through the doors of the castle infirmary with all the poise of blasting fragor. Every conscious head in the room swiveled toward him. None, conscious or otherwise, belonged to Adley.

"Where—" he heaved, clutching the stitch in his side that had developed while he'd sprinted through the halls to get here. "Is—Adley—Farre?"

The healers stopped what they were doing to blink at him. A couple had been tending to patients, changing dressings and administering medicines; one was stripping sheets from the beds lining either side of the long room, while a few others cleaned and stocked supplies. Early morning light shone in through the high windows, bathing the infirmary in a soft glow much too pleasant for the business that went on between these walls. As many people died here as lived.

It seemed ages before a healer answered. "We sent her to her room ten minutes ago." She paused, and Kellen's deep breathing filled the quiet. "Your Highness, are you all right?"

"Fine, thank you," he said in a rush and sprinted

back the way he'd come, not giving his lungs any time to recuperate.

Maybe it was just Kellen's imagination, but the corridors reserved for the King's Children felt bleaker than the rest of the castle. While the stone walls were pale brown elsewhere, they seemed darker here, as if all light and warmth had leached away. He stopped in the middle of the hall and looked at dozens of identical wooden doors, only now realizing that he had no idea which room belonged to Adley.

Kellen started knocking, one door to the next to the next. Luckily, it was late enough that all the King's Children were out of bed, and when he heard shuffling inside one room, he knew he'd found her. "Adley?!" he called through the wood.

The door swung in. Adley's face was covered in nicks and scratches, and there was an impressive cut on her cheek, but she didn't look as beaten-up as Kellen had expected. She must have been truly fortunate when half the pit collapsed. If she'd been on the wrong side of the room, she would be a broken body under a bunch of stones right about now.

She regarded him warily. "Kellen?"

"You have to come with me," he said. "Now."

"Now?"

"Right now."

He must not have been hiding his alarm very well, because she went from confused to worried. "What's going on?"

"My father has ordered your execution at high noon today."

The warmth seeped out of Adley's face, her skin turning ashen. "Why?"

"There isn't time—"

"What happened?" The way she said it, Kellen could tell she already knew.

"He found out. About you and Lesa."

Adley made a small, distressed sound.

"I can get you out of the castle, but you have to come with me now, before my father sends men for you."

"No, I'm not leaving her."

She turned around and limped back into her room, Kellen following close behind. If things had been a little less dire, he would have dwelled on all the books. They were stacked everywhere, not just on shelves but the floor and chair, spilling out from under the bed and towering precariously atop her dresser. It was about the last thing he had expected to find in her living quarters.

"What happened to your leg?" Kellen asked as she hobbled across the room and took a bow from its hook on the wall.

"Stabbed in the ankle," she said, slinging the bow over her back. Then she pulled down a quiver and set to counting the arrows inside.

"What are you doing?" When she didn't answer, Kellen added, "You planning to shoot my father?"

"If I have to."

"You're daft." She only continued to count, so Kellen

grabbed her arm, forcing her to a stop. "Adley, listen to me. The best thing you can do for Lesa is leave. You can't help her from the dungeons, but you *can* help her if you're free."

Her fingers stilled over the arrows, and she looked up at him. "You sound like you have a plan."

"Maybe. Do you trust me?"

It was a few seconds before she replied. "Why are you helping me?"

Kellen had ten different answers for that, and he wasn't sure what was most true. To spite his father. To feel better about himself and his whole miserable life. Because Adley had become something close to a friend, the only friend he might have found since Holland. And like Holland, he didn't feel the need to be someone he wasn't around her. He couldn't watch her lose her head and do nothing to stop it. He'd been doing nothing for nineteen years, and he was sick of it, sick of being complicit in his father's crimes. He was tired of ambivalence, tired of knowing the difference between right and wrong and ignoring the wrong because it was easier that way. Because when it came down to it, everything that belonged to Kellen was wrong. He had a tainted family name, a title that didn't suit him, a pit where fighters courted death. He'd been trying for so long, swapping personas and hoping one day something would fit him right. But nothing ever did. Maybe if he helped Adley, he'd have something worthwhile.

He remembered Holland's voice as she'd said, *When will you learn? Some things are worth the pain.*

Maybe Kellen was finally learning.

But he couldn't say any of that. He didn't know how.

Kellen straightened the lapels of his coat and tugged at his gold-embroidered sleeves. "My father is a bastard, my brother is worse, and I enjoy pissing them both off," he said. "Now *let's go*, while there's still time."

Adley hesitated for only a second more before she threw the quiver across her back and limped out of the room after Kellen, moving at an impressive pace for someone who had recently taken a knife to the ankle.

After traveling down four flights of stairs, they came to a thin passageway. Kellen stopped short, putting up a hand. He peered around the corner at a group of councilmen who had their heads bent together, which meant the meeting had come to an end and their window was closing fast.

"We can go another way," Adley whispered.

"No time," Kellen breathed, assessing the men. "I'll be right back."

He went to step into the hall, but her hand came down on his shoulder. "What are you going to do?"

Filling himself with false confidence, Kellen looked back and winked, then he loped out into the hall, hands shoved in his pants pockets. When the councilmen noticed him, they went stiff under their layers of fur and wool. If Kellen didn't regularly use this passage to avoid the castle staff, and if he didn't know for a fact that no one ever traversed it because it was too far out of the way, he wouldn't have thought anything of it. But a warning prickled at him. Whatever these men were up to, it was nothing good.

"Lord Bayllin, glad I caught you," Kellen said. "I had a question about the counteroffer we were discussing."

The lord's shoulders relaxed. "I'm pleased to hear you're taking this matter seriously, Prince Kellen. What can I help you with?"

"Princess Tayliah Anejide. Is she considered an attractive woman?"

Lord Bayllin stared at him. "I beg your pardon?"

"I have no idea what the princess of Jareen looks like. That won't do. If I marry her, we'll be expected to produce heirs, and I'd like for my children to inherit my good looks."

The council members exchanged glances that were both baffled and amused, and Lord Bayllin said, "I assure you, Prince Kellen, Princess Tayliah is a beautiful woman."

"I'd like a portrait."

"Your Highness?"

"Find me a portrait of the princess. I shall not agree to marry her until I see one."

"Prince Kellen," another lord said, his mouth ticking down. "This is serious."

"Oh, I agree," Kellen concurred. "So get me a portrait. Write to the queen of Jareen. Commission one if you must. You will not have my decision until then." He paused, but no one moved. "What are you waiting for? Go."

"Now?" another council member asked.

"Yes, *now*."

"Prince Kellen—" started Lord Bayllin.

"Did I not tell you to go?"

The men exchanged a few more glances before they inclined their heads and shuffled away.

Once their footsteps had faded, Adley appeared from the stairwell. "Come on," Kellen said. As he led the way to the tunnel that would get them out of the castle long before anyone missed them, Adley kept shooting him looks. They came so often that once Kellen's silver was lighting up the uneven dirt walls of his escape route, he finally asked, "What?"

"A portrait of the princess of Jareen?" she said.

Kellen's answering smile was crooked. He squeezed around a boulder sitting in the middle of their path, a ball of silver bobbing in the air. The cool light glinted in Adley's hair as she used one arm to balance herself on the giant rock and hobbled around it. Kellen held out a hand to help her through, which she ignored.

"You're smarter than everyone thinks," she added.

"That's quite a large claim."

She gave him what might have been a smile, but it was faint and his silver was casting odd shadows, so he couldn't be sure. Even still, Kellen wondered if in another life, one where she wasn't a stolen child and he wasn't the son of a throne covered in blood, they might have been friends since the beginning.

CHAPTER
FORTY

Darek propped his head up on one hand while the other cradled the dip at Ren's waist, bare beneath the cover of cotton. Her head rested on a pillow, and early morning sunlight shimmered in her black hair, which was even more mussed than usual. A woody, vanilla-scented perfume clung to the dark sheets tangled on the bed.

Ren swept her eyes over his face, lingering on the fading bruises. "Your nose hasn't healed," she commented, pressing a palm to his cheek. Silver glowed at the edge of his vision.

"What are you doing?"

"Shut up."

Darek didn't feel anything other than her skin on his, which surprised him a little. Silver was without noise or scent, but he hadn't also expected it to feel like air. Half a minute passed before she withdrew her hand.

"That should help."

Darek furrowed his brow. "What did you do?"

"I gave you a bit of my silver. It won't be in your system for long, and it's not like you can wield it, but your nose should heal a bit faster now."

Darek studied her black eye, which was much darker than it should have been for how new it was. He'd heard stories of wielders capable of healing, both themselves and others, but it still seemed so extraordinary on top of everything else silver could do. It made him wonder what other secrets the magic was hiding.

"Why didn't you offer before?" he asked.

"Because you were annoying me before."

His lips quirked. "So does this mean I don't annoy you anymore?"

"It means you're not annoying me at this specific moment."

"High praise coming from you," he said, tucking a stray piece of hair behind her ear just as an excuse to touch her. He still didn't quite believe she would let him, would shed her armor and allow herself to become so vulnerable. But even without the protective layers, Ren had still tasted like the hells. She was fire and furious energy. She was belligerent and exasperating, and she drove Darek mad. He didn't know if he could ever leave her, but even if he could, he didn't want to. She was a drug. One hit—that's all it took. One hit, and he was hers.

"Where did you come from?" he asked her.

"I think it's a little late for a sex talk."

He laughed softly, his fingers running through the strands of her dark hair. "Speaking of . . ."

"Freya has something I can take."

Darek nodded. He was far from ready to be a father,

and the last thing any of them needed was a miniature version of Ren running around.

"I'll start taking it regularly if you want," she added.

He held her gaze for a moment, then he smiled and lowered down to brush his lips with hers. She arched up, returning the brief kiss. When he pulled back, he asked, "Will you tell me about the Compound?"

She tensed. It was a small shift, like a change in the breeze, and maybe if he hadn't been touching her, Darek wouldn't have noticed at all.

"What do you want to know?" she asked, her tone too casual.

"Why did you and Freya open it? Why did you help take charge of a group of orphans when you were sixteen?"

"Maybe I'm fond of the kids who live here."

"Ren, please." He had seen her around the cramped building, how she avoided the children when she could and snapped at them when she couldn't. Most of the kids were wary of her, if not downright terrified. Darek couldn't blame them. If he were ten years younger, Ren would have scared the hells out of him, too.

She sat up then, pulling her purple sheet with her, and Darek rolled aside. Leaning back against the wall, she fiddled with the bandage wrapped around her upper arm. "I knew this boy once, but he died. Three years ago. He had a good heart. He didn't deserve—" She broke off. "I don't want to get into it, but for as long as I knew him, he'd dreamed of opening an orphanage. I guess I couldn't let that dream die with him." Ren paused, staring out the window at the blue sky. "He would hate me if he knew I talked Freya into charging a boarding fee, but we both need the money."

"To pay Nevskov?"

Ren shot him a glance. "You know about that?"

"I know you're in debt with him, but I don't know why." Darek pushed himself up and propped one shoulder against the wall. "Did you borrow money from Nevskov to help Freya buy the Compound?"

"No," Ren said.

"Then what—"

She sat forward, turning to square him off. "It's none of your business, Darek."

"How much do you owe him?" he pushed.

"It doesn't matter."

"Yes, it does."

Ren leveled him with a cold stare. "No, it doesn't. I can take care of myself."

"Is seven hundred thousand going to cover your debt?"

"You're grating on my nerves," she said, her hands gripping the sheet. "Leave it alone or get out."

Darek clenched his jaw. Why was she always doing this? Why did she insist on pulling away? And why in all the gods' names did he want to push her up against the wall again?

"I won't apologize for showing concern," he said.

"I don't need your concern."

"I don't care."

Ren's green eyes flashed, and he glowered right back.

He wasn't sure if they were going to scream at each other or kiss, and he didn't think she knew either.

A fist banged against the suite door.

"Not now!" Ren shouted, but the knocking only became more frantic. Muttering something unkind about how she detested everyone in the Compound, Ren scanned the room. "Where's my shirt?"

Darek leaned over the edge of the mattress and snatched his crumpled top from the floor. "Here," he said, tossing it to her.

She pulled his shirt on, doing up the buttons as she swung her legs out of bed. It looked so much better on her than it did on him, the dark-blue fabric swallowing her frame, and the hemline hitting at the middle of her thigh. It was ridiculously sexy. How was it possible that she was so infuriating and so attractive at once?

Darek kept his gaze locked on her until she disappeared from view. She pulled open the door, laying the annoyance on thick as she asked, "What do you want?"

A boy responded, his voice high and terrified, "Prince Kellen's outside with a King's Child."

CHAPTER
FORTY-ONE

Holland's house was quiet, but Kellen knocked anyway. He knocked until his knuckles were red and smarting, until he accepted that Holland wasn't home and he needed another plan. Not that going to Holland's was much of a plan to begin with, but it was something. It was all he had.

"Kellen," Adley said low, staring out at the well-kept street and the river beyond. Sunlight glinted off the still water, no riverboats or gondolas in sight. The whole neighborhood was quiet, not yet ready to wake. "Tell me what we're doing."

Breath puffing in the crisp air, Kellen didn't answer right away. A shiver rolled through him, and he shoved his hands across his chest, tucking them beneath the red coat that had been warm enough for the castle, but was far too thin for winter in Denfell. "Listen to my whole plan before you call me mad, all right?"

Adley watched him skeptically.

"We're going to ask the rebels for help."

Her mouth popped open. "Are you out of your—"

Kellen held up a hand. "I told you to listen. You know, for a King's Child, you're awfully bad at following orders."

She blew a breath out through her nose, looking like she wanted to give him a rude gesture, and Kellen nearly smiled.

"I have no idea what the rebels have planned, but they've obviously been getting bolder. They're openly defying the crown now, and if we give them an incentive to make a move during the execution today, I think they might agree to help us save Lesa."

"*Us*?" Adley asked.

Kellen stopped. "What?"

"You said *us*."

Kellen replayed his words. He hadn't realized. "You," he said. "I meant help *you* save Lesa."

Adley gave him that look again, the one she had lobbed his way earlier, right before she'd told him she could see through the image he'd spent nearly two decades perfecting. "So what's the plan then?" she asked.

Kellen explained, and though he'd expected to spend some time convincing her, she agreed after only a short pause.

"Are you sure?" he asked.

"Yes," Adley said. "If I can save her, yes. I'll do anything."

Out on the Battgandon River, a fishing boat drifted by, likely transporting that morning's catch to Traders' Hall. As quiet as it was, the soft splash of the oars striking water had no trouble reaching Holland's front door.

"You really do love her," Kellen said.

Adley observed the fisherman as he passed, her hair

ruffling in the slight breeze. A flash of light brightened her eyes. "Have you ever had pickled fish?"

"I—what?"

She tore her stare from the river. "Never mind. I trust you know how to find the rebels? Because I've been searching for weeks, and I've got nothing."

"Holland will know where they are."

"The baker's daughter?"

"The one and only."

Kellen loped down the front steps, his boots clicking against the stone, while Adley trailed close behind. "You've been sleeping with a rebel?" she hissed, incredulous.

"Look, I didn't know she was a rebel until a couple weeks ago."

She shook her head and muttered something under her breath that Kellen couldn't hear.

The two of them made their way to the Golden Strait, Adley limping beside him as they walked along the river, the winter breeze numbing Kellen's cheeks. It was still a little too early for the city to be fully awake, but Katarine Vespar's cherry tarts had already come and gone by the time they got to Noble Finch. A bell tinkled as they stepped inside the colorful shop, the scent of butter and sugar heavy in the air. Curls held back by golden pins, Holland stood behind the counter with a white box in one hand, the other lifting a chocolate éclair off its tray. She glanced up and dropped the pastry. Slowly, she set the box on top of the counter, her eyes darting from Kellen and Adley to the customers in the shop.

Kellen stepped forward quickly, feeling sick with himself for ever making that ridiculous threat. "No, Holland, that's not why she's here," he said in a low voice. "She needs our help. Well, *your* help, really. I'm a bit useless at the moment."

Holland shot another wary look at the King's Child. "Go away, Kellen. Take her with you. She's scaring my customers."

"Please, Holland," he begged.

She bit her lip, glancing around the shop. The few workers stationed behind the shimmering glass countertops concentrated on organizing the pastries, doing a decent job of pretending like they weren't listening. The patrons, however, stared openly at Kellen and Adley as if they expected them to break into song.

"Fine," Holland said. "Outside. You have three minutes."

Once they were back in the cold and Holland had yanked the door shut, Kellen looked around, checking that the street was empty. "We need you to take us to the rebel leader," he whispered.

Holland blinked at him. "You need me to do what?"

"I know you know who it is, and I know this sounds like a trap, but I swear it's not. We need their help. Will you take us to them?"

She didn't say anything, and Kellen ran a frustrated hand through his hair. Why did he have to go and mess things up so royally? He thought he might have finally been grasping on to the person he wanted to be, but what if he'd gotten here too late? He feared he'd lost her trust for good, and he had no idea how to fix it.

"Please. You know me. I'm an idiot, and I say stupid things that I shouldn't, but—you know me."

She stared at him silently as a carriage rolled by, clopping horse hooves loud in the morning air. And just when Kellen didn't think he could take it anymore, her hazel eyes softened. "Okay," she said.

He let out half a breath. "*Okay*?"

"I'll take you. Let me grab my coat."

She disappeared inside the bakery and reappeared thirty seconds later, buttoning a cream jacket over a dress the color of robin eggs and summer skies. Last Kellen heard, the rebels were operating out of the Atterton District, but Holland led them across the bridge, taking them deeper and deeper south, until they found themselves in Hessler. They wound their way through crooked streets as gray as soot, collars high and shoulders hunched. Kellen asked, "Is Ren the rebel leader?" He remembered that Holland had once told him Ren helped run a boardinghouse in this neighborhood.

Holland snorted inelegantly. "Ren isn't the leader of anything."

They stopped in front of a three-story building that looked on the brink of collapse. The paint was so cracked and faded it was hard to tell what the original color had been. The roof was missing a good number of shingles, and a few wooden support beams sagged dangerously. Holland knocked, Kellen and Adley at her side.

It was awhile before the door jerked open. Behind it was Ren, left eye sporting one hell of bruise, and face hard as steel. She was in a huge dark shirt that definitely belonged to a man and slim black pants, her feet bare, with a knife in one hand. No corset. She pushed past Holland and slammed Kellen against the building, her forearm pressing into his windpipe. A very tall and very shirtless man shot out the door after her and leveled his sword at Adley's throat, but Adley didn't even acknowledge him; she was too busy glaring at Ren. Kellen assessed the bruise on Ren's face. So she was the rebel Adley had found—and lost—last night.

Sharp metal kissed his neck.

"Ren, wait," Holland said.

Ren ignored her. "Give me one reason why we shouldn't kill you both."

"If you kill me, who will be your partner during the annual dance competition?" Kellen asked.

Ren's brows shot up. She gave one disbelieving laugh. "You have got to be joking."

"What?" wondered the Jareen girl who'd been with Ren at that first pit fight.

"You?" Ren asked him. "You're the South Terth pit lord?"

"Okay, I'm confused," said the boy Kellen had first met in Holland's kitchen two weeks ago. He had the same dark features as the man currently pointing a sword at Adley's throat. Brothers, then.

The older of the two brothers shot Holland a dark

look. "Why did you bring them here, Holland? How do you even know them?"

"That's a bit of a long story," Kellen said. "I'll tell you all about it as soon as Ren here removes her knife from my neck."

Ren didn't relax her arm or her blade. If anything, she increased the pressure on both. "I don't think so."

Kellen's hands began to glow. "I could make you release me, you know."

Ren went quiet, and an odd look overtook her face. Her eyes flashed.

"Ren, don't—" the tall man said.

And suddenly, Kellen's magic wasn't alone, because Ren's fist was also glowing silver, and two ribbons were snaking down to his wrists, the magic pinning his hands to the wall. "You want to bet on that?" she asked.

Kellen looked from Ren's bright hand to her face and burst into a hysterical sort of laughter. "And you said there wasn't much to know about you."

She was such a little liar.

CHAPTER
FORTY-TWO

Ren sat on top of the kitchen counter with her hands braced beside her, bare feet dangling over the dull floorboards. It was as far as she could get from the King's Child who had attacked her the night before. Ren watched the girl through narrowed eyes, satisfied at the sight of a long gouge on her cheek, which she definitely hadn't been sporting before the pit crumbled, and the girl gave her a cool look in return.

Word of that day's execution still hadn't reached the Compound, but Ren had already heard the news from the prince, who was also a pit lord. And he was friends with Holland. He'd even met Markus once, though at the time Markus hadn't realized who he was. A week ago, Ren had danced with him.

She'd almost kissed him.

The lot of them—Ren, Darek, Markus, Holland, Freya, Prince Kellen, and the King's Child named Adley—were all huddled in Ren's suite, listening to the prince talk. "Lesa's execution will be public," he said.

"What does this have to do with us?" Darek asked.

"We were hoping you'd help stop it," said Kellen.

"No," Ren said. "No way."

"Why would we help you?" Darek asked, his guarded stare flitting between the prince and the King's Child. "We don't owe you anything."

"Darek," Holland interjected. "Just listen to what they have to say."

"You're right. You don't owe us anything," Kellen agreed. "But if you would think about it for two seconds, you'd realize you need our help as much as we need yours."

"We need your help about as much as I need a heart attack," Ren said.

"Are you really that arrogant, or are you just stupid?" Adley asked her.

"How's your ankle?" Ren wondered.

The King's Child stiffened, and Ren gave her a tight smile.

Kellen stepped toward Adley. "I wish you would sit down."

"Leave me alone. I'm fine." Adley moved away from the wall she'd been propped up against, and to her credit, she hid her limp well. "I'm going to tell you why you need our help. Everyone knows your endgame. You want to take the throne from King Mattheus. But it's one thing to blow up ships and put on magic shows. You make one move against the king's life, and a King's Child will be on you before you can draw your sword." At the edge of Ren's faded red couch, she paused, supporting her weight against the back. "You need my help. If you stop the execution, I'll deal with the King's Children while you make your move for the throne. All I ask in return is that you save Lesa's life." She gave Darek a meaningful look that made Ren feel like she was missing something. "I want you to know: that morning, at Rosewater Inn, I didn't hurt any of those people."

The room was silent. Everyone looked to Darek, who'd tied his hair back and thrown on a shirt. He was leaning against the counter next to Ren with his arms shoved over his stomach, his expression unmovable.

"You can trust Kellen," Holland told him. "I've known him for a while, and he may be a Lyandor, but only in name. If he trusts Adley, I think we should, too."

Darek only watched her, his jaw hard.

"Do you really think I would have brought them here if I didn't believe their intentions?" she added.

That cracked something in Darek. His brown eyes turned to the prince and the King's Child like he might have actually been considering the offer.

"You can't think this is a good idea," Ren said.

"I think we should stop the execution."

Ren threw up her hands. "Unbelievable."

He shot her a look and directed his next question to Kellen. "It'll be public, you say?"

"Of course," the prince said. "Killing someone discreetly isn't my father's style."

"The execution of a King's Child—half the city will be there," Darek said.

"At the very least," he agreed.

"What are you thinking, Darek?" Holland asked.

"I'm thinking it's time for us to lay down our cards. We won't get another opportunity like this, and we're running out of time." To Adley, he added, "But if you so much as think about turning on us, I swear to you I will kill your friend myself."

Adley met his steel-cut stare. "You have my word."

"This is crazy," Ren muttered, but no one listened. Of course they didn't. She'd been saying the same thing since the night she met the Hollistair brothers, and they never listened.

"I hope your plan is more sophisticated than storming the stage and taking off my father's head," Kellen commented. "Because it won't work."

"You don't think I know that?" Darek bit back. "Every rebellion has tried something similar, and I'm well aware it has never worked."

"What's your play then?"

Darek didn't answer. He only fixed Kellen with a stony, untrusting look he'd leveled on Ren on more than one occasion.

"Oh, come on," Kellen said. "I think I've proven myself to you. I'm on your side. That's why I came here."

As ludicrous as it sounded, Ren believed him. He was a prince and a Lyandor, and his father had killed her parents, but she believed him. Maybe it was because she'd met him three times now, not knowing who he was, and he'd always been kind and charming and quick-witted. That first night, he'd tried to get her to back out of the fight—he'd warned her away from Shale. He was so unlike his father, so unlike a Lyandor.

Darek's stare shifted to Holland, where she stood with her back to the low-burning fire. Above her head, a square of sun fell across the wall and the top half of Ren's stolen painting, the rose garden vivid in the morning light. "It's fine, Darek," she assured. "I swear."

He looked back to the prince. "We've been working to discredit you and Heath as heirs to the throne."

Kellen crossed his arms and dropped down onto the arm of the shabby couch, an amused tilt to his chin. He kicked one ankle over the other, as if settling in for a show at the Royal Theatre. "Color me intrigued. Go on."

"It started before either of us were born. My father was a young, unknown businessman and a budding revolutionist, as were Ren's parents and Holland's father."

Ren frowned. She'd known her parents were acquainted with Darek's father, but she hadn't been curious enough to ask how. The Avevian family had been relatively well-off, so Ren had assumed that was the connection. Business contacts, even friends—but revolutionaries? She watched Darek's profile with a wrinkled brow.

"When the king and queen announced their engagement, our parents saw it as an opportunity," Darek continued. "My father adopted *Jai Farrow* as a false name and arranged a business meeting with the queen. He's very good at his job, so it didn't take long for their initial joint investment to bring in profits. Soon, your mother was meeting with him more and more, until my father wasn't just a business associate, he was a friend. He stayed for hours at a time, rather regularly. It continued for years, until after you were born. As you know, the queen's guard keeps meticulous records of all her visitors, stored in the castle archives."

Kellen blinked. He looked both taken aback and impressed. "You made it seem as though she'd been unfaithful."

"Yes. To sell the lie, my father still visits her at least once a year to check on the well-being of his 'sons': you and Heath. I had to get fake papers and go to Lan Covve in his place three weeks ago, but her visitor logs will still show that a man named Jai Farrow came to see her."

Ren's head was reeling. A memory flitted by, one where she had bit into a bright persimmon in the Hollistair's kitchen. So that was why Darek had been so secretive about his trip to the countryside. She understood why he hadn't told her his plans back then, but she'd thought he was beginning to trust her. Even when she'd figured out Heath wasn't a silver wielder, he still hadn't told her. Ren didn't want to admit that it stung just a little bit, so she did what she'd done best for nine years and shoved the hurt away.

Kellen was calculating as he mulled it over. "It's smart. If my father's supporters thought he'd been playing them for fools, they would be furious. They'd demand he abdicate the throne, and they certainly wouldn't throw their weight behind me or Heath if we tried to take it. No one would, not if they believe we don't have a legitimate claim." He studied Darek with intelligent blue eyes, and now that Ren knew his identity, it was hard to believe she hadn't seen through the mask from the beginning. "I have to hand it to you: it would ruin us. My mother might protest the claims, but if her visitor logs show what you say they do, I doubt she would return to the city. It might not be true, but people still talk. Could you imagine the scandal? And *I'm* supposed to be the dishonorable one." The prince gave a cocky smile that Ren didn't really buy. It was like he was putting on a show. "One question: how did you plan to explain our silver?"

"I didn't. I planned to get rid of it. I paid off a tea merchant to mix hycanthian flowers into the teas the castle staff bought for you and Heath, so that when the time came, you couldn't disprove the accusations. I also got my hands on the choreography for the Crown's Demonstration. I was prepared to alter it to look like someone at the Royal Theatre was helping you and Heath fake your silver for the performance. Imagine my surprise when Ren realized your brother doesn't have magic."

Kellen tipped his head back and barked a laugh. "You rebels don't get nearly as much credit as you deserve."

"Sorry," Freya piped up. She was seated cross-legged on the carpet, embroidered skirts pooled around her. "What are hycanthian flowers?"

"They can only be found during two weeks of the year in the Kaskidan Mountains," the prince explained. "Their blue petals hinder a silver wielder's power, as long as we ingest enough. But it's tricky business. Too little does nothing, and too much will bring about a nasty bout of illness. The quantity has to be just right for it to suppress a wielder's magic without any side effects." Prince Kellen held up a palm and produced a ball of shimmering magic. "Too bad it didn't work. Pretty lucky for your revolution that Heath doesn't have silver."

"I'd say *you're* the lucky one," Darek countered. "When I found out about him, my backup plan was finding a way to kill you. Can't prove you have silver if you're not alive to wield it."

Still sitting on the arm of the couch as if he hadn't been informed of a plot that included his murder, Kellen closed his fist, snuffing out his silver. "It's a good thing I'm a rebel now, isn't it?"

"Good for you, maybe," Darek grumbled.

Kellen chuckled. "I'll grow on you."

"No, you won't."

"Probably not," the prince agreed and shifted his stare to Ren. "What's your role in all this?"

"I'm here for the gold," she said.

Darek shot her an annoyed look. He even had to lift his chin a little bit to do it. Ren liked being taller than him. She was going to have to sit on countertops more often.

"Ren has been making appearances around the city to spark rumors," he said. "We want to give the people a reason to rally behind us when we do try to take the throne. Ren's silver is that reason."

Kellen ran a finger under the cuff of his shirt. "Did my father . . . did he send men to kill you nine years ago?"

"Yes," Ren replied, resentment churning in her stomach. His brother's face flashed through her mind, severe lines and cold blue eyes she'd seen in a dream. "He burned my house down. I made it out. My parents didn't."

The prince cleared his throat, threading a lean hand through his blond hair. "I'm sorry," he said, lifting his eyes to hers. The look there was genuine and not like he was doing that thing people did when they felt bad for her.

Ren shrugged, as if she didn't think about it every day of her life. "It was a long time ago."

"You're my brother's shadow then."

"So I've been told. Lucky me," she said dryly.

"I've always wondered: do you know why you ended up with silver?"

Ren shook her head. "Your guess is as good as mine."

"Darek would tell you the gods have something to do with it," said Markus, who'd been watching everything unfold from the lumpy sitting room chair. Darek directed his glower at his brother.

Ren groaned. "Can we not start with the gods today?"

Straightening up, Darek pulled a watch from his pocket. "We don't have a lot of time."

They migrated to the scarred sitting room table, where they worked out their plan. It was the strangest combination of people Ren had ever been in the company of, but they made a surprisingly decent team, and when they were all satisfied, they stood from their seats to set out on their various tasks. Ren retrieved her coat from the back of the couch, preparing to head to the Underground with

Freya, where they would buy six quivers of arrows and plenty more knives.

"Holland, Markus, go tell the others. The execution square at high noon," Darek instructed, rolling up a map and handing it to his brother. "Give them this and tell them to memorize it. I want everyone there and ready for a standoff. This is going to get messy." Just as Markus reached the door, Darek added, "Except Riko. His stubborn ass will want to be there, but the man can barely walk. Lock him inside if you have to." Markus nodded, stepping out into the hall. "And be careful!"

Before Holland could leave, Kellen jumped to his feet and placed a hand on her arm. "Can I talk to you? It'll only take a moment."

Holland retreated with him to the bathroom doorway, her arms shoved defensively over a lacy sky-blue bodice. Ren's suite was small enough that she overheard their entire conversation, and she didn't even have to strain her ears to do it.

"I should have said this earlier, but . . . I'm sorry for what I said to you," Kellen started. "I've wanted to apologize a thousand times, but I didn't know how. I feel dreadful. I don't have an excuse. Maybe Heath has rubbed off on me." He shrugged, pushing his hair away from his face. "I don't know, but I am sorry. Truly."

"Get a grip, Kellen," Holland told him. "What you said was stupid and unkind, but you're nothing like your brother. If you were, do you think I'd have gotten anywhere near you?"

"Holland," Darek interrupted, growling out her name. "Please tell me this isn't what I think."

She slowly rotated in his direction. "Darek . . ."

Apparently, it was all the response he needed. Ren didn't think it was possible, but his face darkened. "You went to bed with a Lyandor, of all people? How could you be that stupid?"

Holland cast her eyes at Freya, Adley, and Ren, who were still gathered in the sitting room and not even trying to look disinterested. "We can't do this now," she said.

Darek's sharp jaw ticked, then relaxed. "You're right. It's not important anymore. Just go."

Avoiding everyone's gaze, Holland left in a swish of blue lace and red hair.

Kellen was aiming for the door, headed back to the castle so he could ride to the execution with his brother and father, when Darek stepped in his path. "I'm trusting you," he said, like he couldn't quite believe the words had come out of his mouth.

"I know," the prince replied. He was gone a second later.

Before departing, Ren stared around the room. Darek was quiet and closed off in the middle of the kitchen, sparse shelves and wooden cupboards at his back, eyes boring into the floor. Adley sat on the couch and laid her arrows across the short table, broad shoulders stiff and a chunk of hair falling over her face. At Ren's side, Freya had on a slight, nervous smile.

Observing them all, Ren wondered just how much everything was about to change.

At high noon, the revolution would reach its tipping point.

PART FOUR

CHAPTER
FORTY-THREE

When Kellen returned to the castle, guards were pounding up and down the stairs, the staff jumping out of their path as they thundered through the halls, while gossiping courtiers in jewel-toned fabrics stood in clusters and observed the commotion through keen eyes. It was barely contained chaos. Not only had everyone heard of Lesa's execution, but they all knew Adley Farre had somehow escaped. A breathless guard dashed up to Kellen, informed him that the king wanted him in the throne room, then retreated as quickly as he had come.

With his hands shoved in his pockets, Kellen forced a casual stride through the bustling halls, pivoting as sets of guards ran by, weaving around castle workers. Pale stone arched high above his head, and late-morning sunlight drifted in through the windows—a rare clear winter day. When he arrived at the throne room, the guards stationed outside the doors let him in without a word.

Steps echoing, he made his way down the long chamber toward his brother, who was pacing back and forth like a displeased cat. His father sat in a throne ten steps above the rest of the room, the queen's place empty beside him.

At his back, a round, misted-glass window cast a shimmering haze across the floor, like crystal refracting light. The throne itself was large enough for two men, its spiked back extending toward the vaulted ceiling, and the entire thing was the color of Kellen's hair: pure gold from top to bottom. Lion heads made up the front of the arms so that whenever his father lay down his hands, it was as if he was petting the animals.

The throne room was stunning, impressive, and intimidating. Kellen hated it.

As he drew nearer, Heath stopped pacing and set his blue eyes on Kellen, but their father was the one to speak. "It has come to my attention that you may have aided in the escape of Adley Farre."

Heart picking up speed, Kellen drew his face into a confused expression. "That sounds like an incredibly stupid thing to do."

"Yes, I would agree," said his father, his voice swimming around the empty room. "And yet, you have not been in your chambers for quite some time, and no one seems able to place you, save for a group of councilmen who saw you in a ground floor corridor less than ten minutes before Farre was discovered missing. Before that, the healers said you visited the infirmary, looking for her. Would you care to explain?"

Kellen swallowed a mouthful of nerves and said, "I've spent some time with Adley Farre. She trusts me. I thought if I was the one to bring her to the dungeons, she would be less resistant."

Every shred of his father's warmth vanished, until he looked as cold as the snow outside. "You must think me quite the fool."

"Father, no."

"Do you want to know what I believe? I believe you helped Farre escape by whatever means you employ to disappear from this castle every night with your guards none the wiser."

"I didn't—"

"Explain yourself."

His brother added, "And spare us any more of your lies."

"Be quiet, Heath," their father commanded. "I am sick of the both of you."

Heath jerked his head up. "What have I done?"

From his seat on the golden throne, the king stared down at his eldest son. "You, Heath, can't summon so much as a wisp of silver, let alone wield it. I have spent the last twenty-two years of my life covering up your failures because I cannot have the people of this kingdom knowing I fathered *you*, a Lyandor who can't wield." His upper lip curled. "It's despicable. You disgust me."

Heath's gaze went hard, something stirring inside him, a deadly thing that only came out when he knew no one important was looking. "Why have you let me live, then?" he asked, his voice low. "If I'm such a stain on the Lyandor name, why don't you just kill me?"

"Believe me, I've thought about it. But if I did, who would inherit my throne? Kellen?" Their father scoffed. "At least you have a spine. If I put your brother on the throne, he'd lose it in a week. Wouldn't you, Kellen? Don't act like you wouldn't sign that joke of a treaty."

He seemed to want some kind of response, so Kellen said, "I think it's worth considering—"

The king gave a harsh laugh. "That's what I thought. I will go to war before agreeing to the terms of foreign rulers, and *I will win*." He looked between his sons, disappointment riddling his aging but still handsome features. "I don't know what I did to deserve the two of you as heirs."

Kellen had heard some variation on these words once a week for the past nineteen years, and the pain of them was more like a mild sting, a bite from a nonvenomous spider. But their father had always treaded more carefully around Heath. He may never have been kind to the crown prince, but Kellen hadn't expected him to snap so completely. The rebels must truly be getting under his skin. Kellen honestly thought they should be proud.

"My sons. One defective from birth; the other as soft as a fucking dandelion. It's pitiful."

Heath hadn't so much as twitched a muscle, and his eyes were very, very hard.

"Come now, Heath, what's the matter?" the king asked. "Is this about Ghan? Are you upset your plaything has been bedding someone else? I suggest you get over it."

"Father . . ." Kellen said, watching his brother.

Heath's shoulders were so rigid that he might not have been breathing, his gaze locked on their father like a predator.

The king turned on Kellen. "I'll deal with you later. I know you're responsible for Farre's escape. It's so very typical of you, Kellen. I suppose you feel bad for her? I shouldn't be surprised. I should be more surprised you haven't joined the damn rebellion by now. What a bleeding heart you have.

"And you," he said, back to Heath. "I have been patient with you. I have nurtured and coddled you in the hopes that your silver will manifest. But you are weak, and you will be *lucky* if your disgraceful head ever wears my crown."

Heath's fingers twitched at his side.

"Go get in the carriage, both of you," the king said. "We'll continue this after the execution."

King Mattheus turned and glided across the room, his boots tapping against the stone floor, cloak undulating as if caught on an angry breeze. Kellen and Heath trailed their father down to the ground floor and outside to their waiting carriage, neither of them speaking a word.

Once they'd piled inside, the horses took off, beginning the trek toward the execution square in the Welsley District. As they clopped into the city with curtains drawn closed, the silence in the carriage was tangible, the air as difficult to breathe as a lungful of water. Heath sat straight in his seat, doing nothing, saying nothing. It reminded Kellen of that expression: "the calm before the storm." That was Heath, and Kellen was more than a little concerned.

The carriage rolled to a stop. Sitting forward, the king straightened the crown atop his head. He lifted his hand to rap the roof, the signal that they were ready to exit.

"Father?" Heath asked. His voice was distant, removed.

Hand poised to knock, King Mattheus turned his disdainful gaze on the crown prince and snapped, "What?"

Heath pulled out a dagger, and before Kellen could think to react, Heath shoved it through the king's chest.

Kellen jerked back, banging into the side of the carriage. Heath's knuckles were colorless on the handle of the blade, the angles of his face like frigid ice as he yanked the dagger free. Blood soaked down the front of their father's shirt. Gaping wordlessly, the king put a hand to his chest, pulled it away, and looked at his wet fingers. His eyes rolled up into his head, and he dropped sideways, then let out his final shuddering breaths and moved no more.

Kellen was unable to look away from the blood flowing out of his father's body. It soaked into the carriage bench, the stain blossoming and dyeing the pale upholstery red. He had the strangest thought that it was the same color as his coat.

Hesitantly, Kellen reached out a shaky hand and placed two fingers at his father's neck. Nothing. No pulse met his touch. His father's heart had gone still.

The king of Erdis was dead.

CHAPTER
FORTY-FOUR

"What have you done?" Kellen breathed, withdrawing his hand. A hundred different thoughts coursed in his head, but it was the only one he could grab on to. The copper tang of blood brushed his nose.

"What I should have done a long time ago," his brother responded, wiping the bloody blade on his pant leg.

"He's our father." Kellen's eyes pricked. He blinked away the moisture. While he'd never particularly liked or admired the man, and he'd been prepared to help the rebels cut short his reign, he hadn't wanted this.

"He was never a father to you. I don't know why you care."

Sheathing his knife, Heath plucked the large lion ring off the king's hand and slipped it on his forefinger. Then he transferred the gold crown from their father's head to his own. In the shadowy carriage, the rubies were nearly black. Kellen gaped. "Have you lost your mind? You think you get to wear the crown now? Heath, you killed the king of Erdis. You committed patricide. No one is going to let you be king, even if you are heir to the throne."

The look Heath gave Kellen made his blood run cold.

"I may not have magic in my veins, but politics is a game, and I play better than anyone. I have spent years arranging the pieces to my advantage. Half the Royal Guard is under my thumb. I have the loyalty of the majority of the council, who have agreed to support my claim, regardless of the circumstances." Heath leaned forward, and Kellen held his breath. "This kingdom is mine. The people will kneel before me. Do you honestly believe I would settle for anything less?"

Kellen was afraid to ask his next question. He pressed his back into the carriage door. "In this game of yours, what piece am I?"

"You're a wildcard. Unpredictable and, as it turns out, untrustworthy."

"What's your next move then? Are you going to kill me, too?"

"I don't want you dead, Kell." He actually sounded like he meant it. "But I can't have you running around, helping traitors escape and ruining all my hard work now, can I?"

Heath rapped hard against the top of the carriage, and the door popped open, two guards appearing. When they spotted the king's bloody and lifeless body, they both started, but not enough. Surprise passed between them, but not panic, and it filled Kellen's chest with dread.

Heath addressed the guards. "Mattheus Lyandor is dead. I am your king now." The guards scarcely paused before inclining their heads, just two more pieces on Heath's board. They were all only players in a game Kellen hadn't known existed. "Inform the others. I want eyes on my brother at all times. If he tries to use his magic, break his hands, shoot him—I don't care. See to it this execution goes as planned."

"Yes, Your Majesty," the guards replied in unison.

"After you, Brother," Heath said, shoving Kellen out of the carriage.

Then the new king of Erdis stepped into the cold winter air. Buffed boots hit cobblestone, and he straightened to his full height, a black-and-gold cloak swaying around his body and the sun winking off his crown. The door clicked closed on their dead father.

CHAPTER
FORTY-FIVE

The winter wind picked up the shortest strands of Adley's hair, those pieces that always fell out of her braid no matter how tightly she tied it, and tossed them around her face. Crouched on a rooftop high above the execution square without any buildings to block the breeze, her cheeks had gone numb in the cold. Since her shooting gloves only covered a few fingers, she kept her hands shoved under her arms to keep them from losing feeling, too. She scanned the square below, first clocking the visible King's Children, then the leather uniforms hidden in shadow, working out the path her arrows would take.

The sun was high in the sky, and there wasn't a cloud in sight. Conditions were not ideal. The sunlight might impair her vision, especially up here with so many surfaces to bounce off, but the most pressing issue was the wind. It was stronger than she liked, and she'd have to account for it, down to its exact direction and speed. Not to mention the distance. She was perched farther away from her targets than most people could reasonably shoot an arrow.

But Adley was not most people, and she never missed.

With six extra quivers of arrows and her bow laying on the rooftop beside her, she stared down at the packed square. Kellen had been right: more than half the city was here, as if this were a play put on by the Royal Theatre. Honestly, sometimes Adley wondered if Denfell and the Lyandors weren't perfect for each other after all.

A hush fell over the crowd as a prison wagon rolled up to the side of the execution platform. The horses came to a stop, and two guards pulled open the back door, reached inside, and yanked a blonde girl out. If Adley hadn't known it was Lesa, she might not have recognized her. She was too far away to see details, but both her eyes looked swollen, blood crusted at her nose and mouth, and the strands of pale hair around her face were tinged red.

Adley made herself breathe. As Lesa walked up onto the elevated platform with her hands shackled behind her back, Adley called on eleven years of training and willed her mind into clarity. She picked up her bow with one hand and reached over her head to pull out an arrow with the other.

And then she nearly dropped them.

In a crown of rubies and gold, Heath Lyandor—not King Mattheus, but his eldest son—treaded up the platform steps, Prince Kellen following behind, looking nervous as all hells and like he was trying not to trip over his own feet.

The crown prince stepped forward. "People of Denfell. It is with a heavy heart that I am addressing you not as your crown prince, but as your king. King Mattheus, the gods rest his soul, passed in his sleep last night."

Murmuring broke out across the execution square, a chorus of raised voices that traveled from corner to corner like the sound of a tide pulling away from shore. Adley felt her mouth hanging open, but she couldn't seem to close it.

Heath raised his arms, his cloak falling back, and the gold buttons on his black jacket twinkled as they caught the light. "Settle down. Settle down. As the king of Erdis, I pledge my loyalty to you, so long as you pledge yours to me." He paused. The crowd had gone quiet, and his heavy cloak rippled in the breeze, the threat of his words tainting the air like a sour stench. "You are here today to witness the execution of the King's Child Lesa Ghan. She is sentenced to death for treason."

Adley forced her shock away, ran her fingers over the feather on the end of her arrow, took in a steadying breath. There would be time for shock later. Now, she had work to do.

The executioner came forward then, his maroon jacket straining at his muscles and a heavy ax in his grip.

Adley nocked her arrow, the weapon's weight familiar and welcoming in her hands.

The guards shoved Lesa to her knees, pushing her neck down onto a curved block of stone. Even as she was forced to kneel, she kept her spine straight, shoulders back, fearless and defiant until the last.

Adley stood, ignoring the protest from her injured ankle. She lifted her bow, drew the arrow back, and pulled the string taunt.

Red-and-gold banners flapped in the whistling wind.

The clock struck twelve.

Adley took aim.

The executioner lifted his ax and swung.

CHAPTER
FORTY-SIX

As the clock hands inched upward, Darek positioned himself at the edge of the platform, as close as he could get to the contingent of royal guards. When Heath Lyandor stepped out on stage in his father's crown and declared himself the king of Erdis, it had caught Darek off guard for a moment, but only a moment.

Focus, he told himself. *Nothing has changed.*

He slipped a hand beneath his overcoat to grip the hilt of his sword, his eyes scanning the square. Two dozen King's Children were visibly present, as Adley had predicted. A dozen was standard for an execution, an event that rarely got out of hand, but with an ever-growing rebellion, she'd said more would be on duty. Most were flanking the execution platform, but Adley had warned there would be others out of sight, and she'd marked their positions on a map.

Off to the side of the platform, a group of older men in thick cloaks and lush furs observed the scene. They were the king's council, Prince Kellen had explained, and they attended all official proceedings. The men would remain unharmed today. Darek needed them alive.

He turned his attention to the crowd, clocking rebels and friends among ordinary citizens with collars raised against the breeze. When he spotted his brother, his heart lurched. He hadn't been able to convince Markus to stay behind with Freya, so he'd found Jaston and made him promise not to leave his brother's side, but it did little to ease the worry eating at his gut like a carnivorous moth.

Heath addressed the audience. "You are here today to witness the execution of the King's Child Lesa Ghan. She is sentenced to death for treason."

At the front of the crowd not twenty feet from the stage, Ren stood directly before the executioner's block. Her profile was to Darek, framed by a long curtain of disheveled dark hair and an expensive burgundy coat, shoulders tense, pale cheeks red from cold.

The executioner stepped forward, and Lesa Ghan was shoved to her knees, her head pushed down onto the block. The square was silent as a boneyard as the clock tower chimed noon. The executioner heaved his ax over his shoulder and brought it down in a swift arc toward the King's Child.

Ren threw up her hands. A wave of silver raced for the stage, where it formed a barrier between Lesa and the executioner. His ax slammed into the shield of magic, metal groaned, and the man lumbered back. An arrow found his neck. The executioner tumbled sideways and dropped off the stage.

The audience descended into a mass of shoving and screaming. Someone rammed into Darek's side, his back, his other side. Adley had already taken out the guards who'd pushed Lesa to her knees, and now she was going after the King's Children. They went down one by one, each with an arrow buried in their chest or neck. The rebels charged toward the platform, swords clashed, knives flew, arrows disappeared into corners and gaps, King's Children tumbling out. Behind the executioner's block, hands shackled at her back, the blonde King's Child smashed her head into a guard and kicked another in the face. Prince Kellen had disappeared. Still facing the raised stage, Ren pulled her arms into her body, bracing herself, then shoved her glowing palms out a second time. A wide wall of silver barreled forward and rammed into a line of guards, flinging them off the back of the platform so violently that they struck the walls of a nearby building and went limp.

Heath stood motionless above the chaos. Every line of his body was rigid, ice in his eyes as they locked on Ren. She stared back, silver brewing in her palms, and her mouth set in a grim line. When Heath spoke, his voice was contorted with a rage so cold it burned. "Seize her." His command echoed through the square.

Darek freed his sword, shoving it through the nearest guard, and an arrow struck the man to his right. Another guard went down, wood stuck in his chest, and then another, arrows loosed in such quick succession it was as if Adley were shooting three at once. Again and again, she found her target, until Darek's way to the stage was clear.

Out in the crowd, guards were shoving for Ren, crashing through bodies and trampling over fallen limbs. Silver struck down the men leading the pack, but there were too many of them—and too many people blocking her path—for Ren to take them out with another powerful burst. She was surrounded in moments, the guards spreading out to encircle her, a sword no matter which way she turned. Silver brewed in her palms as maroon uniforms closed in.

Darek abandoned the execution platform and pushed toward Ren instead.

CHAPTER
FORTY-SEVEN

The King's Children had to be eliminated first.

Adley didn't see faces as she released her arrows. Names did not exist. They were targets. They were scraps of fabric pinned to poles in the training yard, flapping in the breeze on a cold winter night.

She found leather shirts and let her arrows fly.

At the edge of the platform, the tall rebel named Darek pulled out his sword and cut down a royal guard. The man beside him lifted a blade. Adley sighted him, drew her string back, and fired an arrow into flesh and bone. She worked her way down a line of guards who all had their sights on Darek, her arm going to her quiver again and again. She moved with swift grace, her calloused fingers and her tensed muscles, her mind and body, all guided along by instinct and eleven years of brutal training.

The crown had made her what she was.

A lethal weapon. An archer who didn't miss.

I bet they never saw this coming.

Her arrows rained down on the square.

A bright light rolled through the crowd below, pushing bodies back and throwing them into the air. The silver created a wide, empty circle in the middle of the square, with Ren at the center of it, crouched down with her hands pressed to the ground, hair rippling as though caught in a storm. Adley had only seen the girl's magic twice before, but she'd seen enough. Ren was a natural disaster with a pretty face.

Adley exchanged her empty quiver for a full one. She slung it over her shoulder, withdrew an arrow, and nocked it, then turned back to the execution square.

That was when a prickling crawled across her neck. She twisted out of the way just in time for a dagger to fly past her head instead of through it.

Five King's Children were gathered on the rooftop behind her, weapons drawn, the sky a clear, sharp blue at their backs.

"Hello, Adley," said Ethen Delano.

CHAPTER
FORTY-EIGHT

Ren lifted both arms out to her sides, and two rivers of silver burst from her hands. It knocked back a few guards, but just as many dodged the arcing light, rushing for her with swords drawn. She sent her magic for the nearest weapon. The force knocked it from the man's grip, and then Ren drew her shining fist back, hardened her silver around her knuckles, and punched him in the face. He fell like a brick. Another guard attacked, and she twisted away from his blade moments before it could run through her stomach. Turning on him, she raised a hand, flicked her wrist, and wrapped a cord of silver around his throat. Her fist closed, her wrist jerked, and the man's neck snapped.

And still a dozen guards were circling. Breathing hard, crisp air scraping through her throat, Ren whipped her head around, taking in the maroon uniforms and flashing metal. Silver built and swirled in her hands, her red coat flapping at her legs, and hair whipping around her face. She twitched her fingers, calling up as much magic as she could. And then she dropped into a crouch. Her palms struck the cold ground, and a wave of silver burst from her hands. It sped across the cobblestones, rippling like water spilling outward, creating an empty circle in front of the platform as everyone within a thirty-foot radius was thrown off their feet.

Ren hadn't straightened out of her crouch when something pierced her left shoulder. She cried out as hot pain raced down her arm, a short arrow buried in her skin. She glanced up at the platform, where Heath Lyandor, the new king of Erdis, had a crossbow in his hands and a group of guards at his back. He loaded a second arrow and lifted the weapon, his severe eyes locked on her. The rubies in his crown glinted.

"Ren!" a deep voice yelled from somewhere in the scrambling crowd.

She had less than a second to react, and it wasn't enough time. She was still doubled over, processing the fact that she'd been shot, when Heath fired. Ren threw a hand up. She sent silver speeding forward, but the light went wide. There was nothing to stop the arrow as it hurtled straight for her heart.

CHAPTER
FORTY-NINE

Adley let her arrow fly. Lyle Mcillen went down first. The others surged forward, and a second knife drove her way. She pivoted, reaching back to free an arrow and nocking it as she turned. She took out another Child.

Two down; three to go.

Ethen raised his sword as she released a third arrow. He cut it from the air, rushing forward, his weapon a blur at his side. Adley swung her bow into his face, and the strike sent him lurching sideways. Blood dripped from his mouth, his feet stumbling.

The other King's Children were closing in. A sword came at her left. She ducked, nocking an arrow, and from her low vantage point, shot up into the woman's chin. The King's Child fell, an arrow through the center of her head.

A blade arched down toward Adley. She rolled, and metal clanged against the rooftop. She kicked out a foot, sweeping the Child's legs from beneath him. He thudded to the ground, and before he could twist away, Adley shot an arrow through the side of his throat, clipping the artery. Blood gushed from his neck, shining red in the winter sun. He'd be dead in minutes.

Ethen was the last one left. He spit red onto the ground and stalked toward her. A laugh bubbled out of him, off-key and a little deranged. "Is that any way to treat the King's Fang?"

"You?" she asked, taking a step back. Again, her hand went to her quiver, sliding an arrow out. He was a foot taller and one hundred pounds heavier than her, but if she could keep some distance between them, she could win. "You didn't stop the rebellion. You never captured their leader." By this point, she'd worked out that Darek was more or less in charge, and he certainly wasn't locked up in the castle dungeons. "What is Heath playing at?"

Ethen stalked forward, twirling his sword at his side, the metal winking in the light. "The *king* is a generous man. He rewards those who serve him."

He ran at her. She drew her bowstring back and fired. Feet never slowing, he cut the arrow down with his sword. Adley shot another and another. The fourth did the trick, its steel head piercing leather and flesh to bury deep in his bicep. Ethen's feet faltered. He grunted, yanked the arrow from his arm—even though he knew better—and tossed it down with a snarl. Then he was coming for her again, and Adley only had time to grab an arrow, but not to nock it. Instead, she curled her fingers around the shaft and jammed it at his face. Her wrist met his raised palm. He wrapped large fingers around her wrist and forced her hand back, but Adley had been expecting that, which was why she'd dropped her bow and palmed a second arrow while he was distracted by the first.

She shoved it into his eye.

A roar ripped from Ethen's throat as he staggered back, a long, thin piece of wood protruding from his face. Blood streamed over his cheekbone, around his nose, and down to his lips. It dripped from his chin like red tears. His sword clattered onto the stone rooftop.

Adley swept up her bow, reaching back for an arrow to finally end this, but before she could draw it free, Ethen came running at her full speed. His huge body slammed into hers, the breath leaving her lungs in one painful gasp, bow falling from her grip. It was all she could do to keep her feet beneath her. When he grabbed the front of her jacket and began to push, she latched on to the arrow sticking out of his eye and twisted. He groaned out an agonized, animalistic sound, but he still didn't let go. He just curled his fingers around her wrist, found the tender place where bones met, and squeezed hard enough that she was forced to drop her hand.

Ethen shoved her backward. Adley dragged her feet, kicked out, and landed what punches she could, but nothing affected him. He kept pushing until she was teetering on the edge of the roof, the toes of her boots and his hold the only things to keep her from tumbling over. The freezing wind whipped at her back, and she didn't need to glance down to see the gray street below.

Face covered in blood and swelling skin, Ethen held her on the roof's edge, his chest heaving. His remaining eye blazed with fury. "Goodbye, Adley," he growled and pushed her off the building.

CHAPTER
FIFTY

The arrow was inches from Ren's chest when a bolt of silver knocked it aside. Pushing through the chaotic crowd, Darek tracked the magic to the edge of the square and found Kellen. The prince pulled his hood forward and turned away, disappearing into the fray as if he had never been there at all.

The execution square was a clamor of swords and screams and stomping feet. While rebels engaged with royal guards and people fled through gaps in the buildings, Heath yelled like a madman. He sent two King's Children after Ren. A man and woman charged forward, sunlight bouncing off their leather uniforms, and no arrows were coming from the sky to stop them.

Where the devils was Adley?

Darek had been spotted by a guard, and the man was approaching quick. Having lost his sword when Ren's magic threw everyone off their feet—himself included—Darek whirled, searching for a weapon. He spotted one twenty feet away and ran for it, the guard on his heels. Scooping up the sword in one motion, he pivoted in the next and swung out before the man's blade took off his head. Their weapons clashed in a whine of metal on metal.

Darek feinted right and swung left. Steel met flesh, and the guard staggered back with a gasp. Darek struck again, and his sword found the man's stomach, piercing clean through. He yanked his blade free, the guard fell, and Darek turned back to Ren.

Despite the arrow embedded in her shoulder, Ren was using both arms to fling daggers at the King's Children bearing down on her. A sheen of silver clung to the knives, hurtling them through the air, but the Children ducked past the weapons, impossibly swift. The man careened into Ren and knocked her to the ground, then twisted around to wrench her arms above her head. Ren screamed. He pinned her hands down, and when she kicked her legs and bucked her hips, he yanked on her injured shoulder. She cried out again, trapped and unable to use her magic as the woman stalked forward, sword flashing in the light of the high sun.

Darek's heart lurched. Ren was one of the strongest, most stubborn people he'd ever known, but no one was unbreakable, not even her. She may have been a survivor, but she wouldn't survive a sword through the chest. Darek had only had three weeks with her, and in that unfairly short amount of time, he'd been harsh and judgmental and wrong—so wrong—more than he'd been right. He'd never told her that he admired her strength, that she was not as wretched as she believed, that a good person in pain was not the same as a bad one. She needed to know that she deserved so much more than she'd been given. He should have told her.

Darek pushed his legs harder.

The King's Child raised her sword for a killing blow.

CHAPTER
FIFTY-ONE

Kellen was turning away from the square and hoping no one had seen him use his silver when he threw a glance at the rooftop Adley was shooting from. He held his hood around his face and tilted his head back, squinting against the light bouncing off the windows. Then he saw them: two people, not one. Adley and a man shaped like Ethen Delano. He had something long and thin sticking out of his head, but that didn't stop him from barreling into Adley and shoving her toward the edge of the rooftop.

Kellen broke into a sprint. He kept to the walls of the buildings that formed the square, darted through hysterical people who were fleeing down the side streets. He jumped over a fallen guard and crashed into a screaming man. "My daughter! Please! Have you seen my daughter?" he begged, grabbing on to Kellen's sleeve.

Wrenching his arm free, Kellen shoved past the man, who turned to the next person and repeated the question. A second later, and the man's pleas were lost in the roar of the crowd.

Kellen craned his neck back, and his heart dropped. The King's Child held Adley at the edge of the rooftop, only the toes of her boots still clinging to stone. Kellen was less than one building away. He ran faster.

The man let go, and Adley fell.

Kellen bolted into the shadowed alley and threw up his hands. Silver shot for Adley, fanning out beneath her plummeting body. Twenty feet from the cobblestones, her back hit the shimmering surface, the arrows in her quiver crunching on impact. His silver gave a little, but held, and Kellen lowered her toward the ground. He looked up, but Ethen had disappeared, leaving behind nothing but empty blue sky in the gap between the buildings.

Kellen set Adley down on the street, his silver fading beneath her body as she stared heavensward, gasping for air. When he knelt beside her, she found his gaze. "You couldn't"—she sucked in a breath—"have made something softer?"

He grinned down at her. "You're welcome."

CHAPTER
FIFTY-TWO

Darek broke through the crowd and sprinted for the King's Child holding Ren to the cobblestones. The other one called out a warning, but Darek was already there, running his sword through the man's back. His grip on Ren went slack, and he tipped sideways. Before he'd hit the ground, the woman was surging forward, murder in her eyes as she swung up her sword. Ren threw her palms out, and silver hurtled for the King's Child, lifted her off her feet, and flung her into the nearest wall. Her body struck the building with bone-shattering force.

Ren fell back onto her elbows. Darek moved around the fallen King's Child and offered her a hand. Breathing heavily, strands of hair stuck to the sheen of sweat coating her face, Ren reached up with her good arm, allowing him to pull her to her feet.

She grimaced. "If I had known I was going to get shot doing this, I would have asked for more gold."

Despite their current circumstances, Darek very nearly laughed. "Let's go overthrow a king," he said.

Up on the platform, Lesa had disappeared—Darek didn't particularly care where to—and a handful of guards had formed a human shield around Heath. They were about all that remained of the Royal Guard who had accompanied him to the execution, and all two dozen King's Children had fallen, thanks to Adley's arrows. But more would come, and soon. Word of the uprising had undoubtedly reached the castle, and as usual, the rebellion was running out of time.

Darek ran one way; Ren went another. As he charged onto the stage, the guards began to shuffle Heath off the opposite side, but Ren blocked their path. Silver churned in her hands. "Not so fast," she said. "You wouldn't want to miss the grand finale, now, would you?"

She lashed out, her silver razor-sharp as it snapped at two guards. Crimson slid from bloody smiles across their necks, and the men crumpled. Ren's magic wrapped around Heath's throat, slithered down over his black-and-gold cloak to bind his torso. Stalking up the steps, Ren forced him back onto the platform, the guards giving her a wide berth as she pushed their king to center stage.

Heath was glaring at her, a look of resolute hatred on his face that made the winter breeze feel warm. "*You.*"

"Let me guess," Ren said. "You've been seeing me in your dreams?"

A growl bubbled out of his throat. Clenching his fingers, he twisted his wrists like he was trying to get the magic to obey *him* and not Ren. "You're supposed to be dead," he hissed. "Why aren't you dead?"

"Believe me, I've been asking myself that for years."

Darek stepped forward to face the square. Fallen and injured bodies lay across blood-spattered cobblestones, some in uniform, others not. Two people dragged a groaning man into a side street, his limp legs scraping over the ground. A man picking his way through the crowd kept asking if anyone had seen his daughter. Someone somewhere was crying.

Darek didn't peer too closely at any of it. He only took in a relieved breath as he found his brother, who was clutching his arm, a bloody streak on his neck, but looking otherwise fine. A good portion of the audience had fled during the conflict, but the place was still plenty full.

"Your attention!" Darek called.

There was no need to repeat himself; most of the square was already looking at him.

He took in a breath. Decades of planning had led to this moment. Everything his mother had worked for—had died for—sat on this precipice with him, and he was more than ready to jump.

This is it.

"You have all been deceived." He paused, taking another step forward so that he was standing at the edge of the stage. "Heath Lyandor and his brother, Kellen Lyandor, are not silver wielders."

Voices rippled through the crowd. The few people who hadn't been paying attention snapped their heads toward the platform.

"King Mattheus lied to you. Heath and Kellen are not his sons. They are not the rightful heirs to the Erdis throne."

A man with a neat pepper beard pushed through the

line of guards protecting the council members and stormed up the stairs. "What is the meaning of this?"

"King Mattheus and Queen Ellisa were unable to conceive, so they came up with a solution," Darek told him. "If you check the queen's visitor logs, you'll find that over the past twenty-three years, Her Majesty has been meeting regularly with a man named Jai Farrow. He fathered the princes. As such, they have no claim to the throne."

"This is preposterous!" Heath exclaimed. He jerked his shoulders, but Ren's silver held.

Darek looked at him. "Prove me wrong. Wield your silver."

Wrath as pure as blood churned in his blue eyes. "I am the king of Erdis. I will not be forced to perform like a show pony."

Heath suddenly staggered sideways.

"Would you look at that?" Ren said. "I *can* get tricks out of you if I pull on your leash just right."

Heath cursed at her. Her returning smirk was edged with ice.

Another councilman appeared on the stage, this one dark-haired and younger. "Your Majesty, I'm going to have to demand you show us your silver."

Heath glared at him. "It is not your place to demand anything of me, Lord Martene."

"Heath!" barked a third council member, a tall, bald man. He treaded up the steps, his fur cloak swaying. "If this is as preposterous as you claim, then you should have no problem producing silver. If you refuse, I am inclined to believe this man."

"My brother can't show you his silver, because he doesn't have any," Kellen said as he joined the group now gathered on the wooden platform.

It was about time. Darek had been starting to worry the prince wasn't going to show.

"The rebel isn't lying. We don't have silver. Since we were boys, my father has been passing his magic off as our own." Heath looked absolutely murderous as his brother stepped up to him and plucked the crown from his head. Kellen turned to address the crowd. "On behalf of my family, I would like to formally apologize for this deceit. Heath and I have no legal claim to the throne."

Everyone in the square started shouting—at each other, at Darek, at Kellen and Heath, probably even at the gods. The rest of the council filed onto the platform, half of them angry, the other half only wary. Heath managed a string of obscenities before he abruptly broke off. A choking noise rasped through his constricted windpipe, and he clawed at the silver wrapped around his neck.

"Dear gods, please shut up," Ren said.

Darek replaced Kellen at the front of the stage and raised his arms, yelling over the noise. "People of Denfell!" It took a lot more yelling before the crowd settled down again. "King Mattheus did not father Heath and Kellen, but he did father a child with another woman. Legally, she has a claim to the throne, and she could be your queen, if you'll have her."

He looked back at Ren. One arm was dangling by her side, and the fabric at her left shoulder where the arrow stuck out was wet with blood. She held her right hand in a fist at her chest, keeping her silver wrapped around Heath. There was a question in her wrinkled brow, suspicion in the narrow set of her eyes. Her stare struck him hard, like a right hook, and he held it, knowing he might be about to ruin everything between them.

Please don't hate me for this.

He turned to face the square again.

"Ren Kolins is heir to the Erdis throne."

CHAPTER
FIFTY-THREE

What?

Ren jolted in surprise, pain shot through her shoulder, and she nearly lost her hold on her silver. The magic started to fade, but she quickly called up more, brightening Heath's binds. She shoved her lips together, her fist tightening, nails biting into her palm. Heath cursed, but Ren barely heard it. She didn't hear, didn't see anything but Darek, his back to her and an enraptured audience at his feet.

"Ren is a silver wielder, magic passed down to her from her father, King Mattheus Lyandor," Darek continued. "You may have heard rumors about her in recent weeks. I'm here to tell you those rumors are true. She has shown you they are true."

And that was when Ren began to realize, with a sinking feeling, that this had been the plan all along. The Hollistair brothers hadn't offered her seven hundred thousand gold coins to inspire the people. Of course they hadn't. No amount of *inspiration* was worth that kind of money. They'd promised her a fortune so they could position her as heir to the throne. She remembered that first day in the

Underground, the scene she'd caused when she formed a silver castle and lit it on fire. Who else could have done that, other than a Lyandor? Everyone knew magic was passed down by blood, so how else could she have it, when all the wielders were supposed to be gone? Her appearances hadn't been stirring an uprising; they'd been stirring rumors, rumors Darek and Markus had probably helped spread themselves. It didn't matter that it wasn't true, as long as it *looked* true.

Ren wasn't sure how she hadn't seen it before.

A bald councilman grabbed Darek by the arm and pulled him back. "You couldn't have told us about her before announcing it to the entire city?"

"If the people want Ren on the throne, that's where she should be," Darek told him. "You serve the citizens, councilman. It's time you were reminded of that."

"Godsdamn bleeding rebels," the man growled. He turned to confer with the rest of the council. "We are on the brink of war. Every minute the throne remains empty puts us at risk. I can think of five separate countries who would jump at the chance to steal the Erdis crown."

"And we can't risk another uprising from within," a young councilman said, his eyes shooting between Darek and Ren. He turned his back on them and said more quietly, "It'll be all our heads."

"But we don't know a thing about this Ren Kolins," yet another man protested.

They all started speaking at once, and Ren stopped listening.

Kellen leaned toward her. "Did you know about this?" he asked quietly.

She shook her head.

Darek appeared at her side. "Ren—"

"Don't."

The men argued for a while before they all seemed to come to a resigned sort of agreement, and then the bald one approached Ren. "If you'll give us Heath, we'll see to it that he's dealt with."

Ren didn't want to, but she looked at Darek. This was his revolution—he'd made that painfully clear—and it was his decision. When he nodded, she released her silver. Heath staggered forward, sucking in gulps of air, a hand at his throat.

Kellen passed over the ruby-studded crown. "He killed King Mattheus," he told the councilman, lowering his voice to add, "Be careful. You can't trust the people at court."

The councilman's face went tight, and his eyes shifted to the men gathered on the platform. "We need some time to discuss this," he said, looking back to Ren. "Where can we find you?"

"We'll come to you," Darek answered. "You have twenty-four hours."

The councilman's lips twitched down, as if annoyed that a rebel was issuing orders. He gave a terse nod and shoved Heath at two guards. They pulled his hands behind his back, but before they could march him offstage, he jerked toward Ren, leaning into her face. His hair hung over his forehead, blue eyes wild and deadly like a rabid animal. "You stole my magic from me," he said in the voice of a snake, poison on his tongue. "Trust me when I say I'll be getting it back."

The guards dragged him away, shoving him down the stairs and toward a waiting carriage. She watched him go, a shiver trickling down her spine. Heath may not have had magic, but they were going to need a strong cage to keep him locked up. Or an iron box. They could throw it in the sea, let him rot with the sunken ships.

When Darek tried to talk to her, she turned away and plodded down the steps, the crowd parting for her like she was already their ruler. Hunching her shoulders in and ducking her head, she left the square as quickly as her feet would carry her without breaking into a run.

The only reason she went to the Hollistair house was because it was closer, she had an arrow stuck in her shoulder, and Freya was waiting there to stitch her up. Heavy boots thumped in the street behind her, fabric rustled, but she kept her eyes on the wide road ahead.

Ren swung open the mansion's front door and stepped into a towering foyer, a white staircase before her, and an unlit chandelier above. It smelled like Darek, like spices and musk. She slammed the door hard. The bang rang through the empty mansion.

Freya jumped up from a bench at the edge of the room, her jewelry tinkling as she rushed forward. "You've been shot!"

"Have I? I hadn't noticed."

"Come on."

Wrapping a hand around her uninjured arm, Freya led Ren out of the foyer. They'd gotten halfway down the hall when the front door creaked open and boots tapped against the marble floor, but still Ren didn't glance back. She couldn't look at Darek right now. If she did, she might actually hit him.

A fire warmed the kitchen, a line of bandages, needles, and other healing supplies laid out on the table in the center of the room. Freya directed Ren to a chair and handed over a bottle of clear liquor. "Here," she said. "You're going to need it."

Ren took a swig, grimacing as the alcohol burned her throat. A second gulp quickly followed, and when Darek stepped into the kitchen, she downed more. She swallowed and shot him a glare.

"I need to cut away your clothing," Freya told her.

"You owe me a new coat," Ren barked at Darek.

Knife in hand, Freya ripped into the burgundy fabric at Ren's shoulder, and pain coursed up her neck. She flinched, drinking more from the bottle while Freya cut off the sleeve of her jacket and then the shirt underneath. Ren was left in half a coat, arm bare from the neck down.

"Please, Ren," Darek said. "Let me explain."

"I don't want to hear it."

Freya took the liquor from Ren and splashed it over her hands, then traded the bottle for a sharp knife. "This is going to hurt."

"Do it."

Freya took a breath, eyes narrowing in on the arrow, and cut into Ren's shoulder.

Ren couldn't help it. She screamed.

Freya didn't stop. She kept carving away at skin, and it was all Ren could do not to pass out. But then the knife was gone, and Freya's finger was in the wound, and that was worse. As she felt around for the arrowhead, Ren's vision went white and the kitchen swam. Someone placed a hand on her other shoulder, and she didn't think it was Freya, but at the moment she didn't care. King Mattheus could have risen from the dead and walked through the kitchen door, and Ren wouldn't have spared him a thought. She just wanted the arrow, the sheer agony, gone.

Freya's finger disappeared, and Ren gasped. She rested her head back against the chair, drawing in labored breaths.

"It didn't hit bone," Freya said.

Peeling her eyes open, Ren blinked away tears. The hand was still on her shoulder, and Darek was hovering in front of her, looking more concerned than he had any right to be. Ren couldn't jerk away—she wasn't sure she had the energy to move—but she growled, "Don't touch me."

He removed his hand and backed up a step. "I'm sorry, Ren."

"You should have told me."

"I know. I was going to."

Freya twisted the arrow, and pain shot through her shoulder. "Godsdamnit, Freya," Ren snapped, picking up the bottle to take another drink.

"You want this arrow out or not?" Freya shot back.

"Do me a favor," Ren said through gritted teeth. She slapped the bottle down on the table. "When you pull it out, shove it into Darek's arm next."

"You can't tell me you would still be here if you'd known what we wanted you to do," Darek said, growing heated. "Don't try and pretend like you wouldn't have walked away."

"Well, you're the expert on me, so you would know."

"You know what?" Freya said. Abandoning a gentle hand, she gripped the arrow and yanked it free.

Ren's entire left arm, plus a good portion of her neck and back, gave a blinding throb, and a sound somewhere between a groan and a scream ripped from her throat.

Freya slapped the bloody arrow—tip thankfully still attached—against the table. Grabbing a needle and thread, she turned to Darek. "You know how to stitch up a wound?"

"Yes," he said.

Freya shoved the supplies at him. "I'm not going to listen to you two yell at each other."

She left the kitchen. The door swung in and out in her wake, oscillating like a clock pendulum.

Darek threaded the needle and bent toward Ren, but she snatched it from his hand. "I can do it."

"Ren, you cannot stitch up your own shoulder."

"Watch me," she said, lowering the needle toward her wound.

Darek grabbed it before the tip touched her skin. "Let me help you."

"Stop pretending like you care."

"Are you really so stubborn that you'd rather walk around with a hole in your shoulder than accept my help?"

She shot him a glare that was sure to convey just where he could shove the needle. "Fine."

He came in close and bent over her again, and Ren hated that his jaw was so sharp and his eyes so brown and he was so absurdly tall that she wanted to kiss him despite everything. She hated him even more for being so damn attractive. "You should have told me," she repeated as he dug the needle into her shoulder. She felt the pull of the string, the sting of pain, but it was faint and distant compared to before.

"I planned to," he said, concentrating on his work. "I truly did. It wasn't supposed to happen like that."

"Then why did it?"

Through thick lashes, he met her stare for only a second. Then he returned his gaze to her shoulder and said, "I was scared of losing you."

"Don't kid yourself, Darek. You were scared of losing your war, not me."

"That's not true," he protested.

"Isn't it?"

"I can't say the rebellion isn't important to me. Since my mother died, it's one of the only things that's mattered. This kingdom is days from war, and an empty throne put us all at risk. Letting the next in line take it wasn't an option. If we didn't get one of our own into the castle, we might have had another tyrant for a ruler. Framing you as heir was the simplest solution."

"I was an idiot to think—" She stopped herself before the words came out.

He tied off the stitches, setting the needle down and picking up a jar of cream. When he rubbed some on her shoulder, the pain faded, replaced by a soothing numbness, but somehow she could still feel his fingers whispering against her skin.

"To think what?" he prompted.

"To think that you'd care about me." The confession was like sour milk on her tongue. "What was it you said that first night we met? I'm a coward with a few tricks up my sleeve?"

Darek dropped his hand, stricken. "No, Ren—"

"I gallivant around Denfell, taking everything that doesn't belong to me and nothing I deserve?"

"I don't believe any of that. You have no idea how sorry I am for saying those things to you. I've never regretted words more."

Ren looked away.

"It kills me knowing that I made you feel worse about yourself. You were in pain, and I didn't see it, and I can't tell you how sorry I am for that." When she didn't say anything, didn't meet his eyes, he went on, fervent, "I hope you'll forgive me, but I want you to forgive yourself more. Let go of this guilt you've been holding on to. It's eating you alive."

Her eyes bored into the marble floor. What right did he have to talk about her pain, her guilt? To act like he knew her? To act like he cared? "I don't know how I'm supposed to trust anything you say."

"I care about you, Ren."

"You don't. You can't—" She broke off again, before she could say, *You can't possibly care about someone like me.*

"How many times do you need me to say it? Give me a number. I'll repeat myself hoarse until you believe it."

She shook her head.

"I care about you," Darek insisted. "I was scared of losing you because I woke up in your suite and realized I'd rather be lying on your absurdly small couch than at home in my own bed."

"Stop—"

"You really are a talented thief. I never saw you coming. Everything was fine, and then the sun came up one day, and suddenly, I couldn't stand the thought of a river separating us. If I'd told you what I had planned, you'd have walked away, and I would never have seen you again. And, Ren, that thought scared the shit out of me."

Ren pushed herself to her feet, shoulder throbbing with the sudden movement. "Stop it! You lied to me again and again, from the beginning. You think because you say some nice things, I'll be okay with it? All is forgiven, and now we'll ride off into the sunset? That's not the way this is going to work."

"I didn't lie to you!"

"You didn't tell me the *truth*. You wanted me to become the bleeding queen!"

"I was going to tell you!"

Ren rolled her eyes. "Oh, you were going to tell me? I didn't realize. Never mind then. Should we kiss and make up now?"

Darek's jaw was hard. "This self-righteous attitude is pretty rich. I didn't do anything you wouldn't have done. Isn't that the way it's always been with you? Do whatever it takes to get what you want, everyone else be damned?"

She sharpened her gaze. "That's the thing, Darek. You were supposed to be better than me."

Ren left him standing in his kitchen. As the door swung behind her, she peeled off the remainder of her coat and deposited it on a hall table. What she was left in was a one-armed top tucked beneath her corset, which was certainly a look and not an altogether terrible one, at that. What remained of her shirt covered her burn marks, and Ren didn't know whether to be thankful that the arrow had struck her unscarred shoulder, or annoyed.

She trudged down the hallway with a strong desire to hit something, but as it was daytime and she had a serious injury, the fighting pits were out of the question. A card game, it was.

Ren was heading for the door when murmuring called her up short, drawing her to one of the many sitting rooms instead. The door was ajar, revealing tall ceilings and white walls carved with delicate patterns. The King's Child they'd saved was lying on a navy-blue couch, eyes closed as Freya cleaned and wrapped her injuries. Perched on a footstool, Adley watched them with her bottom lip stuck between her teeth. Markus was there, too, hovering by a window and curling a sketchbook in his hands. There was a fresh white bandage tied around his forearm.

Ren didn't enter the room, but leaned her uninjured shoulder against the doorframe.

She couldn't have been standing there for more than a minute when Kellen Lyandor sauntered up and propped himself opposite her. Ren eyed him. His white shirt was untucked, a few too many buttons undone and the sleeves pushed up, blond hair hanging over his forehead. He looked like he'd just rolled out of someone else's bed.

Neither of them spoke for quite some time, until Ren asked, "Why are you a pit lord?"

"Because I'm a dreadful prince," he answered. "Why are you a pit fighter?"

"Because I need the money."

He cocked his head, a smile lifting his lips. "I have a feeling there's more to it than that."

"Perhaps," was all she said.

They fell into a comfortable silence, and this time, Kellen was the one to break it. "If you become queen—"

"I won't."

"But if you do," he said, "I could help you."

"I swear if you're proposing marriage, I'm punching you in the throat."

Kellen's face drew into an expression of mock disappointment. "You ruined the surprise. I had a whole ordeal planned. Champagne, flowers, a flock of doves."

"Well, there's always next time," Ren said. "My threats don't expire."

"That, there is," Kellen agreed. He ran a hand through his curling hair. "In all seriousness, I'm aware of my reputation, but I do know how court works. Forgive me if I'm being presumptuous, but I don't think you're prepared for this. I want to help."

Ren raised a brow. "Are you offering because you have nowhere else to go?"

"That, and I hope I might right some of my father's wrongs. Maybe this will be a way to do that."

She looked toward the kitchen—toward Darek. "I don't want to be queen."

"My father did want to be king, and look how well that worked out."

Her attention returned to Kellen. "What are you saying?"

"I'm saying you might surprise yourself. And on the bright side, if you're terrible at the job, you won't have it for long. Tall, dark, and brooding back there"—Kellen jerked his chin down the hall—"will lead another uprising to overthrow you. Everyone wins."

"What an incentive," she said blandly.

He pushed off the doorframe. "I know it might not mean much coming from me, but I don't think you'd make a half-bad ruler."

He turned and headed down the hall, but Ren called to him before he was out of sight. "Kellen?"

He looked over his shoulder, his golden hair falling into his eyes.

"Your father's wrongs don't belong to you."

He held her gaze for a moment, then his mouth pulled into a smirk. It was the kind of look that had caused scandal for many a fair maiden, and Ren couldn't help but return it, just a little bit. "See you at the fighting pit?" he asked.

"I don't think they let queens do that sort of thing."

"Haven't you heard? Queens can do whatever they want." Kellen winked and meandered off.

Turning back to the sitting room, Ren caught Adley running a hand over her face and through her disheveled hair, which was tied back in something that barely counted for a braid, the brown strands mostly waving free. The King's Child glanced up, finally noticing Ren. They stared at each other, something passing between them, and Ren nodded. It was a moment before Adley did the same. She returned her attention to the unconscious blonde on the couch, fingers brushing over the other girl's cheek.

Love. Such an odd word for a King's Child. If Ren hadn't been staring at the proof, she wouldn't have believed the girl capable of it. How messed up was it that one of the throne's attack dogs seemed more human than Ren felt most of the time?

Freya got to her feet and joined Ren in the doorway, a red crystal pendulum hanging around her neck. Ren had given her the necklace after stealing it off Kellen during their dance at the Royal Carnival, when he was just the South Terth pit lord and not also a rebellious prince. Gods, was that really only yesterday?

"Darek wants me to be queen," Ren said.

"I'd gathered," said Freya.

"Should I?"

Freya only smiled and lifted Ren's injured arm. Ren groaned as her friend wrapped a bandage around her shoulder, bracelets jangling on her small wrists.

"I hate him," Ren pronounced.

"No, you don't."

"Freya, I mean it. I really hate him."

Freya pulled the bandage tight across her shoulder, looping it around her chest to secure it. "Look, you might hate him right now, and that's fine. He did a shitty thing. But you and I both know that you're eventually going to forgive him, because he means more to you than you'll admit." Ren opened her mouth to protest, but Freya shot her a look. "You think I don't know how you feel about him? You push away everyone who tries to get close. I know you've tried to push him away, but he won't let you, will he? That means something. So you can stay mad at him if you want. Go put your fist in some guy's face if you need to get it out of your system. Or you could speed things up by just forgiving him now. It would save everyone a lot of angst."

Ren sighed. It was incredibly annoying how Freya could always see inside her, picking apart all these jagged pieces and unearthing the truth beneath it all. She needed to find a less intuitive friend. "If I do this, it won't be without you."

"Well, obviously," Freya said. "You think I'd let you move into a castle and not take me?"

"The kids are all going to freeze to death if we close the Compound."

"Careful, Ren. It's starting to sound like you care." Freya tied off the bandage and gently lowered Ren's arm.

Ren's nose crinkled. Just when the aching had subsided, her shoulder was at it all over again. "I don't care about the kids. They're pests. They've been nothing but a pain in my ass, and I'm glad to be rid of them."

Freya gave her that look, the one she reserved especially for Ren, both endeared and exasperated at once. "I'll find someone to take over the place."

"Make sure it's someone Aidann would have liked."

Freya's answering smile was soft. Her hand drifted up to the bright stone at her chest, and her eyes went back to the sitting room, where Adley was using a wet rag to clean the blood from Lesa's pale blonde hair. Freya was quiet, her stare far away.

"Is something wrong?" Ren asked.

She smiled once more. "I'm fine," she said, and then she returned to the sitting room to gather her soiled healing supplies.

Ren abandoned her spot in the doorway and went to talk to Darek.

Two glass doors were thrown open to the balcony outside his bedroom, where he rested his elbows on an iron railing and stared out at a city ten different colors of spun sugar. The Battgandon River sparkled like a fistful of jewels, and fading afternoon sunlight gilded the colorful edges of the Atterton District. A breeze drifted through the open doors, ruffling a set of heavy ivory curtains.

Stepping out into the cold, Ren walked across the

balcony and leaned back against the rail beside Darek. "So listen. I've decided to forgive you."

He looked at her, and there was hope in his eyes.

"But you can't keep something like that from me again."

Darek straightened off the rail. He'd pulled on a thick sweater, a pale shade not so different from his curtains. The color offset the warm bronze of his skin, and Ren found herself wondering why he always wore dark colors when he looked this good in light ones.

"Next time I plot a revolution, I'll be sure to give you all the details," he said.

"Next time you plot a revolution, count me out."

He laughed. Gods, she wanted to curl up in that sound and live there.

"Can I ask what brought on this change of heart?" he questioned.

Because you're still here, Ren thought. *No matter how hard I try to get rid of you.*

She shrugged. "You're a good kisser."

Darek's brows shot up. One long step carried him to her, and he leaned in, curling his hands around the railing on either side of her hips. He brought his body close, and she tilted her chin back to meet his eyes. "Was that a compliment, Kolins?"

"It's been known to happen from time to time."

A strand of hair blew into Ren's face, sticking to her lips, and Darek peeled it away. Then he rested his hand at the top of her neck. His thumb idly skimmed her jaw. "You can abdicate the throne," he told her. "I never planned for you to do it forever. Just long enough for us to put another system of government in place."

"Another system?"

"The monarchy is poison. We want the people to have a say in who leads them. Not rulers, not kings or queens, but leaders enacting the will of the people. It won't be easy, and it won't be perfect, but it'll be a start."

Ren dropped her eyes and twisted her fingers around the ties on his sweater. "I don't want to be a Lyandor."

"You can be a Kolins."

"No." She raised her chin. Darek's gaze roamed her face, and now that his nose was nearly healed and the bruising almost gone, Ren could clearly see the freckle at the edge of his nose. She almost reached up to touch it, but stopped herself. "I want to be an Avevian."

It was her family name, and while she would never be anyone but Ren, she thought maybe it was possible to be both people. She didn't have to choose.

Darek's expression softened as much as it could for someone as hard as him. "Avevian, it is." He paused. "I have something else to tell you, but you have to swear not to yell at me again."

"Oh gods," she moaned, dropping her forehead against his chest, his hand burying in her hair. Her shoulder protested at the movement. "Now what?"

"I didn't exactly come up with the idea to pass you off as heir to the throne."

Ren pulled back. "What?"

"My father says that your parents joined the rebellion before you were born, and discrediting the Lyandors had always been the plan, but it wasn't until they realized you had silver that the part involving you came about. When you were old enough, they were going to give you a choice. Let you decide if you wanted to be part of the revolution and hopefully become queen."

She stared up at him, brows lifted. A gust of wind ruffled his knotted hair, and he watched her, saying nothing as she dropped back against the railing. She gazed past him at the mansion's bright-blue paint. Was it really possible that even if her parents hadn't died nine years ago, she'd still have ended up in exactly the same place? Would she be standing on Darek Hollistair's balcony if that fire had never happened? Was this one of those things where every possible road led to the same destination?

Ren rolled her eyes at herself. She was beginning to sound like a romantic. Before she knew it, she was going to start believing in things like fate and destiny and winter sprites.

"Do you think your father could tell me about them?" she asked.

"I think he could," Darek replied. He leaned forward then and pressed his lips to her forehead. Ren's eyes fluttered shut. She took in a deep breath.

After a long moment, he eased back. "I should check on my brother." Grabbing her hand, Darek guided her across the balcony and into the mansion.

Having left the blonde King's Child to rest in the sitting

room, everyone was gathered in the library, where someone had lit a fire and drawn open the bay window curtains. Outside, the street was empty, the sky blue, brightly painted houses lining the road across the river. Markus and Freya were seated in chairs before the hearth, talking quietly. Adley stood at the library's massive shelves, her fingers brushing over the books, while Kellen, his shoulders relaxed and hands shoved into his pockets, leaned against a wall and watched the room. Holland had shown up at some point. She exchanged a curt nod with Darek.

When Markus noticed his brother in the room, he stood and walked over to him, a sketchbook still curled in his hands. He said quietly, "Mother would be proud of you."

Darek clapped him on the shoulder, tugging him in for a hug. "She would be proud of both of us." He pulled back and stepped around Markus, his gaze roaming over the library. "I know we're all tired, but I think we should talk about what happens next. King Mattheus never did sign that treaty, and there's no knowing how political tensions will change with Ren on the throne. We might still have a war to prevent."

"War can wait," Ren said, pulling open a couple drawers until she found what she was looking for. As she turned to face the room, she held up a deck of cards. "Who wants to play a game?"

Adley looked at her like she'd lost her mind. Darek, Markus, and Holland exchanged wary glances, and Freya smiled, shaking her head in that way of hers. Kellen didn't seem to notice. He only pulled out a chair, plopped down, and pushed his hair out of his face with a grin. Everyone else slowly followed, except for Adley. She started to back out of the room, but Kellen snatched her sleeve and tugged her into a chair.

Ren was last to take a seat. She tapped the deck against the table.

They made her swear not to cheat, but what would be the fun in that?

ACKNOWLEDGMENTS

My heart is full as I sit here thinking of all the people who have been instrumental in bringing this book to life. I am deeply grateful for each and every one of you.

First, to my mom and dad. Your support is unparalleled. I'll never find words enough to express my thanks for everything you've done for me. I love you with my whole heart. I'm sorry I moved so far away.

Kelsy Thompson, you are a brilliant editor. Thank you for loving this story fiercely, asking the tough questions, and reminding me of my characters' injuries. With your insight, this book has become so much more than I could have dreamed.

Hilary Harwell, my agent and unwavering champion, I feel so lucky to have you in my corner. You never stopped believing in Ren, even when I wasn't so sure her sarcastic remarks and pointed looks would make it onto bookshelves. Thank you for seeing promise in this story and helping shape it into what I always wanted it to be. Thank you for your dedication and support. Thank you for your prompt responses to my emails.

Without my writing group, the Guillotine Queens, I certainly wouldn't have made it here in one piece. Brittney Singleton, Jessica James, Kalyn Josephson, Kat Enright, Sam Farkas, Jessica Bibi Cooper, Tracy Badua, Alyssa Colman, Ashley Northup, and Amy Stewart, I couldn't have asked for a more loving, talented, supportive group of people to call friends. There's no one I'd rather navigate the highs and lows of this business with. Thank you for being there for me, for reading my work, and for your kind words. Most importantly, thank you for all the fish.

An extra mention needs to go to Britt and her husband, Jeff Singleton, two of the most generous people I've ever had the privilege of knowing. Britt, I'm so grateful to have you in my life. Thank you for being a CP when I barely knew what a CP was. Jeff, thanks for the headshots, and sorry about all the complaining.

To Denise Amador, Shelby Cleland, and Ally Shoemaker, your encouragement and support while reading my early work bolstered my confidence. You made me believe I really could do this whole publishing thing. Thank you for being some of the best friends a girl could hope for.

I want to take a moment to mention the entire bookstagram community and all the friendships I've made there. Thank you to Jacey (@wistfulandwandering) and Chloe (@d.earchloe) for reading this story when it was just a little baby book. Your enthusiasm is appreciated more than you know. Cait, I cried at all the nice things you said about my writing. I'm so happy you got to read this book.

A heartfelt thank-you to the whole team at Flux for your tireless work.

I'd be lost without all the wonderful friends in my life, old and new, from California to North Carolina. I'm overwhelmed by the number of people who have been by my side throughout this journey. Thank you for not holding it against me when I forget to respond to your texts.

And to you, dear reader. Sharing this story with you is a dream. Thank you.

ABOUT THE AUTHOR

Jennifer Gruenke is a graduate of UC Santa Barbara, where she studied communication and writing. She grew up among the redwoods of Northern California, and now lives in Charlotte with her books and the houseplants she hasn't killed yet. If she's not writing or reading, you're most likely to find her in a café, music venue, or the aisles of Trader Joe's.